Graphic Lies
by
Linzi Carlisle

Books by Linzi Carlisle
Village Lies
Graphic Lies
Old Lies
Nocturnal Lies
Skipping Christmas in Holly Crescent
The Little Cat who thought she was a Dog

TABLE OF CONTENTS

PROLOGUE

Narrowing his eyes, he contemplated the dolls lined up against the tree, savouring the moment of victim selection.

His eyes landed on the baby doll and he picked it up before savagely pulling its arm out. Pausing to smile at the boy watching him he produced the knife he'd taken from the kitchen and stabbed the doll, the blade sinking in easily to the soft plastic. He stabbed it again, this time slicing the blade across its plump belly. Taking the lipstick he'd stolen from his foster mother's bedroom, he smeared it around the knife marks before spreading its redness across the body with his fingers, grunting in satisfaction.

Panting slightly, he selected another doll, this one a mature figure complete with breasts and long hair. With trembling fingers, he picked up the small red dress and put it on the doll, before pulling it down to expose her breasts and sliding it up above her plastic buttocks. This time he stabbed the doll multiple times, excitement rising as he spread the red lipstick across her breasts and buttocks. Taking the ball of twine from his pocket he unravelled a length, cutting it with the knife, and tied the doll up, securing her to a root of the tree as small growling sounds escaped his throat.

Turning to his friend he handed him the twine and watched proudly as he too cut the twine and used it to secure the broken baby doll beside her counterpart in the same manner.

Standing back, he admired their handiwork and, retrieving his instant camera from his bag, took a photo.

Feeling hot with excitement he was about to choose his next victim when the call for tea-time came, reaching his ears only faintly at this distance from the house. With a last wistful glance at the dolls, he headed for his tea nodding to the other boy to follow him, the photo in his pocket a reassuring presence promising a return to those heady moments of pleasure later that night.

LONDON'S CALLING

Some of the photos she'd been tagged in on her Graffic account were of obscure items like a key or a doorway, even rooms in private homes, but in every photo containing the bound girl, her head was covered by a hood.

Sasha stopped on one of the photos, shock hitting the pit of her stomach. The girl was wearing her sweatshirt. She expanded the photo, looking intently at the image and phrase printed onto the pale pink hoodie. She and Chantelle grinned happily at whoever had taken the photo of them. In a retro font, the words *Coolest Aunt Ever* swirled across the corner of the image in shades of darker pink and lime green.

Please tell me this isn't Chantelle. She repeated the words like a mantra as she clicked on her sister's name.

'Sash, hi, everything alright?' Tess's voice was bright and breezy, a mother happy to have her daughter home safe and sound after her horrendous ordeal of being held prisoner and almost dying.

'Hi, Tess, yeah fine, I'm at a service station, stopped for a drink and the loo, you know how it is. I thought I'd give you a quick call, see how you're all doing. How's Chants?' She held her breath.

'Oh, she's fine, right here on the couch being spoilt with a tea tray and huge bar of chocolate, which I'm about to steal.'

Sasha exhaled in relief, smiling as she heard the scuffle and laughter at the other end of the call. 'Well give her a big kiss from me, and one for you too. And, Tess, stay safe okay? All of you. Love you.'

Relief that it wasn't Chantelle in the photo was mixed with foreboding about who it could be. How could this girl possibly be wearing a hoodie that her niece had given her, which was personalised, and presumably the only one of its kind in the world? Her gut twisted. Someone had to have been into her flat and taken it. She studied the photos again, frantically looking for the one of someone's living room.

No wonder it had seemed vaguely familiar. She felt her heart rate increase as her eyes took in the books on the coffee table, the artwork on the wall behind the couch – the couch with its cushions featuring proteas and sunbirds – covers she'd brought back from her trip to South Africa – and as if she needed any further corroboration, the photos on the butler's tray displayed the smiling faces of herself with Tessa and Chantelle, as well as one of her and Eric. *She was staring at a photo of her own living room.*

Shaking, she put her phone down on the table and tried not to spill her tea as she took a sip. The sounds around her were drowned out by the ringing in her ears as panic threatened to overwhelm her.

The touch on her shoulder was gentle but Sasha jumped, this time spilling her tea, as she looked at the man smiling down at her.

'Whoah, careful, didn't mean to startle you! Are you okay? Sasha, it's me, Miles.' His concerned eyes looked down at her as he pulled his hand from her shoulder, an unsure smile on his face. 'Eric's friend?'

Her head cleared. 'Miles, of course. Sorry, I was a million miles away. I haven't seen you for ages. How are you, what are you doing here?' Relief flooded her, as well as pleasure, at seeing a familiar friendly face.

'Oh, work stuff, you know, heading home now though. But what about you? You're a distance from home. Look, I could do with a coffee and let's get you a fresh cup of tea. We could catch up if you've got a few minutes?' At her nod,

Miles went off to get the drinks and Sasha relaxed, thinking back to when she'd first met Miles.

She'd been at her local pub with a girlfriend, they were sharing a bottle of wine she recalled. At some point, she'd been walking back to her table when Miles had bumped into her. He'd been really sweet, they'd got chatting and he'd asked to buy her a drink to make up for bumping into her. She couldn't remember how it had happened, but at some point, he and his friend had joined her and Zoe at their table. Eric was boasting about his friend's luck in inheriting a villa somewhere while his friend had looked embarrassed and told him to be quiet. They'd both had a lot to drink, judging by their slurring, but it had been fun. Miles had turned out to be quite shy, his louder friend taking over the conversation, and she and Zoe, on a trip to the ladies, had giggled about the two men. 'Miles is so cute, Sash, I just want to take him home and cuddle him. And maybe a bit more.' Zoe's mischievous eyes had twinkled at her and Sasha had kept quiet. She'd thought he was cute too. But Zoe deserved some fun and Sasha wasn't going to spoil it for her.

'Go for it, Zo,' she'd urged her friend. 'I'll keep his mate busy.' Zoe had needed no further encouragement, squeezing herself in beside Miles, her shiny dark hair falling across her face as she smiled at him. And by the end of the evening, it hadn't been hard to keep Miles's friend busy. Eric had proven himself to be hilarious, albeit terribly drunk, and had laid claim to Sasha in no uncertain terms.

She hadn't had that much fun for ages but when Zoe announced that she wasn't taking no for an answer, that Miles was coming back to hers for a nightcap, Sasha had watched them go, wondering if she'd imagined the slightly regretful look in Miles's eyes.

She pulled herself from her reverie as Miles placed the mugs on the table and sat down. 'Penny for them?' He looked at her enquiringly.

She laughed. 'Oh, I was just remembering when we all met. I haven't spoken to Zo in ages, how is she? How are you guys doing?'

But Miles shook his head. 'It didn't work out. But what about you and Eric? I heard you two had had a falling out or something?'

Sighing, Sasha smiled. 'It's a long story and I'm sure you don't want to hear it.'

Miles placed his hand gently on hers. 'I tell you what, why don't I take you out to dinner this week, just friends, and you can tell me all about it.'

That was why she'd liked him, he was a sweet guy. 'You know what, Miles? I'd really like that.'

After a pleasant few minutes spent chatting Sasha said that she had to get home, explaining that she'd been away for a while, visiting her sister. They made arrangements for dinner two nights later and Miles walked her to her car.

Stopping suddenly, Sasha turned to Miles. 'Miles, you know, sorry, I feel a bit stupid asking you this but, d'you think you could meet me at my flat and just come inside with me for a minute?' Seeing his concerned face, she hurriedly proffered an explanation. 'It's just that I've been away for quite a while at my sister's, and you know how it is, can't be too careful and all that.' She laughed, embarrassed, but Miles reassured her.

'Sasha, of course, no problem at all. I understand, honestly, it's not so great walking back into your home after you've been away for a while, especially if you're on your own. I'll meet you there, we'll go in together and make sure everything's alright.'

Relieved, Sasha opened her car door and turned to him. 'Miles, thank you, I really appreciate it. You remember my address?' At his nod, she parted with, 'See you outside Turnpike Lodge then.'

Driving back, Sasha found herself wondering what had gone wrong between Miles and Zoe. Of course, Zoe was pretty exuberant, extremely attractive and full of confidence. Maybe she'd just been too much for Miles, he was obviously quite a gentle sensitive guy – the total opposite to Eric, now that she came to think of it. Eric and Zoe would probably have made a better match. Which meant that she and Miles... Smiling, she shook her head, that's the last thing you need, Sash, after what's just happened with Cal. No, Miles was a sweet guy who would make a good friend and she needed one right now.

~

'Not bad timing.' Miles grinned, opening her door once she'd parked. 'Here, I've got those.' He carried her bags as Sasha found her key. Images of Cal filled her mind as the memories came thick and fast. The last time she'd been here had been when she'd had to go into hospital, her endometriosis having reared its ugly head. She'd needed a laparoscopy, the subsequent findings resulting in the necessity of the removal of one of her tubes and ovaries. Cal had stayed in her flat while she was in the hospital, and she found herself subconsciously sniffing the flat's stale air hoping for a remnant of his smell.

'Where shall I put your bags, Sash, in your room?' Miles was heading down the short passageway from the lounge towards Sasha's bedroom as he spoke.

Confused for a moment, she wondered how he knew where her room was but then realised how stupid she was being. The front door opened into the lounge, which in turn was open to the kitchen. Of course Miles was heading down the passage, there was nowhere else to go. As if reading her mind, he stopped and looked back. 'Which door's your bedroom, Sash?'

Annoyed at her paranoia, she headed to her room, opening the door and trying not to think about the fact that Cal had slept in this bed not so long ago. 'Thanks, Miles, just drop them on the floor, I'll sort them out later.' Casually she opened the door to her spare room which served as her home office, as well as her bathroom, making sure nobody was hiding in either room. 'Can I make you a quick drink before you go?' She checked the cupboard in the passageway before opening the lounge doors to her small balcony. 'It's a bit stuffy in here, needs some fresh air, don't you think?'

Miles's hand on her arm stilled her. 'Sasha, you're worried, what is it?'

She almost told him. But what could Miles do? And what did she truly know at this point? No, she needed time to figure out what the photos were all about. And she needed time to get to know Miles if she was going to confide in him about everything. 'It's nothing, honestly, it just feels a bit weird coming home to the empty flat, I feel as if I've been away for months not weeks. Now, how about that coffee?'

But Miles had to go. Holding both her arms, he stood in front of her. 'Dinner on Thursday, yes? I'll come and collect you. We can walk along to The Reading Man if you like? They've opened up a great looking restaurant in their conservatory, we could check it out. And you can tell me everything that's been going on in your life since we last saw each other.'

'Sounds perfect.' Smiling, she nodded, agreeing to his suggestion of seven o'clock so they could have a drink first, and finding that she was already looking forward to it. 'Miles, thank you, it was very kind of you to do this. Sorry that I've delayed you getting home, you must be tired.' On impulse, she stretched up and pecked him on the cheek, then felt bad seeing his cheeks flush deep red, as he looked away.

Closing the door behind Miles, Sasha shivered, pulling her cardigan across her body, autumn had slunk her way in that was for sure. About to close her lounge doors, she stepped out onto the balcony, looking around at her familiar view. There was something comforting about being able to see across the street to her neighbours, to see their movements through their open doors, or on their balconies. A bus went by beneath her, its fumes reaching her nose, and the lights of the kebab shop on the corner flashed, the scent of cooked onions and spices mixing with the bus's fumes. Two girls shrieked with laughter as they walked along arm in arm and, as she smiled and looked back across the street the elderly lady, whose balcony was filled with plants, waved at her and smiled as she watered her miniature jungle. Sasha smiled and waved back. It was good to be home.

Taking out her phone, she snapped a photo of the familiar street scene and posted it to Graffic with the caption *#noplacelikehome*. With a last glance around she headed back inside and closed the evening chill out.

It was going to be pizza for dinner, she knew that without looking in her empty freezer. She ate way too much pizza but was craving it suddenly, which usually meant... Oh no, she now became aware of the slight dull ache deep inside. Please no, not already. But a check revealed no sign of any problems. Nevertheless, a hot bath felt very appealing and would ease her pain as well as calm her. She turned on the taps, lit a scented candle, and flicked through her vinyl collection. Fleetwood Mac, perfect, just right for her mood. Enjoying the process of positioning the needle over the record, of hearing its little click, the slight whir of the record as it rotated, she gently lowered the needle with a perfection born from practice to begin playing the second track, her favourite. Sasha hummed along as the first strains of Dreams reached her ears. She stripped her clothes off and sank into the steaming bath water, sliding down until she was fully submerged.

I'M JUST A DOLL, SITTING IN FRONT OF A BOY

'Come back to mine, Brian, I'll make it worth your while...' Stacey's eyes glinted mischievously as her hand crept upwards along Brian's thigh.

'Stace, don't, someone will see.' He pushed her hand away, laughing, and leaned in to kiss her. This girl was just too damned irresistible. 'I'll come back for a couple of hours, but I can't stay the night. Okay?' At her nod, he signalled for the bill and, once it came, dropped some notes on the table before helping Stacey into her jacket. They left the restaurant with their arms entwined around each other, stopping for the odd kiss and cuddle as they made their way to Stacey's flat.

An hour later they lay amidst the rumpled bedlinen, naked, sated, and sharing a cigarette. Brian leaned over Stacey to pour more wine as she held her phone up to take a photo of their entwined legs. *#mysecretlover* She smiled as she posted it to Graffic.

'Brian, stay tonight, please?'

He kissed her nose, sighing. 'I'd love to, baby, but my wife's on the warpath at the moment. We had quite a blow-up yesterday and if I stay out tonight, she'll probably chuck me out.'

'Good!' Sitting up, Stacey picked up her wine glass. 'Let her chuck you out, or better still, just leave her anyway. Why d'you stay with her? Live with me, we could get our own place together.'

Brian threw himself back on the bed, clasping his hands behind his head. 'It's a little delicate, darling, you see my wife holds the purse strings.' He gave a wry smile.

'Yep, I'm essentially a kept man. It's a small price to pay, Samantha's a decent woman. Without her, we wouldn't be eating out at all these restaurants, or drinking these fine wines, and you certainly wouldn't be wearing that new, extremely sexy, as well as inordinately expensive, underwear I just bought you.'

Stacey flung herself back onto the bed beside him. 'Well, how rich is she then?'

'Oh, trust me, she's more than just rich. Family money, darling, rich parents, and her an only child. Yes, my wife is a terribly wealthy woman and I wouldn't want to upset things, I'm quite happy with how my life is.' He looked at his watch. 'And now I must go.' Standing up he dressed quickly.

The front door opened and a slim woman walked in pulling her hair loose so that it fell in a silky sheet down her back. 'Hi, Stace. And who are you?' She studied Brian's face as she waited for his reply.

'Hi, Claudia, this is Brian, I told you about him.' She turned to Brian. 'This is Claudia, she's from Croatia.'

'Hi, Claudia from Croatia.' Brian grinned, switching on his charm involuntarily. 'Now just what has Stacey told you about me?'

'Not much, there is something to know?' Claudia's eyes raked across Brian from head to toe as Stacey looked on feeling left out and a little uncomfortable.

She wrapped her arms around Brian possessively. 'Only that he's my handsome lover who'd leave his wife for me if only she wasn't so rich.'

'Come on, Stace, leave it out, baby. I must go.'

Stacey stood at the door watching Brian walk away. 'Tell your wife she can keep her money, it's you I want,' she called out.

'Now you know I can't do that.' Brian grinned, holding his hands out in supplication.

'What was all that about?' Stacey's flatmate made mugs of tea for them as Stacey flung herself down onto the couch.

'Urgh, that was me showing how desperate I am. Thanks.' she took the tea, cradling it in her hands.

'So now you tell me about your handsome lover and his rich wife, yes?' Claudia sprawled in one of the armchairs, also cradling her tea, ready for a girly chat before bed.

~

Warm and relaxed from her bath Sasha threw on leggings and an oversized jumper before ordering her pizza - with extra chicken, onion, and green peppers - her favourite. By the time she'd drunk her first large glass of wine it had arrived, fresh and hot from her local pizzeria. Still refusing to think about the unsettling images she'd seen on her phone, she watched a re-run of an old Friends episode, laughing with familiarity, as she ate her way through half of the pizza. But now, with the remains of the pizza in the fridge and her wine glass refilled, there were no more avoidance tactics at her disposal. It was time to look at her Graffic account again.

There were eight photos in total. The unknown girl appeared in four of them, each time in a different location. Sasha studied the photo of her lounge, noting that everything was in its usual place, the only difference being the girl herself, sitting straight-backed in the middle of the couch. Feeling uneasy, Sasha jumped up, removing all the cushions and frantically checking for signs of anything left behind. Finding nothing, she replaced them, sitting back down gingerly, it wasn't a nice thought that someone had been sitting right here, presumably against her will. Or was it just a prank? Was someone toying with her?

She continued to study the photos. In one of them, the bound girl was lying on a bed with a plain white duvet cover. It could have been any bed, but she felt sure that it was hers. Walking to her bedroom she tried to work out where the photographer would have stood to take the photo. A corner of the bedside table was in the picture, and on it, just visible, part of a book, its cover worn and damaged. She knew, without having to look, that it was her bed, the book in question being The Thorn Birds by Colleen McCullough. She'd been re-reading it before Chantelle had gone missing and no one else would have kept such a damaged copy, surely. She'd kept it for sentimental reasons, loving the fact that its worn spine, loose pages, and battered red cover showed how much she'd loved it, how many times she'd read it over the years.

The girl was wearing shorts, her legs tanned from the summer sun. Her head, hidden by the hood, was twisted to the side, a small measure of defiance against whoever had placed her there. One foot was visible and Sasha noted the blue-painted toe nails, slightly chipped.

The other two photos with the girl were not taken in her flat, that was obvious. In the one, the girl appeared to be curled up in something, a dark carpet of some kind around her, so possibly the boot of a car. And in the other, she was sitting on a camp bed. The full horror of this photo engulfed Sasha as she noted the chain around the girl's ankle, leading to somewhere off-camera.

Sasha looked at the notes she'd made, nodding, it was a start, although with further studying she might be able to discover more details. In capital letters, she wrote CHANGE LOCKS. She'd phone a locksmith first thing in the morning. Moving quickly to her front door she double-checked that the bolt was securely across and the chain on. Wanting further peace of mind, she pulled the hall table across and pushed it against the door, before collecting some wine glasses and placing them strategically on the table. If anyone tried to enter her flat tonight, she'd certainly hear them.

Curling back up on the couch with another glass of wine, Sasha turned her attention to the remaining four photos. The key was a close-up photo of a keyhole with the key inside it. Attached to the key was a red ribbon, tied in a bow. The visible part of the door was painted white, like hers, but she'd need to study her door's keyhole to see if she could match it to hers. She'd do that in the morning. The photo of a doorway had her puzzled. It definitely wasn't her own front door. So someone else's then. Maybe the girl's? Was it a family home, or did the girl live alone?

A selection of underwear was the focus of the third photo. But not just any underwear, this was sexy lingerie, lacy bras, sheer knickers, all of them in bold colours. There was no way of knowing if they belonged to the girl. Feeling tired now, Sasha studied the last photo, recoiling in disgust.

This was a man's room, she decided. The blue-striped bed cover looked masculine, its faded, crumpled, appearance revealing a lack of any interest in domesticity. The plain bedside table contained nothing but a glass of water and the only other item in the photo was a chair in the corner of the unadorned room. What had caused her to recoil was the occupant of the chair. Not a person, but a doll. And not just any doll, but a sex doll, that much was obvious.

The doll's blonde hair gleamed in the light from the camera flash, her garish red lips smiling grotesquely, thick eyelashes surrounding blue eyes which appeared to stare directly at the camera. The doll was dressed in bra and knickers, and written in black ink on her stomach was one word – a name – Sasha. Controlling her anxiety, Sasha expanded the photo and studied the underwear. The rich purple silk was edged with black lace, the bra a half-cup, exposing the doll's nipples, whilst the knickers were tied at the sides with black ribbon.

Her stomach churned as she walked to her bedroom and pulled open her underwear drawer. She already knew she wasn't going to find the set in there. Rifling through, her suspicions were confirmed, but she turned the whole drawer out onto the bed nonetheless. The empty silk bag that had held the exquisite lingerie set was there, lying limply, its contents missing. Throwing everything back into the drawer she replaced it, before checking the other drawers, and then, in case she'd put them in the wrong place, *which she knew she hadn't*, she checked the shelves in her wardrobe. Nothing. In desperation, but knowing she wouldn't find them there, she pulled down the holdall she'd used for the overnight trip she and Eric had taken to a country hotel, for which she'd purchased the underwear specially. The bag was empty, which she'd known it would be.

She couldn't face the implications of what it all meant, not tonight, not after everything else that had happened in such a short space of time, and not after losing Cal... Cal, who would have been here, supporting her, talking it all through with her, comforting her... If he hadn't turned out to be married with a child on the way.

Angry and depressed, Sasha needed oblivion. But first, she stripped off the bedding and re-made her bed, removing all traces of whoever had lain on it. And then, in a determined mood, she walked through to the kitchen, poured herself a tumbler full of whisky and downed it, before pouring another one and doing the same. Now she was ready for oblivion, at least for tonight.

THE FOLLOWING

Groaning, Sasha rolled over in bed, reaching for her phone to switch it on and check the time. Her head was killing her but her plan for oblivion had worked, she'd slept solidly. Gingerly getting out of bed she reached for her robe and wrapped it around her, feeling the chill of autumn in the room.

While she waited for the kettle to boil, Sasha retrieved some frozen bread from the freezer and placed two slices into the toaster. She needed to go shopping for some basic groceries but she had all she needed for right now – well, almost, she reconsidered, that is if she went without butter and milk.

Having swallowed two painkillers with a glass of water, she spread some peanut butter onto the dry toast and took her breakfast through to the lounge. Pulling back the curtains she allowed the sunlight to stream in and warm the room, before settling on the couch. Sipping her black tea and taking bites of her toast, she opened her Graffic account and studied the photos again. This time she focused on the captions.

@sashablue So you think you're a detective now. Let's see how good you are. #sashablue #findthegirl #beautifulart #cansashasaveher #livingart

Someone was clearly goading her, but the question was whether it was genuine or a hoax. Whichever it was, her private space had been invaded and she searched quickly for a local locksmith. Having made an appointment for an hour's time, she decided to take a quick shower and get dressed.

~

The locksmith was one of those friendly old guys, a real Londoner, rare these days, and he carried out his work accompanying it with a monologue requiring no actual responses. He accepted his black tea graciously, his concerned eyes darting occasionally to Sasha's face.

'You're sure you're alright darling? You don't mind my asking now? Me and the wife have got daughters, two of them, they'd be about your age I'm guessing, and there's not a day goes by we don't worry about them. You can't be too careful these days, girls living on their own, boyfriend troubles, you name it. Now you make sure you don't give spare keys to just anyone, you hear me? I'm always telling my girls the exact same thing. If you're not careful next thing you know you've given a key to the neighbour to water the plants and one to your fella, then you break up but he's still got your key, the neighbour moves away and forgets to give you back your key and before you know it the whole thing starts over again and all and sundry have got keys to your home in no time at all. No, you keep yourself safe, that's what's important, who cares if a plant dies, better that than losing a key and risking your safety, that's what I say. And talking of safety, don't even get me started about all these photos you youngsters share of your lives. It's not safe, I'm always telling my girls that, too many bad people out there knowing everything there is to know about you. Now, while I'm about it, I don't like the look of this old bolt, I'm thinking I'll just put you another one on this door, just to be on the safe side. No charge, I'm in a good mood.'

He waved away Sasha's thanks, his eyes glancing around her living room. 'I see you've got doors opening to a balcony there, mind if I take a look?' Without waiting for an answer, he went to the doors, examining them and tutting as he wriggled the handles. 'Wouldn't take much to open these from outside. And before you say it, I know you're on the first floor, but like I tell my girls, better safe than sorry. No, we need to make these more secure, I'll pop a bolt on here for you too. I couldn't live with myself if I didn't, and that's the truth.'

He opened the doors, stepping out onto the balcony. 'Nice. You can't beat good old Shepherd's Bush, that's what I say, lovely part of London, that it is. Still got the old community spirit round here. Morning darlin' beautiful day!' He waved to the old lady across the street, out watering her plants. 'What's it, about half an hour's stroll and you're in Notting Hill? Lovely. Now that was a good film, you've gotta love a good film made in London.'

Sasha smiled, amused at his non-stop soliloquy, feeling better. There really was nothing better than a salt of the earth person to raise your spirits.

When he left, after insisting that she call him for any concerns she might have, Sasha decided to put the whole Graffic worry out of her mind and go and stock up on groceries.

~

She was in the queue at Waitrose when her phone pinged with a message. Smiling when she saw who it was from, she opened it.

Just checking you're okay? See you tomorrow night! Miles.

Her fingers moved quickly over the keyboard. *That's sweet of you. I'm fine, thank you! Looking forward to our meal x*

He was so thoughtful. She wondered again what had gone wrong with him and Zoe. She'd have to give Zoe a call and catch up. She really needed to get her social life up and running again, her time in Parva Crossing when Chantelle had gone missing having rather taken her out of the loop, although if she was honest, she'd been a bit of a hermit for a while. She briefly thought of Eric, wondering what he was doing now, admitting to herself that she was surprised at how easily he'd accepted her request to leave him alone. Eric didn't usually take no for an answer, if anything he saw it as a challenge. She'd told him they were finished because of her and Cal, *and that had worked out well...* But Eric hadn't treated her right, she'd been a convenience to him she knew that. Hurriedly placing her groceries onto the counter, she pulled her purse out to pay for her shopping.

Arriving back at her flat, Sasha put her shopping away before stepping back out to look at her front door. She pulled up the photo of the key in the keyhole and compared it. The brass escutcheon and keyhole cover were identical. Whoever this was, they wanted her to know that they'd had access to her flat. Relieved that she'd had the lock changed she went back inside, locking herself in securely with the bolts nonetheless.

She sliced the Waitrose mini-baguette open and slathered unsalted butter on it, before adding slices of Emmental cheese and fresh tomato. A sprinkling of seasoning on the tomato and her lunch was ready. Grabbing a bottle of sparkling water, she decided to sit out on her balcony. It was worthy of a photo, she thought, positioning her plate on the small table and allowing her phone camera to blur out the background as it focused on her baguette. She posted the image to Graffic with the caption *#perfect lunch* before beginning to eat, studying the captions on the photos that she'd tagged in.

@sashablue So you think you're a detective now. Let's see how good you are. #sashablue #findthegirl #beautifulart #cansashasaveher #livingart

It had to be a reference to Chantelle having been missing, and her efforts to find her. But who would have known about that? Was it someone who knew her personally? Who knew that she worked as a kind of private investigator, solving people's problems? Had someone read in the news about her involvement with the poison pen letters in Parva Crossing? It felt like a challenge – and it felt like a game, a very sick game. She clicked on her notifications as a new one appeared. Chilled, she saw that she'd been tagged in another photo. This time the girl, still hooded and bound, was in a standing position and holding a carrier bag. The carrier bag was a Waitrose bag. Standing up abruptly she took her plate and bottle inside, locking the doors. Someone had followed her to Waitrose. What else could it mean?

The photo had been liked a few times, and she refreshed her screen, noting the increase in likes. This sicko had a following it seemed. In disgust, she clicked on one of the hashtags, #findthegirl, horrified to find several posts with the same hashtag. The photographs were all of girls, hooded and bound, in poses similar to those of the original images. In disbelief, she tried to assimilate what she was looking at. Were these girls also captive? Or were they just posing themselves in the same way? What was this? Was it a cult following?

But the camera never lies, didn't someone famous say that once – before the world took it on as one of its most oft-repeated sayings? Life had changed though – and now the camera did lie. The problem was that everyone shared their lives on camera now, everyone lived photographic lives, and it became difficult to know which of the graphics depicted real lives and which depicted lies...

Returning to the original photos, she now paid attention to the name of the original poster. @maluspassuum. It told her nothing, she thought, shaking her head in irritation.

Clicking on the account, Sasha's eyes scanned the images, but they were few, only the ones in which she'd been tagged. This was a new account and it seemed it had been set up with her in mind. She noted that @maluspassuum was following her account and that, horror of horrors, he/she/*it*? had followers, fifty-four, to be exact. Could whoever this was consider themselves to be some kind of artist, with their use of the hashtags *beautiful art* and *living art*? Clicking on the hashtags, in turn, brought up thousands of images, some of them of the bound girl or imitations of her.

A thought struck her, could it be that this person was purely some kind of freaky, eccentric, artist? Someone who set up fake scenes perhaps, but used real people? So, a sort of pseudo-realist then? Someone who liked to shock through their work – and shock would be guaranteed with the focus on a hooded and bound female.

It was almost believable. She smiled wryly. But what kind of an artist accesses someone's private home, uses the owner's clothing and furniture as props, and poses their model there? Or was she out of the loop? Were there such people?

No. She was clutching at straws, hoping to find an explanation for the photos, as well as the invasion of her private space, to make herself feel less threatened. This person was not an artist. This person had targeted her directly, both in her home and online. This person wanted something from her, the question was what?

Feeling the need for a distraction, Sasha decided to touch base with Zoe. Maybe she'd be up for a drink later. She sent her a message, hoping that Zoe said yes. It would be great to see her friend again as it seemed like forever since they'd last been out for a girls' night.

She still hadn't heard from Zoe by five o'clock and wondered if she should give her a call, maybe her friend had missed her message. But just as she was deliberating this, her phone pinged.

Sasha! Hi, sorry not been in touch. Took a last-minute holiday! Not sure when I'll be back, might stay longer! xx

Sasha read the message three times, her brow creasing in confusion. It didn't sound like Zoe, she was usually far more casual. She certainly never called her Sasha, always Sash. And a last-minute holiday? Where to? Might stay longer? Who did that? What about her job? Maybe she was with someone, a new bloke, that might explain it. Yes, her brow relaxed, that was probably it, she'd met some hot guy, maybe on the rebound after Miles, and they'd taken off on a trip together. It must be going well and they were talking of staying a bit longer. Wondering where they were, Sasha smiled to herself, trust Zoe to have all the fun. She typed a reply.

Zo, am so intrigued. Where are you? Who's the lucky guy? Tell me! And let me know when you're coming back. xx

Oh well, so no plans for this evening then. She could have contacted some of her other friends but most had family commitments, husbands, kids, the usual, that's why she and Zo got on so well and spent a fair bit of time together, both of them being essentially single and childfree.

Pouring herself a glass of wine and putting the leftover pizza into the oven on a tray, Sasha tried to relax. Still no reply from Zoe, but if what she suspected was true, then Zoe was probably too busy enjoying herself, which was fair enough. Well, at least she was out with Miles tomorrow night. She'd try to put the whole photo problem out of her mind, at least for tonight. Maybe she'd talk to Miles about it, see what he thought. But she found it hard to stop thinking about it. If the girl in the photos had truly been taken captive, then wasn't it down to Sasha to do something about it?

Maybe she should go to the police. But with nothing more than a few photos perhaps they'd just think she was wasting their time. Her phone pinged and she read the message.

Will tell you all about it when I'm back!

Well, her friend didn't want to give anything away. She'd just have to wait until Zoe contacted her. But wait, maybe Zoe had posted a few pics to her Graffic account?

Clearly not, was the answer to that a moment later, as she smiled at Zoe's last few photographs depicting her usual eclectic mix of images – an arty shot of a bowl of pasta accompanied by a glass of wine, Zoe's feet, presumably, modelling a fantastic-looking pair of heels, a sunset over the London rooftops - all typically and wonderfully encapsulating Zoe's life in beautifully created graphics. No, Zoe was having too much fun to even post photographs – that had to be a first.

Sasha closed her Graffic app. For now, she should rather concentrate on securing her next case, that is if she had any enquiries, she did after all have bills to pay. Opening up her business e-mail she scanned the messages.

COME ON, BABY, LIGHT MY FIRE

He switched off the phone, satisfied that he'd allayed suspicion. He hadn't expected her to try to contact his captive so quickly. Heading to the kitchen, he prepared a sandwich and took a bottle of water from the pack on the counter. Taking it up the stairs, he entered the small room. The woman's sobs stopped abruptly.

'We can talk about this. Please. Why are you doing this to me? Just let me go, I swear I won't say anything, we can forget all about it.'

Ignoring her, he placed the meal on the table before leaving the room and re-locking the door.

Back in the living room he sat down and took a long drink of his lager before looking at his Graffic account. He hadn't expected a following and didn't know whether to feel proud or annoyed. Scrolling through the photos posted by his followers he wondered at people's behaviour. What on earth possessed these people to copy his photographs? They were lies, how dare they? He'd gained more followers, he noted, a total of seventy-nine now. Dropping his phone on the coffee table he leaned back, feeling panicky.

What had he started? Where was he supposed to go with this? All he'd wanted was her attention, for her to notice him, *to become part of his game*. But as of yet, she hadn't responded in any way. A thought occurred to him and he quickly tapped out a short message and hit send. That should make things clear.

~

In the town of Dartford, in Kent, upstairs in her friend's bedroom, Sara was getting bored. 'Seriously, Molly, I've taken, like, about twenty photos, they're all good I promise you.' Molly had become way too obsessed about this whole Sasha thing and all that find the girl stuff.

'Oh, just one more,' her friend pleaded. 'I need to get my legs at the right angle.' But the sound of steps coming up the stairs put an end to it.

'Dinner's ready girls, come on down before it gets cold.' Molly's mum called through the closed door, not really caring what they were getting up to. At sixteen she'd been a lot worse, if she thought back, always out with her friends at bars, clubs, you name it. Now all they seemed to do was stay in and stare at their phones, taking photo after photo in search of the elusive perfect selfie. Well, at least it kept them out of trouble. She banged on the door again before heading back downstairs, hearing her husband's key in the lock.

'Alright, babe? How was your day?' Steve kissed his wife on the mouth, pushing a strand of her hair behind her ear. 'You look tired.' It wasn't really a question.

Smiling, Cat rubbed his arm before heading for the kitchen. 'Dinner's ready, love.'

With the lasagne virtually polished off, and nothing but crumbs remaining from the garlic bread, Steve poured himself and Cat another glass of wine. 'That was delicious, babe, I always say you make the best lasagne, isn't that right, girls?' He raised an eyebrow at Cat in amusement, as he glanced at the girls who were engrossed in their phones. 'You girls can clear the table, alright? Molly? D'you hear me? You and Sara make sure you clean everything up. Come on, babe, let's go and sit in the conservatory.'

'It's getting a bit chilly to sit out here, you can tell summer's gone, can't you?' Cat rubbed her arms, shivering a little in her thin top, as Steve leafed through the local paper. 'Did you see in there, they caught that bloke from the robbery all those years ago? Turns out he's from Dartford, charming. So we're not just famous for Mick and Keith anymore, we'll be known as the town with the getaway driver, Reg Turner, as well.' She sipped her wine, enjoying the relaxed feeling creeping over her. A glance through the window revealed that the girls were still in the same position, glued to their phones, oblivious to everything around them.

Steve caught her glance and, on a whim, jumped up and was in the dining room within seconds. His hands grabbed both phones from the girls simultaneously as they screeched in surprise. Holding them aloft out of their reach, he asked them again. 'Are you going to clean up the dinner table for your mum? You can have your phones back when it's all done. No arguments.' Ignoring their pleading he re-joined Cat, grinning in amusement, and put the phones on the small table.

Hesitating for just a moment, Cat picked up her daughter's phone, wondering what exactly was so fascinating the whole time. She swiped her way through countless open applications, shaking her head at the information overload. She stopped and looked at the gallery of photos on the screen, before holding it out for Steve to see. 'What the hell d'you make of this?' Steve leaned over and the two of them scanned the pictures.

'Mum, what are you doing?' Molly screeched at Cat, snatching her phone back. 'It's private, Mum, I don't snoop on your phone.' Upset with her parents, she grabbed Sara's phone and stomped off.

'Now hold on.' Steve called his daughter back. 'We pay for your phone, don't forget that. And why so upset, Molls? If you've got nothing to hide then tell us what all those photos are. Your mum and I don't like the look of them. Looks like people tied up there, what the hell, Molls?'

'Fine!' Molly marched back to them. 'Here, see? It's called living art. It's all about art, but with people and other things. They're artists, that's all, and they're not all tied up.' She was right, the gallery of images contained people, as well as reptiles, trees, anything alive basically. 'We were doing some research for our art project. Can I go now?'

'Alright, calm down, you can't blame us for being worried, that's our job. It's probably time for Sara to be getting home, isn't it? Make sure you watch her 'til she's in her house, okay? You know the rules.'

Miffed, but feeling exonerated, Molly left and gave Sara her phone back. 'That was a close one. I told them it was for our art project. I'll see you tomorrow, okay?' Molly stood at the front door and checked on her friend as she crossed the road and walked down to her front door. Sara waved as light flooded over her from the open doorway and Molly went back inside.

Molly crept upstairs to her room and closed the door. Clicking on the account for @sashablue she studied the photos. After a few minutes of web searching, she knew who Sasha Blue was and what she did. She was some kind of detective, well investigator, she guessed, sorting out people's problems. She read with interest the news articles about Sasha's niece, how she'd gone missing. She'd been kidnapped or something, by some sicko, and her friend had been murdered. There had been two other murders around the same time, in the same little village, and Sasha Blue had been there helping to solve it all. So why was someone tagging her with all these photos? For the first time, Molly considered the fact that the photos might not be just for fun. Maybe the girl in the photos was a prisoner and being held against her will.

She scrolled down her feed, finding nothing of interest, so clicked on the account of @maluspassuum. Weird name. Sitting up straighter she studied the new photo. No one had even liked it yet. He must have just put it on. Feeling a little weirded out, Molly's finger hovered over the heart, not sure if she wanted to be the first one to like it. She looked closer at the photo. The girl had been seated at a dinner table, laid as if for a romantic meal, and was wearing a sexy silver top. Two candles were burning in jars on a server behind the girl, casting an eerie glow over her. She was holding a glass of wine and the image was grotesque, her head being covered by the hood. It was the candles that caught Molly's interest, causing her to breathe rapidly. Most people would hardly notice them, slightly out of focus as they were, but she was sure she'd seen them before. She quickly sent Sara a message.

~

He blew the candles out and cleared the table of its accessories, picking up the glass of wine she'd been holding for the photo. As he admired his latest artwork he sipped the wine slowly, noting with disappointment that Sasha still hadn't reacted, although two of his 'followers' now had.

~

Molly's phone pinged and she clicked on the link Sara had sent her. There they were! She knew she'd seen them somewhere, good old Sara. *You light my fire, handmade candles by Moon Goddess.* The jars contained red wax, and the label was unique – a heart on fire, brilliant yellow on a red background, with a logo of a moon in the corner. She read the caption below the image. *The perfect gift for your man. Hot, sexy, candles to get your evening sizzling. Fire up your night with these gorgeous candles from Moon Goddess.*

What d'you think, Sar? He wouldn't have bought them for himself! His girlfriend must have bought them! She quickly slipped her phone under her pillow, not having finished her message, and picked up her book as her mum knocked and entered her room. 'You going to bed, Mum? I think I will too.' Sudden pain in her right side made her grimace. Clutching her side, her pale face alerted Cat to her daughter's sudden plight.

'Moll? What's wrong? Are you okay, love?' Cat rushed over to Molly, concerned. 'What's wrong? Where does it hurt?'

'Here,' Molly held the right side of her abdomen. 'I think I'm going to be sick.'

Cat grabbed the waste bin, holding it under Molly's mouth just in time. 'Steve, Molly's not well!' She smoothed Molly's hair back, helping her daughter to lie down. 'When did it start, Molls?'

Molly groaned, feeling awful. 'I've had a bit of an ache for a day or two, nothing major, but it just got worse now.' She retched again and Cat helped her up, holding the bin for her, as Steve rushed in. The concerned parents looked at each other.

Cat took the bin to the bathroom to deal with its contents, while Steve soothed his daughter. But as Molly gasped and held her side, he looked at her white face and called his wife. 'Cat, I think we need to get her to hospital, don't you?'

With the decision made, Cat helped Molly down the stairs while Steve fetched the car keys. 'My phone,' Molly groaned.

'Don't worry about that right now, darling, let's just get you to hospital, find out what's wrong, okay?' In too much pain to argue, Molly nodded, allowing herself to be helped out to the car.

~

Sasha awoke with a start. The television was still on, she must have nodded off. She picked up her plate and empty wine glass, taking them to the kitchen as she yawned loudly. Switching off the lights as she went, she picked up her phone and headed to her bedroom. Pulling her clothes off, she brushed her teeth and slipped an old tee shirt on, before crawling into bed. Picking up her phone to check it one last time, she was surprised to see a black screen, odd, she didn't think she'd switched it off. But having pressed the button a few times, to no avail, and tried plugging it in, she sighed, it looked like it had died on her. Great, just what she needed. Well then, she'd read her book and deal with the phone problem tomorrow. She picked up The Thorn Birds, opening it at her bookmark, and read a chapter before turning out the light.

A MISSING WIFE AND ALL THINGS NICE

Bright sunlight streamed in when Sasha opened the curtains the following morning, and she felt surprisingly upbeat – which was odd, she conceded, considering the current state of her life, bad choices in men as well as some kind of stalker obsessing about her. Maybe it was because she had a dinner date to look forward to with Miles – not a date, she reminded herself, just two friends catching up. She went to switch her phone on before remembering it had died the night before and wasted a few minutes fiddling with it before acknowledging that it was dead. Guess I know what I'll be doing today then, she thought.

Powering up her laptop she first checked her mail again. None of the three cases that she'd read about the night before had caught her attention but she did need the money so maybe she should take the case involving someone's stolen garden gnomes. Honestly though? Was this what it was about? And hadn't the writer of the e-mail pretty much stated that they knew who the thief was? A new e-mail appeared and she read the title with interest.

My wife has gone missing.

She opened the mail and read its contents.

Dear Ms Blue,

I wonder if you could contact me as a matter of urgency?

My wife has disappeared, she's not been home for the past two nights, but the situation is rather delicate and I feel no need for the police to be involved. Perhaps you could phone me to arrange an appointment at your earliest convenience?

Yours,
Dr B. G. Ozean

Well, this was intriguing. And no need for the police, a delicate situation. So, he suspected that she was cheating on him and didn't want to be embarrassed, no doubt. *Oh, Sasha, how cynical you've become.*

She e-mailed a reply, giving her mobile phone number but asking him to phone after lunchtime, by which time she'd better make sure that she had a new phone up and running.

Dressed and breakfasted she caught the tube to Oxford Circus, exiting onto Oxford Street, loving the vibe as she always did. She fell into line with the other shoppers, walking along and looking into shop windows. A top caught her eye and, on a whim, she headed into the store, it would look good with her jeans and boots, she could wear it tonight. For dinner with Miles. The thought made her stop in her tracks, why was she thinking about what to wear for tonight? It certainly wasn't a date, Miles was, what exactly? An old friend? No, hardly that, more of an acquaintance if she was honest. He'd just asked her out of kindness, concerned for her after their surprise meeting. But still, it wouldn't hurt to look nice. She tried the top on, loving the sheer, pale grey, chiffon fabric falling in loose folds to her hips, over the tight black camisole. The v-shaped neckline was edged with a hint of lace and the small pearlized buttons at the opening added just a hint of allure. It was perfect, discreetly sexy. Pleased with it, she draped it over her arm. Maybe she'd just check out the footwear seeing as she was here, her boots were getting a bit old and the new winter footwear was in, she may as well have a look.

The boots were gorgeous. Biker style, which she loved, but with a feminine twist. They were perfect, she'd get them. Refusing to face the fact that her bank balance was drastically low, or that she was looking forward to her evening with Miles, and to wearing her new clothes, she paid for the items and turned her attention to the actual reason she'd come shopping. She needed a new phone. Remembering where the store was, she headed down towards Tottenham Court Road.

~

Miles hummed to the radio as he drove to his next appointment, today was a good day. And he was looking forward to his evening with Sasha. It wasn't a date, he was just being a good friend. You tell yourself that all you want mate, his inner voice spoke, you know you always fancied her. It was true, he'd liked Sasha from the moment they'd bumped into each, literally, in the pub that night. But somehow, he'd ended up with her friend Zoe and Sasha had ended up with his friend Eric. Eric, always so confident, used to getting what he wanted, and he'd wanted Sasha. But Sasha hadn't wanted him in the end. He sighed happily. Well, things were turning out differently now, weren't they? He frowned as he thought about the way Eric had treated Sasha. She'd deserved better, she should have been treated with respect not used as a convenience when it suited – but she'd chosen Eric, he mustn't forget that. He was sorry about Zoe, but she'd been so pushy, always wanting more. She'd been fun, he supposed, but he'd had to put a stop to it in the end.

He'd done it when Eric had told him that he and Sasha had met with a problem. That she'd sent him packing. Surprisingly for Eric, he hadn't gone into details. just saying that she'd come around, he'd give her a bit of time and then they'd pick up where they'd left off. Typical bloody Eric, overconfident as usual. But maybe, just for once, Eric wouldn't get what he wanted. Miles relaxed his jaw, after all, *he* was the one taking Sasha out to dinner this evening, not Eric.

~

Steve and Cat waited anxiously for Molly to return to her room. The doctors had told them they'd done the right thing and, having monitored her for a few hours, had decided to remove her appendix. Cat had phoned her school but, as her phone pinged with a message from Molly's friend Sara, Cat realised she'd completely forgotten to let her daughter's best friend know. She tapped out a reply. *Sara, sorry I didn't let you know. We're at Darent Valley Hospital, Molly's having her appendix removed. She should be back from surgery soon. I'll let you know. Cat.* They both jumped up as Molly was wheeled in and, having been told that everything had gone fine, sat by her bedside, holding her hands in relief.

~

It was such a nightmare getting used to a new phone. Sasha growled in frustration as she loaded apps, signing in with passwords and generally getting herself set up. She drank the last of her tea and asked for the bill just as her new phone took its first call. It was Doctor Ozean.

'Yes, this is Sasha Blue, thanks for calling, Dr Ozean.'

Having asked a few quick questions, and asking the doctor where he lived, Sasha checked her watch. She could come along now and meet him.

Taking the tube from Tottenham Court Road she arrived only a few minutes later at Chancery Lane station. Exiting by the steps, she paused to take in the beautiful ancient Tudor exterior of Staple Inn Hall, before turning and heading quickly towards Leather Lane. Turning down the street Sasha did her best to resist the lure of the many market stalls, all seemingly selling something that she'd no doubt decide she needed if she so much as stopped and looked at them. As if sensing her fragile resistance, stallholders held out their wares, a stunning crocheted poncho, an embroidered denim jacket, scarves in floaty fabrics, a leather handbag to die for. She stopped abruptly, all resistance gone in a flash. 'How much for the bag?'

'Twenty pounds, love. Going cheap. Cheep, cheep.' The man turned from her to call out his corny sales pitch at other passers-by before turning back to her to reel her in and seal the deal. 'Tell you what, babe, I'll let you have it for fifteen pounds. Going, going-'

'Done!' *Sasha, what are you doing? You need to earn money not spend it.* She handed over the cash and continued on, cutting through to Hatton Garden as soon as she could to avoid any further temptation.

He would have to live at the furthest most end, she thought, searching for property numbers as she walked along. At this rate, she'd be in the Clerkenwell Road before she knew it. And then there it was, Hatton Heights, a small apartment block discreetly accessed via a narrow passageway beside the inevitable jewellery store. Ringing the bell for Dr B.G. Ozean, Sasha was buzzed in, and she climbed the stairs to the top floor.

Dr Ozean was waiting for her at his open door and was not what she'd pictured – not yet middle-aged, with long hair tied in a pony tail and an earring glinting in his left ear. A white tee shirt hugged his chest, with similarly slim-fitting jeans leading down to bare feet. And painted toenails. *Wait. What?* 'Sasha, come in.'

They shook hands and he offered tea or coffee, which Sasha declined, all the while desperately trying to stop her eyes from dropping to his feet.

'So, Dr Ozean-'

'Brian, please.'

'Brian, tell me everything you can about your wife's disappearance, and why you don't feel it's a police matter.'

Sitting cross-legged on the couch, Brian began.

'We, Samantha and I, we've been having some problems lately. It's a little embarrassing. She seemed to get it into her head that I was spending too much time at the university where I teach. I also run research projects and select students of mine work with me. This work understandably runs into the late hours sometimes, necessitating sustenance, which may or may not be taken at a local hostelry. Samantha, well, she was convinced I was having an affair.' He paused, looking at Sasha as if waiting for the obvious question.

When Sasha didn't bite, he continued. 'Well, as much as my wife was convinced that I was cheating on her, I had my own suspicions. You see, Samantha runs a small business specialising in rare sheet music. She sometimes works closely with clients, hunting down a specific item for them. She's been spending a lot of time 'in the field' as she puts it, lately, with one client in particular. Only two weeks ago this apparently necessitated an overnight trip to somewhere in Hampshire, supposedly to view some antique pieces. He, the client went with her. Well, you can understand my scepticism.'

With still no response from Sasha, he carried on. 'And, well, then last week she and her client had to view a valuable sheet of music which someone had discovered in their loft in, now where was it, somewhere on the coast, Deal, that's it, way down in Kent. Lots of old houses there apparently. So, as you'll guess, they ended up having to stay overnight again. Add to that two late dinners out, an unfortunate evening three nights ago when I worked so late that I decided to sleep in my rooms at the university, and, well, I might as well say it, we had quite a tiff over it all the next day. My research student had to sleep over as well, I couldn't have the poor girl travelling alone so late. But Samantha didn't see it quite that way.'

Stopping abruptly, Brian looked at Sasha, clearly expecting a response.

'So what you're saying is, Dr, er, Brian, that you think your wife has gone off with this client of hers, is that it? And I take it you've tried to contact her? Do you know his name?'

Brian shook his head. 'No idea. I left a message on her phone but I just assumed she was ignoring me when she didn't reply. Oh, her laptop's here, there might be something in there that might help.' He waved towards a laptop sitting on the dining table as his phone rang and, excusing himself, walked out onto the small balcony.

People are certainly strange, mused Sasha, marvelling at his casual indifference and feeling a little irritated with his apparent lack of concern. Surely his wife wouldn't have left her laptop behind if she'd left him? She opened up the laptop and powered it up, one ear to the open balcony door, having been alerted by Brian's slightly covert stance.

'I'll take you out tonight, how's that?' His soft words reached her straining ears. 'Anywhere you like, you choose. And how about I stay over?' He glanced at Sasha as she turned back to face the screen.

'Sorry about that, we're at a crucial stage in our research.' Brian appeared silently beside her. 'In fact.' He looked at his watch. 'I'm going to have to go soon, so if there's anything else you need at the moment?'

'Well actually, Brian, I do need a few things. First of all, when exactly did you last see your wife? Why did she leave her laptop here? Did she take any clothes with her? What's missing? I'll need a recent photo of her and I'll need to have a look around if you don't mind.'

Half an hour later, with a fee having been agreed, Sasha took her leave, accompanied by Samantha Ozean's laptop, with promises to be in touch as soon as she'd found out anything.

'I just want to know that she's alright,' Brian stated as she left. 'She's probably just trying to teach me a lesson and will back home soon, but, well, just make sure for me, that's all.'

A strange marriage that one, Sasha thought as she descended the stairs. He was definitely sleeping with someone, in all likelihood one of his students. Was it simply a case of both partners having affairs? Or had something happened to the wife? Judging by her photo she was a few years older than her husband. Sasha knew not to judge on appearances but Samantha Ozean's rather frizzy, dull-coloured hair, large framed glasses hiding a gentle-looking face, and austere blouse complete with cameo brooch of all things, did not give the impression of a woman likely to have an affair. She also, Sasha conceded grudgingly, didn't exactly look like the type of woman who'd be married to Brian.

That feeling she got when she first began to get a grip on a case came over her. The slight excitement quickened her steps as she returned to Chancery Lane underground station. What had really happened to Samantha Ozean? She only had Brian's word that she'd possibly left him. She wondered who had the money in their marriage? Was it Samantha? Was that why he'd married her? She'd have to look into Mrs Ozean's finances.

Back at her flat, she showered in readiness for her evening. Dressed in her new outfit and satisfied that she'd got the look just right, casual, not overdressed, and not too much make-up, she realised that she was ready far too early. Miles was collecting her at seven so she had an hour to spare. Pouring herself a glass of wine she sat at her desk, hoping to spend the hour searching the missing wife's computer, as well as to catch up with her notifications.

~

Zoe had cried herself out of tears, numb now to her situation and surroundings. Her pleas had fallen on deaf ears, he refused to speak to her, let alone allow her to try to reason with him. Worse than that, she was sure he was drugging her, leaving her confused and hardly able to stay awake. She mutely accepted his offering of food and the usual bottle of water. What she wouldn't give for a huge glass of wine right now, to be sitting in a pub somewhere laughing with friends. The thought of her friends all going about their normal lives filled her with despair. Surely someone had noticed that she was missing? If anyone had, it would be Sasha, she told herself, and Sasha wouldn't just let her disappear off the face of the earth without an explanation. And what about her work? She'd been working at the art gallery for over a year now, Flavia must know she wouldn't just leave her without a word. No, she must stay strong, someone would be looking for her, it was only a matter of time. She spooned the soup into her mouth, wishing she could throw it across the room but knowing that she had to eat something.

~

There was another photo. Her heart sank. Sub-consciously she'd been hoping that it would all go away, that whoever it was would tire of their sick game. Unable to see the girl's facial expression, it meant there was no way of knowing if she was a part of the game, or, if it wasn't a game, a victim being made to do this against her will. She wore a revealing silver halterneck, her lower half not visible, seated as she was at the table. Sasha tried to expand the photo, peering at the girl's hand as it gripped the wine glass. From the whiteness of her knuckles, it was clear that she was far from relaxed, her fingers clamped tightly around the stem. Why a dinner table this time? Was there any meaning to the staged scenes? Candles burned in jars behind the girl, so a romantic suggestion then? She shook her head. Decision time was coming. Either she must respond to this freak and see what happened, or she must go to the police – but she had no evidence of a crime having been committed, they were just graphics and words – and as such, were just a miniscule part of the whole social media animal. She desperately needed to talk it over with someone. The buzz of her intercom made her jump and, having confirmed that it was Miles, Sasha picked up her bag, locked her door behind her, and headed down the stairs.

~

'Mum? Dad?' Molly's voice was weak.

'We're here, darling, everything's fine. You're going to be fine. You just need to rest now.' Cat smiled at her daughter, squeezing her hand and smoothing her hair from her face, anything to have contact.

'You gave us a fright there, Molls.' Steve's voice was gruff, every inch the concerned father, as he leaned over and kissed her forehead.

Molly smiled, her eyes still closed. 'What time is it?'

'It's just gone seven, you've been asleep for hours.' Cat stopped as a nurse came in to check on Molly.

'How are you feeling, Molly? Have you had anything to drink yet?' She raised Molly's bed behind her pillows enough for her to drink, handing her a beaker with a straw. 'You can have some soup a little later, and maybe a yoghurt, I'll be back to check with you in a couple of hours. She looked at Steve and Cat apologetically. 'I'm afraid I'll have to ask you to leave now, visiting's ended. Molly will stay in for one or two nights, the doctor will advise tomorrow.'

~

Miles breathed in Sasha's perfume as she reached up to kiss him on the cheek, her hair brushing against his face. 'Hi, Miles, how are you? I'm so looking forward to this evening, you have no idea.'

She let go of his upper arm, surprised to note how muscular he was. And tall. She hadn't noticed before, maybe she'd been wearing heels. The slight flush that appeared on his cheeks reminded her of his shyness.

Miles smiled happily as they began to stroll along the pavement. 'It's really good to see you, Sasha, I've been looking forward to it as well. You look really nice. How have you been?'

'Oh, okay I suppose and thank you. It's been a bit weird being back home on my own. And I've had some stuff to sort out, a few crappy things going on. And I've got a new case that I'm working on – a missing wife supposedly. But anyway, I'm just looking forward to relaxing with a huge glass of wine and a friend.' She smiled up at him, giving his arm a gentle squeeze.

The Reading Man was a typical London pub turned gastro eatery and with the addition of its dining conservatory had begun to be recognised as a restaurant in its own right. Miles seated Sasha on a couch inside and headed to the bar to get their drinks while Sasha looked about her happily. She loved the book-lined walls and the bookshelves separating the tables and seating, which lent the whole place a feeling of intimacy. Each little area felt like its own private space, that of a study or library, and Sasha picked up a book at random. 'Look, Miles, Somerset Maugham, I love his short stories.' She placed the book down on the coffee table, taking her glass from Miles and thanking him. 'I adore this pub, great choice. And I'm so looking forward to our meal.' She picked up her phone and pointed it at him to take a photo. 'Smile.'

'No way.' Miles laughed and turned away. 'Take a photo of the pub, not me, I hate having my picture taken.'

Sasha shrugged. He was just shy, she supposed. She took a photo of the book on the coffee table, with the bookshelves behind it, and posted it to Graffic with a few hashtags about books, acknowledging ruefully that she was as guilty as everyone else when it came to feeding the animal that so hungrily devoured every shared morsel of people's lives.

They drank and chatted companionably, with Sasha trying to draw Miles out of his shell. She was surprised to learn that he worked for a rental property agency, having had no idea what he did for a living. 'So what do you do, drive around showing clients property every day? Homes, offices, that kind of thing?'

Miles grinned. 'Well, kind of. That's in between finding suitable properties, writing up their details, taking photographs. Then there's the vetting of potential tenants, whether private or commercial, and none of it's very exciting,' he ended with a smile. 'I can pretty much work from home, which is cool. I like the freedom of the work as I get to organise my hours, make appointments to suit, and I like being out and about. That's it really.' He stopped as a waitress approached to tell them that their table was ready. 'After you.' He stood and waited for Sasha to go ahead, carrying their drinks for them as she followed the waitress.

He really is a gentleman, thought Sasha, he's so nice. She sat down, thanking the waitress for the menu, and opened it, before smiling across the table at Miles. 'This is such a treat, Miles, thank you.'

One huge gastronomic delight later, Sasha leaned back in her chair, groaning and holding her stomach. 'I feel so full, I won't need to eat for a week. Miles, this meal has been delicious.' She shook her head as the waitress offered her a dessert menu. 'No, thank you, I'm way too full, maybe next time?'

'Next time, hey?' Miles grinned. 'I like the sound of that. Maybe we should just come here once a week for a massive meal and forget about food in between.' His eyes twinkled at Sasha.

'Maybe we should,' she responded softly, smiling at him. She was finding Miles increasingly attractive as the evening wore on but wondered if it was related to the number of glasses of wine she'd drunk.

As if reading her mind, Miles picked up the bottle, their second, and tilted it in her direction. 'Top-up?'

As she sipped her wine, Sasha decided that now was the time. 'So, Miles, what exactly went wrong with you and Zoe?'

Shifting in his chair slightly, Miles sighed. 'I suppose I'll have to tell you if I want you to tell me what went wrong with you and Eric. Not that there's much to tell, we started off okay, but we were too different. I'm not such a big social guy, parties and all that, but Zoe liked all that, always wanted to go out here and there, meeting up with people. I tried to go along with it, but I just don't fit into that kind of lifestyle. So...' He paused, and Sasha spoke, suddenly understanding what had happened.

'So, Zoe started going out without you.' She spoke softly, realising that it could be painful for Miles. Zoe must have met someone else, that would be it, but she couldn't bring herself to voice her thought to Miles. 'She was always the party girl, any wild nights I've ever spent have always been at Zo's instigation. She's great fun and I adore her, but I can only handle so much Zoe at a time.' A thought occurred to her and she broached the subject carefully. 'Miles, d'you know anything about Zoe going off on holiday?'

He frowned. 'No, nothing, although...' he looked uncomfortable.

'What is it?'

'Well.' He laughed. 'It's probably nothing, but it ended quite abruptly. I suspected she might have met someone else on one of her nights out. To be honest, I needed it to be over, but I wasn't sure if she'd got the message. I tried to call her at work a couple of days ago but her boss said she was taking some leave.' His eyes suddenly flashed as he put two and two together. 'She did meet someone, didn't she? She's gone on holiday with him, whoever he is. Well, that didn't take long, did it?' He looked hurt, and Sasha, feeling sorry for him, put her hand on his across the table.

'I honestly don't know, Miles, all I've had from Zoe is a couple of short messages saying she's on holiday. She didn't tell me where, or who with, in fact, over all she was pretty vague, but Zo can be like that when she's busy having a good time.'

Shrugging and raising his eyebrows, Miles drained his glass. 'Well, she's not my business anymore, I just hope she's happy. Listen, what d'you say we move back to the bar, find a nice corner and get ourselves a couple of cognacs?'

'I say yes.' Grinning, Sasha finished the last drop of wine in her glass before standing up as Miles promptly held her chair out for her. 'But I do fancy a ciggie. And now you're going to tell me to give up, that it's bad for me.'

'There's a lot you don't know about me, Sasha.' He smiled, steering her towards the door out to the pub's rear terrace. 'One thing being that I do enjoy the odd smoke, especially after a good meal, and I'd say the one we've just had qualifies hands down. Take a seat, I'll be back in a sec.'

She looked around, deciding on a small table and chairs partially surrounded by hedging as it would offer a little shelter from the breeze, which was quite chilly.

'Here we go, cheers, and thanks for such a great evening.' Miles placed the two shot glasses down on the table. 'I thought these would warm us up while we're outside. I've no idea what it is but I'm told it tastes like marshmallows or something, kind of like dessert I guess.'

'Mmm.' Putting the glass back down, Sasha lit a cigarette for Miles and passed it to him, before lighting one for herself. 'Cheers, and thank *you*, Miles.'

'Thanks.' Taking the cigarette, Miles spoke casually, as if unconcerned about what she might tell him. 'So, what happened with you and Eric then?'

Sasha nodded, fair enough, he'd told her about Zoe. 'Phew, I'm not sure where to begin, to be honest. I'll have to give you the short version otherwise we'll be here all night. Eric and I, well, it was always a relationship based on Eric's terms. We'd go out when Eric wanted to go out, we'd stay in when he wanted to stay in, and I'd see Eric when he wanted to see me. At first, I didn't notice too much, he was good fun and when we went out it was always a good laugh. The trouble was we always drank too much, especially Eric, and I noticed it getting worse. Don't get me wrong, I'm no saint, but Eric would become a different person with too much booze in him. And then there'd be like whole weeks, or even longer, three weeks one time I remember when he just wouldn't contact me or return my messages. He'd basically just ignore me. And then, out of the blue, with no explanation, he'd pitch up, or call, wanting us to go out, and refusing to take no for an answer. And of course, I'd always give in because Eric's this big ball of crazy fun. I guess that's what made him hard to say no to.'

'That's no way to treat you, Sasha, you deserve better than that. Bloody Eric.' Miles looked pretty annoyed with his friend. 'So what happened when you two had your falling out? According to Eric, it's only a glitch, you're still together, just giving each other some breathing space.'

'He said that?' Sasha was incredulous. 'He's so deluded. He suddenly turned up in Parva Crossing, where my sister now lives, after I hadn't heard from him for ages. Her daughter, my niece, went missing, and I was up there trying to help, oh, well, of course, that's when you and I bumped into each other when I was on my way home. Anyway, I was staying in a pub up there and Eric just arrived and took over, behaving like a complete moron and being so overbearing. He got trashed, like seriously out of his head, and passed out. Anyway, everything about it was just, I don't know, inappropriate somehow, he behaved like such a slob, in front of everyone, he didn't seem to care at all that my niece was missing, pretty much mocked me for thinking I'd be able to help. He acted like

I'd gone off on a holiday and he was joining me. Anyway, it was the last straw of what was already a damaged relationship. In my mind, we were pretty much broken up already, if we were truly ever together.'

Miles's face was sympathetic as he looked at her. 'That's typical Eric, he's never changed, Sasha. He has this total overconfidence about himself, that he can do whatever he wants, get any girl he wants, you name it. And then, when he's got what he wants he treats them badly. He *will* try to see you, you'll have to be prepared for that.'

'Unbelievable, talk about thick-skinned. Oh, don't worry, I'll be prepared, there's no way Eric's coming back into my life.' Sasha gave a small, cynical laugh. 'I probably shouldn't let any man into my life for a while, my track record lately has been a disaster. There was a guy up there, in Parva Crossing, he was also staying at the pub, he kind of lived there, an artist. We got friendly, he was helping me with my missing niece. I really liked him and I thought he liked me. He had me so fooled, Miles. He's married. And he's going to be a father. I don't know how I could have let myself get sucked in so easily.' She stopped suddenly, feeling embarrassed. 'Sorry, I've said way too much.' Was it her imagination or had Miles just looked a little upset at her revelation?

'It's fine, truly. But let's go in and get that cognac.' Once they were settled on a couch with their drinks, Miles spoke again. 'It sounds like you've had a rotten time lately, no wonder you looked so upset that day at the service station. Was that because of everything you've just told me or was it anything else? Sorry, I'm prying.' He put his hands up apologetically. 'It's just, well, you seemed worried about something, you were so jumpy. I got the impression that something on your phone had upset you, but as I say, I'm being too nosy.'

Sasha took a deep breath. It would be such a relief to talk to someone about it all. 'Actually, Miles, you're right, something *had* upset me. Oh, I've needed to talk to someone about it so badly. It's these photos.' She took her phone from her bag and opened up her Graffic account, clicking on the first photo to show him, watching his reaction.

'Sasha, what is this?' Miles looked up questioningly. 'Who's this girl with the hood on?'

'There's more.' She clicked on the name of the account holder who'd posted the photos, bringing up a grid of all those she'd been tagged in. 'I've been tagged in all of these, and the same hashtags are on every photo. And look, there's even a blow-up doll in this picture, with my name written on it.' She stopped suddenly, finding that she just couldn't bring herself to tell him that the sex doll was wearing her own underwear.

'No wonder you were upset, this is terrible. And you've no idea who she is or anything?'

Shaking her head, Sasha replied. 'Nope, but look at the top she's wearing. That's my top, Miles, my niece gave it to me. It's got a picture of the two of us on it. But the worst thing of all is, some of these photos were taken in my flat – the images aren't lies, they're real.'

'Could it just be a game of some kind? Or, look, all this mention of art, maybe it's some new creative idea? Are you sure someone hasn't just done some clever photoshopping?'

Leaning back, Sasha felt filled with relief. 'You know, I never even thought of that. Maybe you're right, oh, Miles, what would I do without you?'

Miles slipped his arm around her shoulders, giving her a gentle squeeze as he looked at her. 'You don't have to do anything without me. I'm here for you, Sasha, whatever you need.' He removed his arm, looking slightly embarrassed.

'You're a good friend, thank you.' She looked at the photos supposedly taken in her flat, as a thought occurred to her. 'But how would someone have photos of my flat in the first place, if they were going to doctor them? I mean, it really does look like she's sitting on my couch and lying on my bed. I'm not sure that could be done, could it? Hell, I don't know, I'm not an expert in that stuff. Maybe I should just go to the police with all this and see what they say, but they'll probably just think I'm being overly dramatic about a few arty photos.'

'I don't know anything about all that photo stuff either, but it seems like they can do anything these days. As for the cops, it's your decision, but you don't want them to say you're wasting their time, it might be better to have a bit more information first. And you've received no other contact from this person? He, if it is a he, hasn't tried to get in touch with you at all?'

'No, not that I know of – his only contact has been through the graphics he's posted.'

'What about messages? Have you checked? I'm just taking wild guesses here, like, I sometimes find old messages on Facebook and stuff, that I never knew were there. It might be worth looking, well, actually you must look. We need to have all our facts before we decide what to do.'

We. She liked that, she didn't feel so alone. 'That's something I didn't think of, Miles, you're full of ideas. I don't use any of those message things on social media. Um, let's see, how do I do this?'

'Here, may I?' Miles took her phone from her and quickly brought up her Facebook app, opening up the messages. 'Here, look, you've got quite a few messages that you haven't opened.' He handed her phone back to her. 'Scan through them, see if there's anything there of interest.'

With her eyebrows raised, she shook her head. 'No... loads of weirdos, how to make money, some bitcoin stuff, asking for money, and, oh listen to this one, hip broadening cream, it seems to be from some guy in Africa, Zambia by the looks of it, calls himself Doctor Chongolo. Formulated to redefine the shape of a woman. Who the hell would want to broaden their hips and thighs? Most of us spend our whole time trying to reduce them.' Laughing, she handed her phone back to him. 'Try your magic somewhere else.'

Miles's fingers moved deftly over her phone screen as Sasha watched. He had nice hands, big, manly, hands, but his touch looked so gentle. She glanced up at his face discreetly, feeling a tingle of attraction.

'Here, see here, He pointed. 'And then you can view them.'

Her eyes quickly scanned the names and her heart sank as she recognized the unusual name @maluspassuum. 'It's him,' she whispered, clicking on the message. 'You were right.' *Involve the police and she dies*. She held her phone out so that Miles could see. 'I can't believe I missed this. If it hadn't been for you, I'd never have seen it, it just hadn't even occurred to me.'

'Let's see when he sent it. Yesterday. Well, I don't know what this all means, but involving the cops sounds a bit dodgy, maybe we should keep them out of it, at least until we've found out more. What d'you think?'

'Crap. I've got a bad feeling about this. If it was just some kind of game, or art challenge or whatever, he wouldn't go sending me this, would he? What should I do? Should I reply? Acknowledge him? Or ignore him? But then what happens to the girl?'

Miles looked serious. 'We need time to think it all through, decide what to do. Right now we should finish our drinks and I need to get you home. But let me help you, okay? Look, I've got appointments tomorrow, but I'll be free later in the afternoon. How about I come by tomorrow and we put our heads together?'

'Thanks, Miles, that sounds great.' She touched his hand briefly as she spoke, before picking up her glass and draining the last of her cognac.

It was quiet as they walked along the pavement to Sasha's flat, most people being back in their homes for the night. She shivered slightly as a breeze picked up and Miles, noticing it, wrapped his arm around her shoulders, pulling her into him for warmth. On a whim, she slipped her arm around his waist, *well it was more comfortable*. They stopped outside the main door to the house containing her flat and released their arms, finding themselves facing each other. Miles gently placed his hands on her shoulders. 'It's been a great evening, Sasha, sleep well, okay? Try not to worry, I'm here for you, we'll work this out.'

'It has been great, Miles, thanks for the meal, and the drinks, I enjoyed myself. And I won't worry about it, not tonight. I'm not even going to think about it I promise. I'll see you tomorrow then? You're sure?'

He nodded, before leaning down and gently kissing her on the cheek. 'I'm sure. Go inside, you're getting cold.' He watched her until she was safely inside the front door and then turned, walking off down the road.

TELL ME YOUR NAME

Stimulated from her evening with Miles and with her mind still sub-consciously running over her new case, which would actually help her pay her bills unlike the game she'd been dragged into on Graffic, Sasha poured herself a whisky and opened up Samantha Ozean's laptop.

Half an hour later she was convinced that Samantha had no secrets and nor was she having an affair with her client – or, if she was, she'd hidden her tracks extremely well. Unable to access her bank account, Sasha could still deduce enough from various downloaded statements to tell her that Samantha Ozean was pretty well off. Scratch that. Samantha Ozean was actually terribly wealthy.

A quick online investigation into the value of rare sheet music told her that as much as six figures had been paid for works by Chopin and Loewe and four figures for an Elvis Presley piece. Nonetheless, this wasn't common and she doubted that Samantha made fortunes from her work. So where did her money come from? She continued to search.

Family money. There it was. Samantha was the daughter of wealthy American parents, the mother having been an acclaimed artist in her youth, with works hanging in several top modern art galleries around the world. Sasha checked out some examples of her art, raising her eyebrows at the auction prices. Amazing that collectors would pay such fantastic sums for what she saw as blocks of colour with seemingly random objects glued onto them. Maybe she should have held onto some of her creations from nursery school she thought, shaking her head. The father had owned a string of nightclubs in New York and the couple had been players on the party circuit – and regularly photographed in scandalous situations. They'd died tragically in a car accident whilst holidaying at Martha's Vineyard, the well-known playground of the rich and famous, and Samantha had inherited their vast wealth, having been an only child.

So Samantha had moved to the UK at some point and met Brian. Further research told her that they'd been married for seven years, a decent enough amount of time she supposed. But if Brian was involved in her disappearance why come to Sasha? To lay the groundwork? To establish himself as a concerned husband? So that when the police inevitably became involved it would seem that he'd taken steps to find his supposedly errant wife?

Her thoughts turned to Brian's financial situation. It didn't take her long to decide that his work would not earn him a huge income, which left her in no doubt that his wife funded their lifestyle. He hadn't seemed overly concerned about her disappearance and was, she was pretty sure, having an affair with a student, whom he was probably with tonight judging by what she'd picked up from his phone conversation earlier.

Social media searches for both resulted in nothing apart from Samantha's Graffic account which contained a few images of music sheets. Here were two people who didn't share their private lives online, which made a change she supposed.

Taking a break, Sasha pulled on an oversized cardigan and stepped out onto her balcony with her whisky. Lighting a cigarette, she leaned on the railing and mulled over the case. It would be easy enough to contact the client Brian had inferred his wife was with, the correspondence between him and Samantha was all there in her laptop. But still, Sasha's gut feeling was that Samantha was not the type to have an affair. She stubbed out her cigarette and went back inside, yawning. She'd make contact with the client in the morning so that she could exclude him from further investigation. Right now, she needed to get some sleep.

~

Molly spent a fitful night in her hospital bed, her dreams vivid flashes of people, girls, bound women in poses, and flames, but each time she woke the images faded away just out of her grasp. She felt as if she was forgetting something but it eluded her every effort to recall it. She was feeling hot and uncomfortable and reached for the water beside her bed. It was then that she realized she didn't have her phone with her. Blast. It must still be in her bedroom. Mum had come in, she remembered that, but what had she done with her phone? She'd put it somewhere out of sight, why couldn't she remember? Her belly hurt, her shoulder too – they'd told her it was from the gas they'd pumped into her for the surgery. Feeling fed up, she visited the bathroom, before trying to sleep again.

~

Sasha lay in bed, pushed her new case to the back of her mind and thought back over the evening she'd just spent with Miles. It had been even more enjoyable than she'd anticipated. To think how different things could have been if Zoe had hooked up with Eric that night, and she, Sasha, had ended up with Miles. For about the hundredth time, she wondered why Zoe hadn't wanted to make it work, why she'd gone out of her way to meet other people and ultimately to meet a new guy – a guy she was now away on holiday with. It was all pretty sudden, even for Zoe, gregarious party girl though she was. She thought about how Zo usually filled her Graffic page with pictures of just about anything, from food and drink to shopfronts and hotel rooms and anything else that presented itself – Zoe truly lived a graphic life. If she was on holiday, she'd have usually been posting photos like mad, but Sasha hadn't seen anything. Tired, and a little sloshed, she decided to check again in the morning, she needed to sleep now.

Although she slept, Sasha's night was as fitful as Molly's – they probably even shared some of the same images in their dreams – But Sasha's dreams were interspersed with sudden flashes of Zoe. Zoe laughing on the beach when they went to Brighton together for a crazy weekend, her long, tanned legs stretched out on the pebble beach. Zoe drunk, chatting to a guy in one of the bars they went to, her bright pink bra strap falling off her shoulder and the guy lifting it back up. Miles's fingers moving over Sasha's phone, but it wasn't her phone, it was her body and she was naked. More images of the bound girl in the photos appeared in her subconscious mind, she was walking through a doorway, then suddenly Sasha was at a dining table with Miles, candles burning on the server, lingerie lying over everything, on the chairs and the table, even on the dinner plates, and it was all hers. She was naked again, with Miles, lying in her bed, except she wasn't real, she was a plastic doll. She awoke with a start, the last image, that of the blow-up doll, hovering in her mind for just a moment, and tried to remember what she'd been dreaming about. It had seemed important but even as she tried to grasp at the wisps of her subconscious imaginings, they were gone.

Groaning, Sasha massaged her temples, she'd overdone the booze last night. She wondered how Miles was feeling, they'd downed quite a bit throughout the evening but it had been fun. She checked the time, surprised to find it was only six, but didn't think she'd be able to go back to sleep. Instead, a mug of hot tea seemed appealing, plus some toast, maybe that would ease her hangover.

~

Zoe shivered in her shorts, didn't the bastard realise she was bloody freezing? She wondered again what he was going to do to her. What did he hope to achieve? He couldn't keep her locked away forever – and when he let her go she was going to destroy him. The sound of the door being unlocked stopped her thought process and she curled up in the corner of the bed furthest from the door. 'It's freezing, are you going to give me some warm clothes? Blake? That is your name, isn't it? Blake Selim? You won't get away with this, someone will be looking for me.'

'No one's looking for you, I've taken care of that. No one knows you're here, only me. So it looks like I will get away with it.' He smiled at her. 'I haven't decided what to do with you yet, for now, you're serving a purpose, so just do as you're told and I won't hurt you. You wouldn't want me to hurt you would you, Zoe?'

Shaking her head, Zoe's mind filled with images of his victims, the young women he'd abducted and tortured. They should have kept him locked up. But of course, he'd been a minor, they'd locked him up for a few years, kept an eye on him for a few more, and now here he was, living a new life under a new name and no one had the slightest clue what he'd done.

'Here.' He handed her the tray. 'I made you eggs on toast, I was having some myself.' His gaze softened. 'And I'll get you some warmer clothes, as long as you don't cause any trouble I'll look after you, alright?'

Nodding, Zoe accepted the breakfast, annoyed with herself at feeling hungry, as well as at her helplessness.

~

Back in bed and cosy under her duvet, Sasha munched on her peanut butter covered toast as she returned to her thoughts about Zoe's social media. Zoe put everything out there, it's just the way she was, she shared, she laughed, she loved, she lived, and she shared some more. So why, all of a sudden, had Zoe gone quiet? Why, five days ago, had Zoe completely stopped posting anything to her Facebook or Graffic accounts? Could it be something to do with whoever she'd gone away with? Was she having such a fab time that she didn't want to stop, even for a second, to post a photo? Maybe...

She drank her tea, leaning back against her pillows, wondering why she was focusing on Zoe so much when surely the main issue was the person stalking her on Graffic. She felt rattled from her bad night, so many weird dreams that she couldn't quite bring to mind now, and Miles. Had she dreamt of Miles? Yes, she thought that perhaps she had - that was embarrassing, but at least no one else knew. Miles. He must have Graffic, he'd been very familiar with how it worked last night. She could do a little spying, get more of an idea about who he was, after all, that never hurt at the beginning of a new relationship. Except that it's not a new relationship, she reminded herself, they were friends, just friends.

She didn't know his last name. Shocked, Sasha stopped typing, she'd never find him and he could have called himself anything on Graffic, people had all sorts of odd account names. She scrolled through the list of people Zoe followed, thinking that she might find him that way, but to no avail. Clicking on Zoe's profile, Sasha scrolled quickly down, looking for photos of Zoe and Miles from their time together. Odd, she'd never noticed it at the time – Miles never looked at the camera, there wasn't one proper photo of him out of all the pictures Zoe had posted throughout their relationship. He really *was* shy. Facebook then, he'd be on as a friend of Zoe's. Except he wasn't. Okay, but that could make sense, if they'd split up maybe she'd unfriended him, or vice versa.

But then the thought occurred to her – she and Eric were still friends on Facebook – clearly neither of them had felt the need to change that – so either things had got seriously bad between Zoe and Miles or he simply wasn't on Facebook. Feeling a little like a stalker herself, she put her phone down. She only had to ask Miles, and he was coming round later. The thought made her smile. Maybe she should have some casual food prepared in case he was hungry, nibbles, that sort of thing. She could pop to M&S at the Westfield, they had a great food hall. She tapped out a quick message. *Thanks for last night. It was fun. See you later if still ok. Sash x*

She followed this up with a short e-mail to Samantha Ozean's client, deciding to wait for his response before taking her next course of action.

~

Steve and Cat arrived at the hospital hoping they'd be able to take Molly home but when they entered her room the nurses were busy attending to her and they were asked to wait outside. They watched anxiously as the doctor went in to see Molly, wondering if there was anything to worry about. He left the room a few minutes later and they approached him. 'Doctor, is everything alright with Molly? Will we be able to take her home today?'

The doctor looked at their worried faces and smiled reassuringly. 'Nothing to worry about, but Molly's picked up an infection. It happens rarely, she's one of the unlucky ones. She had a bad night, and she's in some pain, so we'll have to keep her in a little longer while we treat the infection, but we have it under control. You can go in and see her now.'

Thanking him, they rushed in. 'Molls baby, how are you feeling? The doc said you had a bad night. You feeling okay, darling?' Cat leaned over her daughter, kissing her cheek, as Steve took her hand.

Molly was tearful. 'It hurt so much in the night. At first, I just thought it was the gas they'd told me about, but then my belly felt hard and hot and the pain was like a knife stabbing me. The nurses were kind though and gave me painkillers. It's an infection, it's all red and horrid. And now I have to stay in longer.' She looked up at her parents desperately. 'Did you bring my phone? I need to call Sar, she'll be wondering what's happened to me.'

'Sorry, baby, you poor thing, but you just need to rest and get better. Where's your phone love? I didn't see it in your room? Are you sure it's not here? Maybe in this cupboard?' Cat opened the door and quickly checked through Molly's few bits that had been put in there.

'No, it's not there, Mum, it's somewhere in my room, I just can't remember what I did with it.'

We'll find it, don't worry, you just do as you're told and rest.' Steve thought it might be a good thing if Molly didn't have her phone for a day or two, she spent too much time on it and without it, she'd be forced to rest. He went off in search of drinks while Cat produced magazines, scented wet wipes, linen spray, and hand cream, all picked up in a rush at Boots chemists.

~

Feeling better after her breakfast, Sasha took a shower and dressed, ready to tackle her stalker mystery. She enlarged and printed out all the photos, printed the profile page of @maluspassuum, plus a separate page of the hashtags, one for the chilling direct message he'd sent her, and then, rather laboriously, printed the many photos of his 'fans', making a note of their names at the top. She removed the few papers on the large corkboard in her small office and pinned up everything as chronologically as possible. Standing back, she surveyed her work – it was a true panoply of graphic lives. It was a start. From here she could try to make sense of it.

Her phone pinged and she opened the message from Miles. *Thanks, Sash, it was definitely fun! Yes, still on for today. 4 p.m. ok? M x* She sent back a quick confirmation and checked the time. She should go and shop now if she didn't want to run out of time. Grabbing her bag and keys, she slipped her phone into her back pocket and left her flat to catch the bus for the short ride to Westfield.

~

He left the shop with his bag containing warmer clothes for Zoe, checking his watch. It wouldn't be as much fun with her not wearing the bitch's stupid little pink personalized top, but still, he'd had his fun with that. He still wasn't sure what he was going to do with her. For now, she added spice to his game, so she served a purpose, but eventually she'd have to be disposed of. That would be a pleasant experience. He felt a slight shiver of excitement at the thought. He was still in disbelief that he'd been recognized. He saw so many people and no one had ever even looked at him twice. It was ancient history and with a new name and location, plus being so much older, he'd thought he was safe. But it wasn't a train smash, it had given him the perfect idea for how to reel in the little lady detective. She'd have to respond eventually and then they could really start having some fun. The thought aroused him and he got back into his car, looking around to see if he was alone. Slipping his hand inside his jeans he quickly brought himself release, moaning as he stared at Sasha's picture on his phone.

~

Back in her flat with her shopping put away, Sasha made herself a quick sandwich, eating it as she surveyed her corkboard. She made mental notes of what she knew so far. Two photos of the girl were taken in Sasha's own flat, one possibly in the boot of a car, one sitting on a camp bed. She stopped, considering the photo. The chain around her ankle indicated that this was where she was being held, but where was it? She knew the key with the red ribbon on it was in her own keyhole but had no idea if the red ribbon, tied in a bow, was supposed to hold any significance. Well, at least he wouldn't be able to get into her flat now, she thought with relief.

She concentrated on the photo of the doorway. It meant nothing to her, and she still didn't know if all the photos were supposed to hold significance to her or not. Was this one a clue? Find the doorway and you find the girl? But how in hell would she find one doorway out of all the doorways there must be in just London alone? And was it even in London? Waitrose. The shopping bag the girl was holding in the one photo. She made a note to check out where all the Waitrose stores were, although he had to have been following her that day so maybe he bought something there, which meant he had to be relatively local, as did the place the girl was being held. So perhaps she would be able to find the doorway, but it would take a lot of walking and could take forever. Crazy idea. Okay, she wouldn't think about that yet. She moved on.

The underwear photo was weird. It was totally sexy stuff, hot colours, but did it hold any meaning? Who didn't have some hot lingerie these days, in every colour you wanted? The shops were full of them. It must mean something, she just wasn't sure exactly what yet. Her eyes moved on to the photo that she found particularly repugnant. The room looked so unappealing, the crumpled bed cover, the bare furnishings. But the blow-up doll, wearing Sasha's own set of underwear and with her name written on its belly, disquieted her greatly. She put the rest of her sandwich down, her appetite gone. *Please don't tell me he's having sex with it, pretending it's me.*

That left his most recent photo, that of the girl being made to sit at a dinner table and hold a glass of wine. Were the candles meant to indicate a romantic setting in some way, she pondered? And what about the highly revealing top she was wearing – had he forced her to wear it? She again noticed the girl's strained knuckles, feeling sympathy for her awful situation. Sasha squared her shoulders. She would find this girl – if it all wasn't just some stupid lie created by someone with a warped mind.

Checking her mail, she found a reply from Jake Bedingham, Samantha Ozean's client. He'd had dinner with Samantha four nights ago, before flying home the next morning. He'd left the acquisition of the music sheet in Samantha's capable hands and hadn't heard from her since but hadn't felt concerned as these things usually took time.

Well, that was something she hadn't checked, Sasha mentally ticked herself off – she was too distracted, her head was all over the place. Samantha's client lived in the States and had flown back there three days ago. She scanned her notes, confirming that Brian had seen Samantha before going to work three days ago. Her disappearance was clearly nothing to do with having an affair with her client. What about friends? Maybe they could tell her something, perhaps Samantha had confided in one of them. Making a note to find out about Samantha Ozean's friends, Sasha jumped in the shower to prepare for Miles's visit.

~

Miles let himself into his flat, feeling tired. His day had been busy and his clients difficult. He took a shower, washing off the grime of the day, his spirits lifting as he thought of his visit to Sasha in an hour. His phone rang as he was dressing and he picked it up, seeing that it was Eric, feeling a flash of irritation. 'Eric, how are you, mate?' He made his voice cheerful while wishing he could have ignored the call.

'Hey, Miles, long time no see, mate! How about a drink tonight? I need to sound you out. I reckon Sasha's sweated enough, it's time for me to swoop back into her life and lift her off her feet. I need some ideas. Flowers? Dinner? Or maybe just drinks to start with? What d'you say? You up for it? I came by last night but you weren't in. Come on, let's down some pints and talk about our women. How is Zo, by the way, did you guys get back together? Were you out with her last night?'

'No.' Miles's voice was clipped. 'That's ancient history now. But I'm busy tonight. Sorry, mate. Another time, yeah? I'll call you.'

But Eric wasn't going to let his friend off the hook that easily. 'Oh yeah? Busy hey? New bird is it? Come on, Milo, spill the beans to Eric, you know you want to.'

Miles felt his irritation rising and thought frantically about what to say to Eric. He didn't want to tell him that he was going to Sasha's. One mention of that and Eric would invite himself or just pitch up and that would ruin it. 'I'm helping a friend out, that's all. Like I said, I'll call you, okay, mate? We'll have a few drinks in a day or two, how's that?' Grudgingly, Eric accepted Miles's refusal and they ended the call.

As he walked to Sasha's flat, Miles pondered the Eric situation. Would Sasha take him back? Surely not, she'd sounded pretty over him. But if Eric did manage to weasel his way back into her life it would leave Miles out in the cold again. He couldn't let that happen, not just as he and Sasha were getting closer. He popped into the wine shop, picking up two chilled bottles of Sauvignon Blanc from South Africa and arrived at Sasha's only a few minutes late.

'Miles.' Sasha opened her door to him and smiled. 'Come in, oh wow, that wine looks good. I think I've just about recovered from last night, I was definitely feeling a little fragile this morning.' She led the way into the kitchen, turning back to him. 'Is it too early for a drink? You decide.'

Making a pretence of looking at his watch, he grinned. 'Well I'm up for it if you are.' At that, Sasha took two glasses from the shelf and Miles opened one of the bottles, pouring them both a glass.

'I've been busy putting together a board with everything I know about my stalker, as I'm calling him, it's in here.' She led the way into her small home office and stood back as they both gazed at her handiwork. 'It hasn't got me anywhere yet, but I'm determined to make sense of what's going on and I must find that poor girl. Miles, this isn't a game, his message about not calling the police confirmed that. He's sick, he's holding a girl against her will, but it's like he wants me to find her, otherwise why put the photos on of things like a doorway? I mean, am I supposed to recognize it? The chances of finding it by trawling through every street in London are pretty slim.

'Oh yeah, but I had this sudden idea. This picture here, of the girl holding the Waitrose carrier bag. I'd been to Waitrose that day, so he must have been following me, how else could he have known? And that made me think – if he was following me and he was able to produce a Waitrose bag for the girl to hold in the photo so soon afterwards, then it must mean he lives in my area, don't you think? Maybe he shopped in the same store as me, maybe he was behind me in the checkout queue.' She looked up at Miles hopefully, as she sipped her wine.

'Well, he could easily just have Waitrose bags at home, I do, so even if he did follow you, he could have travelled back to somewhere else before taking the photo, he might not have gone shopping there.'

'Well, yes, but then why do the photo? Surely he's giving me a message. He's saying I followed you today, I was close to you. Ugh.' She shivered. 'It gives me the creeps. It's just, I don't know what he wants from me. D'you think it's time I engaged with him? And look, he had seventy-nine followers after that photo and I checked again just now – he's got ninety-one. Ninety-one people are following him thinking it's all just some stupid new game, or at the very least believing it to be art.'

Miles whistled. 'Wow, that's incredible. I get what you're saying, but are you sure you want to engage with him? It could be dangerous, Sash. We don't know what he's capable of.'

'Well, unless I can find him and find the girl, I can't think what else to do. And screw him, to be honest, Miles, he started it after all. I don't know why he picked me, did our paths cross in the past? Does he bear a grudge against me for something? He obviously knows what I do, although I'd hardly call myself a detective, not exactly, but his one comment, *so you think you're a detective now*, well, I feel that must be all about what happened when my niece went missing. I was involved, in some way, in finding out stuff, you've no idea what a freak show it was. There was quite a bit in the papers about it, you may have seen some of it?'

'I did, I read it all with great interest, you were amazing. Look, he's definitely taunting you, is there anyone you can think of who you've had a problem with lately? You mentioned a guy in Parva Crossing that you were close to?'

Surprised that Miles had remembered the name of the village, Sasha thought about Cal, then laughed. 'No way, no, not Cal. Whatever happened between us, however badly he behaved, he's not like that. We spent loads of time together, he was always on my side, always happy to help, no, he's a good person underneath, I can't take that away from him.'

'But when a man's in a corner... you say you were close, maybe he's got a bit of a thing for you, even if he is married. Has he tried to contact you at all?'

'No, and I've deleted his number and blocked him, he won't be able to contact me easily. Let's go and sit in the lounge while we're talking, it'll be more comfortable. But it doesn't feel like him. This is someone with some serious issues, women issues for sure.' Sasha settled into the couch, curling her legs up, as Miles joined her.

'Okay well, is there anyone else?' He stopped, clearly thinking and struggling with something. 'Look, I know this sounds crazy but what about Eric?'

'Eric? You must be kidding!' Sasha laughed. 'Miles, Eric's many things, but a kidnapper he's not. And even if he was, he'd never be able to orchestrate something like this. Eric's just one of those guys who takes the easy path through life. He takes what he can get, believing it to be his right, women included, but only because he turns on the charm not because he uses brute force. No, this person must be a stranger to me, even if he thinks he knows me somehow.'

'Has Eric tried to contact you at all since you've been home?' Miles's expression belied his casual tone.

'No, and I hope he doesn't, he's the last person I want to see right now.' She groaned, this isn't much fun for you, is it? I'm sorry you've been dragged into it all, you're a good friend.'

There it was again, *friend*, was that all she was ever going to see him as? Smiling, he reached for the wine bottle to top them up. 'Happy to help, you need someone in your corner. And I'm in it, Sash, I really am.' He wondered whether he should mention Eric's call earlier, but decided against it. Maybe he could deal with that problem himself.

'Miles.' Sasha put her plate down, feeling full, her nibbles selection having proven to be rather huge in the end. 'You must be on Graffic? And Facebook?' She felt embarrassed, how could she not know his last name?

But Miles shook his head. 'I know it's weird but I've never wanted anything to do with all that social media stuff. It's normally all you girls who like it anyway, isn't it?' He grinned at Sasha's shocked face. 'I'm teasing you about the girl thing. But no, all that personal stuff, count me out.'

'But then how did you know about Graffic, and the messaging, and on Facebook? I mean, you were like a total expert compared to me?'

'Oh that, well, I have to know about it for work, of course. Obviously, we use social media for our clients, to either attract property owners or to show properties in the hopes of attracting tenants.'

Well now she didn't know whether to ask about his surname or not, if he had no personal social media footprint, she wouldn't be able to look him up anyway. But still, she could just ask... 'D'you know what's funny? This morning I suddenly realized we weren't connected online in any way and I thought I'd look you up. I thought I'd find you on Graffic or Facebook but as I typed your name, I realized I didn't know your last name. Crazy huh?'

'That is crazy, I can't believe it. But my name's a bit bleak, to be honest, rather depressing, definitely on the miserable side.' He was grinning.

'What are you on about?' Laughing, Sasha poked him in the side, to which he slipped his arm around her shoulders and squeezed her. 'Bleak, that's it, my name. Miles Bleak. Now you see what I mean.'

'Well, I don't think you're bleak, or depressing, or miserable. I think you're nice, and quite the opposite of all that. You make me smile anyway, and happy, Miles Bleak.' Sasha was still encircled by Miles's arm and she tilted her head slightly to look up at him so that their faces were centimetres apart. *They were going to kiss, she knew it...* Her phone rang and the moment was gone.

Feeling awkward, they pulled apart as Sasha reached for her phone. Distracted by the moment that had just passed between them, she answered without looking to see who it was. 'Sasha, baby, it's me, Eric, tell me how much you've missed me and I'll be at your door in thirty seconds with wine, chocolate, and flowers.' Thirty seconds? Did he mean that literally? *If so, that meant he was outside her flat.*

'Eric, what are you doing calling me?' She glanced at Miles, rolling her eyes, noticing his rather irritated expression. Well, she didn't blame him, she felt the same. 'I'm sorry, Eric, I really can't talk, there's nothing to say and to be honest I'm busy right now.'

'No, Sash, don't be like that, come on, let me in, we can chat, drink some wine. I need to talk to you about something. It's important, it's about Zoe, something she said, I can't make sense of it, it's about Miles.'

'Zoe and Miles? What about them? God, Eric, you'd say anything to get me to see you. No really, I told you, I'm busy.' Frustrated, she looked at Miles who was trying to snatch her phone.

'Eric, it's Miles. She doesn't want to speak to you, mate. What? Well, not that it's any of your business but I'm helping her with something. No, I don't know anything about that. Nope, no idea. Listen, I've got to go, I'll see you for a drink like we said. Yeah okay, tomorrow, no problem.' Ending the call, Miles apologized to Sasha. 'Sorry, I wasn't sure if you wanted me to intervene or not, I just took your phone without thinking, you looked like you needed help.'

'It's fine, thanks, Miles, it's probably the best thing you could have done. Maybe he'll give up and leave me alone. I don't know what he was on about though, about you and Zoe?'

'Oh hell, who knows? He probably wanted to tell you that we'd split up, make out he was concerned or something. I'll meet him for a drink tomorrow evening. I forgot to tell you that he phoned me earlier. Okay, I'll be honest, I didn't forget, I wasn't sure whether to mention it or maybe I just didn't want to bring Eric into our friendship. You know what I mean, don't you? Am I making any sense?'

'You are, and I get it, I do. Eric tends to take over everything, and we're just getting to know each other properly which is nice. We don't need him barging in and being the centre of attention, which is what he always ends up doing. And you're helping me, Miles, you really are. If it was Eric, he'd have mocked me, laughed at this whole thing. He'd never have taken it seriously.'

Suddenly Sasha laughed. 'D'you know what I've just realized? We're Blue and Bleak. What a pair of depressing individuals.'

'Oh no, what a pair.' Grinning, Miles picked up the wine bottle and, finding it empty, raised an eyebrow at Sasha. 'Shall I open the other bottle? Yeah?' He stood up and went to the kitchen to fetch it.

What a pair. That sounded nice. And trust Eric to spoil the moment earlier – what had he been on about though, about Zoe? And Miles too? No, Miles was probably right, it was just his way of reeling her in, making out he cared about other people's relationships when he didn't even know the meaning of one himself. 'Oh, thanks.' She took her filled wine glass and leaned back against the cushions. Miles was quite the mystery man, one minute shy, the next taking control. She kind of liked that... A roar of an engine and screeching tyres interrupted her thoughts.

Miles stood and looked through her balcony doors. *Bye, Eric.* He turned back to Sasha. 'Let's go and look at the photos again, see if we've missed anything.'

'This one.' He pointed to the photo of the girl curled up on dark carpeting. 'What d'you think, any further ideas?

'No.' Sasha stared at it, willing the image to speak to her. 'It has to be the boot of a car, which gets us exactly nowhere, aren't all boot carpets dark grey or black? I suppose it's something we can investigate fairly easily.'

'How about this one?' Miles turned his attention to the photo of the bed with the blow-up doll in the chair beside it. 'Apart from the fact that your name is written on the doll, is there anything else in this photo that holds any meaning? Anything at all, Sash?' He glanced at her, making her feel uncomfortable.

She supposed if she wanted his help, she'd have to be open with him about everything and couldn't keep some things secret, that would serve no purpose. 'Oh God, Miles, I didn't tell you before. It's just too horrible to think about.'

'Sash, what is it? What aren't you telling me?' Miles looked so concerned that Sasha knew she could tell him and he'd understand just why she found it so disturbing.

'That underwear on the doll, it's mine. I'm so embarrassed and revolted. It's mine, Miles, I swear to God. I've searched my flat, it's missing. He took it from here. He went through my stuff.'

He pulled her to him gently, resting his chin on her head as he looked at the photo. 'Sash, it could be anyone's, just because you had some like it doesn't mean he took it. There must be loads of women's underwear out there that's similar.'

Sasha pulled away to look him in the eyes. 'Trust me, it's mine. I know. I know because it was really expensive and I bought it for a night away with, well, with Eric. It's not the sort of underwear women have just hanging around in their cupboard generally, this was a luxury brand. It even came with its own silk bag to keep it in. Here, I'll show you.' Taking his hand, she led him into her bedroom and pulled open her underwear drawer, realizing as she did so that she was revealing her whole lingerie collection. Blushing slightly, she took out the silk bag. 'See? The same purple silk and the black lace across the bag. It even has the black ribbon to tie the bag with.'

Miles took the bag from her, nodding, before walking back to the other room and standing in front of the photo. 'I'm convinced. You'll have to excuse me doubting you, I'm a bloke, we don't know about these things. But I can see it all matches. Sorry, I didn't mean to embarrass you, this must be so uncomfortable for you. Here.' he handed the bag to Sasha. 'So what d'you think he's saying? Well, other than the obvious, I guess.'

Nodding grimly, Sasha looked at the photo with anger. 'He's telling me he has some kind of control. That he owns a part of me, at least in his imagination. He's playing with me, literally and figuratively. He's been into *my* flat, he's been through *my* things, and he's getting his kicks with a sex doll which is wearing *my* underwear. With *my* name on her belly. Sorry.' She tried to calm down, realising that her voice had risen. 'It's so twisted and perverse it makes my skin crawl.'

'I understand.'

Miles avoided her eyes, and she realized it was embarrassing for him too.

'Not wanting to labour the point or anything, but what about this other underwear photo? Does this look like an average collection to you? I mean, and I don't want to pry, but would yours look like this if you laid it out?'

Laughing to ease the awkwardness, Sasha shook her head. 'Not really, and I doubt many women's would, to be honest. Yeah, there'd be a few sets of the sexy stuff, but plenty of the comfy stuff too, white cotton knickers, that kind of thing. Unless you're a hooker, of course.' She stopped, grabbing Miles's arm. 'D'you think she's a prostitute? Maybe he abducted a prostitute, that could be it. If only we knew from which area, then maybe we could go around and ask the girls if they know of anyone missing. Hell, they might even know who she last went off with.' She calmed down, 'I'm getting carried away, aren't I? I've been watching too many TV shows.'

'No, it makes sense, except for the fact that we have no idea of the area. And, well, we still don't know why he's targeting you. What is the connection between him and you, and why this sex angle?'

'I suppose he's calling me a whore. Which is charming. I think I need to send him a message. I need to engage him somehow, see if I can get a response that gives something away. Yes.' She nodded excitedly. 'This has to be my next step.'

They returned to the lounge as Sasha voiced her ideas aloud. 'What d'you want with me, you sick pervert? Or, why no police, what have you got to hide? How about, who's the girl and why must I save her? No, I need to get this right.' She drank some more wine, trying to find the right words.

'You should keep it simple, just be you and write what comes naturally – let him feel what you're feeling.'

'Okay.' She tapped on her phone, bringing up the profile for @maluspassuum. 'I feel really nervous, it's like I'm in the room with him, making contact with him. It's like I'm opening up something, I'm letting him in.' She typed out her short message and sent it, leaning back and letting out her breath, unaware that she'd been holding it.

They sat and stared at Sasha's phone, willing it to ping with a reply, but it remained silent. 'He might not reply, or he might only reply tomorrow or next week. We'll just have to wait now.'

Miles yawned and, embarrassed, apologized, but Sasha felt bad. 'Miles, you're probably knackered. We were out late last night and you've been working all day, plus doing all this with me. I'm being selfish taking up all your time like this.'

Sheepishly, Miles nodded. 'I am tired, but it's not your fault, honestly, don't feel bad. But I suppose I should go and get some sleep, I've got quite a day tomorrow and then, well, you know I'm meeting Eric at the pub. Knowing

Eric that won't just be a couple of drinks.' He rolled his eyes. 'I should probably be going then.'

Sasha stood at the door as they said goodbye, both promising to update each other with any ideas or developments. Not quite sure what to do, she decided that a friendly kiss on the cheek would be the best thing. But it appeared that Miles had thought the same and as they both leaned in, they found themselves inadvertently kissing on the lips. It was just for a second, then they pulled apart, laughing and apologizing.

'I'll see you soon, okay?' Miles's dark eyes seemed to bore into hers and she nodded mutely, closing the door behind him and locking it.

PLAYTIME

He seemed excited Zoe thought, when he brought her food and water, a little preoccupied with something. Maybe she could get him talking, it was worth a try. 'I didn't thank you for the warm clothes earlier so thank you, I feel much better. And the blanket's nice, soft and warm, maybe I'll sleep a bit better.' *That may have come out wrong, he might see it as criticism.* 'I just mean that I'll be warmer that's all, the bed's not that uncomfortable. Anyway, I appreciate it.'

He still didn't speak, just stared at her, his eyes slightly glazed. She tried again. 'Did you have a good day? Do anything interesting?'

'A good day? I spent half of it running around buying you stuff. I've got more important things to do you know.' He left the room, slamming the door and locking it.

Back in the lounge he sat on the old couch left behind by the owner of the property, and looked at his phone again, re-reading her message. *Why are you doing this, you sad, pathetic, little excuse for a man?* That was all. It wasn't much, but she'd finally taken the bait and she hadn't been able to resist goading him, he thought happily. Now they were playing. He pondered his reply, not in any hurry. Let the bitch wait.

~

Sasha walked back and forth between her office, the lounge, and her kitchen, now and again topping up her glass of whisky. She felt wide awake and mumbled to herself as she moved, trying to make sense of everything. Her phone was in her hand and she checked it almost manically, waiting for his response.

Realising that she'd allowed the sicko to distract her from her current case she forced herself to go through Samantha Ozean's laptop again, this time making a list of her friends. She could only come up with two possible names, which was hardly surprising as friends didn't generally communicate via e-mail, preferring calling or instant messaging on their phones, or social media. She'd have to ask her husband, she decided, having sent e-mails to the two names asking if they knew anything.

As if by coincidence a message came in from Brian Ozean with a photograph attached.

Apologies, I hadn't been home, stayed in my rooms at the university last night. I just came home to find this shoved through my letterbox. I find it rather alarming although it makes no sense. What's going on, Sasha, what's my wife got herself tied up in?

Withdraw statement so police drop case. Then wife comes back. We kill her if you tell police of this.

No, thought Sasha, his wife hadn't got herself tied up in anything, this was essentially a ransom note, albeit a rather badly written one. Feeling slightly ashamed, she realized that she'd allowed Brian Ozean's casual indifference and lack of concern over his wife's whereabouts to rub off onto her. And what's more, this was now the third night that she'd been missing. What hadn't Brian told her? What statement? And how serious was this threat to kill his wife if he told the police? She should call him but, aware of her current drunken state, she replied with her a typed message instead, telling him she needed to see him again as soon as possible.

By midnight @maluspassuum still hadn't responded and she resigned herself to the fact that his reply would come on his terms, not hers. If he wanted to make her wait, he would and there was nothing she could do about it. He was in control.

Quite drunk by now, as well as angry, but still functioning, Sasha made a decision. There was something she could control. She brought up each photo she'd been tagged in on her Graffic account and, one by one, wrote the same comment in capital letters. THIS IS NOT A GAME. THE PERSON WHO POSTED THESE PHOTOS IS A SICK PSYCHO & NEEDS HELP. Nodding, she moved onto the hashtags, bringing up photo after photo of the young girls who'd misguidedly copied the original images in which the woman was posed. She altered her comment slightly and systematically posted it in the comments of every posed image. STOP THIS IT IS NOT A GAME. THESE ARE GRAPHIC LIES. @MALUSPASSUUM IS A SICK FREAK.

She finished the last one just after two in the morning and, satisfied that she'd done all she could for now, blearily turned off lights as she made her way to bed.

~

The sound of his phone's notifications woke him. He must have fallen asleep he realized, as he came to, cold, and still on the couch. He re-read her reply to his message, *Why are you doing this, you sad, pathetic, little excuse for a man?* Then he turned his attention to her comments on the photos. He read them with rising anger. Bitch! Stupid little stuck-up whore. Who did she think she was? Trembling with rage, he climbed the stairs to the bedroom and stood looking at the doll in the corner.

'Hello, Sasha, you nasty little bitch. So you want to play do you?' He grabbed the doll, throwing it onto the bed, and straddled it before slapping it on the face. Pulling the bra straps down over the arms, he stared at the red nipples, feeling his erection taking hold. His hands shook slightly as he untied the ribbons on the knickers and he pulled them off roughly, leaning back to gaze at the dark hair between its legs. 'You think you're too good for me, do you?' He wanted to say more but his eyes were blurring, a red rage glazing over them, and he turned her over, losing his train of thought. He thrust inside the doll, grunting, and released his rage before groaning and slumping on top of it.

~

Molly woke up feeling much better and hopeful that the doctor would let her go home. She was so bored being stuck in her hospital bed, and without her phone she felt lost. She was beginning to think her mum and dad were deliberately not bringing it in. Activity at the door made her look up hopefully, but it was the nurse coming to check on her vitals. That done, Molly was informed that she needed to start walking and that she should begin by walking up and down the corridors. Well, it was something to do, she guessed. She pulled her robe on over her pyjamas, grateful that her mum had brought them in for her, and slipped her feet into her slippers. That done, she took a slow walk, being nosy and having a good look into every room as she passed by.

~

Miles was running seriously late. He'd had a bad night, for one reason or another, and he had appointments with clients. His stomach rumbled with hunger. Great, he needed to eat something before his first appointment. Checking his fridge quickly he found what he'd expected – milk past its sell-by date, a crust of bread in its plastic bag, a tub of margarine, and some ham in a plastic container, which he definitely couldn't face opening right now, knowing that it had long since expired. Miles my boy, you've been off your game lately, too busy with other distractions, *pleasant though they are.* He'd stop at the supermarket on his way home later before he met up with Eric. The thought made his heart sink. He was tired, a night in relaxing would have been nice.

He rushed out of his flat, slamming the door behind him, and got into his car, trying to think where the quickest place to get something for breakfast would be. He had a shop premises in Kensington Church Street to show to someone, so if the traffic wasn't too bad, he'd be able to grab something from one of the many food places on Kensington High Street.

Wiping muffin crumbs from his mouth, he gulped down the last of his coffee, straightened his tie, and left his car. He'd made it with a minute to spare. His phone pinged. Sasha. Tempted to read her message, he resisted, he'd have to save it to look forward to later.

~

She was not going to drink a drop of alcohol today. Gulping down water, Sasha gave herself a talking to. Starving hungry and with a hangover from hell, she decided that a cooked breakfast was needed, which would require an outing.

It was quite a mild autumnal day and she felt better as she walked along towards the Green. There was a great café there which served a delicious cooked breakfast. Once seated, with her order placed, Sasha drank her juice as she tapped out a short message to Miles. Next, she called Brian who told her he would be home all day and she arranged to visit him early afternoon. Finally, Sasha opened her Graffic account and noted the number of notifications. Her drunken actions last night had obviously hit a few nerves. About to go through them she was presented with her breakfast and thanked the waitress, feeling ravenous. Life didn't get much better than halloumi, avocado, poached eggs and toast.

Unable to resist the urge, *it looked so perfect*, she took a quick photo and posted it to Graffic with the caption *#lifeisgood*. Yes, you're right, she silently answered the mocking voice in her head – she was playing into the lies that people posted about their lives – and no, her life wasn't exactly good right now if she was honest, seeing as she was being stalked by a psycho.

~

'Mrs Townsend, it's Sara, I wanted to know if it'll be okay if I go and visit Molly after school?'

'Hi, Sara, yes, of course, my darling. And you must call me Cat. D'you want a lift? I'm going up in a minute but Steve can pick you up and bring you when he finishes work if you want?' Cat smiled into the phone, Sara was a sweet girl, and a good influence on Molly.

'Okay, thanks that would be great. So I'll wait for Steve then. Thanks, Mrs, er, Cat. And tell Molls I'm missing her.'

Cat arrived to find Molly's room empty. Where was she now? She hoped there weren't any further problems. But a quick enquiry at the nurses' station informed her that Molly was taking a walk, which meant she could be anywhere, and Cat started walking along the corridors in search of her daughter. The sound of laughter from one of the rooms made her stop. That was Molly's distinct laugh. She popped her head around the door and found Molly sitting on a patient's bed. He and Molly were chatting away, oblivious to Cat's arrival. She cleared her throat to get their attention.

'Mum! This is Maddox, he's also had his appendix out.' Molly smiled shyly at the boy, who looked to be about the same age as her. 'Maddox, this is my mum, Cat.'

'Nice to meet you, Cat.' Maddox winced slightly as he sat up straighter. 'Molly's been cheering me up. I'll see you later then, Molls, yeah?'

Pleased to see Molly looking so much better, Cat walked with Molly back to her room. 'He seems nice, love, it's good to see you laughing. Oh, and Dad's coming up in a couple of hours and bringing Sara.'

~

Cat and Steve said they were going to go and get a bite to eat and give Sara and Molly a chance to catch up. 'Oh, Sar, it's so good to see you.' The two girls hugged, both smiling broadly.

'I was so worried about you. Everyone at school's worried too. Look, we all signed this card.' Sara handed Molly the card, together with a small gift bag. 'I didn't know what to get you, Mum said you probably weren't allowed sweets and stuff, but anyway, I know they're your favourite.'

Molly pressed the bar of Dairy Milk to her nose, breathing it in. 'I've missed chocolate, thanks, Sar. And if I suck it 'til it melts then it's not really solid food, so that's ok. And, aww, Sar, this is so cute.' She smiled as she held the small white teddy bear embroidered with the words *best friend*. 'I love it, thanks. Mum and Dad keep forgetting my phone. I don't believe them, I think they're leaving it at home deliberately. But I think I'm going home tomorrow so that's okay. Oh, and I met this cute boy, his name's Maddox, Mad for short. So cool. He lives up East Hill and goes to the boys' Grammar just across from our school, how convenient is that?'

The girls giggled and chatted and then Molly said, 'Come and meet him.'

Back in Molly's room, Sara having agreed that Maddox was totally cute, Molly asked her about the Graffic photos. 'Has anything else happened, Sar?'

Sara took her phone out, glancing at the door. 'We'd better keep an eye out for your mum and dad. She's been commenting on everything, that Sasha, she sounds really angry about it. Look at this.'

The two girls pored over the images and comments. 'I knew it. He's a sicko. He's probably got this girl tied up in his basement somewhere. I can't believe she's called him a psycho, he's going to lose the plot with her. But why hasn't he said anything back?'

It was only later, after Sara had left with Cat and Steve, that Molly realised she hadn't talked to Sara about the candles in the photograph. Her message to Sara, on her phone, was probably still sitting there waiting for her to send it, well, apart from the fact that her phone's battery must have died ages ago.

~

For some reason, Zoe's absence was niggling away in the back of Sasha's mind. Sure, she'd received those couple of short messages from her, but that was it. No photos to make her jealous, no follow-up messages, and nothing posted on her social media. It just wasn't like Zoe, no matter how loved up she might be. On a whim, as she drank her tea after her breakfast, she decided to walk along to Notting Hill. It wouldn't do any harm to call into the art gallery where she worked.

She walked along enjoying the warmth of the sun and headed up Portobello Road, smiling at the banter of the stall holders and trying to remember which of the small art galleries Zoe worked at. Frame, that was it, she paused for a moment, admiring the tasteful display in the window, and then entered. A tall, heavily made-up woman approached her, dressed from head to toe in black with her hair hidden by a turban-style headdress, every inch the archetypal gallery owner right down to the glass of wine in her hand.

'Welcome,' she breathed. 'Art is food for the soul, are you hungry, dear? Tell me that you're famished and I'll feed you.'

Sasha grinned inwardly, everything Zoe had said about her boss was bang on.

'Er, hi, I'm Sasha, a friend of Zoe's.' She got no further.

Clutching Sasha's arm, the woman gasped. 'How is she? Is she alright? She left me all alone, disappeared without a word. I've been so worried.'

'Well, that's why I'm here, to be honest, I wondered if you'd heard from Zoe, but I'm guessing not, er, sorry, Zoe did tell me your name?'

'Flavia, dear. Tell me you know when she's coming back to me, I can hardly cope without her.'

For goodness' sake, this woman was way too dramatic. It didn't look like Flavia was rushed off her feet. 'I'm not too sure, she's sent me a couple of messages but they were so vague. She said she was taking a holiday. I wondered if she'd met someone?' Pausing, Sasha looked at Flavia hopefully, maybe she'd remember something.

'Well, Zoe is a beautiful woman as you know, and a great draw for my gallery, handsome clients are just putty in her hands. So vivacious, you know?'

Sasha nodded, that much was true. 'So nothing stands out for you? No handsome client showing an extra interest in her? Maybe inviting her out for dinner or something?'

Flavia pouted, her hand on her hip. 'Oh, Zoe's always being asked out to dinner, of course, she had a boyfriend, but there were problems there, as far as I recall... Oh, d'you know, you've jogged my useless memory. I did receive a message from her, maybe a few days ago? Now, what did it say?'

Sasha tried to control her impatience, could this woman be any more vague?

'Yes, oh now I feel silly. That's right, she was taking some leave. But it was such a short message, quite abrupt I think, not like her at all. I'll confess dear, I'd been at the wine, one does that sometimes, it goes with the business.' She lifted her hand holding the glass of wine, 'We offer the clients a glass, it does wonders for sales. Would you like a tipple?'

Sasha declined politely, wondering what else she could ask. 'So nothing else? Just that she was taking leave? And you can't think of anything else that happened before this? Anything at all?'

Flavia took a long drink from her glass before waving in the direction of a small mezzanine level. 'Only that Zoe had been busy overseeing the opening up of our upper level. D'you know, we didn't even know it was there? It was boarded up and painted over. Why would someone do that? A beautiful space hidden from the world. The stairs were there, of course, but leading to nothing except a tiny landing. And Zoe, such a clever girl, she had the idea of hanging some large pieces up there. And that's when she found it, the hammer went straight through! It was quite exciting I must tell you. We looked through and we could see the space, and a window.'

Nodding, Sasha wondered how to extricate herself, she wasn't going to learn anything here.

'I'm in awe of her. She came in the next day, put on an overall, and started hammering down the boards. Of course, I told her we should leave it for a builder, but she was determined to investigate.'

Feeling that she should at least express some interest, Sasha enquired. 'And did she find anything in there? It does sound quite fascinating, no wonder she wanted to take a look.'

'Oh, you girls, I can't think of anything worse, such a load of rubbish. Boxes of stuff, old books, all sorts of rubbish, and yellowed newspapers, stacks of them. All belonging to someone from years ago, about thirty years ago I think she said, from the dates on the newspapers. She spent ages going through it all, said she found it interesting to read the old news articles, heaven knows why. She seemed quite obsessed about it all. Oh.' Flavia grabbed Sasha's arm. 'It was the very next day that she didn't come into work. She was going to call someone she knew, he worked in property development, she said he would recommend a builder for us. Well, I'm still waiting, as you can see.' Pouting again, Flavia flounced to a nearby table and poured herself a fresh glass of wine.

'Do you mind if I take a quick look around up there, that is if the boxes of stuff are still there?' It was worth checking it out at least.

'Be my guest, dear.' Flavia turned her attention to the door, where a man had just walked in. 'Welcome. Art is food for the soul...'

Sasha nipped up the stairs, having had her fill of the woman. There were just three boxes of stuff, nothing quite as dramatic as Flavia had indicated. The newspapers had been tied with string once, but it had broken with age, and a number of the papers were strewn around where Zoe had clearly been looking at them. But nothing caught her attention. The front page of some had been torn off, but there was no way of knowing whether Zoe had done this or whether they'd been that way when she found them. Sasha poked in the boxes, picking up a couple of old books and leafing through them, before deciding to leave, but paused at the last minute. Maybe she'd take the few papers that had pages missing. If she didn't hear any more from Zoe maybe she'd look into them further although it seemed unlikely they'd offer any help.

Flavia was in full swing with her client and Sasha thanked her for her time, holding up the newspapers. 'D'you mind if I take these?' A wave of her arm indicated that Flavia had lost interest, and Sasha left the gallery, not sure if she'd wasted her time. Probably, but it had been an experience. She'd head to Brian Ozean's now, she decided, glancing at her watch.

Once in Brian's apartment, Sasha wasted no time in getting to the point. 'This–' She pointed at the note on his dining room table. 'This is a ransom note, Brian. Your wife isn't playing games, someone's taken her and they've had her for four nights now. What's the statement they're talking about? What haven't you told me?'

But Brian was non-plussed. 'I've no idea, honestly, Sasha, you've got to believe me.' He looked at her incredulously. 'D'you mean, d'you really think Samantha's been kidnapped? Someone's taken her? So she's not having an affair?'

'Yes, I do think someone's kidnapped her and no, I don't think she's having an affair. Her client left for the States before she disappeared. I e-mailed a couple of her friends last night but I haven't heard back from them. I'll need a list of all her friends from you, with phone numbers preferably, but I don't think that's going to help us now. And Brian, their threat of what they'll do if you talk to the police should not be taken lightly, you're going to have to trust me on that. Believe me, you shouldn't tell anyone about me either. If we need the police involved it's better that it's through me so that the kidnappers are unaware. So you need to talk to me, you need to tell me what this statement is that someone wants you to change.'

Brian ran his hands through his hair as he paced the floor, looking anguished. 'I don't know. It sounds like something you'd see in a movie. I don't make statements, I teach. I research too, but I haven't released any papers for about two years. None of this makes any sense. I swear I'm telling you the truth.' He looked at Sasha in horror. 'My poor wife, you have to help her, please, just bring her home. I don't think I could bear it if anything happened to her.'

So he did care for his wife after all. He sure had a funny way of showing it. But something Brian had said sparked an idea in Sasha's mind. He was right, it was like something you'd see in a movie, usually leverage to force a witness to change their statement. But Brian hadn't made any statements of any kind he assured her. He'd witnessed no crimes and made no statements to the police.

Leaving with a list of Samantha's friends, Sasha headed home with one recurring thought in her mind – mistaken identity. Could whoever had taken Samantha have mistaken her for someone else?

IS THERE ANYBODY OUT THERE?

Zoe had never felt so degraded in her life. She'd fought him as best she could, but he was way stronger than her. He'd had to drag her into the bedroom though, she'd refused to make it easy for him. Sure that he was going to do something awful to her she'd pleaded with him, telling him it wasn't too late, they could sort this out. It was all just a misunderstanding, surely.

When he'd told her to take her clothes off, she'd started crying, to her annoyance, hating that she was showing weakness. She'd caught sight of the sex doll on the chair and gasped. 'What the hell? Why is that here? Why does it have Sasha's name on it?'

'Shut up and undress her.' He'd hit her around the head, making her dizzy, and she'd complied with trembling fingers. The smell of semen hit her as she removed the doll's knickers and she'd thought she was going to throw up. It must be his, which meant he was more seriously deranged than she'd realised.

Now she was lying on the bed, wearing the purple and black underwear, her head once again covered with the hood. *This is it, girl, he's going to rape you.* She lay still, trying not to panic, fighting the claustrophobia from the hood. She could feel the hard, dried, gusset of the knickers, and tried not to think about what it meant. But he made no move to touch her, just instructed her how to position her body, one hand over the left side of her belly, one arm stretched out, legs bent a certain way. She tried to comply, but she could sense his irritation and flinched when he repositioned her left hand.

And then all was quiet. Apart from the sound of his breathing, which was harsh and ragged. She could sense him moving around the bed, stopping now and then for a moment. It reminded her of the other times when he'd sat her somewhere, or made her stand for ages. What was he doing?

She strained to listen for sounds. His breathing sounded so close and yet she was sure she'd heard a movement somewhere else in the room. Not sure if she was being brave or stupid, Zoe moved her hand from where he'd positioned it, hearing his sharp intake of breath. Her hand was pushed back onto her belly and a slight scent reached her nostrils. She breathed in deeply through the hood, it wasn't aftershave, more like some kind of soap, she decided, and not one she'd smelt before. And then there it was again, a slight sound of movement as if someone was retreating, but she could still hear, or sense, his breathing right beside her. Could there be someone else here with him?

'Get up,' he commanded her suddenly. 'Take it off and put it back on her.' He pulled the hood off and she caught a quick glimpse of excitement in his eyes before he hit her again. 'Don't look at me, do as I told you, hurry.'

There had been someone else there. In the moment that he'd removed the hood her peripheral vision had picked up the slight movement of the door as it swung back towards the door frame as if pulled closed by someone. *He hadn't been alone.*

~

Miles rushed into his flat, hands full of supermarket shopping bags. His day had been nonstop and he felt quite knackered. What he wanted to do was to heat himself up a microwave meal and just watch television but Eric wouldn't let him off that easily. He may as well just go and have a drink with him but his heart sank at the thought of the grilling he was going to get about why he'd been at Sasha's.

He stood under the hot needles of water in the shower, washing the dirt of the day away, and pondered what he should say to Eric about Sasha. Should he tell him they were becoming close? No, if he did that Eric would double his efforts to get Sasha back and he couldn't let that happen. He'd play it by ear and see where the evening went.

He took a taxi to Maida Vale, entered the pub and, after stopping at the bar, headed through to the riverside terrace holding two glasses. 'Miles, mate.' Eric jumped up and the two men did a one-armed hug as lager sloshed from the glasses in Miles's hands. 'It's good to see you, how's it going?'

Miles fended off questions about Sasha as best he could as Eric became steadily more inebriated, which had been his hope. He was quite fond of Eric, they'd been friends for a few years now, and he found himself enjoying the evening as it progressed. He survived the third degree about Zoe and managed to convey to Eric that Sasha just wasn't in a relationship place right now. Eric's jealousy over Miles's visit to hers had been fairly easy to allay when he'd explained that he was helping her with one of her investigations. This Eric had found hilarious, his rather condescending comments about Sasha and her job irritating Miles, but he'd smiled and played along.

He'd sensed Eric's eyes studying him on and off throughout the evening and once or twice Eric had seemed on the point of saying something but had appeared to think better of it, distracted with ease by Miles's regular trips to the bar for more drinks. They polished off some pretty good burgers with fries, and all in all it had been a good evening.

~

Sasha's phone had been quiet since the flurry of likes to her comments on the photos. Maybe she'd got the message across to the naive followers of the sick pervert's account. She decided to cross-check her list and see if any of them had deleted their photos. With delight, she found that a few had. Good, that had been her aim. She'd post a statement in the form of a graphic, on her own account, maybe that would encourage a few more to delete their photos. It would have the additional benefit of making him mad, which was also good.

She fleetingly wondered whether she should send Miles a message, but didn't want to appear needy. He'd told her he had a busy day, plus he was out with Eric this evening. No, she'd wait until she had something to tell him at least.

Opening up her laptop, Sasha's fingers hovered over the keys as she wondered where to begin her search. If her hunch about Samantha Ozean's disappearance was correct and it was a case of mistaken identity, then did that mean, crazy thought it sounded, that there was another Brian Ozean somewhere? Typing in his initials and surname she hit enter.

Her eyes scanned the results one by one and on the second page Sasha inhaled sharply. Bruce Gavin Ocean – or to be more accurate, Dr B. G. Ocean. What were the odds, she thought excitedly? Two doctors with the exact same initials and a similar surname – a surname so similar that someone could easily make a mistake, especially if their grasp of English was poor, which it quite likely was, considering the badly written ransom note. Add in the close proximity of the two differing letters on the keyboard and it would actually be hard *not* to make a mistake.

Dr Bruce Ocean worked at a London hospital but also had private rooms. Having skimmed through his website, Sasha next used an online address finder and found herself staring at the details of his home address as excitement buzzed through her. She fetched herself a glass of wine on autopilot, before staring at his address again in disbelief.

Dr Bruce Ocean and his wife, Delia, lived in Hatton Place. This was beyond unbelievable. Had someone confused him with Dr Brian Ozean of Hatton Garden, resulting in the abduction of Samantha Ozean when they'd intended to abduct Delia Ocean?

Her fingers flew over the keys as she brought up everything that she could find about Dr Bruce Ocean. She opened a separate tab for image results and found a number of captioned images of the doctor *out and about in his local Hatton Garden area*. Returning to the online articles Sasha quickly sifted through and discarded a number of stories referencing his clinic or his attendance at conferences, and found herself left with news stories about his position as a witness in a forthcoming trial. This was it – she'd found what she was looking for.

Clicking back and forth between the stories, Sasha absorbed the information. He was listed as the sole witness in a case concerning a drugs and prostitution gang. The details were fairly substantial, telling Sasha that a gang member had been stabbed and had required emergency medical attention. A doctor had been called in for urgent surgery, one Dr Bruce Ocean, and he'd since identified the man as his patient when shown his photo by the police. The gang member, a high-ranking one, was charged with murder based on Dr Ocean's corroborative evidence. On the night in question problems had arisen with a rival gang over a new shipment of girls and drugs and three gang members had been killed in the fighting, together with two of the girls, but another of the girls had succeeded in stabbing the gang member in question. His injury was severe and his fellow members had dropped him off outside the emergency rooms. This was when Dr

Bruce Ocean had been called in to carry out an emergency procedure and was thus able to attest to his treatment of the man's injury on the night in question.

Sasha read on with rapt interest. The police had arrived and taken the girls into safe custody but the other gang members remained at large. The girl who'd stabbed the gang member requiring medical attention had also been a witness but was killed in a hit and run accident a few days later.

According to the writer of the main article, the other girls were refusing to talk for fear of retribution, and the case was now hanging solely on the witness testimony of Dr Bruce Ocean.

The very Dr Bruce Ocean who was quite likely enjoying a relaxing evening with his wife Delia, with no idea that a Dr Ozean's wife had been abducted in error, for this was surely what had happened. It would have been such an easy mistake to make, she thought – to first try to find out a little about the doctor via the internet – thus being armed with the knowledge that he lived in the Hatton Garden area – and then to mistype just one letter in his surname so that the wrong address displayed on the screen – an address that raised no alarm bells because it was within the anticipated area.

Sasha gasped. This was huge. And dangerous. She thought about poor Samantha Ozean being held somewhere by a bunch of unscrupulous and evil people. Little did the gang know but Dr Ocean wouldn't be changing his statement because Dr Ocean hadn't had his wife abducted, nor had he received a ransom note telling him to do so.

This was more than she could, or should, handle on her own, Sasha acknowledged. She'd get in touch with her police contact in the morning and tell him everything she knew.

There just remained a quick online search for the wife who was conspicuously absent in the photos showing Dr Ocean. Maybe she just liked to keep out of the public eye – which would add substance to Sasha's certain theory that the wrong wife had been abducted. Finding nothing and realising that her glass was empty, she refilled it just as her phone pinged.

The freak had replied. Part of her didn't want to open the message, it was opening up much more than just the message itself, it was opening a dialogue between them, and she wasn't sure how comfortable she was with that. But knowing that she really had no choice, not if she was going to try and figure everything out, she clicked on it and read it.

She could almost feel his rage. *Why? You arrogant bitch. You made a choice once. It was the wrong one. Now you pay.* There was an underlying feeling of impotence to the angry reply. What choice had she made? Had she come across this person somewhere? She mixed with so many people through her work, and even while she'd been in Parva Crossing, she'd crossed paths with lots of people. But it was hard to believe that anyone she'd ever known could behave like this.

Another ping on her phone and she saw the new notification. He'd posted another photo. The girl, well, woman, yes, definitely a woman now that she could see her virtually naked body, was strategically posed on the bed – and she was wearing Sasha's underwear. It was too small for her, the cups of the bra unable to fully contain her breasts. She was hooded as usual.

He's done this in response to my message, she thought. I've made him angry. She hoped that he'd only posed the woman and not hurt her. This was a fit of sexual anger directed at Sasha personally. The thought scared her. Gratefully, she thought about Miles. At least she had a good man in her corner. She looked at the photo more closely, wondering about the positioning of the woman's left hand. It was an unnatural place to put her hand, awkwardly resting on her lower belly, her elbow at a sharp angle. Everything was controlled by him, and presumably had meaning to him, so why the position?

Finding her glass empty yet again she re-filled it, observing that her ideas came to her when she occupied her mind with other things. Laying out the old newspapers from the art gallery, Sasha pondered Zoe's interest. Did Zoe tear off the front pages, and if so, what was it that was so interesting from thirty years ago? And what did she do with the pages? Flavia had said that she'd been going to call a property developer that she knew. Well, unless Zoe knew loads of property developers, it had to be Eric. That posed a problem. The last thing Sasha wanted to do was to contact Eric.

But Miles could ask him. Maybe Zoe had mentioned the newspapers she'd found? Something kept worrying away in the back of her mind if only she could grab at it. In a moment of clarity, she realised something. A woman had been taken against her will, of that she was sure, and was being made to pose for the photos – photos which most definitely weren't arty graphics but images of abuse – and at the same time, Zoe had suddenly taken off on a last-minute trip, leaving Flavia in the lurch, which wasn't like her, even if she did love adventure. But no, it couldn't be, that was madness. Zoe couldn't possibly be the woman in the photos. Could she?

She looked at the latest photo again. Zoe was always tanned. And Zoe had big boobs, bigger than Sasha's. And Zoe had a tattoo on her belly, on the left side. The woman in the photo had her hand over the very spot where Zoe's tattoo of a rose was. Shock jolted through her body as she studied the photo. It could be Zoe. But Zoe was on holiday. Zoe had replied to her messages.

With a sickening realisation she acknowledged that if Zoe had been taken by him, then the sick bastard, whoever he was, could also have her phone. What if he'd been replying to her messages, pretending to be Zoe? Was she just projecting her concern over Zoe's sudden absence into this other sick scenario? Or were her fears justified?

She wandered through to her office and stood looking at the enlarged graphics on the board. Suddenly, as clear as day, she was seeing an image of Zoe on a bar stool, her bright pink bra strap fallen from her shoulder. And here was a photo of brightly coloured underwear, bras and knickers laid out, in colours that Zoe adored. Including a bright fuchsia pink set. The cups of the bras were quite large, they could easily be Zoe's. Frantically she stared at the photo of her bed and the woman lying on it. She zoomed in on the blue-painted toenails. With sickening dread, she nodded to herself. Zoe always had her toenails painted exotic colours, and blue was one of her favourite choices.

She had to tell Miles. But looking at her watch she wasn't sure if he might still be out with Eric or if he was in bed already. Whichever way, it was late and she'd have to leave it until the morning. The trouble was, she was feeling defiant now, helped by what was now her third glass of wine. Maybe she should send another direct message telling him she knew the girl was Zoe. Or she could send Zoe another message saying she knew she'd been taken and that she was going to find her. Of course, if it was true then Zoe would never see the message, but *he* would. And if she was wrong, well then, she'd just get a pretty confused reply from Zoe, wouldn't she? Except she wouldn't know if it was Zoe. She slumped in defeat, realising the impossibility of the situation. The only way she could be sure that Zoe was okay was if she actually spoke to Zoe.

A sudden noise outside on the pavement made her move to her double doors and peer out from behind the curtains. Eric was looking up at her balcony. 'Sasha! Sasha, baby, I know you're there, I can see you.'

His shouting would disturb the neighbours, she thought frantically. But she couldn't let him in, he'd never leave.

'I need to talk to you, just let me in.'

She stood behind the curtains deliberating on what to do. Finally, she opened the door and stepped out onto the balcony.

'Eric!' she hissed. 'Please just go home. We've got nothing to talk about and it's late. You're disturbing people.' She watched him lurch drunkenly, stumbling as he held onto the streetlight for support. 'And you're drunk. Go home, Eric, I mean it, just go home, you can hardly stand up. And you can throw away my key, in case you had any ideas. I changed the locks. I'm going back inside now and I'm going to bed. Goodnight.' She closed the door and pulled the curtain back across before quickly switching the lights off. She could hear Eric's muffled voice going on, something about her key. Maybe if he saw her flat was in darkness he'd give up.

She stood silently, trying to gauge what he was doing. All was quiet. After a few minutes, she peered out, relieved to see no sign of him. He was seriously becoming a nuisance, and really, there was nothing he could say to her that would change their situation. She'd tell Miles tomorrow, maybe he could have another word with him and tell him to leave her alone.

She could block his number. Why hadn't she thought of that? Bringing up Eric's number, she did just that, feeling relieved. She seemed to be making a habit of blocking men's numbers these days. Fleetingly she thought of Cal. She'd blocked his number as soon as she'd found out that he was married. Feeling sad, she remembered how much she'd liked him. Her record with men wasn't looking too good these days.

But there *was* Miles. Kind, sweet, and gentle Miles. She was developing feelings for him. Which was weirdly inappropriate, considering the reasons for their spending time in each other's company. Leaning back on the couch cushions, the only light that of the street light penetrating the fabric of the curtains, she thought back to last night. They'd kissed. Okay, it had been an accident and had only lasted for a second, but it had been nice. *Very* nice. Had he thought so too? He was so hard to read, his shyness hiding so much.

Yawning, she thought about going to bed. But first, she'd send that sick freak a message, and Zoe too. It was time to rock the boat a bit more. Switching on a small table light, Sasha put her empty wine glass in the sink and grabbed a tumbler, sloshing some whisky in and adding ice. She needed some Dutch courage.

Satisfied with her work, she threw back the last of the whisky and went to bed.

~

Brian and Stacey fell through the front door into her flat, laughing. 'Shhh.' Stacey giggled, exaggeratedly putting her finger to her lips and glancing at her flatmate's bedroom door.

The door swung open and Claudia emerged from her room holding a bottle of whisky. 'Hi, guys, I am also just home, we will have the night hat?'

Giggling again, Stacey corrected her flatmate. 'You mean nightcap, Claudia, and yes, we will have one, thank you.'

The whisky made, an already drunk, Brian maudlin, and the two girls looked at each other as he began to speak sentimentally about his wife. 'Someone's taken her, Stace. I mean, who would do that? My poor Samantha, all alone somewhere, scared and cold. And I can't withdraw the bloody statement, can I? I never made one, I don't even know what they're on about. I shouldn't be here, I should be at home.' He struggled to stand as Stacey pulled him back down.

'No, Brian, you're in no fit state to go home. Stay here, let me take care of you.'

'What is this statement?' Claudia's eyes narrowed. 'What are you talking about? Stacey said your wife has just left you, gone off with some other lover.'

Stacey interrupted. 'Well poor Brian thought she'd left him, but then he got this strange note in the door, something about withdrawing a statement. But I'm sure it's all a mistake. She's probably got herself a boyfriend, after all, I've taken Brian.' She stroked Brian's hair as he lay in her lap.

'No mistake.' Brian spoke softly. 'She's been kidnapped and there's nothing I can do to get her back. If they'd just asked for money...' His eyes closed drowsily.

'My poor Doctor Ozean, such a drama queen.' Stacey leaned over and kissed his forehead, watched by Claudia.

'Stacey, your Brian is doctor? You call him Doctor Ozean, why is that?'

'Well, that's his name.' Stacey was puzzled.

'Ozean.' Claudia repeated the name, her eyes gleaming, before leaning forward to pour more whisky into their glasses while Brian snored gently. 'Where does he live, Stacey, your doctor man? I forget.'

'I don't recall ever telling you. Did I? Ugh, I'm feeling horribly drunk, don't give me any more to drink after this. He lives somewhere in Hatton Garden, you must have heard of it – the place famous for jewellery? Hatton Heights, I think that's the name. I bet it's really gorgeous, his wife must have paid for it, of course, with all her money.' Noticing Claudia's incredulous expression, Stacey grinned. 'You look surprised. I'll have to take you there, it's filled with jewellery shops and you've never seen so many diamonds.' Yawning, she swallowed a mouthful of her whisky and groaned. 'I need to get Brian to bed before I fall asleep.'

'Yes, yes, I also need to sleep. But I don't understand why he wants his wife back if he is with you? If she comes back, he will leave you, no?'

'No.' Stacey laughed at Claudia's confused expression. 'He wants her back because she gives him money and then he spends it on me. She's loaded, you know, rich.'

'Yes, is very clear to me now.' Claudia gave a small laugh. 'Stacey's doctor lover from the Hatton Gardens will pay for wife to come back then will spend money on Stacey. You take your Doctor Ozean to bed now.'

THOSE WERE THE DAYS, MY FRIEND

He'd felt all-powerful when he'd sent his reply to her. That would put her in her place. Tell her who was the boss. Feeling the beginnings of arousal, he'd taken pleasure in causing his prisoner pain. It was the little bitch's fault after all. He'd used his belt, as he had when he was younger. She should thank him, he hadn't even begun to cause her any real pain. The sight of the raw welts on her back, her cries as she tried to hunch away from him, excited him further and he left her, going down to the room to join his Sasha.

By now highly aroused, he'd thrown her on the bed, touching himself as he slapped her around the head. 'You arrogant bitch whore, who's in control now?' He could feel himself close to release and stopped, savouring the moment, as he repositioned the doll for entry. He smoothed her hair and kissed her gently. 'Sasha, you're mine, look what you do to me.'

The buzzing of his phone disturbed him and torn between achieving his release or checking to see if she'd replied, he did the latter, knowing it would excite him further if it was from her.

He read her message in disbelief. *You impotent little man. You think you're in control. Is that the only way you can get it up? You're not a real man and would never be my choice.*

Pure rage engulfed him. The little slut thought she was better than him. Hatred coursed through him. He punched the doll's head, taking satisfaction in watching it fall to the side. He punched its breasts, its stomach, before flipping it over and punching at its buttocks. Her words repeated themselves on an endless loop in his head, *you impotent little man... the only way you can get it up...*

He looked down at himself. He was limp, his shrunken penis now soft and pathetically flaccid. With a roar, he collapsed on top of the doll, curling up and howling at his emasculation.

~

With phone numbers exchanged, Molly and Maddox said goodbye. Both were being discharged from hospital and Molly waited impatiently, fully dressed, for her mum to come and get her. Cat arrived and helped her daughter to the car while Molly chattered away about Maddox. 'He's such a great guy, Mum, he's really nice and he goes to school across the road from me, at the boys' Grammar.'

Making the appropriate noises, Cat wondered if this was when the trouble started. Up until now, Molly hadn't shown too much interest in boys, but it had to happen at some point. And he had seemed like a decent boy. Parking the car, she helped her daughter into the house and upstairs to her bedroom.

~

Her phone was on her bedside table. She definitely hadn't left it there. And it was dead. Putting it on charge, Molly fired it up and checked her messages. She'd been about to send Sara a message when she'd doubled over in pain. But the message had disappeared. Sara's Etsy link was still there and she clicked it. There were the candles by Moon Goddess. She compared them to the candles in the photo of the girl at the dining table again. They were out of focus, but still, Molly was sure they were the same. She had to tell @sashablue. Which was a bit embarrassing. She was just a kid – wouldn't this Sasha just think she was being stupid? Maybe they could meet, that way she'd be able to make sure that Sasha took her seriously.

It would be an adventure. She and Sara could go up to London for the day. But would her mum let her? Not likely, not after just getting out of the hospital. Maybe if she waited a couple of days, did everything right, she was already feeling better and would be even stronger then. And perhaps Maddox could come with them too. Yes, that's what she'd do. But first, she had to convince her mum that she was better. She'd be a model patient.

~

It wasn't just a hangover, no, she had enough experience with those, especially lately. This was a general heaviness throughout her body, a feeling of utter weariness. Please no, Sasha pleaded, as she felt the gnawing pain taking hold inside. She hated her body for its betrayal, but hated her endometriosis more, knowing it was the real monster inside her. It had been the curse of her life. Ha, she acknowledged the pun, even as she pulled herself out of bed and went to the bathroom.

It was just a little spotting, maybe it would pass, she thought hopefully. Stress was a major factor, that much she'd learnt over the years, and she was certainly stressed out right now. Toast, tea, and strong painkillers, and she began to feel a little more normal. She checked her phone, but he hadn't replied, was probably still fuming. Nothing from Zoe either, or from him – if he had Zoe's phone, which she feared would prove to be the case.

Trying to ignore her extreme tiredness, Sasha made a call to D.S. Tony Palmer. She should try to meet him as soon as possible and fill him in on her case. His voicemail kicked in and she left a message asking him to call her urgently. Not wanting to waste any time she decided to go in search of Dr Ocean.

~

He awoke, still curled up on the bed, freezing cold, with his jeans and underpants around his ankles. In disgust, he pushed the doll away so that she fell onto the floor. Pulling his pants and jeans back up, he shook his head, trying to clear it. The little bitch queen had destroyed him again, taken his pleasure, acted like she was in control. He had to show her that she wasn't.

He ignored Zoe when he entered her room, roughly covering her head with the hood, before finally addressing her, coldly. 'Take your clothes off. Now kneel on the bed facing the wall.'

Drained of attempts at resistance, Zoe did as he instructed, shivering as the cold air hit her bare flesh. She wanted to ask him for some cream for her back but didn't dare, sensing his anger. The welts from the beating he'd given her had wept in the night, and the discomfort had kept her from sleeping.

She felt him on the bed beside her and cringed, waiting for him to touch her, but nothing happened. The chain around her ankle tightened suddenly, almost unbalancing her.

'Keep still,' he barked.

Zoe listened to the sounds, trying to work out what he was doing. He was moving around the room, stopping every so often. And then the sound of the chain, its feeling of looseness, and her clothes were thrown at her.

'Get dressed.'

Once she was sure he'd gone and she'd heard the door being locked, Zoe removed the hood and frantically pulled her clothes back on. Hungry and thirsty, for he'd brought her nothing to eat or drink the night before, she looked around frantically. Nothing. She began to cry, giving in to her mounting panic.

~

About to leave her flat, Sasha hovered indecisively for a moment, not sure whether to phone Miles or not. She still wasn't quite sure on what footing their relationship was and didn't want to come across as too hopelessly needy. But Miles was a kind person, she'd sensed it in him from the moment they'd bumped into each other at the service station. She decided to call him.

'Sasha, hi, everything okay?'

She could hear that he was in his car. 'Miles, sorry, you're driving. I can call you later.'

'No, it's fine, I'm pulling over. What's wrong, you sound a little anxious?'

'Well, oh, look, it's about Eric. I hate having to bother you, but he came round last night.'

'What?' Miles's sharp response was edged with concern. 'You didn't let him in did you? Did you speak to him? What happened, what did he say, are you alright?'

'I'm fine, really. No, I didn't let him in, he was outside, late evening, it must have been after you left him last night. He was drunk, but that's nothing new for Eric. I spoke to him from the balcony, told him to go, and he did.'

'Did he say anything?'

'No, just drunken stuff, nothing of importance, you know Eric. I, well, I blocked his number, I thought it best to stop him from keeping on trying to contact me.'

'You did the right thing, Sash, he was drunk last night, completely off his head by the time I left. The guy's got issues, he was getting quite out of control at the pub. Maybe he'll get the message this way. Look, I've got a busy day, but I could come round later? We could go out for something to eat again?'

Smiling into the phone, Sasha nodded. 'I'd like that. I need to ask you to do something for me, it's about Eric, but I'll tell you later. Oh, and I've got some ideas about the missing girl. Oh, I may as well say it, Miles, I think it might Zoe.'

'Zoe?' Miles sounded shaken. 'Surely not, Sasha, you must be mistaken, she's on holiday, you said so yourself.'

'I know it sounds crazy, but there are things that make sense. It could be her, Miles, oh God, what if it is? Poor Zo, being held by that sick freak.'

Miles spoke brusquely. 'Look, I have to go, I've got appointments, but listen, don't tell anyone about this, we don't want to cause a panic. We need to get our facts straight, okay? We'll talk about it tonight.' His voice softened. 'You look after yourself, okay?'

'I will, and thanks, Miles, you too. I'll see you later then.' Feeling better for having spoken to him, Sasha made a quick call to Dr Ocean's private rooms before taking the tube to Oxford Circus. Crossing through Cavendish Square Gardens she headed along Harley Street looking for The Cavendish Care Clinic. The autumnal sunshine felt good on her face and the unexpectedly long walk helped ease her cramping. She felt her energy returning and quickened her pace as her phone rang.

'Tone, hi, thanks for calling back.'

'No prob, Sash, long time no speak. Good job up in Parva Crossing, by the way, I read about it in the paper, right old village of horrors you found yourself in there, sounds like you're a fully-fledged private investigator now. So what's got you all hot and bothered then? Got yourself involved in the crime of the century have you?'

Listening to Sasha's rapid speech bringing him up to speed, Tony interrupted. 'Whoah, slow down, baby. This is sensitive stuff. I was involved in the case so I should know. And this Mrs Ozean has been missing for five nights you say? Where are you now?'

The brass plate on the wall confirmed that she'd reached her destination, as did the distinctive logo of the three interlinked identical letters. 'I'm at his rooms in Harley Street, I'm about to go in and speak to him.'

'No, no, hold on, I'm not far away, give me five minutes, okay? I'm on my way, just wait for me'

Dammit, she was right here. Well, she could just pop in and confirm that Dr Ocean was still in his rooms, no harm in that. Opening the door, Sasha's feet sank into a plush carpeted elegant hallway as the gentle strains of classical music reached her ears.

'Can I help you?' A rather austere-looking woman with stiffly coiffed hair looked up from her desk.

'Yes, hi, I phoned earlier. I believe Dr Ocean is here at the moment?'

'I'm afraid not. He's just left to go home for the day so if you'd like to make an appointment for another time?' The woman waited, pen poised over her diary.

'No, thank you but no, not to worry.' Sasha backed out of the room under the receptionist's stern gaze and left the building, perching on a wall to wait for Tony.

She didn't have long to wait, a loud hoot alerting her to his arrival and she jumped in the car before he could get out. 'He's not here. We should go to his home, it's in Hatton Place.' Sasha told Tony everything that she knew while he drove, his whistles of surprise echoing her own feelings of incredulity at the unbelievable and unfortunate coincidence.

'We'll walk from here,' Tony said as he pulled into a parking space. As they walked, he called Dr Bruce Ocean to advise him that they were on their way and upon arrival at the mews property the two were buzzed in immediately. They climbed the stairs to the first floor and were invited into the living room.

'D.S. Palmer, good to see you again, this is my wife, Delia. Er–' He held out his hand to Sasha.

'Sasha Blue, nice to meet you.' At his perplexed expression, she added. 'Private Investigator. I'll let Tony fill you in.' She studied Dr Bruce Ocean and his wife, covertly, while Tony spoke. Dr Ocean looked older in person, the photo on his clinic's website giving an impression of a younger more vibrant man. His wife was an attractive woman but extremely shy, sitting close to her husband and merely smiling in welcome.

The couple sat in silence as Tony took them through what had happened. Finally, he turned to Sasha. 'Anything to add so far?'

'Not really, I think you've covered everything. Only to say that Samantha Ozean has now been missing for five nights and six days and we have no idea as to how she's being treated which is a huge concern. This gang mean business as they've already disposed of the only other witness who can put their man away. So the question is what do we do about it? What do we do about Dr Ocean's statement and what happens if, or when, they realise their mistake?'

'Well surely you can't expect me to change my statement? The man walks if I withdraw my statement and you surely wouldn't suggest that I do so?'

Sasha and Tony glanced at each other.

'Dr Ocean,' Tony spoke carefully, 'You might feel differently if it was your wife who'd been abducted. Look, no one's suggesting that you change your statement, absolutely not. At the moment we just want you to be aware of the situation and to take care, especially you, Mrs Ocean.'

'Do you mean I'm in danger?' Delia Ocean spoke for the first time, her voice strained. 'I told Bruce it was dangerous to get involved. What if they realise their mistake and take me too?'

Sasha addressed her calmly. 'There's no reason to expect them to realise their mistake yet, but perhaps you could leave town for a few days, just to be on the safe side?' She looked at Tony. 'That would be alright, wouldn't it?'

Tony nodded. 'Yes, that may be wise. Do you have someone you could go and stay with, a relative perhaps?'

Dr Ocean held his wife's hand as the couple made murmurings about her sister and Tony decided to wrap things up.

'We'll leave you to make arrangements then, and I'll stay in touch, Dr and Mrs Ocean, but please just be cautious and if you notice anything suspicious call me immediately, okay?'

Back outside in the narrow mews, Tony turned to Sasha. 'We've done what we can, informed them of the situation and if Mrs Ocean goes to stay with her sister that gets her out of harm's way while we sort this mess out. Shall we see if your Dr Ozean's at home then?'

'Let me call him, we can walk in that direction it's not far.'

Brian Ozean answered his phone immediately, sounding harried. 'Sasha, you're going to tell me there's no news on Samantha, aren't you? Where are you, can you come round? Okay, great, see you in five minutes.'

'Brian, this is D. S. Tony Palmer, he's involved in the case. We've uncovered quite a lot since I saw you yesterday'

Shaking hands with Tony, Brian Ozean looked flustered. 'Look, I've just got in, I, er, I had another late night at the university last night.' He glanced rather sheepishly in Sasha's direction. 'Well anyway, look, this was shoved through my letterbox.' He held out the torn sheet of paper. 'I'm afraid I ripped it when I opened the envelope.'

Tony took it and he and Sasha read the short note demanding a ransom of half a million pounds for his wife's safe return and that instructions would follow.

'I mean, what the hell's going on?' Brian's face was a mixture of confusion and frustration. 'One minute I've got someone telling me to withdraw my statement and I haven't a clue what they're talking about, the next they're asking for half a million pounds. Meanwhile, my poor wife's being held somewhere and God knows what they've done to her. Samantha doesn't deserve this. What do I do? I don't have that kind of money. Samantha does, of course, but I can't access it, how ironic is that?' He laughed bitterly.

Looking questioningly at Tony, Sasha suggested they sit down and let Tony talk.

'Okay, Brian, it seems that some huge unimaginable coincidence has resulted in a case of mistaken identity. To be honest I'm still trying to wrap my head around it and what I'm about to tell you must go no further. We think that members of a drugs and prostitution gang planned to kidnap the wife of a doctor who's a witness in a case against one of their members. Yes, I know it sounds far-fetched. Their plan was to exert pressure on him to change his witness statement in exchange for the safe return of his wife. The only thing is, they took the wrong wife. It seems that this doctor has an unbelievably similar name to yours and by a further coincidence happens to live quite close to you.'

'What? You've got to be kidding me! Some gang has kidnapped my wife in error? Well, get the other doctor to bloody well withdraw his statement. You can do that can't you? Samantha's locked up somewhere and terrified out of her mind. I might be a crap husband but I do care about her, she's a good person, she wouldn't hurt a fly. She must be so frightened.' He sobbed, rubbing his face, before looking up at them beseechingly. 'You've got to sort this out, please. You've got to get my wife back before they hurt her.'

'Brian,' Sasha said softly, 'we're busy trying to connect the dots here. Until this moment it was about a witness statement but the ransom note you've received throws a different light on things. Something's changed and we have to work out what and why. It's not about the witness statement any more, it's now about money. We're going to need as much information as you can give us about anything unusual that's happened lately, as well as the name of the student you're having an affair with.'

'What? Oh hell, I–' slumping into the couch, Brian seemed to shrink before their eyes. 'Okay, nothing unusual has happened lately, nothing except Samantha's disappearance.' He stopped for a moment, gazing off into the room. 'Her name's Stacey, Stacey Turnbull.'

'Were you with her last night, Brian?' Sasha studied the man's slumped posture as he nodded shame-facedly.

Tony chimed in. 'Did you mention your wife's abduction or the demand note that you received about changing the statement?'

'No, I– oh hell, I don't think so.' Brian raked his fingers through his by now unkempt hair. 'We'd had a lot to drink, I can barely remember what happened. I think I passed out.' He looked up at them beseechingly. 'I might have said something about it, I think maybe I was rambling on a bit, but Stacey would never tell a soul.'

Sasha and Tony exchanged a grim look. So he *had* talked about it.

'Was anyone else there?'

'Anyone else? She's got a flatmate, some foreign girl I think, I'm sorry, I can't remember. She might have been there at some point.' He shrugged helplessly. 'I'm not much help to you, am I?'

They left Brian's, armed with his student's address. Tony made some calls, informing his colleagues of the situation regarding Samantha Ozean, before phoning Stacey Turnbull, who was at home, and telling her they were on their way to see her.

As they headed along Gray's Inn Road to Stacey's flat, Sasha ran through her thoughts with Tony whilst simultaneously bringing up Stacey's Graffic profile. 'D'you think Brian could have set this whole thing up? Maybe he and his girlfriend are in on it together? Maybe they found out about the similarity in the doctor's names and used the initial witness statement ransom to muddy the waters before getting to the real point, which was for money? I mean, think about it, we've got Brian Ozean having an affair with a student while he's married to an older woman who happens to be extremely wealthy. And then we've got the sudden change from a demand about a witness statement to a demand for money, Tone, it doesn't make sense.'

'Wait until we've got all the facts, Sash, sure and steady does it. Now, Brian and Stacey's little love nest should be coming up... ah, here we go.'

'Definitely a love nest, check this photo out that Stacey posted.' Sasha held out her phone once Tony had parked the car and showed him the graphic of entwined legs, the red-painted toenails on the hairy, masculine feet clearly visible.

Peering at the image, Tony grinned. 'My secret lover? What kind of bloke paints his toenails? Is that for real?'

'Yep, I could hardly stop staring the first time I visited him, but it seems Stacey finds it quite hot.'

Tony whistled. 'Blimey, whatever floats your boat, eh? I reckon my girlfriend would be seriously worried about me if I started prancing around like that. It never ceases to amaze me at the things people shove out there for all the world to see.'

They left the car and rang the bell of the door, nestled between a dry-cleaner's and a coffee shop, where they were welcomed in by a confused looking Stacey. 'Afternoon, Officers, I'm not quite sure what this is all about?'

'I'm D.S. Palmer and this is Sasha Blue, a private investigator. We'd just like to ask you a few questions. Why don't we sit down?'

Tony explained why there were there, adding that Sasha had been contacted by Dr Ozean to assist with the disappearance of his wife. At this Stacey looked a little discomfited and even put out. She confirmed that she was in a relationship with Brian Ozean and when asked what she knew about Mrs Ozean's financial status she rather awkwardly informed them that Brian had told her that she 'held the purse strings'.

'So you knew she had money of her own? Did Dr Ozean ever indicate just how much money she had?'

'Well, he did kind of say she was really rich, like, loaded I suppose. He said that's why he couldn't leave her.'

'And did you ever tell anyone else about that, Stacey?' They were interrupted by the sound of the front door opening. A woman strode into the lounge, pulling her hair loose from its long ponytail. About to throw her leather jacket over the back of a chair she stopped, realising that Stacey had company, and stepped back out of the room.

'Sorry, that's my flatmate, Claudia, she's from Croatia. Er, what were you asking me? Oh, did I tell anyone? Well no, why would I?'

'What about your flatmate, did you tell her?' Sasha leaned forward intently, aware of the sudden silence in the flat.

'Oh, I don't know. Maybe? But, I mean, it's not like I'd go round shouting it out, would I? What for? She might know, okay, maybe it cropped up one night. Yes, I think it probably did, maybe Brian was going on about it or something, and I might have mentioned it to her. And we were talking about it last night a bit because Brian was upset and going on about his wife being kidnapped or something. He was drunk-talking, going on about ransoms and kidnappings and how he'd pay anything to get her back safely, all kinds of stuff. But she's just gone off with someone else, hasn't she? Brian can be a bit over dramatic sometimes. Anyway, we drank a bit too much last night, I remember Claudia asking about his name and finding it funny, I don't know why, and I told her I'd take her to Hatton Garden, where he lives, to see all the jewellery shops, I don't think she's ever been there. But what's all this got to do with anything? Look, I'm feeling really confused here. Didn't his wife just go off with some bloke somewhere? Brian told me they had a row one morning about him being out all night and he said that she was the one always out with a man.'

Not wanting to give Stacey any further information, Tony instead asked her if she'd heard of Dr Bruce Ocean, to which she shook her head, before asking her to write down the dates and times of when Brian had visited.

Glancing at Tony as he wrote in his notebook, Sasha quietly stood and left the room. She gently pushed open the first bedroom door before entering and finding it unoccupied. It was clearly Stacey's room, adorned as it was with photos of herself with family members as well as a framed photo of her and Brian. The next door was open, revealing the bathroom. That left Claudia's bedroom. Tapping the door quietly and eliciting no response, Sasha stepped silently in – it was unoccupied – Claudia must have left the flat moments after returning.

There was nothing personal on display in the slightly smaller bedroom, unlike in Stacey's room. Moving to the dressing table Sasha glanced out of the window as she heard the rumble of the trains from nearby King's Cross, glimpsing the canal between the buildings. Pulling open the drawer and looking inside she hurriedly flicked through the untidy contents – a couple of printed photos of Claudia with a bunch of guys in a pub, assorted business cards, hair clips, a map of the underground, another photo of the same men sitting outside a pub. Spreading the photos out on the dressing table, she pulled out her phone and took a quick picture before dropping them back into the drawer and closing it.

Returning to the living room, she found Tony standing up about to leave, and joined him in thanking Stacey for her time. They left, Tony having given Stacey strict instructions not to speak to anyone about their visit.

'There's something odd about her flatmate, Tone.' Sasha rushed to keep up with Tony's brisk pace as he headed for his car. 'She was listening to our questions, I'm sure of it, and then she must have slipped out of the flat within minutes of coming in. What d'you think?'

'There's not much to think right now, Sash, she didn't do anything wrong, all she did was go back out again. You can't let your imagination run away with you, it's all about getting our facts straight. She'll need to be questioned, of course, but right now I've got piles of work to do on this and I need to get my team up to speed pronto on everything we know so far. How about you meet me at the station tomorrow morning and we can go through all the points, once I've got it all laid out, see if we can figure out what the hell's going on? You're already involved at the request of Dr Ozean and I'm happy to have you assist with this.'

Back in her flat and feeling energised about the case – there was something right in front of their eyes that they were missing, she just knew it – Sasha shoved her vacuum cleaner round the flat at breakneck speed, embarrassed about how dirty the floors were. Blasting her tunes, she sang along as she cleaned her flat, completing her chores in record time. Pleased with her accomplishments, she made herself a sandwich and a cup of tea, before settling down on the couch, hoping for a few minutes' rest before taking a shower.

But then she remembered that she was waiting for the stalker's response, as well as Zoe's, and checked her phone.

I am in control. My latest photo will be you soon enough, you little bitch. Then you will see what a man I am. Prepare for pain. Whore.

Her mouthful of sandwich turned to sawdust, and she forced herself to chew and swallow. This person, whoever he was, hated her with a vengeance. Who could she possibly have treated so badly in her life that they would say these things to her? Of course, she had enough experience to know that there was no reason for her to actually know this person at all. It was probably all a figment of his imagination, but still, he had to know of her in some way.

He was sounding increasingly violent as if he was losing his grip, which was dangerous. Well, Sash, you wanted to rock the boat. She looked at the photo of the bound girl, her naked back covered in welts from some kind of beating. Gasping, she realised that she was probably responsible for this. She'd never intended for him to take out his anger on the girl, but of course he would, why hadn't she thought of that? And if it was Zoe… 'Oh, Zo, if it is you, I'm so sorry, babe, I never meant for this,' she whispered, feeling pained.

He'd positioned the sex doll next to the hooded girl and had placed a bag over the doll's head so that both woman and doll were facing the wall with their heads covered. The chain around the girl's, or rather, woman's, ankle, had been twisted to encompass the doll's ankle too. Written in black marker pen on the doll's back was one word. *Sasha*. It was a chilling message. He intended to take her captive.

Suddenly Sasha was aware of just how vulnerable she was. When she was safely in her flat, with her door locked, he couldn't get to her, but what about the rest of the time? She hadn't seriously considered any kind of threat to herself before, seeing the whole sick thing as some kind of challenge.

~

He'd punished her enough. He didn't want her to die on him, well, not yet. But he did need something from her, and maybe the promise of food and drink would ensure that she behaved. Taking her phone, and the sandwiches and water, he unlocked the door.

'Drink.' He handed her the bottle, allowing her to thirstily gulp a little of the water, before removing it from her.

'If you do as I say you'll get the rest of the bottle and some food. But if you mess with me in any way, if you say the wrong thing, I'm going to hurt you. Do you understand? And I'll take this food away.'

~

About to take a shower in preparation for her evening, Sasha stopped undressing as her phone rang. It was Zoe.

'Zo? Are you alright?' Her heart was thumping, either Zo was fine, or calling for help.

'Sasha, babe, I'm fine, how're you doing? Sorry I haven't been in touch, I'm in Crete. Yeah, I met this guy and we went on one of those last-minute deals. I'll tell you all about it when I'm back.'

'You're in Crete? And everything's okay? It's just, you've been so quiet, no photos, you know, I was getting worried. Oh, Zo, it's so good to hear from you.'

'Oh, you know what it's like, new man and all that.' Zoe laughed. 'Yeah, we're in a room above a taverna. Remember that place we stayed in here? It's *exactly* like that, fab breakfasts, gorgeous room, great room service! Do you remember? Oh, I split up with Miles...'

There was a muffled sound on the other end of the line. 'Zo? Are you still there? Zo?'

'I'm here. I've got to go. Take care, Sa–' The phone went dead.

~

'I told you to do as you were told.' He slapped her again.

'I'm sorry. Please, I was just trying to be natural, it's the way Sash and I are.'

Reassured and pleased that he'd accomplished his aim, he gave her the sandwiches and water and left the room.

Shaking, Zoe huddled on the bed. Would Sasha even know what she was on about? Had she been too subtle?

But with him holding the phone, and with a knife pressed into her side, she hadn't dared risk saying too much. He hadn't seemed to suspect anything, she just had to hope that Sasha's memory was in good working order.

~

Phew. Zoe was alright. She wasn't the girl in the photos. Relief flooded Sasha as she continued to undress and step into the shower. But as she lathered shampoo into her hair, she replayed the conversation in her head. *Remember that place we stayed in here? Fab breakfasts. Gorgeous room. Great room service.* They hadn't stayed in any place in Crete like that...

~

Greek Island addicts, she and Zoe had taken countless trips to the islands as soon as they were old enough to travel without their parents, finding bargains that their meagre salaries could afford. But the only place they'd stayed in Crete had been a hotel. They'd stayed in Corfu in a room above a taverna and it had been the crappiest place they'd ever stayed. They'd actually laughed about how bad it was, concerned only about having a good time and getting a suntan. The room had been bare, apart from twin beds and a cupboard. There had been no breakfast after their first day, and that one breakfast had consisted only of tea and some kind of sweet biscuit. And as for room service, it had been non-existent, they'd had to make their beds and even buy their own loo rolls.

~

Realising that she'd stopped mid-lather of her hair, Sasha quickly finished her shower and stepped out, feeling shaken. Zoe had been giving her a message. And not just a message, it had been a cry for help. She tried to think back to how Zoe had sounded. Had her voice been strained? The more she thought of it the surer she was. Zoe had told her incorrect facts deliberately. Zoe had been taken captive by him. And Zoe needed her help. The problem was that she had no idea where her friend was being held or by whom.

FROM ENVY TO EROS

Sasha virtually pulled Miles into her flat when he arrived.

'Sash, what is it? Are you okay?' Miles held her arms, looking down at her with concern.

'No, Miles, I'm so not okay you have no idea.' She garbled away almost incoherently until Miles took charge.

'Let's sit down. Now, start from the beginning, and tell me everything.'

Once she'd finished telling him everything about her conversation with Zoe, Sasha sat back and looked at him expectantly. 'So you see? It was some kind of code. Zoe's not on holiday.' She jumped up, pulling him with her. 'Come and look at the board again, I've added the latest photos. Zoe's got a tattoo, right there, where her hand's placed. It's hiding it so that I wouldn't recognise it. And the sick bastard made her wear my underwear. Look, it's too small for her. And Zoe always wears super-hot, sexy, underwear, it's just always been her thing, and look at this picture of all the bras and knickers, they could easily be hers, in fact, I'm sure they are. Oh, and the nail varnish, see here? It's blue, one of her favourite colours.' She stopped, breathless, waiting for Miles to catch up.

Miles took his time, considering everything that Sasha had said. But he shook his head slowly. 'Sash, it's all circumstantial. Everything you're saying could equally apply to someone else. Are you sure you're not allowing your concerns over Zoe's sudden trip to cloud your judgement? I mean.' He held her hand gently as he looked at her with his soft eyes. 'Anyone could have blue painted toenails and coloured underwear, couldn't they? And large breasts? Sash, none of this means it's Zoe. She called you, you should be relieved, not imagining the worst. She probably just forgot which island you stayed on together, you know she can be a bit scatty.'

'But the room above the taverna, the breakfasts...' Her voice trailed off. Frustrated, Sasha realised that Miles just didn't get it. There was no point in going on about it. 'I'm just being over-sensitive, you're probably right, I've got an overactive imagination at the best of times.' She tried to laugh it off. 'Let's go and get something to eat.'

As they walked to the restaurant, Miles addressed the latest message and photograph from the person calling themselves @maluspassuum. 'I don't like it, Sash, not at all, there's a threat there and I worry for your safety. We don't know who you can trust at this point so you have to promise me you'll be extra careful, okay?' At her nod, he continued, 'And I want you to promise me something else, if anything happens, if you find out anything, or are thinking of going off investigating something dodgy, you call me. I just feel better knowing where you are, you get that, right?'

'I do.' She smiled. 'And thanks, Miles, it does feel good to know that you've got my back in all this.'

They sat in the little Italian eatery just along the road from Sasha's flat and whilst Miles ordered the alfredo, Sasha opted for one of their thin crust pizzas.

The waitress grinned and asked, 'Usual toppings?'

Laughing, Sasha thanked her and they sat back to wait for their wine to arrive.

'I take it you're a regular here?' Miles smiled at her, before looking around. 'It's nice, intimate with tasteful décor. And the smells from the kitchen are driving me crazy right now, I'm starving!'

Laughing, Sasha agreed, 'And your comments on the décor remind me that you describe properties for your job. It must get tricky when the places aren't up to much though. Or do you only deal in upmarket accommodation?'

'No, we deal in all sorts, although we do politely decline the ones that aren't above a certain standard. But there's a demand for every type of property, so we have to keep an open mind. And I've learnt over the years to become quite creative with my descriptions. Things like, *great office space on upper landing*, that means it's the only place you could squeeze a desk in, or, *second bedroom ideal for small home office*, in other words, it's not quite big enough for a single bed. Oh yeah, and gardens are tricky, I often find myself using the phrase *small outdoor area, easy to maintain*, in other words, virtually no garden.'

'I can imagine. It must be quite amusing to come up with that stuff. What's the name of your agency, I never asked you?'

'Oh, we're small, I doubt you've heard of us, we've only got the one office. We're called HWS Properties. Stands for Home and Work Space. Not exactly imaginative but it gets the job done.'

'You're right, I haven't heard of it, but I probably don't know half the names of property agencies in London. But to go back to your earlier question, I have come here quite a bit, I must confess, usually with a friend or two, and Zoe and I often come here.' She stopped talking, it felt wrong to even mention Zoe casually at the moment. 'But it's also handy when I don't want to cook but need to get out of the flat for a change of scenery. Sometimes my work keeps me quite isolated so it's good to be among people.' She grinned suddenly. 'And their pizzas are to die for. Especially when they're topped with chicken, onion, and green peppers.'

'Hmm, I'm beginning to realize that's a favourite of yours,' Miles reached his hand across the table and gently stroked hers, causing Sasha's belly to flip slightly. 'Now, what did you need to ask me about concerning Eric?'

'Oh hell, I feel quite awkward even asking you, as well as pathetic.' She glanced at him before looking away. 'It's just, Eric's becoming a problem, I can't have him keep turning up at my flat. I don't know why he's behaving like this, it's not like him to be honest. The getting drunk part is, but the rest of it? Eric's never been needy, so I think it's turned into some kind of game for him now. You know, like, Eric can dump the chick, but if the chick dumps Eric, then all hell breaks loose. He won't stand for it. Anyway.' She looked back across at Miles, apologetically, 'I wondered if you could try talking to him?'

'Say no more. Sash, honestly, consider it done. I'll deal with Eric, I promise you. I'll make sure he doesn't try to contact you again or cause you any problems at all.'

'There's just one more thing, it's probably nothing, but could you try to find out from him if Zoe called him about the art gallery? It's a long shot, to be honest, but her boss said that she found these old newspapers in a disused mezzanine. I'm not quite sure why but I think there could be some significance to them, I just can't figure out what. Maybe she talked to Eric about it and if you–' Surprised at the flash of irritation that passed across Miles's eyes, she stopped mid-sentence, feeling awkward.

'Sash, let's just forget about Zoe and Eric, alright? I'll deal with him, you have my word, but let's just enjoy our evening.' He smiled across the table at her. 'I know detection and following the clues is what you do, but you'll drive yourself crazy if you're not careful.'

Maybe she'd imagined his look of irritation. He was right, she was probably clutching at straws anyway. Thanking him, and trusting him to be true to his word with regard to Eric, Sasha decided to just enjoy the evening. She'd keep her fears for Zoe to herself, for now, Miles clearly thought she was getting carried away there.

'Cheers.' She lifted her glass, tapping it against Miles's, as their food arrived.

Replete and relaxed from their evening, they wandered back along the street to Sasha's flat. She'd ask him in for a drink. Why not?

'You're quiet,' Miles commented. 'What're you thinking about?'

'Okay, if you must know, I was thinking about asking you in for a drink, but if you need to get home…'

'No, a drink sounds good, it'll round off the evening, thanks.'

They were definitely becoming more comfortable with each other. Miles seemed to have lost his initial shyness, and there was a closeness between them wasn't there? Maybe when this was all over, they'd still see each other, without the excuse of trying to hunt down a mad man and find a missing girl.

'Whisky or red wine?' Sasha stood in the kitchen, holding up the two bottles, her eyebrows raised.

'Whisky sounds good, thanks.'

Miles took his filled glass and they smiled at each other.

Putting some music on low, she turned to him. 'Quick smoke out on the balcony?'

They leaned over the railing as they smoked their cigarettes, taking in the quiet evening.

'Miles.' She may as well be brave. 'When this is all over, you know, the missing girl and the freak, *and it will be over*, we'll find her, and him, well, it would be really nice to see each other for no reason other than pleasure.' Glad that he couldn't see her blush, she continued. 'It's just, well, I'm enjoying being with you, spending time with you.'

'I'd like that, I'm enjoying being with you too.'

She realised that Miles had moved slightly closer and was looking at her with an intensity she hadn't seen before.

~

Eric stood hidden in the shadows further up the street, watching the couple as they kissed. Fuck Miles, what was he playing at? He was pulling Sasha away from him, making it harder for him to get to her. And he did need to get to her, he had things to say to her, things she needed to hear. Why was she choosing Miles over him? It was a bad choice, he needed her to know that. Jealousy consumed him as he watched them leave the balcony, closing the door behind them. He turned and walked away. He'd have to deal with Miles.

~

Not sure whether to be disappointed or relieved, Sasha kissed Miles goodbye, with promises to speak the following day, and threw herself down onto the couch with a fresh glass of whisky. Wow, that had been some kiss. Slow, sensuous, and totally sexy, she melted again at the memory of it. He hadn't tried to take things further, for which she was grateful although slightly disappointed. Her body was playing its usual tricks with bad timing, so it saved her from having to explain anything to him right now.

It was the worst part of a new relationship for her, having to explain to the new man that her insides were rubbish, that she was a liability, and that a man with any sense would run a mile. She envied the women who lived such carefree lifestyles, who, once a month, grumbled about the inconvenience and the slight pain – pain that was relieved by popping a simple painkiller. They had no idea what it was like living with endometriosis, the constant worry, the sudden debilitating pain that came out of nowhere. And that was before the lack of energy, the uncertainty of when her body might let her down, and how embarrassing it could be. It was exhausting, and she wondered again whether she should just tell her specialist to remove everything. He'd mentioned the possibility to her at her last procedure and the idea was becoming more appealing, after all, it caused her nothing but pain and was unlikely to ever be able to produce a child.

Even as she had these thoughts, she was aware of the pain returning, deep inside, even the whisky not having numbed it. Picking up her phone for distraction she was surprised to see that she'd received another direct message on Graffic. Not *him*, please, she didn't want to face his hideous anger, not tonight.

But it wasn't from him, it was from someone she didn't know, called Molly. She read the message.

Hi, Sasha, you don't know me, but I've seen the photos of the girl. I think I know something important. It's about one of the photos. If I'm right, you'll be able to trace her. Can I meet you? I can come to London. Molly.

Intriguing. Sasha sat up straighter and read the message again. She clicked onto the girl's account and studied the images she'd posted. They were mainly the usual teenage girl photos, posing with her friends, a smattering of life quotes, nothing out of the ordinary. Apart from, and her heart sank, she'd copied the pose of the bound woman on the bed.

Did she really know something or was she just thrill-seeking? There was only one way to find out. She checked the time, wondering whether to call Miles, but decided to leave it until tomorrow, as cramping pain shot through her abdomen. Standing up she rubbed her lower back, it was getting her all over this time. She needed to get to bed with a hot water bottle.

~

Well, that was right up there with the crappiest nights of all times thought Sasha the next morning as she surveyed her white face in the bathroom mirror. She was now losing heavily and had spent the night in and out of the bathroom, with what little time she'd spent in bed having been used for everything except sleep. She'd drunk tea, read her book, eaten ginger biscuits, taken more pills, but sleep had eluded her. Thoughts of her friend had constantly entered her mind and her concern that Zoe was the girl in the photos was growing by the minute.

She made a decision. She'd put her phone on silent, have something to eat so that she could take some more painkillers, and then try going back to bed for an hour or two. She had to get some sleep before meeting Tony.

One egg and bacon sandwich and two mugs of tea later and Sasha gratefully sank back into her bed. With her pain abated she fell asleep within minutes, not waking until her phone alarm buzzed, and feeling much better she showered and set off to meet Tony.

She had to admit it, there was a thrill to announcing herself to the young woman at the front counter of the police station as a private investigator helping D.S. Palmer with a case. She took a seat until Tony appeared and ushered her into a lift. Once on his floor, Tony led her to a room with a large board covered in pieces of paper, photos, and other notes about the case. Boxes were heaped on a table, their contents strewn haphazardly around.

'Well, Sash, here we are, the centre of the operation. We've got everything relating to the original case concerning the drugs and prostitution gang. Photos – some not very pleasant – of the scene of the fight with the rival gang. We've got victims as we found them, oh, and here's the girl who was later killed in a hit and run. She would have been a witness in addition to Dr Bruce Ocean of course. Then here's our main man, Jax Milan, the one in custody and believed to be pretty high-ranking. Photos of everything we found on him at the time of his arrest.' Tony waved his arms around as he spoke, pointing at the various sections of the board as Sasha took in the array of images. 'Here are photographs of other suspected gang members. And then we move over here for the Dr

Ocean/Dr Ozean, and respective wives side of things. The missing woman, Samantha Ozean, has huge personal wealth, which would explain the demand for money, but that's not why she was taken in the first place. So what changed? What are we missing? Sash?' Tony looked questioningly at Sasha who had zoned out and was staring intently at something on the board.

'I think I've just found our connection, Tone.' Sasha's voice was breathless with excitement. 'Who's this?' She pointed at a photo of an attractive woman, long dark hair tied back severely, wearing a black leather jacket. Looking at Tony with wide eyes she jabbed at the photo. 'I saw her yesterday. She's Stacey Turnbull's flatmate, Claudia.'

Tony stared at the photo for a moment or two before shaking his head slowly. 'I don't know, Sash, I never even saw her and you only glimpsed her for a second. I'm not convinced. Look.' He softened his tone, noticing Sasha's downcast expression. 'It's easy to get carried away in these situations. There's probably a million women walking around with long dark hair and black leather jackets. As far as we know the woman in this photo is the girlfriend of our man in custody and holds quite a position within the gang, although we've never been able to confirm an actual name. It would be a bit of a stretch of the imagination if she was the chick who walked into Stacey's flat while we were there, don't you think?'

'What? No. But, Tone, it's her, I'm sure of it. I told you there was something off about her. Listen, Stacey's having an affair with Brian Ozean, he of the rich wife. Her flatmate, Claudia, is the spitting image of the girlfriend of your top gang member – not just the spitting image, it's her, I know it. Bruce Ocean is the only witness who can tie Jax to the night of the bust-up when people were killed. But they don't take *his* wife, they take Samantha Ozean instead. Her husband receives the ransom note telling him to change his statement, but he's the wrong doctor, and then today he receives a ransom note for half a million pounds. I mean what the hell, Tone, it all ties in.'

Grabbing a pen, Sasha started scrawling names and arrows on the whiteboard, connecting the different names. When she was finished, they stood back, staring at it all.

'The only people with a connection to your gang man, Jax, are Claudia and Dr Ocean. The only person with a connection to Dr Ozean is Stacey Turnbull. If the gang wanted Dr Ocean to withdraw his statement they should have abducted Delia Ocean, but they didn't, they abducted Samantha – because someone got the name and address confused. It must have been Claudia! Stacey said she's from Croatia and Brian referred to her as some foreign girl. Why did he do that? Maybe her English isn't very good! And then Brian suddenly receives a ransom note for money. This is the connection – Stacey and Claudia – two girls sharing a flat. Stacey admitted that she'd told Claudia about Brian's rich wife. She even said Claudia found his name funny, and that she mentioned Hatton Garden. That's when she realised her mistake over the wife, I'll bet you anything. We've solved this, Tone, I'm telling you, it's all here. It's Claudia – and she'll lead us to Samantha Ozean.' Sasha stood back, eyes gleaming, and looked at Tony.

'Once Claudia realised her mistake in confusing the names and addresses of the two doctors, and once she found out from Stacey how rich Brian's wife was, she probably decided that money was more important than her boyfriend getting out of prison. Especially seeing as drunk Brian pretty much announced to both women the fact that he'd pay money to get his wife back. She knew it was a done deal, all she had to do was get the other guys on board and deliver a ransom demand for money.'

Tony was nodding, his expression still doubtful. 'It could all make sense. If so it's a bleeding comedy of errors.

But it's all supposition, Sash, there's nothing to back any of that up. I've already got an officer checking up on Brian Ozean's other students, as well as Stacey's flatmate, Claudia Novak. If she is Jax Milan's girlfriend we'll know soon enough and she'll be interviewed, like everyone else.'

Exasperated, Sasha nodded in defeat. 'Okay, well I just hope your officer works fast, I mean, poor Samantha Ozean, the woman's been held somewhere for a week now. Just promise me that once you confirm what I've told you that you'll follow Claudia? She'll lead us to Samantha.'

Tony laughed. 'You don't give up do you? Novak's a common name, which complicates things, but we'll check her out, alright? Look, great work so far, Sash, you've been brilliant, babe, you have, but I need to let my team do their stuff. I'll let you know as soon as I have any news.' He looked at Sasha. 'Are we on the same page here? You're not going to go sniffing around and muddling things? If it turns out you're right it could raise alarm bells and put Samantha at risk. Oh and, Sash? Not a word to Brian Ozean about all these ideas of yours, the last thing we need at the moment is him blabbing to Stacey and muddying the waters.'

Begrudgingly Sasha agreed not to say anything and left Tony to his police business, deciding to head home and concentrate on her other missing woman case.

~

He was disappointed to find that she still hadn't reacted to either his latest work of art or his message. She wasn't playing the game. It was no fun if she didn't join in, that's what gave him the thrill. He wanted to enjoy reeling her in. He wanted her to get close, to hunt him down, and he'd be waiting for her, she just didn't know it yet. The thought excited him, images playing in his mind of how it would be, the climactic moment when all was revealed. For a moment, as he felt his arousal, he considered spending some time with his Sasha on the bed, but looking at his watch he knew he'd be late if he didn't leave now.

~

Sasha's exhilaration at what she'd pieced together about Claudia Novak had been flattened by Tony's lack of enthusiasm for her ideas. *Why did everyone always think she was getting carried away with her theories?* It had been further replaced with a heavy lethargy by the time she got back to her flat, her body feeling like it had a sack of potatoes inside it. Switching her mind from the Samantha Ozean case she thought about the cruel photos on her phone. In her mind, she was still convinced that the woman in the photos was Zoe and she owed it to her to follow up on any leads, regardless of the obvious doubts that Miles had. With this in mind, she sent a short reply to the girl called Molly telling her she could meet her if she came to London.

~

Excitedly, Molly read the message. Sasha wanted to meet with her. She sent back a message telling Sasha that she could meet her on Saturday and could she let her know if that would be okay. She then sent a message to Sara, telling her the plan. Finally, and feeling a little nervous, she sent a message to Maddox asking him if he fancied a day in London if he was feeling up to it. And then she waited.

~

Yes, she could do Saturday, she sent back to Molly, asking if Molly had a particular place she wanted to meet. She hoped she'd be up to it, no, she told herself, you *have* to be up to it, Sasha. She'd need to catch Miles up with the latest but didn't want to be on his case the whole time. Maybe he'd drop her a message later.

~

'Are you sure your mum and dad will let you go, Moll? I mean, you've only been out of hospital a few days?' Sara was cross-legged on Molly's bed, an anxious expression on her face. 'And what about Maddox? He probably won't be allowed to go, not so soon after his operation?'

'I've got it all worked out, Sar.' Molly was grinning. 'Mum and Dad are going to a wedding in Deal, down on the coast. They're going on Friday and staying the weekend. So I'm free.' She fell back on her pillows triumphantly. 'And Mad's cool, he says he'll bring his mate, Tyler. Look.' She thrust her phone into Sara's face, 'He's cute, huh?'

Sara studied the photo, agreeing, as the two girls giggled about what to wear. 'Does he know what I look like?' she asked anxiously.

'Sar, you worry too much, look, I sent this photo of us, read what Mad said. He said Ty thinks your mate's a little hottie! So, we just need to decide where to meet Sasha. We should go to the big Top Shop at Oxford Circus. Maybe we could meet her there, or is that too busy? Or what about Leicester Square? It's got to be somewhere easy that we know. Oh, what about that statue down in Piccadilly Circus?'

'Oh yeah, Eros ,isn't it? We could take some cool photos there. Yeah, let's meet her there.'

~

Sasha agreed to the meeting place and time and decided no harm would come from just letting Miles know. She wasn't being needy, he had, after all, told her to keep him updated.

She needn't have worried, Miles was on the phone to her within what must have been seconds of receiving her message.

'Sash, are you mad? How do you know this is real? It could be anyone. It could be *him*. Bloody hell, you're too trusting, Sash. And what did the message say? No, forget that I'm on my way to you now.'

Surprised at his response, Sasha quickly tidied the detritus from her day, having been a little on the lazy side. She hadn't expected him to worry so much, although she kind of liked it.

She buzzed him up and he flew into her flat. 'Sash, what are you thinking? You mustn't just make plans without telling me, it's too risky. We don't know what we're dealing with here.' He stopped, noticing her white face. 'Are you alright? Sorry, I'm being an idiot, barging in here.'

'I'm okay, really, just having some trouble with my beloved endometriosis, it's a long story. It's left me feeling a bit wrung out, that's all. But, Miles, it's all fine, she's a young girl, I've checked out her account and it's all legit.'

'Anything can be faked, Sash, but first, do you need anything? What's this about endometriosis? What can I do?'

Glazing over the details of her condition with a weariness born from experience, she assured him she'd be fine and he relaxed a little. 'Right, tell me everything about this person. What did she tell you?'

Once Sasha had relayed her communications with Molly to him, and showed him her messages for good measure, he calmed down. 'Right, so she could just be a thrill-seeker, as you say, or maybe she does know something, although I can't imagine what, can you? But there's no way you're going on your own, you know that, right? I'm coming with you.'

It was so nice to feel cared for, even if Miles had gone a little over the top. And they could turn it into a nice day out. Once they'd met with Molly they could amble around the West End, do a little shopping, maybe have a nice lunch somewhere.

Miles checked his watch. 'Sash, I'm really sorry, but I'm going to have to go, I've got a ton of work to catch up on tonight. Will you be okay?'

Disappointed, but knowing that the best thing she could do for herself was to have a booze-free evening and an early night, she smiled. 'Honestly, Miles, it's fine, you didn't need to rush round here either, I know you have stuff to do. I'm going to read my book and have an early night. If I can just fight off the pain I'll feel better tomorrow. And if you're sure you want to come with me to meet Molly on Saturday, then that'll be great. We could maybe get lunch somewhere, I haven't been to Oxford Street for a while, it'll be quite nice to stroll along and window shop.'

'Sounds perfect and I'm looking forward to it.' He regarded her thoughtfully for a moment, concern etched on his face. 'I hate to leave you when you're not well though. You get a good sleep, okay?' He kissed her gently on the lips and left her flat.

Feeling cocooned in his care, Sasha locked her door behind him and prepared to spend her evening relaxing and taking care of herself.

THE CAMERA DOESN'T ALWAYS LIE

Ten minutes later she closed her book and picked up her phone. How could she have forgotten all about the photo she'd taken in Claudia Novak's bedroom? Her brain was all over the place – she needed to stay focused and not let her physical discomfort affect her state of mind, she reprimanded herself.

As she studied the photo of the group of men in the pub with Claudia, Sasha tried to recall the images of suspected gang members on Tony's active case board, annoyed that she hadn't thought of it while she'd been standing in front of it. Surely that guy had been one of them? And the burly shaven-headed guy with the big beard, he'd definitely been up on the board. These were the gang members and their photo was sitting in Claudia Novak's dressing table drawer. This was absolute proof of Claudia's involvement, but she could go one further. Sasha enlarged the part of the photo showing the group of men outside a pub. Yes, she thought so, that was the canal behind the pub – only just visible at the end of the narrow passage between the buildings – and if she needed any further corroboration, the colourful painted side of a passing narrowboat provided just that.

Expanding the photo to its limit, she focused on the partially visible sign above the men's heads. Well that wouldn't be difficult to trace, she thought excitedly, it could only be waterman or lighterman, a memory of the fascinating history of the men who'd worked on the barges of London's canals fluttering in the back of her mind. She'd seen it on a documentary, she recalled, trying to remember which was which, some had unloaded the barges and some had transported passengers, back when the canals had been the equivalent of today's motorways.

A one-minute online search later and Sasha was staring at images of The Lighterman's Arms, the rear of which backed onto Regent's Canal. An image of the front of the pub showed the wooden tables and benches which the men had been sitting on.

Hesitating for all of thirty seconds, Sasha deliberated whether to call Tony. No, sod it, he'd doubted her hunch, she thought mutinously, she'd get him proof all on her own, see how he liked that. A quick glance at her watch confirmed that it was still only early evening – the perfect time for pub-goers – if the gang frequented this pub there was a chance she'd find them there – and Claudia. But first to call Stacey, after all Tony hadn't told her *not* to speak to her.

Yes, Stacey confirmed, Claudia was out for the evening, and no, she didn't know where but she was probably drinking with friends as that's what she usually did. Having elicited a promise from Stacey not to mention a word of her call to Claudia, Sasha pulled on her jacket and boots, grabbing a cap as an afterthought and ignoring the painful pull deep inside her belly – this was no time to give in to the broken inner-workings of her body.

Unable to face the hassle of the tube, she hailed a passing cab and gave the driver the destination before leaning back and giving in to a momentary feeling of fatigue. She should have eaten something, should have taken pain killers, should have called Tony... She closed her eyes for a moment.

'You awake, love? You don't look so good, sure you want to be out? You sure you want to be *here*?' The cab driver had turned around in his seat and was studying Sasha with concerned eyes.

'What? Oh, yes, no, I'm fine, really, thank you. Are we here already?' She thanked the cabbie and paid him, pulling on her cap as she left the cab, and found herself amidst the hardened outside drinkers and smokers clustered around the tables in front of The Lighterman's Arms.

A couple of the men glanced in her direction with interest and she kept her head down, not wanting to attract attention – the clientele didn't look particularly savoury. She'd get a drink and then see if she could recognise any of the gang, including Claudia.

The pub was fairly quiet inside and Sasha quickly ordered a whisky and coke, before taking a seat at a bar table in the corner. A few surreptitious glances at the patrons soon confirmed that neither Claudia, nor any of the men from the photos, were inside. So outside it was then, if they were even here. Picking up her drink she walked outside, shivering in the autumn chill. She lit a cigarette to fit in, but not feeling like smoking if she was honest.

This wasn't good, she was a lone female drinker at a somewhat rough pub and guys were beginning to clock the fact – mean-looking guys, the kind you didn't mess with. Her ears picked up a strong accent, men's laughter, as well as a woman's lone voice in the midst of the group, and she turned her head a little to study the faces.

And there she was – Claudia – and she wasn't alone, at least one of the guys from the photo was with her, the one with the shaved head, she was sure of it. The man turned his head, appearing to look directly at Sasha, and she quickly looked down, tapping her cigarette in the ashtray – it was definitely him. She needed to be careful.

Their voices were raised now and it sounded like they were arguing. Frustrated that she couldn't understand what they were saying, Sasha kept her head down, hoping to pick up a word or two that might make sense, but they clearly weren't speaking English. The only word she was able to make out was Claudia's last name, in fact they seemed to be repeating it in virtually every sentence – almost as if they were arguing about Claudia – which didn't make sense. Unless...

Holding her phone under the table Sasha brought up an online translator and tapped in Claudia's surname. The word *novice* appeared on her screen. That didn't make any sense. She tried replacing the letter 'k' with a 'c' and felt a momentary stab of jubilation as she stared at the English equivalent - *money*. They were arguing about money. She'd bet her life on it that they were arguing about the ransom money for Samantha Ozean.

Suddenly the mood of the group changed and they were laughing again – whatever they'd been arguing about had been resolved. This time Sasha clearly picked up the word *zena* and another which made her think of sports cars for some reason. Suddenly it came to her and she played with the spelling until, after a couple of tries, she found herself looking at the Croatian word *bogati* meaning *rich*. The spelling of the word *zena* was a lucky guess and she got it right first time – it meant *woman*.

The group had been arguing about money and were now laughing about a woman and about being rich. This was all the evidence she needed to prove to Tony that she'd been right. She risked another glance towards the group and as she did so Claudia stood, stepping over the bench seat and facing in Sasha's direction. Had Claudia seen her? Recognised her? Lighting another cigarette, as two of the men with Claudia also stood, Sasha realised that they were saying goodbye. She looked down as the three passed behind her seat, straining to hear what they were saying, and picking up on the word *zena* again.

She needed to follow them – what if they were going to wherever they were holding Samantha Ozean? Standing quickly, a wave of nausea flooded her as pain hit her insides and she held the table for support, feeling suddenly dizzy. This was all she needed. Gritting her teeth, she stepped away from the lighted pub seating area and headed into the misty darkness of the cold, waterside street, following the sounds of the departed group's voices.

A towpath turned off from the street and Sasha paused, trying to gauge in which direction they had gone. Dark shapes of abandoned warehouses loomed ahead and she shivered as a light drizzle began to fall. They'd taken the towpath, she was sure, her eyes straining to see them as she followed silently.

Her phone suddenly buzzed loudly and she froze, cursing herself for not putting it on silent mode. Ahead of her the group stopped and she slunk down into the shadows, frantically trying to silence her phone. One of the men left the group and headed back towards her. *Oh crap.*

The railings to her right were broken and Sasha fumbled with her hand, finding a gap and squeezing through before lying flat in the weeds growing out of the unkempt ground. *This was right up there with the best nights of her life.* A sound of laughter and footsteps passed her in the direction of the group and she exhaled raggedly, lifting her head to see a couple pass by, arms entwined.

The man who'd turned around paused before shrugging and hurrying to catch up with his friends and Sasha pushed her way back through the broken railing and resumed her trail. Dizziness threatened to overcome her again and she gasped in huge gulps of damp air. It was no good, she wasn't up to this, what had she been thinking? As she watched, a member of the group switched on a torch and she saw their silhouettes turn in and force their way through another of the broken railings towards one of the warehouses.

Decision made she brought up Tony's number and sent him her location, followed by a brief message. His reply made her cringe. *Bleeding hell, Sash, you're a flaming liability. Get out of there. Not safe. Go back to the pub and wait for me. Team on way.*

Dejected and angry with herself for failing, Sasha made her way back to the pub, went into the ladies and appraised herself in the mirror. Her damp hair was plastered around her white face and dirty patches covered her clothing from where she'd lain on the ground. Grabbing some paper towels, she rubbed ineffectually at the mud stains before venturing to the bar.

The barmaid looked at her questioningly. 'You were in here earlier, you alright, love?'

'Fight with the boyfriend.' Sasha improvised, rolling her eyes, before asking for a whisky.

'Want me to call you a cab, you don't really want to be around here on your own, know what I mean?' The woman couldn't shake her concern, but Sasha shook her head and smiled.

'Thanks, but I'm waiting for my friend.' She retreated to the table she'd sat at earlier and waited for Tony.

Half an hour later an angry-looking D.S. Tony Palmer strode into the bar, glanced around and made a bee-line for Sasha. 'Let's get you out of here, this place is teeming with the bleeding underworld.' He grasped Sasha's elbow and steered her out of the pub and into his car.

'Are you mad, Sasha, or just stupid? These are dangerous people and you're out here at night playing super sleuth all on your own. Now, show me this photo you mentioned.'

Meekly, Sasha handed over her phone and watched as recognition flash in his eyes. 'They're your gang members, Tone, and these photos were in Claudia Novak's bedroom. You thought I was getting carried away earlier about Claudia, and it was only this evening that I remembered the photo I'd taken. When I worked out where the pub was, I just thought I'd check it out, that's all.'

'And what made you think she wasn't just at home in the flat watching television?'

'Okay, I called Stacey, but I got her to promise not to say anything. Look, Tony, I know it was risky, alright? But I just thought if I could prove the link between Claudia and the gang then you'd believe me, and then once I was here, I figured if Samantha's being held by them maybe they'll go and check on her. They were talking about money and a woman as far as I could tell. I didn't really have a plan, it just kind of happened, and then I wasn't feeling so good and, well, that's when I contacted you.'

'Hmm.' Tony looked at Sasha, conflicted between feelings of frustration at her foolhardiness and sympathy at her pinched face as she clearly battled whatever was wrong with her. He slipped his arm around her and hugged her. 'You're one crazy bitch, Sasha Blue, but you know that already. Hold up.' He answered his phone, nodding and speaking rapidly, before turning back to Sasha. 'My team's going in, fasten your seatbelt.' He started the car and drove through the narrow streets, turning left and right seemingly haphazardly before screeching to a halt. 'Stay in the car, that's an order.' With that he was gone.

Had they got them? Had they found her? What was going on? Where the hell was Tony? After twenty minutes Sasha was feeling restless and frustrated and annoyed at being ordered to stay in the car. She'd seen nothing since Tony and his men had entered the warehouse, it was pitch dark outside and she was freezing in the car. Just off to her right her vision was caught by a dim glow of light which slowly began to move haphazardly in the direction of the wasteland behind the warehouse. Fixing her eyes on the moving light she picked up two figures as a passing car's headlights illuminated them for a second or two.

Sitting up straighter in her seat, Sasha tried to assimilate what she'd just seen. One of the figures had seemed large, probably a man, and one quite small and being pulled by the man, she was sure of it. Flashes of light appeared intermittently through the broken windows of the warehouse and she surmised that Tony's men were still conducting their sweep of the building – so they hadn't found them – or not all of them.

Opening the car door, she stepped out and quietly closed it behind her before creeping in the direction of the moving torch. If she could just confirm that one of the men had Samantha, she'd call Tony. But then good sense prevailed. She should tell Tony what she'd seen, he and his men were better equipped to take down a hulking great guy with a female hostage than she was, she acknowledged ruefully. Hitting the call button on her phone she suddenly realised that the moving torch light had disappeared and as a soft, muffled cry reached her ears just ahead of her, blinding pain crashed through her skull and everything went black.

She opened her eyes to find a grim-faced Tony staring down at her as another man helped her to her feet. 'Have you got them? Is Samantha safe?' She touched the side of her face gingerly, grimacing at the pain.

Tony shook his head. 'You never learn, do you? I don't know whether to arrest you or give you a flaming hug. Yes, we've got them and yes, Samantha's safe, she's with the paramedics and she's going to be fine.'

'That's good. I did try to call you, Tone, but he was getting away, that's why I–'

Tony stopped her. 'Come here.' He enveloped her in a big hug before holding her at arm's length and appraising her. 'You need to be seen by a paramedic, alright? I got your call but when you didn't speak, I guessed something was wrong. Two of my guys had spotted the light outside the warehouse and had gone round the other side to head off whoever it was. If he hadn't stopped to bash you over the head, we might have missed him and he could have got away with Samantha, so all's well that ends well, as they say. Apart from your head, reckon you'll have a nice shiner by tomorrow.'

Sasha grinned, before holding her face. 'Ow, that's sore. So are you going to arrest me then?'

Laughing, Tony led her to the waiting ambulance to be checked over and given the all clear. 'Not this time, babe. I'm off to the station to sort out our Claudia and her band of merry men, one of my guys will drop you home. And Sash? Good work.'

Nodding, Sasha asked one last question. 'Has anyone told Samantha's husband, Brian?'

'On his way to the hospital to meet her. Not sure how he's going to explain everything, but that's between them, our job is done. I'll call you tomorrow.' Giving Sasha a quick peck on the cheek, Tony walked off, barking orders at his men.

Sasha sank into the passenger seat gratefully, feeling exhausted, and found herself outside her flat seemingly moments later. Thanking the officer for the lift she climbed the stairs and let herself in, yawning. Not sure which hurt more, her head or her insides, she made herself some tea and toast, pulled off her filthy clothes and replaced them with some pyjamas.

Finally, after swallowing some pain killers, she lay down in bed and closed her eyes. Within minutes she was asleep.

WHODUNIT?

A loud buzzing sound woke Sasha and it took her a moment or two to realise it was her flat's doorbell. Feeling like she was wading through treacle she stumbled to her intercom and buzzed up the delivery man, barely registering where he was from.

At his knock she opened the door to find herself staring at what looked like the contents of a flower shop on legs.

A grinning face appeared between the blooms. 'Someone's popular, what you done to deserve all this then, eh?' His tone changed slightly as he looked at Sasha. 'Cor, someone's been in the wars. You alright, love? You don't look so good.'

Still half asleep, Sasha suddenly became aware of how terrible she felt. She pulled her robe around her tender belly and touched her face gently. 'You should see the other guy.' She flung out the clichéd response on autopilot and smiled at the worried-looking man. 'I'll be fine, thanks. Wow, these are beautiful.'

Locking her front door, Sasha returned to the kitchen and stared at the two enormous flower arrangements before taking out the first card. It was from Tony – *For the most stubborn super sleuth I know. You did good. Tx*. She smiled, he was a big softie underneath his tough act. She picked up the second card and read Brian Ozean's note of thanks for finding his wife safe and returning her to him. Well, that was nice, but she couldn't help wondering if Samantha Ozean would still want to be with Brian once she knew everything. Typing out short messages of thanks, Sasha sent them to the two men.

She should take a shower, she thought, but the heavy sluggishness seeming to own her body was giving her a brain fog and as a grinding pain gripped her insides she doubled over in agony. 'I've got no time for this crap!' she shouted at her empty living room. Feeling clammy and dizzy she was forced to lie down with a hot water bottle, tears of frustration running down her face. Her body just screwed everything up for her all the time. She had so much to do, so much to think about, but all she could do was lie down and all she could think about was her pain.

Not sure how long she'd lain there, but realising that the hot water bottle was only lukewarm, Sasha picked up her phone to see who'd sent her the message which had woken her. She replied, telling Tony that she'd love to go in and see Samantha, if the woman was sure she wanted her to, and also to meet Tony for an update.

Noting which hospital, Sasha pondered her ability to make it there in her current condition. Running a hot bath, she submerged herself for a few minutes before pulling on her gown and swallowing down a sugary drink. Still in need of more energy as well as something in her stomach she grabbed a couple of ginger biscuits. Pain killers were next and then she dressed in a long, loose, jersey dress, her stomach too tender for anything tight-fitting. With a huge jumper thrown over the dress, and her boots pulled on, she left the flat, hailing a cab, and arrived at the hospital half an hour later.

'Bleeding hell, you look seriously rough and that's not all down to that little bump on your head, even I can see that. What's the matter with you?' Tony looked at Sasha's pinched face in concern.

'Endometriosis, Tone, the sneaky little monster that lurks in my body and ruins my life on a whim. But I *really* don't want to talk about it, okay? How is she?' Sinking onto a chair outside the hospital room she looked expectantly at Tony.

'Alright, you're the boss, but I'll just say this – you look like you should be in bed – I'm no doctor but you don't look a well girl, Sash.' At her warning glance, he mimicked a zipping motion across his mouth, before updating her.

'Samantha's surprisingly well, which is a relief, to say the least. She looks in a better state than you do, to be honest. The husband's in there at the moment – I've just filled him in on everything that happened. I don't think he'll be in there much longer though, not now that his wife knows about him and his little affair and the whole sorry chain of events that somehow ended up with her being held for money.'

As if on cue the door opened and Brian Ozean walked out looking crushed. Greeting Sasha, he slumped into the chair beside her. 'You look terrible. She wants me out of the apartment before she leaves the hospital.'

'Well thanks for that, I feel terrible actually. Listen, Brian, I'm so pleased that Samantha's safe but I'm sorry about how all this has turned out for you and your wife.'

He raised resigned eyes to hers. 'Thanks, Sasha. You did what I asked you to do. You found my missing wife and I'm grateful. I'll pay you the balance of your fee today. The strange thing is, I do actually care about her very much but she'll never believe me. I've been a bloody fool, messing around with students, and now I've lost her for good in another way entirely. How ironic is that?' He laughed bitterly. 'I asked you to find my wife only for me to lose her forever thanks to my own stupidity.' Standing up, he shook both their hands and walking off along the corridor, his shoulders sagged in defeat.

Tony and Sasha raised their eyes at each other. 'Not the most pleasant way for a case to end,' Sasha commented wryly, standing up ready to leave.

'No, but you did good, Sash. *We* did good. We've got three more gang members in custody, so it's a great result all round. Jax Milan stays in jail as well and Bruce Ocean is still the witness that will keep him there for a very long time. Claudia Novak's spitting blood and screaming blue murder, but the good thing about that is that she's giving us information on the remaining members who are still out there. We'll hopefully root them out over time. I reckon we should work together more often, you just need to learn to do as you're told once in a while, that's all.' He winked at Sasha to indicate that he was teasing. 'Listen, you look—'

He was interrupted by the door opening and Samantha Ozean appeared. 'Are you Sasha? Thank you. Thank you so much.' Samantha held out her arms and the two women hugged.

'You're very welcome, Samantha.' Sasha smiled gently as they pulled apart. The two women spoke for a few minutes before embracing again and saying goodbye.

They watched her walk back into her room and Tony spoke again. 'You look like you're about to keel over. I'm taking you home, no arguments. I'll even pick you up a pizza on the way home to say thank you, how's that?'

With no strength to argue, Sasha allowed him to lead her to his car and to drive her home. Pulling up outside the pizza takeaway she opened her mouth to speak.

'I know, chicken, onion, and green pepper, don't worry.' He grinned. 'I remember from the last time I bought you pizza.'

Hugging Sasha outside her flat, Tony waved her off. 'I meant what I said about working together again, Sash, we make a good team. But right now, me and the girlfriend are heading off to sunnier climes. So don't even think of calling me about anything, my work number's firmly switched off for the next two weeks while I soak up the sun.' With a final grin, Tony jumped back into his car, hooted and drove off.

Back in her flat and curled up on the couch, Sasha munched on the pizza, its flavours comforting her and, psychologically at least, easing her pain. She hadn't told Miles what had happened to her, it could wait she decided, she'd explain why her face was black and blue when they met tomorrow. She'd take some tea to bed and try to get some more sleep and hope like mad she'd be well enough to keep her meeting with Molly the next day.

~

Molly and her friends exited the train at Charing Cross on Saturday morning and decided to walk to Piccadilly Circus via Trafalgar Square, stopping along the way to take numerous photos. Maddox and Tyler nudged and teased each other as they admired the two girls whispering and giggling in front of them. Passers-by smiled indulgently at the happy youngsters.

~

Sasha was filled with frustration, she'd been so hopeful that she'd be okay but her body had other plans – nothing new there. Miles had assured her that he'd go and meet Molly on her behalf to find out what she knew. He'd promised to come to her flat as soon as he returned, bringing food, and insisted that he would spend the rest of the day caring for her. Realising that it was out of her control, she'd capitulated and, dosed up with painkillers, had fallen into a deep sleep.

Waking with a start, Sasha tried to get her brain to focus. Something had been bothering her. Molly. She hadn't told her that she wasn't coming and that Miles would meet her instead. Cursing her foggy brain, she looked at her watch, her heart sinking, they should have met half an hour ago and he wouldn't have known what Molly looked like. Not sure who to contact first, she decided on a quick message to Molly in case she gave up and left. With that done, she hurriedly messaged Miles and awaited his response.

~

Molly smiled to herself, Sara and Ty looked really cute together. While Maddox went to get them drinks, she slipped away quietly, wanting to take a sneaky photo of the two of them. It was getting busy and crowds of pedestrians jostled her as they crossed back and forth around her. She stood at the edge of the crossing, lifting her phone for the perfect shot, but sighed in frustration as someone stepped in front of them. *Patience Molly*. She took a step back for a better angle, wondering what had happened to Sasha.

Maddox cried out, dropping the cans of cool drinks, and raced between the vehicles. 'Molly!' He rushed to the spot he'd last seen her, pushing his way through the crowd gathering there. Molly lay sprawled in the road, a pool of blood spreading into the tarmac. At the sound of his cry, Sara and Tyler had rushed to join him, and the three youngsters looked at Molly's inert form, and each other, in horror.

As the adults took control, Tyler comforted Sara, but Maddox's attention was caught by the man in the blue jacket disappearing into the crowd. He'd seen him earlier, he was sure, he'd been watching them as they posed for their photos, hadn't he? Or was he just imagining things? He started to tell Sara, but her hand on his arm distracted him as, through her tears, she pulled him towards the police officer.

~

Why wasn't anyone replying to her? Sasha checked her phone again impatiently. She clicked onto Molly's Graffic profile, noticing that she'd posted some photos. Well, she was definitely there, her smiling face looked at the camera as she posed with her friend by Eros. And another photo, this time with a boy, their arms around each other as they grinned at whoever was taking the photo. She'd tagged Sasha in her post, *Solving the mystery, finding the girl!*

Whodunit! Clearly, this was a great fun adventure for her and her friends.

So where was Miles? As she wondered what to do, her phone rang. 'Miles?'

'Sash, oh, Sash, something terrible has happened. I can't get close, I'm not sure exactly–' His voice was drowned out by sirens and she strained to hear him.

'Miles, what's happened? Are you alright?' He sounded odd and she began to panic.

'I'm fine, Sash, but there's been an accident or something, I can't get through, can't see what's happening. Oh no, there's someone in the road, I think someone might have died, there's police and an ambulance. They're shaking their heads, they've got a stretcher but, no, they're not moving the person.'

'Oh no, that's awful. You sound shaken, are you sure you're okay?' At his insistence that he was fine, she had to ask. 'What about Molly? Did you find Molly?'

'No, no sign of her. Well, I realised I didn't even know what she looked like. I was going to look around to see if anyone looked likely and otherwise ask you to contact her. I was running a bit late and when I got here, they were already cordoning off the area. They're moving everyone away now so–' He stopped.

'Miles? What is it?'

'Oh God, Sash, I can just about make it out, I think it's a young girl. They're covering her with a sheet.' Miles's anguished voice made Sasha's blood run cold.

She groaned. 'Oh no, please don't tell me. Please say it isn't her, it can't be. Can it? No, it could be anyone. Miles, please come home, I'm so sorry, you poor thing. You must be so distressed. I'll get in touch with her later, she's probably been caught up in the same chaos as you. I'm sure she's fine.'

As Sasha put her phone down, she felt full of foreboding. *Get a grip Sash, it's just a horrid coincidence.*

But still, the feeling remained. She forced herself to get up and shower and dress, knowing that Miles would be coming and wanting to be ready to comfort him. He'd sounded quite distraught on the phone.

Opening her front door, she took one look at Miles's pale face and wrapped her arms around him. 'Oh, Miles, what an awful thing to happen. You're obviously pretty shaken up. That poor girl, did you find out anything else before you left?'

Shaking his head, Miles buried his face in her hair. 'I didn't even see it happen, Sash. But just being there, seeing her lying there in the road, and when they covered her small body...' His sobs shook his frame. 'It can't have been her, can it? It's just a coincidence, it could have been anyone. Have you contacted her? Heard from her?' He pulled away and looked down at Sasha's upturned face, noticing her bruises for the first time and frowning. 'What happened? Did someone do this to you? Are you alright?'

'Don't worry about me, hazards of the job, let's focus on Molly. I've heard nothing. I've sent her messages, but no reply. But she's probably upset, poor girl, she may have seen it happen. She was there though, she posted photos, look.' Sasha picked up her phone from the coffee table and held it out to Miles. 'She was with friends, so they've probably gone off somewhere. At least she's not on her own, such an upsetting incident.'

'Well, I hope you're right, but, Sash, what on earth were you doing to end up with these injuries and why didn't you call me before?' He listened as Sasha gave him a canned account of her investigation, his eyes narrowing at her repeated mentions of Tony. 'You've not mentioned him before, who is he exactly?'

Seriously, Miles was going to exhibit jealousy now? 'D.S. Tony Palmer is my police contact, we ended up working together on this – we've got a rather symbiotic relationship, I suppose – I help him out and he helps me out, that's all. Anyway, to finish off the story, he bought me pizza on the way back from the hospital and dropped me home.'

Miles slapped his forehead. 'I forgot to get food. But honestly, I don't think I can eat anything, Sash. In fact, would you mind? I think I'll head home if you're okay? But I can stay if you–'

'No,' Sasha cut him off. 'You've had a bad experience, you must go home and get some rest. Have a good sleep and we can talk tomorrow. I'll be fine, I'm just so sorry you went there for me today. I feel so bad, you've been roped into stuff you never should have been.' She noticed his glance towards the flower arrangements in her lounge and the slight shadow that seemed to pass over his eyes. 'The flowers were from Tony and my client to say thank you.'

Sasha closed the door behind Miles and sank into her couch, feeling depressed. She'd found Miles's jealousy to be a little petty if she was honest, plus her concern for Molly was growing the longer she didn't hear from her, despite what she'd said to Miles. She should have asked him if the road accident victim had been wearing clothes that matched Molly's in her photos. But maybe she was getting ahead of herself, time enough to worry about that if she didn't hear from the young girl.

~

Angrily he slammed his fist into the wall. Why had she made him do that? They were all the same, women, girls, they made you do things you didn't want to. A guttural sound came from his throat as he sank onto the floor, wrapping his arms around his knees. She probably hadn't known anything, but he couldn't take any chances, couldn't risk her destroying his game. And she'd just had to post graphics of where she was and what she was doing – *solving the mystery, finding the girl* – how stupid was she, and how dare she steal his words, his fun?

Events had spiralled out of control, no one else was supposed to get involved, but no, these stupid girls had to hijack his game, his perfect game for him and Sasha. He needed to regain control, needed to be in charge again. As the red rage encroached on his vision, he staggered to his feet, knowing just what he needed to do to feel better.

Zoe flinched, a whimper escaping her throat, as the door flew open with a crash. One look at his face and she pressed herself into the wall behind her, dreading what he might do to her.

The first punch knocked her sideways on the bed, pain shooting through her head as tears filled her eyes. Her head was yanked up as he grabbed her hair, her flailing hands trying futilely to protect her face from his vicious onslaught. 'Please,' she sobbed, 'please stop.'

Ignoring her, he pulled on the chain around her ankle, causing her to fly onto the floor, landing painfully on her coccyx. Zoe curled herself protectively into a foetal position, in a desperate attempt to ward off further attack, but his booted feet relentlessly kicked at her until she gave up, lying submissively, her body accepting his anger.

Not sure how long she'd been lying there Zoe gingerly opened her swollen eyes, stretching her limbs and flinching at the pain. She felt her face gently then flexed her arms and legs, relieved to find that nothing felt broken. Wiping the blood from her mouth with the back of her hand she pulled herself up onto the bed, covering herself with the blankets, and lay there shivering. There was nothing to drink, nothing to eat, and no one to rescue her. Her body shook as she sobbed and, not caring if he heard her, she let herself give in completely, her wails sounding deafening in the small room.

He was hard now and he stroked himself through his jeans, not wanting to lose it. Hurrying up the stairs he called out gently. 'Sasha, Sasha baby, I'm coming for you.' She was lying on the floor where he'd thrown her after his last photo session and he roughly picked her up, sneering at the scrawled word on her back, *Sasha*. Placing her face down on the bed he clambered on top of her, spreading her synthetic buttocks. He'd show her who was the boss.

He finished quickly and, leaning over the doll, lifted her hair aside. 'It won't be long now until we're together properly,' he whispered in the doll's ear.

IT'S A CELEBRATION

Sasha awoke the next morning filled with energy and knew that her latest flare-up had crept away to leave her in peace again, for a while at least. There was nothing she could do about her bruised face, time, the great healer, would have to take care of that. Concern for Molly niggled at her consciousness and she hurriedly checked her phone again, dismayed to still find no response from the girl. With no other means of contacting her, there was nothing to do but hope for a reply at some point.

She smiled as a message popped up on her phone from Miles. *How's my girl this morning? Hope you're feeling better? Let me know if you feel like company. xx*

There was no one else's company she felt more like, and she tapped out a quick reply, before heading for the bathroom to shower.

Disappointment flooded through her when she read his message as she towelled her hair. He could only come through later. Hopes for them spending the day together disintegrated but, not one to give in to disappointments, Sasha replied telling him that would be great. Suddenly feeling at a loose end, she wandered through her flat, filling the kettle and placing bread in the toaster. Fine, she'd just be lazy. No, I'll get the Sunday paper, and some treats, she decided.

Pulling her boots on, Sasha walked along to the little coffee shop on the corner, picking up the paper on the way, and returned to her flat with a freshly squeezed orange juice, a large cappuccino, as well as warm croissants. This was more like it, she thought, as she sipped and munched, flicking through the paper.

And there it was. Just a few short lines on page four. She almost missed it, tucked away as it was, down in the left-hand corner. A tragic accident. Piccadilly Circus. Molly Townsend. Fifteen years old. Sasha re-read the paragraph three times as reality sunk in. Molly was dead. Molly, who she was supposed to have met yesterday. *Molly, who said she knew something which might help her find the girl in the photos.*

She pushed the remains of her croissant away, her appetite gone. What were the chances? Could it just be a terrible coincidence? Or was it something else? No, she told herself, get a grip, no one even knew, how could they? Thoughts raced through her head as she pulled up Molly's Graffic account and studied the photos again. There was no way of knowing, now, what time Molly had posted her photos. Could someone have seen her post about solving the mystery, finding the girl? If so, they would have to have been close by, perhaps an hour away at the most. Could it have been *him*? Yes, she nodded to herself, it was possible, Molly had, like so many others, copied the poses of the girl in the photos he'd posted, and copied his tags, which meant he could easily be aware of her and may have kept an eye on her account. *Oh, Molly, you must have invited him right to you, you poor girl. And all for a silly game, as far as you knew.*

Needing to keep busy and distracted, Sasha occupied herself in the kitchen, preparing a meal in advance for her and Miles. Never one for the traditional Sunday roast she decided on quesadillas and chopped and flash-fried chicken fillets in cajun seasoning, as well as peppers and red onion, before grating cheese and assembling the ingredients in tortillas ready for finishing off in the pan later. Enjoying the process, and helped by the sounds of David Bowie on vinyl, she decided to expand the meal a little with some accompaniments, wanting to keep herself occupied. With avocados mashed in a bowl, Sasha added finely chopped red onion before squeezing half a lime over the bowl and adding a sprinkle of salt. After making the guacamole she turned her attention to potato wedges, knowing they would complete the meal perfectly. Once she'd washed, chopped, and par-boiled the wedges she laid them on a tray, drizzling them with olive oil and adding freshly ground salt and pepper. She'd pop them in the oven later and they'd crisp up perfectly. Annoyed that she had no fresh tomatoes she opened a small can of tinned tomatoes, chopping them up then adding onion and a splash of balsamic vinegar. It wasn't exactly authentic tomato salsa but it would do.

Standing back Sasha surveyed her work and, as she sang along to Star Man, realised she'd forgotten sour cream. Frowning she checked her fridge, pleased to find a small tub of cream lurking in the door compartment. A squirt of lemon juice, a sprinkle of salt, and a quick whisk sorted that problem and, as she nodded in satisfaction, she realised that she'd been overthinking the whole Molly thing. She'd got carried away, allowed her ever vivid imagination to run riot. Molly's death was an accident, the newspaper said so, there was no reason to suspect anything else. It was what it was, a tragic accident. Calmness enveloped Sasha like a cloak. Working in the kitchen had been just what she'd needed, and it had done the job, it had cleared her mind and kept her balanced.

Not sure exactly what time Miles was coming, Sasha made some tea and studied the last photos posted by @maluspassuum. They exhibited the most cruelty so far, as well as having a sinister feel to them with regard to the hidden message for Sasha. She wondered if he'd been angered by her lack of response and if she'd been right to ignore his latest offerings. If she was honest with herself, she was beginning to feel a kind of fatigue about the whole thing – what exactly did he want? Maybe it was time to turn the whole thing over to the police – perhaps she should talk to Tony? But his message about involving them had been crystal clear, the girl would die, *Zoe would die...*

~

'Miles, they're beautiful.' Sasha gasped at the huge bouquet virtually hiding Miles's upper body from her. 'You didn't have to do this, really, so sweet of you.'

'I wanted to give you something beautiful, Sash, just like you.' Miles smiled, before managing to somehow embrace Sasha without damaging the flowers. Their kiss was lingering and intimate and Sasha's belly did a few backflips as she felt desire stirring rapidly. There was an air of confidence about him, he seemed pleased with himself, almost triumphant, and she wondered what it was all about.

'Let me put these in water, I'm not sure I've even got a vase big enough. My flat's beginning to resemble a florist's shop.' Laughing, Sasha headed for the kitchen and found a large pottery jug which would suffice while Miles poured them both prosecco, grinning at Sasha's enquiring expression. 'Are we celebrating something? What's going on, Miles, you've got me all intrigued'

'Here.' he handed her a glass. 'I picked this up on the way over, it was a spur of the moment thing. But yes, I suppose there is something to celebrate. I er, well, I've dealt with a problem and I'm feeling pretty pleased with myself. So I went to get wine, saw the Prosecco and, well, here we are.'

Sasha felt mystified. 'Well, are you going to tell me what it was all about then?'

'Maybe later, I think we have something else to attend to first.'

Wow, Miles had turned into Mr Masterful literally overnight. She liked it. His eyes darkened as he looked into hers and she saw his desire reflecting her own. *This is it. We're going to make love.* They reached for each other at the same moment and their kiss this time was less lingering, more hungry, rough and passionate. They pulled apart for just long enough to acknowledge they were on the same page and then kissed again, their fingers tearing at each other's clothing. Sasha half-pulled Miles towards the bedroom where they hastily finished undressing in the glow from the street light outside. Miles pulled the duvet back and pressed Sasha down onto the bed before falling on top of her with a groan. She gasped loudly as his fingers brushed over her sensitive spots, his mouth kissing her neck, his hands exploring her belly, her thighs, and finally... she couldn't hold back the groan as he began to touch her... She reached an arm up to run her fingers through his hair, to stroke his face, to gently touch his closed eyes, while her other hand ran over his taut upper body, his firm arms, feeling the muscles tense as he moved. She lowered her hand to his buttocks as he raised them slightly and suddenly she was flipped over.

The move took her by surprise but, unable to adjust her position and free her trapped arm, she let him take control. She pushed against him greedily but, with a muffled groan, Miles's weight was instantly heavy on top of her. It was a moment before Sasha realised what had happened and, not wanting him to feel embarrassed, she relaxed her body, allowing it to fall sideways, and lay back, smiling languidly at him.

His eyes were still closed as he fell next to her and Sasha reached for his hand, holding it gently as his breathing calmed. It was normal, of course it was, they'd been building up to this for a while now, no wonder. She turned her head to look at him in the semi-darkness, not sure if his eyes were still closed. 'Miles?' she whispered, 'Are you okay?'

His eyes flashed open, surprising her. 'I'm great. And I'm hungry. What about you?' He nuzzled her neck, kissing her, before jumping up and pulling her with him. 'What was all that delicious food I saw in the kitchen?'

Sasha watched him pulling his jeans back on and realised he wasn't going to acknowledge their rather swift and somewhat one-sided coupling, so neither would she. She went into the bathroom and freshened up, finding him gone from the bedroom when she came back out. Her body felt in limbo, still wanting release, her mind a little confused by his behaviour, but she put it aside. Maybe he thought it had been mutual... Hopefully they'd have a repeat performance later, after they'd had food... The thought made her shiver with anticipation. She joined him in the kitchen and switched the oven on before accepting a refill of Prosecco and leaned back into his chest when he wrapped his arms around her.

The last thing she wanted to do was to spoil the mood of their evening but she felt conflicted about the whole Molly tragedy and yearned to talk to Miles about it. As she busied herself with the final preparations for their meal, she pondered what to do, but Miles suddenly swung her around, grinning.

'Guess what?' he asked, looking pleased with himself.

Laughing, Sasha said she had no idea, and looked at him expectantly.

'I've dealt with Eric. He won't cause you any more problems, Sash, he's out of your life. Didn't I tell you I'd sort it out?'

He pulled her to him and kissed her, before releasing her and looking at her, waiting for her response.

'Oh wow, you did? Miles, thank you, that must have been difficult. I can't believe he accepted it, was he annoyed? I know what Eric's like, he hates being told what to do by anyone. What did you say to him?'

Miles placed his finger on her lips. 'It's done, that's all you need to know. Eric's caused us enough problems, we should forget about him now. He was no problem at all. I must say I was surprised, I'd expected him to give me a hard time, but he was pretty easy-going about the whole thing. Let's forget about him, shall we? He's been hovering around in the background of our relationship the whole time so maybe we can move on now, what d'you think?'

'But, it's just, what on earth did you say for him to accept it so readily?'

'I didn't say he accepted it readily, Sash,' he sniggered, gazing across the room, 'but like I say, we're done talking about Eric, okay? Now, how's the food coming along? It smells delicious and I'm starved.'

He's right, she thought, as she lifted the last tortilla from the pan, why think or talk about Eric? And if she was honest, she also kind of liked the way he put his foot down, definitely more and more on the masterful side... Relieved, she carried dishes through to her small dining table, switching on the low-hanging light above it and laying out napkins and cutlery. Turning to Miles as she collected the dish of wedges, she smiled. 'You're right, we should forget all about him. Come, let's eat.'

'Mmm, I have to say, Sash, you're not a bad cook, this is so good.' Miles winked at her as helped himself to more food, heaping a slice of quesadilla with guacamole and sour cream before taking an appreciative bite.

She watched him happily. 'Thank you, I'm no chef but this is one meal I'm not bad at. Oh, you've spilt some on your shirt.' She reached across to wipe the red splash with her napkin, but it was stuck on. 'I'll get a cloth.'

She returned as Miles laughed, wiping ineffectually at himself and looking up at her as he rolled his eyes. 'I've done it again, I'm a disaster. But this tomato salsa is great, the whole combo is, I'm just making a real mess of it I'm afraid.'

Sasha took in the pile of salsa on his plate and the splashes over the table and his shirt. 'You really are. Miles, take your shirt off, let me stick it in the machine, it'll be ruined otherwise.' *And maybe while you've got your shirt off, we could do something to keep busy…*

'No, it's fine, here, give me the cloth, it'll be fine, it's old anyway.' He dabbed at his shirt before wiping the table then jumped up, picking up a dish and going through to the kitchen. Sighing inwardly, Sasha picked up the remaining dishes, carrying them out. *Could this man not take a hint?*

With everything put away in the dishwasher, Sasha noticed Miles check his watch. 'Nightcap?' she asked, holding up the whisky bottle, hopefully. But he smiled regretfully and shook his head.

'I've got a busy one tomorrow, Sash, sorry, you don't mind, do you?' He pulled her into him, kissing the top of her head as she felt her spirits sink.

'No, of course not, you go and get some sleep.'

She surveyed her crumpled bed as she got undressed, the memory of their bodies writhing there just a little earlier still fresh, and sighed before lying down and turning off the light.

She slept fitfully, waking what seemed like every hour, her dreams chaotic and filled with images of her and Miles, of Molly, even Eric. She woke again, the vestiges of her last dream still lingering. She'd been unbuttoning Miles's shirt, but then they'd been at the table, laughing as Miles loaded his plate with sour cream and guacamole, and then he was on top of her, her body arching towards him. Groaning, she turned over in her bed, half asleep and yet filled with longing. Her mind suddenly sparked wide awake and she sat up – something about their meal – something important – she tried to grasp at the threads, but whatever it was it had gone. Looking at the time she realised it was morning and with a heavy sigh pulled herself out of bed. She may as well get up.

WHERE WERE YOU?

'I feel responsible, I can't help it. I don't know what to do, should I contact the parents?' Sasha clutched her phone tightly as she spoke to Miles.

'Sash, you're not responsible, you didn't do anything, she chose to involve herself in something. You shouldn't feel bad.' Miles tried to placate Sasha to no avail.

'Maybe that's the problem, I didn't do anything. If I had done maybe she'd still be alive. It's my fault she was in London, Miles, she came to meet me. And I don't even know why she wanted to see me or what it was she thought she knew. And honestly? What can she have known? She was just a young girl caught up in the thrill of what she thought was a new stupid craze. Even if it was just an accident, she was there because of me. I want to go to the funeral.' There, she'd said it, what she'd been feeling but hadn't vocalised until this moment.

'Sash, really, why on earth would you want to do that? You didn't know her, what can your being there possibly achieve?'

'I don't know, I just feel I should be there. I'm going Miles, sorry, but I need to.'

'Alright, but if you're going then I'm coming with you. Accident or no accident, I want to keep you safe. And it was an accident, Sash, you know that. But I don't like the idea of you being out anywhere alone, not while he's out there.'

She couldn't remember the last time she'd felt so cared for. Well, the thought came unbidden into her mind, Cal, of course. Cal, who'd made her trust him, who'd made her believe he cared about her. Until his pregnant wife had turned up of course. The hurt hadn't gone away. She missed him. Still. But he wasn't part of her life anymore. At least she'd never slept with him. They'd come so close though. She wondered what it would have been like... Sighing, she put the thought out of her mind. She'd really made some great choices with men, Eric, Cal, she certainly knew how to pick them. And now Miles. She smiled, feeling better. Yes, Miles was the real deal, she was sure. Maybe finally she had a chance at a good relationship. She wondered yet again what had gone so wrong with him and Zoe, and then, guiltily, allowed herself to acknowledge that she was kind of glad that it had.

~

'You okay, love?' Steve Townsend looked anxiously at his wife as she fixed her hair back.

Her pale face, with its red-rimmed eyes, turned to him. 'Of course I'm not okay, Steve, how can I ever be okay again? My baby girl's dead.' Cat sank onto the bed, fresh tears falling, as Steve sat beside her, gathering her into his arms.

'Hey, shhh, I know, love, I know.' They rocked together for a while, their sobs the only sound in the bedroom until Steve carefully looked at his watch. 'Babe, it's time, we have to go.' He helped her up and she straightened her dress before following him downstairs and into the waiting car. Neighbours lined the street, their heads down, as the small procession of cars drove off.

Sara held her mum's hand tightly as their car joined the cortege heading for Watling Street Cemetery. She couldn't believe this was happening. Her best friend was dead. She felt like she was in some kind of bad dream, that at any moment she'd wake up and she and Molly would be laughing as they got ready to take the bus to Bluewater shopping centre or something.

~

The parking area was almost full, but Miles squeezed them into a space in the far corner. 'For the last time, Sash, are you sure you want to be here?'

'I do, Miles, I'll stay at the back and won't speak to anyone, but I just want to pay my respects.'

The couple followed the line of mourners to the Chapel, stepping aside to allow others to enter. 'It'll never hold everyone, we'll wait out here.' Sasha looked around, feeling sad as she watched the small group of young girls in uniform enter. They must be Molly's friends from school of course. A young girl, accompanied by her parents, caught Sasha's attention, she looked familiar. Yes, she'd been in some of Molly's photos, that was it. Sara, if her memory served her correctly. As if sensing Sasha's eyes on her the girl looked up at her as she passed, recognition sparking in her eyes. But then she was gone, guided in by her parents.

The service was short and mourners stepped into line behind the hearse as it drove slowly towards the freshly prepared grave. Sasha and Miles kept to the back and once the coffin had been lowered into the ground, turned to leave.

A tug on Sasha's sleeve stopped her and she looked round to see a woman's tear-stained face grimacing painfully at her. 'What are you doing here? How dare you come to my daughter's burial? It's your fault she's dead.' A man stepped forward and held the woman, looking at Sasha angrily. 'I saw her phone, if she hadn't been meeting you, she'd still be alive. What did you want with my daughter?'

Sasha tried to speak. 'I, I'm sorry, I didn't know Molly, I don't know why she wanted to meet me. I'm so sorry for your loss.'

A howl of painful rage escaped the woman. 'Don't speak her name. Go, get out.' She was led away by the man and Sasha and Miles turned and headed for the car.

'I feel dreadful, oh, Miles, you were right, I shouldn't have come, I've made things worse.' Miles slipped his arm around her and hugged her, before unlocking the car.

As Sasha opened her door, a small voice called her name. Turning, she recognised Molly's friend, Sara. She was accompanied by two boys and she looked anxiously around her before speaking.

I'm Molly's friend, Sara, I was with her in London, the day she, well, that day. We all were, me, Maddox, and Tyler.' She motioned towards each of the two boys standing beside her, one of whom had fixed his eyes on Miles. 'Why didn't you come and meet her?'

'I'm so sorry, Sara, I wasn't well, and I'm so sorry about your friend, Molly. Miles tried to go and meet her on my behalf, but he was too late. It must have been so awful for you.'

Miles took charge. 'Sara, we're so sorry about your friend, it must have been hard. So you were all there that day, the day it happened? Such a tragic accident.'

Sara nodded as the boy called Maddox spoke, looking at Miles. 'I saw you there. You were right there.'

But Miles shook his head regretfully. 'I wish I had been, but by the time I arrived, the area was already cordoned off. I wondered what had happened, I had no idea it was your poor friend.'

Sara turned towards Sasha. 'We wanted to tell you what we knew, you see, Molly and I, we worked something out. It was about the–' she stopped suddenly as the same boy put his hand on her arm.

'We should go, Sara, now.' Ignoring her puzzled look, Maddox led her away. The other boy shrugged apologetically before following them, leaving Sasha and Miles looking across the car at each other, bemused. Sasha looked back at the girl who was trying to shrug off the boy's hold on her arm as she strained to look back towards them.

'Give me a sec, Miles.' Sasha hurried after the three, calling out. 'Sara, wait. Take my card, call me any time, okay?' She handed her card to Sara and, with a final sorry smile, returned to the car.

'Well that was a little odd,' Sasha pondered what had happened, as Miles drove.

'Kids, you know what they're like. And shame, they're all upset, they've lost their friend. I'm not sure giving that girl your card is going to help, Sash, you should probably just leave it alone now, you don't want more angry parents after you. Hell, I feel so sorry for them.' Miles shook his head sadly.

'Yes, me too, and you're probably right about my card. Anyway, it's done now. But, well, Maddox seemed pretty sure that he saw you? Are you sure you didn't see them? Maybe you were standing right next to them and you just didn't know it?'

'Sash.' Miles gave a small laugh. 'There's no way I could even get close, I told you, plus I was late. No, he's obviously confused me with someone else.' He laughed again, ruefully. 'After all, I'm not exactly noticeable, I'm just like millions of other blokes, nothing special.'

'Oh, that's not true.' Sasha reached across and squeezed his arm, amused at his lack of confidence in his looks. 'You're noticeable to me, and special.'

His pleased look lifted her spirits. It had been a depressing day, but it was over now.

They sat silently in the car on the drive home, each wrapped up in their thoughts.

What happened back there? Maddox had stopped Sara from talking. Why? He'd been staring at Miles, had seemed adamant that he'd seen him there that day. Could he have been there? If so, why was he hiding it? She glanced sideways at Miles, taking in his gentle face, and he turned his head towards her, giving her a wink. *No, he wasn't hiding anything, she honestly didn't think he had a bad bone in his body. It was like he said, they were kids. Plus, why on earth would Miles, of all people, want to harm a young girl who'd only wanted to try and help Sasha?* She reached out and held his hand as they drove.

A thought occurred to Sasha. 'Miles, why d'you think he's gone quiet?'

'Who's that?'

'You know. *Him.* @maluspassuum.'

'Hell, I dunno, Sash, maybe he got bored? Why, are you missing him?' He grinned at her.

'That is not funny, Miles. No, I'm relieved, but also, well, it's weird. And worrying, I mean, what about the poor girl?' *Zoe. Maybe.*

'Well, why don't you ask him?'

What? You mean initiate new communication? D'you think that's a good idea?'

'Yeah, why not? What have you got to lose?' Miles pulled up outside Sasha's flat, keeping the engine running.

'You're not coming in?' As soon as she asked, she felt bad. Poor Miles, she'd already made him take time out of his working day to take her to the funeral.

'I've got some stuff to do, Sash, plus, look at this road, not a parking spot in sight. Tell you what, why don't I come round again this evening? I could pick up a takeaway if you like?'

'Okay, great, that'll be nice. If you're sure?' At his nod, she kissed him on the cheek, thanked him for taking her and got out of the car.

Back in her flat and once she'd changed into a soft sweatshirt and leggings, Sasha thought about what Miles had said. Should she instigate communication with *him*? Was that what he was waiting for? She picked up her phone, thinking about what she could say to him.

CROSS BONES

He wanted her gone if he was honest. He'd had his fun with her, now he had to decide what to do. He sat stretched out on the bed next to the doll, thinking. She'd be hungry and thirsty, and desperate. Maybe he should use her one last time then think about disposing of her permanently. A final photo for precious Sasha, that's what he needed. Something to anger her.

Excitement rushed through him as he had an idea. Checking his watch, he then searched on his phone for the details he needed. It was a little risky but that gave him an extra thrill. Jumping up, he hurried to her room. 'Strip,' he ordered Zoe. 'Then face the wall.' Once she was naked, he wrote on her back in large letters. Standing back, he admired his handiwork, before throwing an old raincoat onto the bed. 'Put this on.'

'If you try anything, anything at all, I will kill you. We're going for a little drive, and if you're a good girl I'll give you something to eat and drink afterwards. Are we clear?'

Zoe nodded, mutely. Weak from lack of sustenance, she could barely stand, let alone care what happened to her anymore. She allowed him to lead her to the car and, when he opened the boot, put up no resistance as he lifted her in and closed it.

The dull, drizzly, weather was perfect, the roads were fairly clear this time in the afternoon, and pedestrians were few. He followed the directions with ease, pulling into Redcross Way and parking in an empty spot directly across from the gate. Making sure that there was no one around, he quickly pulled Zoe from the boot and marched her across the narrow street. 'Face the gate, drop the raincoat, and don't move.' He placed the hood over her head, before crossing back over, where he took a few photos and, pleased with the effect, hurriedly ordered her to put the coat on. He dragged her roughly back to the car and shoved her into the boot. It had all taken only two minutes.

As he neared the house he pulled into a drive-thru, ordering burgers and chips, plus cool drinks. She should thank him, she was having a treat today. Her last supper. The thought made him giggle.

~

Sasha pressed send, wondering if she'd done the right thing or if she'd been too aggressive, but it was too late now. Deciding to shower before Miles came, she sent him a message telling him she was looking forward to seeing him. Would they make love this evening? The thought filled her with anticipation.

~

The photos were perfect, he thought happily, but which one to use? Finally, having made his choice, he posted the image, together with his usual tags. There, that would show the bitch. Was she clever enough to work out the subtle message from the location, he wondered? Admiring his handiwork, he leaned over and kissed the doll. 'Oh, Sasha, we are having fun together, aren't we?' He sat up and frowned. He wanted her here with him, the *real* Sasha. Soon, though.

He unzipped his jeans, touching himself as he imagined the things that he would do to her. It was a moment before he realised his phone had pinged with a notification. Well, that was quick. But no, she hadn't seen his latest artwork, she was just communicating with him – and not very nicely. She'd pay for that. He read her message again.

Why have you gone quiet you sick little pervert? What have you done with Zoe? I know it's her. What's wrong with you? Not man enough to get a woman the normal way so you have to kidnap one and torture her? I will find you, you little prick, and you will suffer.

Oh, Sasha, my little Sasha, aren't you sweet? Amused, he put his phone down. He'd make her wait for a reply. First, she had to see his latest offering, as well as his fun little red herrings he'd posted on behalf of sweet little Zoe.

~

Sasha checked her phone after her shower. Miles hadn't read her message yet. But she had a notification on Graffic. Feeling apprehensive, she clicked and opened the image she'd been tagged in. Gasping, she stared at the naked woman in the photo. It had to be Zoe. *Oh, you poor thing, Zo.* The words scrawled on her back were clear enough. *You're all whores, Sasha.*

She studied the photo. It was a distinct location, the gate covered in ribbons of every colour, behind it a brick wall, and further back– was that the Shard? A short search on the internet rapidly told her what she needed to know. Cross Bones Graveyard was an old burial ground for prostitutes.

She read with sadness the tale of the unconsecrated medieval memorial for thousands of prostitutes, which later included those from London's poorest and most violent slums – an area known as The Mint – those burials including many infants, and criminals too. The medieval sex workers known as The Winchester Geese were believed to have been buried there, having been licenced by the Bishop of Winchester to work in the local brothels on land owned by him. It is thought that they were either given their name due to their screeching – to attract customers – or for the baring of their white breasts for the same result.

A shiver passed through her body. His message was clear. He viewed Zoe as no better than a prostitute, and Sasha the same. Did he mean them both to die? Is that why he'd chosen this location? Feeling panicky, she was about to call Miles when her phone rang. Expecting it to be him, she answered it without looking.

'Sasha? It's Sara. You said I could call you? Is it a bad time?' Sara's anxious voice concerned Sasha.

'Sara, hi, and it's fine. Are you alright? You sound worried.'

'I'm fine, it's just, well, I've got some stuff to tell you. Are you on your own?'

Strange question. 'Yes, I'm alone. What's up? You can tell me anything. You said you and Molly had worked something out. Was it from the photos?'

'Okay, yes, it's like this. You know that photo, the one where he posed the girl at the table? The dinner table? And there were candles burning behind her? D'you remember?'

Scrabbling for a pen and paper, Sasha answered, 'Yes, I remember.'

'Okay, good, well me and Molly, we recognised them. We thought we'd seen them on Etsy so we looked it up. It was the labels as well, they stand out because they're red and they've got this burning heart, it's yellow, kind of flaming, and there's a moon in the corner.'

Sasha wrote quickly. 'You're sure about this, Sara? That's a lot of detail from a blurry photo.'

'I'm sure. *We* were sure. We'd been looking at candles on Etsy before and we'd seen them. We thought they were nice – if you had a boyfriend anyway. And that's why we thought you'd be able to ask her who bought them.'

'Hold on, ask who?'

'Oh, sorry, Moon Goddess, that's what she calls herself. It says they're the perfect gift for your man. So, you see? Someone bought them for their boyfriend or whatever. Well, probably. So if you ask her she can tell you who's bought them. We figured that you could find out who the girl is that way.'

She was right. It did sound a little far-fetched, but... 'Sara, thank you for this, it's really helpful.'

'I can send you the link if you'd like? Then you can see for yourself.'

'That would be great, my love. You've been an enormous help.' Sasha felt excited, maybe the girls had stumbled onto something after all.

Sara spoke again, sounding nervous. 'There's one more thing I need to tell you, it's a bit awkward. I mean, maybe he's wrong, but...'

Sasha interrupted her. 'Sorry, Sara, can you hold on just a sec?'

'Miles, you're here.' Sasha smiled at him as she held her door open. He entered her flat, delicious aromas filling the air from the takeaway bags in his hands. 'I'm just on the phone with someone, give me a minute.'

'No problem, I'll just put these down.' Miles kissed her as he carried the bags to the kitchen.

'Sara, sorry, you were saying?'

'Oh, it doesn't matter. It's nothing. I have to go, my mum's calling me. I'll send you the link. Bye.' She ended the call, and Sasha was left hanging. *That was strange...*

'Who's Sara? The young girl from the funeral?' Miles wrapped his arms around Sasha and kissed her. Releasing her, he looked inquisitively at Sasha. 'What did she want?'

'Well, it could be something, it's definitely worth looking into. Oh, hold on.' Sasha clicked on the link that Sara had just sent her. 'Miles, come and look, it's about these candles.' She explained what Sara had told her about the girls recognising the candles in the photo of the girl at the table. Together they studied the information.

You light my fire, handmade candles by Moon Goddess. The perfect gift for your man. Hot, sexy, candles to get your evening sizzling. Fire up your night with these gorgeous candles from Moon Goddess.

Sasha switched between the Moon Goddess image and the image with the girl in, tutting at the blurred candles in the background. 'Hold on, I'm going to send this photo to my laptop, see how much I can enhance the candles.'

They sat together on the couch, staring at the larger, clearer, image on Sasha's laptop. 'Look.' She pointed at the image as she spoke. 'Glass jars, red wax, a flaming heart on a red background and that little logo in the corner could be a moon.' Excitedly, she turned to Miles, 'They were right, Miles. These candles look identical. All I need to do is contact the seller and ask her who she sold them to.' *I'll ask her about Zoe*, she thought but didn't say aloud.

Miles peered at the screen. 'Well, yes, they do look similar, I suppose. But Sash, d'you think she'll tell you who her customers were? She'll probably think you're trying to steal her clients, don't you think?'

Why did she feel that Miles was being a bit of a wet blanket about it all? Was it just a man thing? Or could he just not see the similarities? Not even similarities, they were the same candles. 'Miles, trust me on this, this is what I do, I've got a nose for it.'

'And a very lovely nose.' He leaned over and kissed the tip of her nose. 'Up to you, Sash, you may as well try, I kind of get the feeling that you're going to, anyway. But first, what about the food? The smells are driving me crazy.'

'Sorry, I'm getting carried away. Look, would you mind popping the stuff on the table? I'll just send her a quick message.'

They sat at the dining table and gorged on the array of Chinese food which Miles had brought. 'I'm going to have to watch my weight,' Sasha complained, laughingly. 'All this tempting food I keep eating with you.'

Miles laughed, pouring them more wine, as he spoke. 'I've been meaning to ask you, have you heard any more from Zoe?'

Sasha looked at him in confusion, *he still honestly believed that Zoe was off on holiday*. 'Well, no, she hasn't called me, but, Miles–'

He shook his head, smiling. 'Maybe she's too busy enjoying herself to call you, but she might have posted some photos, isn't that what Zoe always does?' He shrugged his shoulders. 'I'm just saying, it's worth checking, but hell, what do I know about all this stuff?'

'No, you're right, I should have kept checking, there's just been so much going on and I was so sure...' Her voice tailed off as she stared at the photos on Zoe's Graffic profile. 'I don't understand, I–'

'What is it?' Miles looked at Sasha's phone as she held it out to him.

'Holiday photos, a beach, a pool, plates of food and stuff, it's all typical Zoe, but...' Her brain was struggling to compute what she was looking at – it felt right but it also felt wrong – relief that Zoe was safe mingled with feelings of doubt. 'I was wrong, wasn't I? Zoe's not the girl in the photos, she's not been taken by him?'

Miles's eyes were sympathetic as he smiled at her. 'It's okay to be wrong occasionally, Sash, you mustn't blame yourself for making a mistake.'

Her phone pinged and she picked it up. 'It's from Moon Goddess.'

She looked up at him despondently. 'An out of office reply. Damn, I'll have to wait. She says she's away for a few days. Arrggh, that is so frustrating.'

Reaching for her hand, Miles stroked it, his eyes glinting. 'I think we need to ease that frustration...'

She let him lead her to the bedroom, removing all thoughts of Zoe and candles from her mind.

Whether it was from her frustration from their last time together, when Miles had left her wanting more, or the feeling that she was in his power, but the way he seemed to control her drove her crazy and she fell back moments later as Miles slumped beside her, their limbs entwined in the ruffled sheets, skin clammy from their exertions.

~

Lying in bed alone, later that night, Sasha relived their coupling, pondering Miles's seeming masterfulness in the bedroom. She found him to be rather an enigma, one minute quite shy and gentle, the next exhibiting a controlling behaviour which she found both unexpected as well as exciting, especially when it came to the bedroom... And then there was the feeling of haste – like there was no time to lose. But she'd been as much to blame this evening as him... It was all good though, they were still learning about each other's bodies, there would be hours of slow lovemaking to enjoy as time went along, she thought, shivering in anticipation.

Her thoughts turned to Sara's phone call earlier in the evening as she tossed restlessly in bed. What had she been about to tell her? And more to the point, why did she change her mind suddenly? What was it she'd said? Maybe he's wrong? Who? And something about it being awkward? What? And why? Miles. Miles had arrived and she'd asked Sara to hold on while she opened the door. Had she told Sara it was Miles? She tried to remember, but her tired brain failed her. Maybe Miles had spoken and Sara had heard his voice? But so what? Miles had been with her at the funeral and Sara had come and spoken to her. Yes, but even then, one of the boys had pulled her away. And why was she even thinking that it had anything to do with Miles? She needed to sleep, she wasn't thinking clearly. She finally drifted off with images of a crowded beach, a swimming pool, and Zoe floating through her mind, her last conscious thought being that she had to go to Zoe's flat.

THE KEY TO THE MYSTERY

Waking the next morning with a sense of purpose, Sasha jumped out of bed, showered, dressed, and gulped down some tea and toast before decisively bringing up the photos Zoe had supposedly posted on Graffic. There had been something wrong about the photos – not one of them included Zoe. And hadn't Zoe said in her call that they were staying in a room above a taverna? Then how did that explain the presence of a pool? It had looked like a hotel pool and, more than that, one of the photos had purported to show the entrance to a hotel surely?

Thinking back to her recent luck in being able to identify the name of the pub from a small section of a sign in one of Claudia Novak's photos, Sasha concentrated on the image of the hotel entrance – sure enough, part of the hotel's name was visible in the corner of the photo – not on the hotel itself but on a shuttle bus. She jotted down the letters *imna bay*, before examining the photo of the pool.

A smiling waiter in a light blue uniform posed with a tray of drinks beside the pool – odd, unless he was posing for Zoe? Zooming in, Sasha tried to decipher his badge, sure that the first letter was '*R*'. It was enough to go on she decided as she brought up a map of Crete – for Zoe either had to actually be in Crete or @maluspassuum was stuck with perpetuating the myth following Zoe's potentially forced call telling her about her holiday.

Bringing up an alphabetical search result of hotels on the island of Crete, Sasha's eyes whizzed down the list until she found what she'd been hoping for – The Rethimna Bay Hotel. Clicking on it she proceeded to select the photo gallery and drew in her breath sharply. Could it be–? She compared Zoe's photos, one by one, with the images displayed by the hotel and sat back stunned but with her suspicions confirmed – the photos on Zoe's Graffic account were a lie – she hadn't taken the photos, she hadn't posted them, she simply wasn't there at all. Someone had made a poor attempt at giving that impression by blatantly pinching the images straight from the hotel's website. Grimly, Sasha stood and pulled on her boots and jacket, locked her door behind her and set off for Zoe's flat. She should have gone there ages ago, she chastised herself, angry at leaving it for so long.

Stepping off the bus, Sasha headed along Zoe's street, thinking back to the night Zoe had misplaced her key. They were both completely trashed, having had one of those girly nights where it had been Zoe's turn to cry into her wine, while Sasha agreed with her that men were bastards. She couldn't remember who the boyfriend in question had been, but he'd dumped Zoe unceremoniously and Zoe had been horribly upset. She'd really liked him and the two of them had polished off bottle after bottle of wine as they'd picked the male psyche apart. Having successfully ripped men to shreds, they'd ended up having a great evening, Zoe had cheered up, and they'd left the pub at closing time to stagger their way to Zoe's, stopping for chips in pitta bread on the way before finally reaching her flat.

That was when Zoe had ended up tipping the contents of her bag onto the step as she'd hunted for her keys. 'They must be here somewhere,' Zoe had slurred, as the two of them had drunkenly sifted through the pile of makeup, pens, tissues, phone, purse, and other assorted items. Sasha smiled at the memory. Eventually, they'd stared at each other in exaggerated shock. The keys were definitely missing. Sasha had suggested they go to hers, which would mean finding a cab or taking a night bus, but Zoe had suddenly clapped her hand to her forehead dramatically. 'I've got a spare,' she'd declared exultantly. But Zoe had been so drunk she couldn't remember where she'd hidden it.

Sasha forced herself to remember where they'd looked. She knew they'd started upending plant pots by the front door, to no avail, shushing each other loudly as a pot rolled noisily across the path, soil falling out in a heap. It had been a bit of a Patsy and Eddie moment, she thought, grinning fondly. They'd opened the creaking side gate and tiptoed along to the back of the old Victorian semi to continue their search. Needless to say, they'd found Zoe's bunch of keys the following day under a bush by the front path where they must have fallen when she'd tipped her bag upside down.

She'd reached Zoe's flat by now and paused to take in the closed curtains at Zoe's ground floor windows. She might as well try the bell, maybe she'd got it all wrong and Zoe really had been away on holiday. She could have got back last night and be sleeping soundly in her bed. But even as she pressed the bell, she knew that Zoe wouldn't answer.

Retracing their drunken steps to the back garden, she stood looking around, hoping for inspiration. There it was – an old wall sconce, crumbling now, but once an attractive feature. A flowerpot sat crookedly inside it, its withered contents evidence of neglect. Lifting the pot, Sasha felt around beneath it and found the key. She returned to the front and unlocked Zoe's door.

The flat had that silent, unlived-in feeling which quickly creeps into a home when its occupant is away. Opening the curtains, Sasha walked silently through the flat, checking the kitchen, lounge, bathroom, and bedrooms. She surveyed Zoe's bedroom. If Zoe had been packing to go on a trip, there'd have surely been evidence of such? Surely there'd be a few discarded items left on the bed or empty hangers on the wardrobe handles? But the room just looked like Zoe had got up on a normal day, gone out for a while, and never come back. There was even a mug half-filled with cold tea beside the bed.

The kitchen proved more definitive. A container of sour milk sat in the fridge, mouldy fruit in the fruit bowl, and the half loaf of bread in the bread bin had turned an interesting shade of green. Instinctively, Sasha moved to collect up the items but then, realising that she may need to involve the police, she left them where they were. Maybe she should call the police right now? But he'd been extremely clear about what would happen to Zoe if she did. She couldn't risk it, not yet.

She scanned the other contents of the kitchen counter, noticing something red next to some opened post. Picking up the key, Sasha froze. The red ribbon was tied through the hole in the head of the key in exactly the same way as with the key in the photo which had been in her own door lock. Could it be her own key? But that made no sense – as if anything made any sense though. She opened Zoe's front door and tried the key. It fitted and turned easily. Okay, so Zoe's key was here and tied with ribbon. *He*, and it had to be *him*, had accessed both their keys.

A memory came into her mind of the night Eric had been outside her flat. He'd been out drinking with Miles and had pitched up outside, calling up to her and being a nuisance. She'd told him to go home. And she'd told him she'd changed her locks, something like that. Maybe she'd told him to throw away her key? What had he shouted up at her? Irritated, she tried to force her memory to cooperate. She'd closed the curtains – he'd been yelling something, yes, he'd definitely yelled something about a key. Or, her key?

She sat on a barstool at Zoe's kitchen counter trying to sense what might have happened to her. Thoughts whirled in her head but she couldn't make the connections. What did the keys mean, if anything? Zoe, her flat, her key, Sasha's key, Eric, Miles... Why did the two men seem to be connected at the heart of everything? A chill settled in her stomach. Eric and Miles. Eric or Miles? Why had that thought even come into her head? Everything, and everyone, seemed connected. But that couldn't be.

She wasn't sure how long she sat there, bizarre thoughts careering around in her head. Eric. He'd been pretty stalkerish, there was no denying it. And Miles? Was there something a little disconcerting about him? He could be a little controlling, at unexpected moments... but wasn't he just looking out for her? And at her behest, she reminded herself. No, she'd just lost her confidence in men, and not surprising after Cal's behaviour, and Eric's before that. Maybe she was subconsciously trying to sabotage the first chance she had at a good relationship? Which would be pretty dumb, so why would she do that? Standing up, Sasha took a last look around Zoe's kitchen before leaving.

~

It was time to reply to his sweet Sasha's rather rude message, he decided, with a little excited knot in his stomach. Time was drawing to a close in their game. Not sure which excited him more, deciding how to take Zoe's life or the moment when he revealed himself to Sasha and took her in Zoe's place, he tapped out his message on his phone and pressed send.

He looked down at himself, disgust at his hardness filling him, even as he headed for the bedroom. She was to blame for how he had to find his release, for what she made him do. He stared at the inane expression on the doll's face with hatred. This would be the last time. Next time she would be replaced with flesh and blood... Sasha's... He couldn't wait to see her terrified face looking up at him beseechingly as he toyed with her. Finally, she would see him as the powerful man that he was. Naked now, he mounted the doll, placing his hands around her neck. Pushing himself inside her, he squeezed her neck, growling as her face distorted and, as the familiar red rage filled his vision, began to bite her face, ripping chunks of silicone and spitting it out. At his release he collapsed, moaning, on top of the disfigured doll, self-disgust suffusing him.

~

By the time Sasha reached her flat, she'd come to a decision. She'd tell Miles what she'd discovered at Zoe's flat as well as about the fake photos posted on Zoe's Graffic account, surely then he'd take her seriously about her fears for Zoe's safety.

She'd been stupid, had let her imagination get carried away, there was no way that either Eric or Miles could possibly be behind something like this, they were, or had been, all part of each other's lives, that was all. She'd had a fairly long-term on/off relationship with Eric and knew him pretty well, she thought, and Miles had obviously been his friend for much longer. By virtue of that, Miles was completely trustworthy, which he'd proven in the way he'd supported her since the moment they'd bumped into each other at the service station. How long ago was that? It felt like ages, but could only be a couple of weeks or so.

About to call him she first clicked on the notification on her phone, her skin crawling as she read the message.

Oh Sasha, my sweet little Sasha, don't sound so upset. Forget about Zoe, it's time for her to go. Then we can finally be together. Then you'll see what a real man does to a woman. You're going to love what I do to you. I'm going to take my time with you. I'll be real slow. And there will be no one to hear your cries. I'm coming for you soon...

Gasping, she fell into the chair behind her, leaning onto the table for support. Nausea bubbled up inside her as the full realisation of his intentions became clear. He'd just confirmed that it was Zoe, and that he was going to kill her. If she didn't find her, and soon, Zoe would be dead. And then he was going to take *her*, Sasha. And God only knew what he planned to do to her. Fear flooded through her body and for a moment she succumbed to it before berating herself for being weak. *This isn't like you, Sasha. How exactly will he be able to take you? You stay alert, you keep your wits about you, you'll know if anyone's behaving strangely. He won't be able to even get close. And you've got Miles.* Feeling a little better, she waited a few minutes until she'd calmed down, and then she called Miles.

He couldn't have been kinder, or more understanding. As soon as he'd finished work and changed, he'd be round to talk it all through with her. She was to take no chances, speak to no one, trust no one. Reassured, Sasha busied herself in the kitchen, her go-to place when she needed to feel safe and at peace. As always it worked like a charm and her head cleared of all thoughts as she chopped and sliced, fried and baked. Standing back a couple of hours later she surveyed the spread in front of her. She'd maybe gone a little overboard. Oh well, she shrugged, they'd have plenty to choose from for this evening's meal.

Showered, and waiting for Miles, Sasha paced her flat, stopping now and then to stare at the photos fixed on her board in her office. An idea was beginning to form in her mind. A possible way to locate Zoe. But she needed to find out how it worked, never having tried out the exact process before. She'd keep it to herself for now though. What she needed, more than anything, was to give herself over to Miles's care for the evening. To let him be the man in charge. She needed to feel safe.

'Sash, baby, come here.' Miles enveloped her in his strong arms, stroking her hair. 'Let's get a drink and then I want you to show me the message.' With wine poured, they sat together on the couch as Miles read the message, silently. He looked up at Sasha, a worried expression on his face. 'You haven't told anyone else about this, have you? You haven't spoken to anyone? It's just, right now we don't know who we can trust. Is there anyone, anyone at all, who you can think of, who might harbour bad feelings against you?'

But Sasha shook her head. 'No, I've only told you, there's no one else to tell. And the only person who might have a bit of a grudge against me is Eric. And that's ridiculous, I know Eric, and whatever he is, he's not a complete psycho. And you've spoken to him, he was alright about it, you dealt with his behaviour, didn't you?'

'I did, and he won't be giving you any more trouble, I told you. Eric's not a bad sort, but all the same, you don't want to be trying to contact him.' At her questioning glance, he clarified. 'All I'm trying to say is, if you try to make any contact you might start him off again and you don't need him hanging around causing you trouble. I'd say you have enough trouble on your plate as it is. Promise me you'll stay away from him, okay?'

'Alright, I'll stay away from him, it won't exactly be difficult, but, Miles, I'm seriously wondering if I shouldn't just take all this to the police now? Surely there's enough to convince them that Zoe's being held against her will and is in danger?'

'No.' Miles's response surprised her in its abruptness, even as his hands encircled her wrists a little too tightly. 'He softened his tone and loosened his grip. 'He made it quite clear what would happen if you went to the police, you just can't risk it, Sash, for Zoe's sake. And much as you think you've got all this evidence, you can't really prove any of it, it's all just supposition, theories, and what the cops would likely dismiss as rambling messages from someone with an overactive imagination.'

His eyes bored into Sasha's as he spoke and he pulled her close. 'Listen, you need to step back from all this a bit, give yourself some breathing space. Let's just relax for a while, okay? Something smells good in your kitchen and it's making me ravenous. What have you been doing in there?'

Miles was being so sweet, trying his hardest to take care of her in every way, although, if she was honest, she did feel a little controlled by him at times. But of course, she knew deep down that he was just trying to keep her safe and that he didn't want her worrying the whole time. At least he couldn't argue with her about the girl in the photos being Zoe now. Strangely, he hadn't commented on her name being mentioned in the message, or about Sasha's uncovering of the fake photos, but it was also no use mentioning it to him anymore, he'd begun to sound a little agitated with her about it lately. Best to let him focus on keeping her safe, this, at least, seemed to make him happy.

After she'd laid the food out on the table, she realised that it looked a little ridiculous. 'Sorry, I got slightly carried away earlier,' she sheepishly explained. 'But hey, whatever you feel like, it's probably here.' The two of them gazed at the array of dishes, samosas, savoury rice, pasta salad, crusty bread, mini pizzas, breaded chicken pieces, a whole asparagus quiche and, finally and completely unnecessarily, a large dish of bobotie. 'You must try it.' Sasha began to cut into the spicy mince dish. 'I fell in love with it when I was in South Africa, it is truly divine.'

Having done justice to Sasha's culinary offerings and made the appropriate appreciative noises throughout the meal, Miles now seemed fidgety and distracted, throwing sidelong glances at Sasha every now and then. Eventually, she asked him, 'Miles, what is it? You're distracted, talk to me.'

'I should stay with you tonight, Sash, I'll worry otherwise. I want to anyway of course.' He leaned over and kissed her. 'But I have to go away tomorrow, and it's bothering me. I don't want you here on your own, I think you should come with me. You should pack a bag in the morning then we'll stop at my place so that I can grab a few bits.' His eyes seemed to darken in their intensity as they looked into hers, awaiting her response.

'Hold on, Miles, tonight, yeah, of course, I'd love you to stay you know that, but to go away with you? Where? And for how long? I know you're worried but I'm fine, I can look after myself.'

Miles slipped his hands around her wrists again and she flinched momentarily, always surprised at the strength within him. 'It's just for two nights, a conference up in Birmingham. Bloody nuisance but my boss is being pretty insistent about it. It could be fun too though? We can lunch out, and we'll have the evenings, and the nights of course... the hotel's pretty cool...' His dark eyes twinkled at her and she felt temptation trying to wheedle its way in.

But she shook her head. 'I can't, Miles, I'm sorry but I have to stay here. I have to try to find Zoe.' She watched his expression change as annoyance flashed over his face. 'Look, it sounds lovely, it really does, and I'd love to go away to a hotel with you. Maybe we can do something once this is over?' She looked at him hopefully and, in an instant, his face relaxed into a smile.

'Well, there's still tonight to change your mind...'

But Sasha shook her head again, laughing. 'I like the sound of that but I can't go, Miles, I'm sorry.'

She began to clear the table, trying to gauge Miles's mood as she did so. Any mention of Zoe seemed to annoy him but then, she had a sudden thought – of course, it would, her friend had treated him badly and then she'd dumped him, or he'd dumped her, she wasn't entirely sure which, now that she came to think about it. Her second thought was – but she's being held against her will somewhere, surely he ought to be a little more sympathetic towards her now? She glanced back at him, from the kitchen, noting his strained expression, the way his fingers drummed agitatedly on the table. Her heart melted, he truly was so concerned for her safety, as he surely was for Zoe's underneath, maybe he just didn't like to show it. As if sensing her watching him he looked up and grinned, before picking up more dishes and bringing them through to her.

With more red wine poured they stood on Sasha's small balcony, shivering slightly in the cold air as they smoked a cigarette. 'Miles.' Sasha touched his arm, gently. 'You've looked up and down the street about ten times. There's no one there.' She stopped to wave at the elderly lady across the street as she stepped onto her balcony for a moment, and who returned her wave before retreating inside and drawing her curtains against the night.

'Who's that?' Miles's voice was sharp, a measure of his anxiety.

'D'you know, I don't even know her name, but we wave and smile across the street virtually every day. It's kind of comforting, she's like the local neighbourhood watch, always popping out and seeing what's going on. I swear, if anyone tried to get in here, she'd be the first to call the police.'

Miles stared broodingly across the street at the old woman's window. 'What about your other neighbours? Who are they? Men? Women? D'you know them?'

Really, Miles was being too ridiculous now. 'Yes, I know them, Miles, and they're all great people. Mike's on the top floor, a graphic designer or something, but he's away half the time, in fact, he's away right now. Then there's Nicole and Saffron below me, they're such a cool couple, completely ditzy and terribly creative, you should see their flat, it's amazing. They're total party animals, always out somewhere, I have no idea when they sleep. The other flat below is empty at the moment so I'll have to wait and see who moves in. But why are you worrying about my neighbours? You can't surely think one of them is my stalker?'

'You can't be too careful, Sash. Look, I'm sorry.' Miles was apologetic. 'I'm getting carried away, aren't I? How about some more wine? Inside though, it's freezing out here.'

If she didn't know better, she'd swear Miles was trying to get her completely drunk, she thought foggily, later, as he poured the last contents of the second bottle into their glasses.

'No whisky, please, I'm finished.' Sasha laughingly protested as Miles walked back into the lounge, the bottle of Glenfiddich swinging in his hand. But her protests fell on deaf ears and each time her glass emptied, Miles refilled it before she had a chance to stop him.

They finally staggered to bed in the early hours.

THE COLD FEET OF FEAR

Had they made love? Sasha's brain was refusing to co-operate with her, and she couldn't seem to recall anything. Images of Miles on top of her filled her mind, his hands gripping her wrists, or was that earlier in the evening? There was a sensation that he'd been angry, but at what? With her? He'd felt heavy on her, she thought she remembered that. Had she imagined his angry mutterings, his roughness, as he'd pushed her away? Her brain hurt with the effort of trying to remember and she slipped into unconsciousness again.

A noise jolted her awake, and she pushed herself up, trying to see in the gloom. 'Shhh, go back to sleep.' Miles loomed over her, stroking her hair.

'You're cold, where have...' Her words trailed away as she drifted off again, Miles's voice murmuring in her ear.

She awoke to the smell of coffee. Miles was up and dressed, and smiling down at her. 'How're you feeling?'

Groaning, Sasha tried to move, her head thumping with the effort. 'I feel terrible, what time is it?'

'It's almost nine and I have to go I'm afraid.'

'We totally overdid it last night, we must be crazy. How much did we drink?' She was sitting up now, holding the strong coffee.

'How much did *you* drink, you mean? You were on a complete bender last night, I couldn't keep up with you.' Laughing, Miles leaned down and kissed her. 'But we had a good time, especially later... hmmm?' He nuzzled her neck as she felt confusion mount. She hadn't been the one on the bender, that had been Miles. Hadn't it? And the good time later? Why couldn't she remember clearly? She didn't even feel like she'd *had* sex…

'No, I–' Stopping, she wiped her hand across her eyes. 'I feel so stupid, I can't remember last night clearly at all.'

'Never mind, take my word for it, baby, it was fantastic. Now, I really must go, will you be okay?' At her nod, he hugged her, planting a kiss on her forehead. 'I'll call you from my hotel later today, alright? Remember, talk to no one about this whole photo thing, trust nobody, and stay safe, okay? I'll be back before you know it, it's only two nights, we can talk about it again then.' He paused at her bedroom door, staring back at her, before turning and leaving.

Sasha collapsed against her pillows as she heard her front door close. The coffee wasn't working, she needed her tea. And she seriously needed some food, that is if she could make it to the kitchen without throwing up.

Managing to pull on some track pants and a long-sleeved tee shirt, Sasha manoeuvred her way to the kitchen. Water. Pills. Tea. Toast. Finally, she surrendered to the couch, curling up as she finished her toast and nursed her second mug of steaming tea.

Something was off about last night, but she couldn't put her finger on it. Surely it had been Miles pushing the drinks and not her? And she would swear that they hadn't made love. But she'd been so out of it… The memory came again, that of Miles gripping her angrily, of pushing her away. Had that happened? Or had she dreamt it? She remembered feeling cold, when was that? There'd been a noise, that's right, it had woken her. Miles had been there, but he hadn't been in bed. She sat up straighter. He'd been by the bedroom door. She was sure now, he'd climbed into bed and his body had felt cold. That's why she'd felt cold. Had she asked him what he'd been doing? She thought so. Maybe he'd told her. Yes, he'd said something about needing to pee, that's right.

But Miles had been extremely cold. You don't get that cold just going to the bathroom. His feet, she remembered now – they were freezing – as if he'd been outside. She leaned back, suddenly relaxing. He'd been out on the balcony checking the street, that would be it. He'd never tell her of course, but he was obviously so worried for her safety.

Sasha, I swear you'd write your own crime thriller if you could, talk about let your imagination run away with you. You both drank too much, you had a great evening, you fell into bed, maybe you fumbled around a bit, maybe you had sex, maybe you didn't. Maybe Miles felt embarrassed about it. And maybe he checked outside on the balcony in the middle of the night. So what?

But still... it did feel a bit odd... like something was all a bit... wrong...

She thought back to the message she'd received – forget about Zoe. How did @maluspassuum know that she thought the girl in the photos was Zoe? Chills rushed through her. Only Miles knew of her fears...

And Sara. Sara had acted strangely when Miles had been there at the funeral. What had she been going to tell her? The boy, Maddox, wasn't it? He'd stopped her. And he'd been staring intently at Miles. And the same thing had happened on the phone. One minute Sara had been about to tell her something, but Miles had arrived and she'd changed her mind.

She reached for her phone. There was one way to settle this. She waited for Sara to answer, hoping that she was just muddling things in her head. The sleeve of her top slipped up her arm and she frowned, looking down at her wrist. Pushing her other sleeve up she noticed the same redness on her other wrist too. Rubbing it, she became aware of the tenderness. Either Miles had been particularly passionate, or... 'Sara, hi, it's Sasha. Can we talk? I'm on my own.'

'Hi, Sasha, yes, I've got a minute before my next class. Is everything okay?'

'All fine, my love, I promise you. I just wanted to ask you something, and I want you to be totally honest with me, okay?'

'You want me to tell you what I was going to tell you the other day, don't you? I'm so sorry, Sasha, I should have found a way to speak to you when he wasn't there. He could have hurt you too and it would have been all my fault.'

'Whoa, Sara, slow down. Are we talking about Miles?'

'Yes, I just felt so bad with him being your boyfriend and everything. I thought Maddox must have got it all wrong but he swears he saw him.'

'Okay, so Maddox saw him. Start at the beginning, tell me the whole story.' Chills were forming in the pit of Sasha's stomach, the hairs on her arms prickling from goosebumps.

'So, like, we all went up to London, you know, to meet you? Me, Molly, Maddox, and Tyler? And we were hanging out, having a laugh. We took it in turns to pose by the statue, taking photos and that. Anyway, you hadn't come so Maddox went off to get us some drinks. Me and Tyler were together and I remember Molly backing away holding her phone up. I kind of knew she was taking photos of us and I was pleased so I pretended not to notice.' Sara let out a strangled sob. 'And then there was the accident, and Molly was in the road, and people were running everywhere, calling for doctors and ambulances and stuff. Sorry, hold on.'

Sasha listened to the sounds of Sara blowing her nose. 'It's alright, take your time,' she said softly.

'Okay, so, Maddox got back over the road to us. He was white as a sheet and he was staring at someone. I couldn't see who but he kept saying, *he was there before, he was right there*. I asked him what he meant but he kept shaking his head. We were standing by Molly and then the police took charge, moving us out of the way. He tried to point the man out to me but he'd got lost in the crowd. He said it was a man in a blue jacket, that he'd seen him staring at us, or maybe at Molly, before. Then he'd seen him moving away, quickly, after the– after the accident. He said it was weird because everyone else was waiting there, in shock. We tried to tell the policeman but he was busy and Maddox couldn't point him out because he'd gone.'

'Sara, what happened was terrible but I'm not quite sure where Miles comes in?'

'Don't you see?' Sara's voice was frustrated. 'Maddox recognised him at Molly's funeral. That's why he wouldn't let me say anything in front of him, you know, about the candles.'

'Well, yes.' Sasha was puzzled. 'But Miles, well, he told you didn't he, he was running late, he didn't manage to even get close. Maybe Maddox glimpsed him among the crowds of people.'

'No.' Sara's voice was determined. 'Maddox saw *him*, Miles, watching us before, and then he saw him rushing away from where Molly fell. He says he's sure that Miles pushed Molly, that he killed her. Don't you get it? He lied to us, he lied to you. And then when I told you about the candles on the phone I heard his voice, so I couldn't tell you what Maddox had said. I thought he might hurt you too.'

The chills in Sasha's stomach had turned into a hard ball of ice, turning her body cold. She needed to think about this. Thanking Sara and promising to be careful, she put her phone down.

If what the kids were telling her was true then Miles had been right there that day. But of course, relief, he hadn't known what Molly looked like. Maybe he'd told a white lie because he'd felt that he'd failed Sasha, failed

Molly? But then she remembered the photos that Molly had posted online. She'd used the hashtags. Anyone tracking her would have easily found her photos, especially if they were actively looking for them. She'd remembered now, that's how she'd thought he, @maluspassuum, could have found Molly. Could Miles be *him*? Bile rose in her throat and she hurried to the bathroom where she vomited her breakfast. Back on the couch, she sat, immobile, feeling numb.

~

Not sure how long she'd been sitting there, Sasha roused herself. She needed to get busy. It could all be a huge mistake or it could be true. Whatever, she needed to keep a clear head and focus on her mission. She'd say nothing to Miles. At least he was away for a couple of days which gave her time.

After a quick shower, Sasha sat at her laptop studying how to conduct reverse image searches. When she was ready, she began.

Two hours later she was still scrolling through the hundreds of images. It was impossible, it had been a long shot. Tired, she made herself a cup of tea before returning to her task. Five minutes later she was staring at an image of a house which made the hairs stand up on her arms. Blinking, she studied it, clicking back and forth between the image of the doorway that he'd posted and the image of the house. Carefully, she enlarged the doorway in the house image and compared them. Printing the enlarged doorway image, she fixed it to the board beside her print of the original doorway. And then she stood back.

They were identical. There was no doubt about it. Excited now, Sasha clicked on the original image to be taken to the website it originated from. There were more photos, each showing either the garden or various rooms in the house. She froze over the image of the bedroom, staring at the blue striped duvet on the bed, taking in the small bedside table and the chair beside it. She didn't need to compare it to the photo he'd posted of the room to know it was the same room. *She'd found the house.*

Finally, Sasha studied the name of the website. It was one of those generic sites that shared properties for rent originating from other agencies – this site was just a middleman and contained little detail about the properties displayed on its pages. Across the main image was a diagonal box, the word *unavailable*, stamped in large letters. Her heart sank. But peering closer she realised that there was a small link for more information and, clicking on it, she waited, holding her breath.

No. No. No. *This information is no longer available* appeared on the screen. Her eyes lifted to the logo at the top of the page – HWS – it was familiar. Why was that, where had she heard or seen it recently? She racked her brain, trying to think. A click on the logo took her to the agency's main page with their name and address at the top. They were based in Kensal Green, which told her nothing. But then it came to her – HWS – Home and Work Space – that was Miles's agency. Shock juddered through her as her body began to tremble.

Miles had befriended her just as she'd begun to be tagged by her stalker. Miles was there when Molly died. Zoe was being held in a property that Miles's agency had let out. Miles, who'd become a part of her life. Miles, who she'd slept with. Groaning, Sasha shook her head from side to side. No, please, no, it can't be true. It must just be some kind of awful coincidence.

She could phone the agency right now and ask them about the property. But wouldn't they contact Miles? Miles could have let the property to someone. Yes, that was a possibility. And he might not even be the agent for that property. She needed to visit the property and check it out, but how to do that without speaking to someone at the agency? Or she could just ask Miles...

If Miles was somehow innocently caught up in this mess, wouldn't he want to know? So that he could help her? Her hand strayed to her phone, her mind fraught with indecision. No. She couldn't take the risk, she needed to do this alone. She returned to the site containing all the photos, studying them intently, looking for clues.

Her attention was caught by the view from one of the windows of the house. It appeared to look onto a cemetery, the glimpse of a white brick building possibly being the chapel. In the foreground of the photo was, presumably, the back garden, nothing more than a weed patch, but it told her that it was to the rear of the property. Frustrated, she studied another image, this time showing the street view. Nothing helpful sprang out at her, just the fact that the house was clearly down a small unkempt dirt driveway between other properties. A good choice – if you were a sick bastard who'd kidnapped a woman. The house to the left of the driveway had a large front window and Sasha's excitement grew as she realised that a neon sign was reflected in the window glass.

Clipping that area of the image, she uploaded it to her software, defining the image as much as possible, before reversing it. Finally, she stared at the results of her work. Picking up a pen, she copied the letters onto a pad: UTH, ING, RRY, LACE. Four words. A neon sign, that would usually be food. Or a bar? And then it came to her. Food. The RRY was the end of the word CURRY. Curry Palace? For once, her love of puzzles, especially crosswords, was paying off. King? But a word ending in UTH... Mouth? South? South. South – something - Curry Palace. She moved to her large map of London, fixed on the wall behind her, and concentrated her attention on the area radiating from the agency office. And there it was. Ealing. The South Ealing Curry Palace was across the road from the house where Zoe was being held.

Back at her laptop, her trembling fingers typed in the name of the restaurant and she sat back in dumbfounded joy as she read the address. She'd actually found it. Finally, she viewed the address on street view and as she moved her cursor the houses across the road appeared on her screen. And there was the driveway leading to the house. Leaping up, she rushed around, grabbing her bag, pulling boots on, and then she stopped. Was she going to just pitch up there? And then what? A weapon. She needed a weapon of some kind. Frantically, she looked around, before pulling the bottom kitchen drawer open and rummaging messily through its contents. A screwdriver went into her bag, together with a heavy pair of scissors.

Of course, she reasoned with herself, if it was Miles, then he wouldn't be there. He was in Birmingham. But if it was someone else, then she had to be very careful. Slamming her front door behind her she rushed down to the street, her eyes searching for a cab. Flashing lights across the street caught her eye as an ambulance pulled away. A police car was parked outside the property with an officer unwinding yellow tape across the doorway. A cab pulled up and she jumped in, taking one last glance at the police car. That was where her elderly neighbour lived, she hoped nothing had happened to her.

'Where to, love?'

'Er, can you take me to the South Ealing Curry House on Nun's Lane, please?'

'Blimey, their curry must be bloody good if you want to go all the way over there, darlin'.' The cabbie grinned over his shoulder at Sasha as he pulled out into the traffic.

Impatiently, she watched their progress out of the window, drumming her fingers on her phone until finally, the cab pulled over. Having paid the cabbie and thanked him, Sasha stood across the road from the driveway and looked up and down the road.

It was quiet, being mid-afternoon, and satisfied that no one was around Sasha crossed the street and headed cautiously along the driveway.

PROOF OF LIES

At the end of the driveway, she was met by tall wooden gates, a heavy padlocked chain holding them closed. She guessed it was locked, but checked it anyway. Frustrated, she studied the gates. The wood was smooth with no footholds and, on either side, the frame butted against the adjacent properties' walls, both six feet at least. She retraced her steps, turning back to try and glimpse the house but it was set further back and all she managed was a view of the roof. She returned to the street, thinking about her next move. She had to get in there somehow.

And then she remembered the photo showing the cemetery at the rear of the property. The wall hadn't looked too high, but the angle may have disguised the actual height. Bringing up a map on her phone Sasha studied the row of houses on either side before choosing the shorter row. She walked past the houses, counting them, and turned right, again counting the houses until she reached the last one. On this side of the road, a wall continued along beside the pavement. It had to be the cemetery wall.

Sasha finally reached the end of the wall and turned the corner, heading for the entrance gates. Once inside she turned to the wall running along the right-hand side of the cemetery and walked beside it, counting the houses when they appeared behind the wall. The numbers matched and she turned along the rear wall, again counting the houses behind the wall until she reached her goal.

For the sake of caution, and to better check out the situation, Sasha first wandered among the headstones, pausing here and there as she studied the back of the house. All the curtains were closed, there was no sign of activity, and she finally approached the wall, looking for a way over. Some ancient headstones rested against the wall and with an apology to whoever the worn epitaph referred to, Sasha stepped onto one of them and climbed quickly over the wall, dropping down quietly into the overgrown garden.

She moved quickly to the rear wall of the house, stopping beside what must be the kitchen window. Silently she waited, listening for any sounds of occupation. Satisfied, she tried to look through the gap in the window's curtains. It was dark inside but she could just about make out part of a table with fast food cartons strewn on it, and the back of a chair, but nothing else. Gingerly she tested the window, but it was firmly closed and, upon closer inspection, she saw that burglar bars were fitted inside.

Next, she did the same with the kitchen door, trying its handle to find it locked, unsurprisingly, before examining the glass. There was an old cat flap in the bottom part of the door and Sasha knelt down, pushing it open and peering through. She reached her hand in, feeling either side, her heart sinking when she felt the bars of a burglar gate. Someone had taken their security seriously here. An added reason to choose this house to keep someone a prisoner in.

She continued along the rear of the house to what must be a toilet window. But it was high and, looking around, she saw nothing she could use to reach it. That left the larger window on the other side of the kitchen, probably the dining room. But again, she couldn't get a clear view inside, was barely able to make out the odd furniture shape in the gloom. The window frame was solid and, although there were no bars at this window, she could see a window lock.

Dispirited, Sasha checked along the left side of the house, but there were no ground floor windows, so she turned her attention to the other side. Here she found another door, old, its paint peeling, and by the looks of it never used. The door felt loose in its frame, and the lock itself moved when she touched it. She thought back to the images of the house, had there been a basement? Or was this just an outside loo? She couldn't recall photos of either, but they weren't the sort of photos likely to attract tenants.

An idea came to her and she stepped carefully along the wall, first one way and then the other, pulling back the overgrown grass from against the brickwork. And there it was, a long narrow window at ground level, which meant the house had a basement. She could gain access to the house this way if she could just get in the door!

Holding her screwdriver, Sasha shook her head, it was way too big, having been brought along more as a weapon than as a useful tool. She tried the point of the scissors in the lock, wishing she'd learnt how to pick locks, it always looked so easy in the movies. She picked up the screwdriver again, this time pushing it into the gap between the door and the frame, and tried to lever it against the door. The wood splintered a little and she could feel movement but knew that she needed something stronger.

With a last look up at the house, Sasha retraced her steps, silently promising Zoe she'd be back soon, and made her way out of the cemetery, noting its closing time as she wondered if she'd make it back again in time. She needed some kind of hardware store or tool store and searched on her phone. Nothing nearby, and time was going. It would also be getting dark soon so she'd need a torch. She made a mental list, as she walked hurriedly along the street looking for a cab. *Crowbar, torch...*

Her phone rang and seeing that it was Miles she hesitated, wondering what to do. Answer it and try to sound convincing? Or ignore it, which meant he would just keep calling her. And he could still be innocent she reminded herself, it could all just be a horrible coincidence. She answered her phone, putting on a bright voice.

'Well, you sound better than you did this morning. How are you feeling?' Miles was chirpy and she felt herself relax a little.

'I'm good, thanks. Much better now. Are you at the hotel? How was the drive?'

'Yeah, I'm checked in, and the drive was fine. Where are you? I can hear traffic.'

'I'm just taking a walk, it felt a bit stuffy in the flat and I needed some fresh air.'

'You sure you're okay, Sash? You sound out of breath and anxious. What's going on?'

Was she imagining it or did he sound suspicious? 'No, I'm fine, it's just cold so I've been walking quite fast.' She laughed, cringing at herself, feeling sure he'd notice her false laugh. 'So tell me about the conference, how's it going?'

'Oh, just the usual, various presentations, and I've met up with a few familiar faces so we'll probably get together this evening and have a few drinks. You know how these things are.' He paused. 'Sash, you don't sound quite yourself, is there anything you're not telling me? Has anything happened, have you found anything out? I wish you'd wait for me to get back, in fact, I insist, Sash, for your safety.'

'No, Miles, really, to be honest, I've wasted the day. I felt pretty finished this morning so I went back to bed for a few hours. I've basically achieved nothing.' *Liar, would he believe her?*

'Okay, well if you're sure, I worry about you, you know that. I'll call you later then shall I, after dinner?'

Hoping she hadn't aroused his suspicions, Sasha finally jumped into the cab that pulled over, asking the driver to take her to the address of the store she'd found on her phone. Ten minutes later she was standing outside the store, reading the notice on the door. Sod's law, of all the days they had to close for stocktaking it had to be today. She checked the time, it was getting too late, she'd never make it back in time now. Taking her last cab of the day she headed for home.

Sitting in the cab, Sasha mulled over the problem of the house in Nun's Lane. She was pretty sure that Zoe was being held there but maybe it would help to have a little more information, she didn't want to break into a house that had people living in it. Bringing up the details for HWS, she called the number but guessed it would probably go to voicemail this late in the day.

Unexpectedly, her call was answered by someone called Sandra, who sounded a little rushed. 'Hi, you just caught me, I was on my way out of the door. What can I do for you?'

'Sandra, hi, sorry to bother you, it's just a quick question. You had a property on your books in Nun's Lane, South Ealing?'

'Yes, I believe so, are you interested? We haven't had any enquiries about it for so long I was beginning to think there must be something wrong with it.'

'Oh, is it still available then? Only I thought it had been let?'

'No, no, that's odd, it should still be an active listing as far as I know. Tell you what, let me take your number and I'll call you in the morning once I've checked for you, okay?'

Having given Sandra her number, Sasha wondered what it all meant. The obvious conclusion was that someone, *Miles*, had removed it from the list and was using it for his own sick purposes.

Before she entered her building Sasha looked across the road at the yellow crime scene tape. Worriedly, she crossed over, wondering what had happened. A policeman was stationed outside the entrance to the flats and she asked him, not prepared for what he would tell her.

In shock, Sasha sat back in her flat, a large glass of gin in her hand. Who on earth would break in and murder an elderly lady, her sweet neighbour whose name she'd never known, who'd waved and smiled at her every day? The policeman hadn't been forthcoming with further information but reading between the lines Sasha felt sure that nothing had been taken, it had purely been a cruel and unnecessary act of evil.

As she sat there with tears welling in her eyes her phone pinged and she opened the e-mail from Moon Goddess.

Hi Sasha, thanks for your mail. I don't usually give out information about my customers, but as you gave me a name and explained briefly what it was about, I'm happy to confirm that Zoe Pullman did buy the candles from me. I hope this helps and that everything works out okay. Regards, Mandi (Moon Goddess).

She was right. The girls had been right. This was irrefutable evidence – it had been Zoe who bought the candles, and it was Zoe who was held captive. How sick was he that he'd used the candles Zoe had bought him in one of his twisted photos?

Sure, now, that Miles must be behind everything, Sasha dreaded his call later. She thought back over all that had happened between her and Miles. Had he been following her when he supposedly bumped into her at the service station as she drove home from Parva Crossing after Chantelle's ordeal? Probably. He'd caught her at a vulnerable moment and played on it and she'd been putty in his hands ever since – she'd fallen for his kindness – she'd opened up and told him everything, shared all her thoughts and concerns. He'd known what she found out almost as soon as she did.

Filled with disgust, Sasha could hardly bear to think about their intimacy. It must have given him such a sick thrill to have been holding captive and torturing her friend, whilst spending time with Sasha and gaining her trust. She'd played right into his hands and participated in his game without even knowing. She thought back over their conversations, knowing now that she couldn't trust anything he'd told her. He'd been the firm voice encouraging her not to speak to the police, she realised. Every time she'd expressed her doubts and concerns, he'd either reminded her of the threat to the girl in the photos – *Zoe* – or convinced her that the police wouldn't take her seriously. She could call Tony and tell him everything. *Why hadn't she done that before?* But then, with a sinking heart she remembered that Tony was away on holiday busy forgetting he was a cop for two weeks. Hell, he'd even joked about it. *'Don't even think of calling me about anything, my work number's firmly switched off for the next two weeks while I soak up the sun.'* She had no other police contacts and where would she even start right now? Who would take her seriously? A friend would though...

With a sudden shock, she thought about Eric. Miles had told her he'd dealt with him – what did that mean? Fumbling for her phone, she quickly called him, but a disembodied voice told her that the number was no longer in use. Was that because she'd blocked him from calling her, or not? Concerned now, she made a decision, realising that whatever Miles had said about Eric wasn't true. Eric had been desperate to talk to her, to tell her something, but Miles had made sure she'd rebuffed him at every turn. With the evening stretching ahead and with nothing she could do right now for Zoe, she decided to go to his flat. It would only take her about ten minutes to walk it.

It felt a little like déjà vu, the flat exhibiting no signs of life, but this time, being later in the day than when she'd gone to Zoe's, the absence of any lights added to that impression. She knocked on the door, waiting anxiously in the vain hope of a response. A light came on next door and a man stepped out, leaning over the small dividing wall. 'Can I help you? Oh, it's Sasha, isn't it? Eric's girlfriend? Haven't seen you for a while? It's Chris, you might not remember me.'

'Oh yes, of course, Chris, hi. Um, Eric and I aren't together anymore, but I've been a bit worried about him. D'you know if he's okay?'

'He's away, isn't he? At least that what his friend said. Didn't catch his name. He was round here the other day, said he was checking on his mate's flat while he was away. Not the chatty kind, couldn't get away quick enough.'

Pulling out her phone, Sasha brought up a blurry photo of Miles that she'd taken when he'd been unaware. 'Was this him?'

Chris peered at the photo, nodding. 'That's him. And I'm judging by your face that's not good news?'

'No, it's not. As far as I know, Eric's not away. Chris, I'm seriously concerned for Eric's safety. The guy in the photo? Well, he's not his friend. I think he may have harmed him. I'm going to go into his flat, he keeps a spare key at the back, I've retrieved it more than once when he's been on one of his benders.'

'I'm coming with you, hold on and I'll get a torch.' Chris disappeared, reappearing seconds later, and the two of them headed for the rear of the flat.

'Thanks, Chris, I appreciate this.' Sasha lifted the garish garden gnome, which Eric had thought a hilarious addition to his patio, and retrieved the key. Returning to the front she unlocked the door and they entered Eric's flat, switching lights on and calling his name.

There was a strange smell, unpleasant, and Sasha was filled with foreboding as they moved through the flat. At Chris's urgent call she hurried to the kitchen, finding him crouched in the small utility room adjoining it.

'Eric! Is he okay? Eric? Oh God, he's killed him.' Eric's prone body lay in an unnatural position, an arm twisted behind him, a leg bent awkwardly. A pool of blood had dried on the floor, together with other bodily excretions, and Eric's face and body were a mass of bruises, his clothing torn and blood-stained. Chris called for help on his phone as Sasha knelt over Eric, staring in horror at the wound in his stomach. Someone had stabbed him, correction, *Miles had stabbed him*, as well as beaten him to death. Sobbing, Sasha leaned over Eric. 'I'm so sorry, oh, Eric, you poor thing.'

Did his eyelid just move? Sasha concentrated on his swollen eye, calling his name and feeling his neck for a pulse. His eye twitched again and his mouth moved slightly as she felt a faint pulse in his neck. 'He's alive. Chris, tell them to hurry, he's alive. Eric, can you hear me?'

While Chris recounted what was happening to the operator, Sasha grabbed a cloth, running it under the cold tap before gently touching it to Eric's face and squeezing a few drops of water between his parched lips. Eric moaned, moving slightly, and his eyelid opened a fraction.

'It's alright, don't try to move, the ambulance is on its way.' Tears poured down Sasha's face.

The sound of sirens heralded the arrival of the emergency services and as Chris directed them to the utility room, Eric's hand suddenly grabbed Sasha's, feebly, trying to pull her to him. He moved his mouth as if trying to speak and she leaned in, trying to hear him. Frustrated, she moved closer, but she was in the paramedics' way and she stepped aside to let them work on Eric.

Once Eric had been stretchered out, the police wanted to speak to her and Chris and, once Chris had told them all he knew and had gone, with reassurances that Sasha would be okay, she tried to explain why she'd come to the flat.

'So let me get this straight.' The officer was struggling to make sense of Sasha's babbling. 'This man was your boyfriend, but your new boyfriend Miles did this, you say? And he's taken your friend captive?'

'Yes, he's been sending me these photos, and I thought it was Zoe, but I wasn't sure, but now I am, and Eric's been trying to get in touch with me, but I thought he was just jealous of his friend, so I asked his friend to speak to him. He said he'd dealt with him. And my friend, she's still in the house, the house I went to earlier–'

The officer stopped her again. 'So you know where your friend is? And her name's Zoe, is that right? You've been to see her? So she's okay then? And this Miles, your boyfriend, he's away, you say?'

'No.' Sasha's frustration was mounting. 'I mean, yes, he's away, and yes, Zoe's her name, but I haven't seen her. I mean, I think I know where she is, but...' sSe stopped, noticing the look that passed between the two officers.

'And there's something else,' she continued, unable to stop the words as they tumbled from her mouth. 'My neighbour across the street, she was murdered last night. Someone killed her and I think it was him, he was cold you see, when he got back into bed, he was freezing cold. I think he killed her because she'd seen him at mine. He was going to take me too, you see, he said so. He told me if I spoke to the police he'd kill her, so you see I couldn't take the risk, I mean, maybe she's still alive, but I didn't know it was him – all this time he's been playing me, controlling my actions without me realising it.'

The officers exchanged another look. He killed her or she was still alive? Don't talk to the police but here she was talking to the police. Boyfriends, ex-boyfriends, friends kidnapped... They shook their heads at each other.

The female officer spoke soothingly to Sasha. 'You've had a nasty shock, why don't you go home, for now, we can send someone with you if you'd like? And then, tomorrow, perhaps you can come down to the station and tell us everything when it's a bit clearer in your mind. How's that?'

Realising how crazy she must sound, Sasha nodded. 'Yes, I'll do that. I'll be fine, no need for anyone to come with me. I'll come and talk to you tomorrow.' Having given the officer her details, Sasha took Detective Inspector Wendover's card, before being escorted from Eric's flat, and walked along the road looking desperately for a cab. She needed to get to the hospital and Eric.

But any hopes of being able to see Eric were quashed. He was in surgery and they couldn't give her any information other than that they remained hopeful that he would fully recover. Having been told, in no uncertain terms, that she would not be able to see him tonight, Sasha headed home feeling exhausted.

It was only once she was in her flat, nursing a whisky, that she saw all the missed calls from Miles. There were messages too, each one more urgent than the one before. She couldn't speak to him, couldn't stand the thought of hearing his voice, but needed to allay his suspicions. She tapped out a short message, hoping it sounded convincing.

~

Miles read the message, frowning. Something wasn't right. How could she have not heard any of his calls? Sasha wasn't that deep a sleeper. She was avoiding him, which didn't bode well, although there was no way she could know anything, surely... A slap on his shoulder jerked his arm, and lager spilt onto the table. 'Come on, Miles, one for the ditch.' He fixed a grin on his face. He needed to get back, he'd leave the conference early. As long as he attended the morning sessions, he should be able to get away with it. He picked up the shot glass, downing it in one before standing up and, ignoring the others' boos, headed for his room.

OH, THE HORROR

Relieved to have avoided speaking to Miles, Sasha thought back to Eric's attempts to tell her something. But what? He hadn't made any sense, which was hardly surprising. Grabbing a piece of paper, she jotted down the odd words that she'd picked up. *Zoe. Miles. Key. Papers.* Frowning, she tried to remember, he'd definitely said Zoe again, something like *Papers Zoe.* Papers at Zoe's maybe?

Excitedly, she sat back. Eric wanted her to find some papers at Zoe's. So he *had* known something, Zoe *had* mentioned something to him – her hunch had been right but Miles had successfully steered her away from any further progress in that direction.

She cast her mind back to her visit to the art gallery where Zoe worked, Frame. Flavia had practically told her, but she hadn't paid proper attention. Zoe had taken some of the papers and she'd told Flavia that she was going to call someone she knew in property development. Without a doubt that had been Eric, it had to have been. Zoe had mentioned something to Eric about whatever she'd found in the papers and that would explain why he was so anxious for her to get the papers from Zoe's flat.

And *Miles? Key?* Could it be that Eric was trying to tell her that Miles had taken her key from Eric's? He'd definitely been shouting something about her key that night she'd sent him away. Had he been trying to warn her, even then?

And then another memory, of Eric calling her while she and Miles were getting cosy on the couch. He'd started to say something about Zoe – that she'd called him? – and something about Miles. She hadn't wanted to listen to him, hadn't paid attention, so sure was she that he was trying to get back together with her. And then Miles had snatched her phone and told Eric to leave her alone. But Eric must have been trying to tell her whatever Zoe had told him. He'd said it didn't make sense...

She needed to find the papers from Zoe's flat, they were part of this, she was sure. Zoe had read something, from about thirty-odd years ago, which concerned her enough to call Eric about it. Was it something about Miles? Maybe she was going to show him but she never got the chance. Did she confront Miles? Is that why he took her captive?

Looking at her watch as she yawned, Sasha knew that she needed to grab a few hours of sleep. She'd go back to Zoe's flat first thing and look for the papers, then buy what she needed to get into the house in South Ealing. Hopefully, the agent would call her with information and if it was as she suspected then the house had never been let to anyone, Miles had just taken it off the books. She pulled her clothes off and crawled into bed, exhaustion overtaking her.

Allowing her mind to wander, she pictured Eric lying in his hospital bed and hoped he wasn't in too much pain. Filled with revulsion at the thought that Miles could have so brutally attacked Eric and left him for dead, she suddenly realised the full horror of what had happened.

It had been the night Miles had arrived with the huge bouquet of flowers – the night he'd been pleased with himself – had wanted to celebrate. As if in slow motion, the events of that evening played back in her mind – and then she saw it – the dinner table laden with quesadillas and accompaniments – Miles's plate heaped with sour cream and guacamole – *but no tomato salsa - and yet he'd had a splash of something red on his shirt*. She'd fetched a cloth and had returned to find his plate now loaded with salsa and splashes on the table as well as all over his shirt.

I've dealt with Eric, he'd announced triumphantly after they'd made love.

He'd viciously attacked Eric before coming to her flat – and taking her to bed – with Eric's blood on his shirt.

The man is a depraved monster, thought Sasha, with abhorrence, curling up into a ball underneath her duvet and trying to switch off her brain.

~

Up early the next morning, barely refreshed from her disturbed sleep, Sasha made a quick call to the hospital to check on Eric. Relieved to hear that he was doing well she hurried straight to Zoe's flat, letting herself in and pausing to consider where Zoe might have stashed the papers. Zoe wasn't stupid, if she'd been going to confront Miles with something she wouldn't have let him get hold of the papers that proved whatever it was she'd discovered. She'd have put them somewhere that Miles wouldn't think of. But where? She looked around as she walked from room to room, trying to imagine that she was Zoe. Where would she keep them?

Zoe wasn't the tidiest of people and piles of magazines sat in stacks on the coffee table as well as on the floor. But a look through them confirmed that they were just magazines. She checked under the mattress, although that felt too obvious, before checking the bookshelves. Next, she examined the various art prints on the walls, carefully examining the backs of them all, but found nothing. The wardrobe shelves yielded no results and Sasha perched on the bed despondently.

A pair of Zoe's heels lay on the floor and, remembering that Zoe was very particular about her footwear, Sasha opened the wardrobe doors again, gazing at the piles of shoe boxes. She began to open them, finding, in each, layers of paper beneath the shoes. Mostly it was tissue paper but when she opened one containing a pair of boots she found, beneath the tissue paper, some yellowing pages.

She laid them out on the bed and read the thirty-year-old horrific headlines.

IT SHOULD BE LIFE FOR THIS SAVAGE CREATURE! LOCK HIM UP AND THROW AWAY THE KEY!

WOMAN SPEAKS OF TORTURE ORDEAL AT HANDS OF SELIM.

SCARRED FOR LIFE. TORTURE VICTIM'S PSYCHOLOGICAL WOUNDS WILL NEVER HEAL.

BLAKE SELIM GRINS IN DOCK AS HIS VICTIMS RE-LIVE THEIR ABDUCTION AND TORTURE.

THE FACE OF A MURDERER. SURVIVORS SPEAK OUT FOR SELIM'S MURDER VICTIM.

DRESSED UP LIKE DOLLS – VICTIMS SPEAK OF SELIM'S SICK FETISH.

His dark eyes stared emptily back at Sasha as she looked at the faded photo of fifteen-year-old Blake Selim. Or, as she knew him, Miles Bleak. Realisation hit – *it was an anagram*. But one she hadn't known to look for.

He'd abducted his first victim, nineteen-year-old Sharon Contell, when he was fourteen years old and living with his third foster family. Seemingly mature for his age, he'd struck up a friendship with her, gained her trust, and then kept her locked up in a derelict Liverpool tenement where he'd repeatedly abused, tortured, and raped her, over a period of two weeks. And then he'd left her there, chained up to die, but not before taking photos of the girl dressed up, by him, to look like a prostitute.

Sasha shook her head, wiping her eyes, and fought the panic building inside her. The poor girl. If it hadn't been for the druggie with a conscience who'd found her, she would have died there.

He'd left his foster family, moved to another town and done the same thing, on and on, until, finally, he'd been caught. By this time, he'd abducted and tortured eight women, one of whom didn't survive, thus adding murder to his sadistic spree. Photographs of all his victims, at various stages of their captivity and torture, often dressed in inappropriate clothing, were found in his possession at the time of his arrest.

And his sentence from the Crown Court? Twelve years, due to the fact that he was a minor, followed by supervision for another eight. And then he was free. Free to reinvent himself however he wished. Free to go about his life, to forge relationships with people, to gain their trust. Free to abduct and torture Zoe. Free to make love to women. To make love to her, Sasha. Free to make her start to fall in love with him.

Against all odds these old newspapers had been left behind in an unused and boarded-off part of a building which had later become an art gallery. Over the years the photographs on their pages had yellowed and faded, and the face staring at the camera would have gradually become obscured by time, if they hadn't, by chance, been discovered by a gallery employee who had tried to fix a painting onto the wall a little too forcefully. It was, Sasha decided, as if the fates had determined that Zoe should know about Miles's past and take action. Well, poor Zoe had obviously tried – and it hadn't turned out well for her. But now it was Sasha's turn.

Setting her jaw, Sasha stood and, laying out the papers on the bed, carefully took photos of them all, before e-mailing them to herself. She then replaced them in the boot box and left Zoe's flat. It was time to go and buy that crowbar. It was time to get Zoe.

~

Detective Inspector Wendover thanked a slightly incoherent Eric, dosed up as he was on analgesics, for all the information regarding his attack, assuring him that they'd be following up on it and locating Miles Bleak to bring him in for questioning. Personally, she thought it sounded like a totally over the top case of male jealousy. Fighting over a girl, one of the oldest clichés in history. It was strange though, he'd also been rather garbled about a girl not answering his calls, possibly missing and in danger. What was it with this bunch?

~

As Sasha exited the hardware store with the heavy crowbar in her bag, her phone pinged with a message. It was a voicemail from the letting agent, Sandra.

'Sasha, hi, Sandra here, calling you about the Nun's Lane property. I've looked into it and there seems to have been an admin error or something. The owner is overseas for a couple of years, hence the listing. But there's no tenant so it's definitely available just let me know if you're still interested. In the meantime, I've left a message for the owner, as well as for the agent dealing with this property, Miles Bleak. Hopefully, he can shed some light on it, but he's out of town for a couple of days. Let me know.'

Oh fuck. Sasha froze for one second, before galvanising herself into action. Stepping out in front of the cab she waved her arms frantically until he pulled over. Jumping in, she gave the same request as the day before and was met by the same retort. *This shit was getting old*.

She checked her watch, checked what time Sandra had called her, and calculated how long it might take Miles to drive back from Birmingham, for she was sure that once he'd received the call from Sandra, he'd guess it was Sasha. Hell, Sandra probably told him her name anyway. Or if she didn't then at the very least he'd rush back to deal with Zoe.

Two hours. At the most, two hours twenty minutes. That's how long it would take him to reach the house. But first, he'd have to get his things and check out of his hotel, so maybe she had three hours tops? But Sandra must have called him about half an hour ago so, basically, she had two and a half hours. Think two, to be safe, she told herself. 'Please can you hurry? It's an emergency.' She leaned forward to the cabbie.

He shook his head, wondering what kind of emergency called for a dash across London for a takeaway curry, but put his foot down nonetheless.

~

Miles listened to his colleague's voicemail during the short break in the first session as coldness spread through him, followed swiftly by anger. His knuckles were white around his coffee cup and he relaxed them, not wanting to attract attention.

So, little Sasha had found the house, had she? The bitch was cleverer than he gave her credit for. But the timing was wrong. It would spoil the game completely for her to go there and rescue her tiresome little friend without him. No, he had to be there. Just thinking about it excited him, seeing her face as he grabbed her, as he tied her up, as he hurt her for the first time...

'Miles, you coming back in, mate? You haven't touched your coffee.'

His mate's voice cut through his thoughts and he glanced down distractedly at his coffee cup. 'I'll catch you up, you go ahead.' His friend shrugged and headed back to the conference hall as Miles brought up Sasha's name on his phone, pressing the call button.

Oh God, Oh God, Oh God. Miles's name flashed on her phone as the cab filled with the sound of her ringtone. With no time to think, and having no choice but to wing it, Sasha answered his call, staring out at the gridlocked traffic in frustration.

'Sash, hi, baby, I missed talking to you last night. How are you? Recovered from our boozy night by now I hope?' Miles's laugh sounded relaxed in her ear as he stepped out of the lift and headed for his room.

Her tension eased at his light and seemingly unsuspecting tone and she responded with a forced laugh. 'I have, hi, Miles, it's good to hear your voice. Sorry about last night, I was so tired I just needed to sleep.' *Good to hear his voice? She wanted to puke.*

He laughed again. 'You're sure you weren't out with some guy, having a good time without me? No, I know you wouldn't lie to me, Sasha.' Opening the door to his room, he entered, picking up his small suitcase and throwing it on the bed.

Was she imagining it, or did his tone sound vaguely threatening now?

'So what are you up to, anyway? I'm about to head back in to listen to someone drone on about social media and how it can influence property trends in different areas. Exciting stuff, huh?' He grabbed his clothes from the cupboard, dropping them messily into the case.

She allowed herself to exhale. He was none the wiser, he didn't suspect anything. Everything was fine. He was miles away and about to sit and listen to a lecture. 'Oh hell, poor you, it does sound rather dull. I'm not really doing anything, to be honest.' She was interrupted by the loud hoot from a truck, the driver angrily yelling out of his window at the car blocking his right turn.

Miles gathered his toiletries from beside the basin, throwing them into his bath bag and zipping it closed. 'Are you going somewhere, Sash? Sounds like traffic.' He dropped the bath bag into his case, closing the lid and, scanning the room quickly, picked up his case and hurried out.

Dammit. 'Yeah, just getting a few bits of shopping, nothing interesting. What's the hotel like, are you wishing I was there with you?' *Cringe. Try and distract him.*

'It's really cool but would be so much more fun if you were here. Hold on, babe.' Miles smiled at the receptionist as he handed her his card. Sasha could hear muffled sounds and then he was back. 'Sorry, they're calling us back in. The hotel's great, nice room, good bar, and the food's not bad either.' He took the lift down to the parking level and threw his case into the boot of his car. 'We put away a few last night and the guys are determined we do the same again tonight. I'm going to try to talk them into a curry first.'

'Sounds like a good plan. Well, I'll let you get back to your conference then. Hope it's not too boring.'

Miles put his key in the ignition. 'I'll try not to fall asleep. I'll call you tonight then, okay? Before I down too many beers. I miss you. See you soon.'

'Bye, I miss you too.' She nearly gagged saying the words, but she needed to keep his suspicions allayed. Relief flooded her whole body, making her feel weak. He had no suspicions. He was in Birmingham. He was only returning tomorrow so she had nothing to fear from him.

Miles turned the key and pulled out of his parking spot before heading for the M40. If the roads were clear he should be there in under two hours.

'Sorry, love, the traffic's really bad. Nothing I can do about it, we'll just have to wait it out.' The cabbie gave Sasha an apologetic shrug before turning back to fiddle with his radio.

At least she wasn't up against the clock now, she thought. The panic she'd felt, at the thought that Miles would be on his way to the house, had subsided. Zoe was her one and only focus now. She willed the traffic to clear so that she could get to her friend.

~

Miles passed the turn-off for Banbury, checking his watch. He'd made good time, half an hour under his belt and less than an hour and a half to go. He put his foot down further, keeping an eye in his mirror for any cops.

~

Finally, the traffic cleared and the cab driver wasted no time in getting moving. He deposited Sasha at the Indian Restaurant fifteen minutes later.

She quickly scanned the road both ways before heading down the dirt driveway. Taking out her crowbar, Sasha forced it behind the chain holding the padlock and, with all her strength, levered it against the gate. Nothing happened. She looked at the dent in the gate made by the crowbar. Stupid girl. She should have bought bolt cutters. Why didn't she think of that? She'd thought she'd be able to break the chain with the crowbar. No chance. Nonetheless, she tried again, just in case, but with the same result.

There was no alternative, she'd have to make her way along the cemetery wall and head through to the rear of the house as she'd done the day before. Forcing herself to stay calm, and reminding herself that there was no need to panic now – Miles was far away in Birmingham with no suspicions whatsoever – she nonetheless walked as fast as she could before starting to run.

At last, fifteen minutes after the cab dropped her off, she was back in the garden, staring at the door to the basement. This time she had no difficulties. The crowbar slipped in between the door and the frame and with a forceful push the door creaked towards her a little. Repositioning the crowbar for the best leverage against the lock she heaved at it with all her strength. The door strained against its old lock, trying to break free from it. She heaved on the crowbar again and, gasping with the effort, watched with delight as the wood splintered and the door opened.

SEE YOU SOON, SASHA

Miles swore loudly. He needed fuel. With just under forty minutes to go, he swerved dangerously, pulling in front of a truck, before turning into the service station. Drumming his fingers impatiently on the steering wheel, he waited for a fuel pump to open up.

~

Sasha entered the house cautiously, listening for any sounds from inside. The stairs to the basement were old and crumbly, the air damp and musty, but she could smell something else, like rotten eggs, or maybe cabbage. She made her way down to the bottom and switched on her torch to see better in the gloom. Jumping, she calmed herself. *It's another bloody sex doll.*

The doll, dressed in a tight top, mini skirt and heels, stared back at her, ghoulishly, in the torchlight. He'd tied it to a chair, using multiple straps by the looks of it. Sasha peered a little closer, wondering what made Miles do this stuff with dolls. *Only it wasn't a doll.* She gasped as the stench hit her nostrils. Stepping back, she tripped over an old broom, falling to the floor and, scrabbling with her hands and feet, moved as far away from the dead woman as she could until her back hit the cold brick of the basement wall, her heart thumping almost out of her chest.

Her torch had fallen onto the floor and its glow shone away from the woman in the chair so that she was just a shadowy figure. *Okay, Sash, get it together. Think.*

Her phone ringing made her jump for the second time. Miles, again. If she didn't know better, she'd start to think he was faking his whereabouts and was already on his way here. She froze, the hairs on her arms and neck prickling. But that is exactly what he *would* do. Miles was cunning, he was devious, and he had years of experience at hunting and toying with women, before taking them captive.

Her hand shook as she answered his call. 'Hello?' She cleared her throat, her voice sounding raspy.

'Sasha, I just had to call you again. I couldn't help wondering where you'd gone shopping, what you were getting. Either I'm missing you too much or this conference is boring me to tears. Are you home yet?'

He sounded normal. But relaxed? Maybe not. She strained to pick up on his tone, as well as the background noises. There was a humming sound, varying in volume.

'Miles, you must be bored to keep calling me. Where are you now?' Her eyes were fixed on the dead woman as she spoke.

'Where am I? You know where I am, Sash. I'm in Birmingham at the hotel. I popped out for a quick smoke, anything to break the tedium.'

Traffic, that's what the sound was, passing traffic, trucks, cars, hence the volume increasing and decreasing in no discernible order. 'Oh, yeah, of course, I just meant, are you in the hotel, or outside? Where do you go for a smoke break?' She tried to tear her eyes away from the horrific sight.

Oh, we go downstairs to the underground parking. It's that or stand out in the rain. How's your weather?'

'What?' *He definitely wasn't standing in an underground parking lot*. 'Oh, fine here. Look, Miles, I must go, okay? Bye.' She cancelled the call, tears forming in her eyes. He was on his way. She had no way of knowing how close he was but was sure he was coming.

~

Miles grinned into his phone, as Sasha hung up on him. Little bitch. Little spoilt princess, Sasha. Whore. He was fairly sure that she knew everything now and had guessed he was on his way. Maybe it was time to ramp up the fun a little.

~

Turning away from the seated corpse, Sasha frantically searched for the card the police officer had given her at Eric's, but couldn't find it. Fumbling with her phone, she searched for the police station details. It was all taking too long. Panic was all she felt now, she couldn't think straight. Her phone pinged and she read the message.

SEE YOU SOON SASHA. I'M ON MY WAY YOU LITTLE BITCH. BUT I THINK YOU ALREADY KNOW THAT. THE GAME JUST GOT MORE EXCITING. TIME FOR THE REAL FUN TO BEGIN.

She was right, he was coming. And all pretence was off now. This was his end game. This was what he wanted – her, terrified and at his mercy – with no one coming to help – no one to even know where she was. Just like with Zoe.

Zoe. She had to get to Zoe. She must hurry. But she needed help. She punched in some words on her phone, hoping they made some kind of sense and, looking at her options on her phone, as well as toggling between her message and her search results, typed at speed in the recipient box before hitting send.

~

Zoe lifted her head from the mattress, her vision blurry. Had she just heard something? She tried to swallow, but her tongue was stuck to the roof of her mouth. Water. She needed water desperately. Weakly, she tried to move her legs, managing to kick one of the water bottles with her foot. But the empty bottle rolled across the floor. The bastard had left her to die. She fell back onto the mattress. She might as well do what he wanted. But there it was again, a faint sound. Was he back?

~

Sandra mulled over what to do about the property in Nun's Lane. It wasn't like Miles to make a mistake. But why hadn't he called her back? Surely he'd have received her message by now? As she pondered this, her phone rang.

Replacing the phone, Sandra sighed. That was all she needed, a furious property owner giving her a hard time. The owner of the house in Nun's Lane had been adamant, they had never had a tenant, in fact, they were anxiously awaiting news of one. What exactly was going on at the agency? Having promised that she'd sort it out, Sandra took the spare key from the file. She'd best go there and make sure that nothing was amiss.

~

The door wasn't locked, she was sure, it just wouldn't budge. Again, Sasha tried pulling the door, sure that it was just jammed from the damp. The crowbar. She needed the crowbar. That meant going back down the stairs – back to the corpse in the chair. She shivered, but made her way down and, having kept her eyes averted while she retrieved the crowbar, returned to the stuck door.

This time she had success as, with a loud crash, the door opened, nearly knocking her down the stairs. She regained her balance and entered the ground floor of the house, dropping the crowbar as her panicked brain tried to decide what to do next.

~

That was definitely a noise, she hadn't imagined it. Was it him? He didn't usually make any noise though, just silently appeared, creepily, when she wasn't expecting him. Maybe it was someone who could help her. Hauling herself upright she forced some saliva into her mouth, managing to swallow, and in so doing, tried to call out. But her voice was a feeble whisper. She picked up the chain around her ankle, clanging it against the floor, the leg of the bed, anything to make a noise.

~

Miles hummed along to the radio as he neared South Ealing. Not long now. It would only take him a matter of minutes to drop the car off at the rented garage and exchange it for his van. He wriggled in anticipation at what awaited him. Two for the price of one. Giggling, he winked at the woman next to him at the traffic lights. The woman gave him a strange look before pulling away as fast as she could.

~

As she started her car Sandra's phone pinged with a mail notification. Checking it as she fastened her seatbelt, she frowned at the sender's name, Sasha Blue. It must be the same woman who'd called her about the property the day before. She must be keen. She laid her phone back on the passenger seat. There was no point in reading it until she'd found out what the story was with the property. Pulling out of her parking space, she touched her brake. Something had seemed odd about the subject, she realised.

She read the subject of Sasha's e-mail. URGENT. LIFE OR DEATH. PLEASE HELP! It was rather extreme, she thought, maybe the woman was some kind of drama queen. Turning off the car's engine, she opened the message, scanning it rapidly. Well, she was either a paranoid drama queen with conspiracy theories, or she was seriously in trouble. She opened the attachment and studied the photos of the old newspapers. *Sasha Blue was definitely not a drama queen.*

~

Wrinkling her nose at the mess of old food cartons and the odour from the overflowing bin, Sasha walked quietly from room to room, recognising the dining room from one of the photos. As she entered the front room her ears picked up a faint sound. She stopped moving and waited. There it was again, like a kitten crying. And then a louder sound, clunking and grating. It was coming from upstairs. Zoe!

'Zoe! Zoe! Are you there? It's me, Sash! I'm coming!' She raced up the stairs calling out to her friend as she tried to decide which closed door Zoe was behind. Flinging the first one open she was met with a familiar scene, the blue striped duvet on the bed with the chair beside it. The sex doll was thrown across the bed, half of its face missing – as if it had been bitten off. Backing out of the room she pushed the next door open only to find an empty room. The next room was a bathroom.

Sash was here. Tears streamed down Zoe's face. She'd found her. 'Sash!' Her voice came out stronger now. 'Sash, up here.'

Shit, there was another storey, of course – she'd seen that from the photos. But where were the stairs? Frantically she looked around the landing, before drawing back the curtain concealing them. She quickly climbed the steep stairs to the top floor to be met with just two doors. 'Zo? Zo, I'm here.'

'Sash, in here.' Zoe's voice was weak as Sasha turned the handle of the correct door. She'd found her friend at last. But the door was locked.

'Zo, hold on, okay? I just need to get something to open the door with. I'll be right back.' *Why had she dropped the blasted crowbar?*

Oh, thank God. Zoe fell onto the bed, relief flooding through her body. *It was over. She was safe.*

Tripping, as she rushed down the steep stairs, Sasha half fell, half tumbled, to the bottom. Cursing, she rubbed her ankle before getting back up. *Be careful, you can't afford an accident, not now.* She moved as fast as she could down the next flight of stairs and looked around for the crowbar. Where had she dropped it? She'd had it in her hand when she'd forced open the door from the basement. She'd dropped it on the floor, right here, hadn't she? *How could it have moved on its own? It couldn't... which meant...*

~

Eric speed read Sasha's e-mail, fury rising in him. He'd kill Miles. He'd kill him with his bare hands if he hurt Sasha. Or Zoe. His eyes scanned the photos of the old newspapers, realising, now, that this was what Zoe must have called him about – if only she'd told him more at the time maybe he could have taken action, but she'd been so cryptic, hinting that she had something to tell him about Miles, but only wanting to tell him whatever it was in person, and then suddenly disappearing off the map, and he, in typical Eric fashion, hadn't taken it as anything serious, that is, until he'd realised that Miles was with Sasha. It was only then that he'd discovered the disappearance of Sasha's key from his flat and had begun to feel that something was amiss, by which point Sasha was refusing to speak to him. Feeling helpless, he looked at his arm and leg, both in plaster, as well as at the drip in his arm. Wrenching off the neck collar, he pushed himself into a sitting position, wincing as the stitches in his stomach pulled.

Picking up the card on his bedside table, he called Detective Inspector Wendover, telling her everything, before calling Sasha's phone, only to have his call end abruptly no matter how many times he called.

~

A chill of fear hit Sasha as she heard his voice. 'Sasha, oh, Sasha, where are you?'

Miles's voice sounded eerily different, creepy, sinister, and terrifying. She looked around, hoping desperately to find something that she could use as a weapon. Where was he? He called her again.

'Sasha. Come to Miles, you little bitch. It's time for us to have some real fun.'

He was upstairs. She must have run down right past him. She crept into the kitchen, quietly opening drawers, hoping for something to hurt him with. She rummaged through the few old utensils, grabbing a fork and an old-fashioned tin opener, sliding one into her back pocket, the other into the top of her boot.

~

Steph Wendover listened as Eric spoke rapidly. Her eyes were busy scanning the e-mail on her screen, sent by the woman called Sandra who'd phoned her just a few minutes earlier. Hitting print, she watched as the photos of the newspapers landed in the printer tray beside her. The woman she'd had down as a bit of a nut job, Sasha, who'd found Eric, wasn't crazy after all. She clicked her fingers and waved her arm urgently, attracting the attention of her colleagues, who came over at her beckoning, before galvanizing into action.

Still listening and responding to Eric, she clicked on the link to the Graffic account, looking at the photos of Zoe in horror. Again, she printed them, even as she was bringing up the details of the property in Nun's Lane.

With an all-unit alert sent out, metropolitan officers rushed for their vehicles, together with officers from the firearms unit, with one directive – to get to number seven, Nun's Lane, South Ealing, and apprehend a Miles Bleak, otherwise known as Blake Selim, believed to be armed and dangerous. Two females were believed to be at risk in the property.

~

'No, no, no.' Zoe started to cry. He couldn't be here, he couldn't. Helplessly, she stood in the middle of the room, unable to reach the door, and prayed that Sasha could get away in time and bring help.

~

Sandra left her car in the street and walked cautiously along the driveway. The police officer hadn't exactly told her not to go in, but then again, Sandra hadn't exactly told her that she was on her way to the property. But with no police officers in sight yet, and knowing that Sasha and her friend were inside, with Miles likely to arrive at any minute, she felt that she had to try and help.

She unlocked the gate, quietly closing it behind her, and walked up to the front door. Unlocking it, she slipped inside, leaving it ajar. A hand was pressed over her mouth and she was pulled into the front room. Struggling to free herself, she tried to prise the hand from her mouth.

'Shhh. He's here.' A woman's frantic face appeared in front of her as she was released. 'Sandra?' At her nod, the woman whispered again. 'I'm Sasha. He's upstairs. He's got my friend locked in on the top floor.

As the two women looked at each other, fear written on both their faces, Miles called out, in a singsong voice. 'Come to Miles, Sasha, I've got some real treats lined up for you.' He giggled, as the sound of his footsteps walking along the landing reached their ears.

'Hide!' Sasha pushed Sandra towards the rear of the house. 'Hide somewhere, he doesn't know you're here.'

'What are you going to do?'

'I'm going to kill the bastard if I get a chance. Did you call the police?'

Sandra nodded, before holding out something to Sasha. 'Take this, you'll need it.'

Taking the car jack from Sandra, Sasha told her to hurry. But Miles's footsteps could be heard slowly descending the stairs.

'Let me help. I'll distract him.' Sandra gave Sasha a quick look, before running to the front door. Pulling it wide open, she shouted up to Miles. 'Miles, I know everything! It's over, I'm going for help.' Turning, she ran out of the door as Miles descended the stairs in a rage.

With his back to her, Sasha swung the jack towards his head, hitting him with a satisfying crunch. Howling, he turned, grabbing her and throwing her against the wall. He kicked her in the stomach and she curled up in pain, even as he lunged after Sandra.

Forcing herself to get up Sasha stumbled for the door, watching as Miles pulled Sandra down to the ground. He lifted the crowbar before bringing it down with full force on Sandra's shoulder. As Sandra cried out in pain, Sasha ran at him screaming. She launched herself onto his back, stabbing at his face with the fork. He flung her off, shaking his head as blood ran down his face.

The crowbar was lying in the dirt and Sasha grabbed it, swinging it at his crotch. He doubled over in agony, falling to his knees, and she slammed it into him again, this time hitting his neck. He lay still. Gasping for breath, Sasha ran to Sandra. 'Can you move?' Sandra nodded. 'Go! Get to the street. Wait for the police!'

Sasha ran back into the house, taking the flights of stairs two steps at a time, and called out to Zoe. 'He's down, Zo, it's ok. I'm going to try and force the door open, okay?'

Trembling, Zoe stared at the door as Sasha began trying to crowbar it open.

With a final effort, the door gave, flying open, and Sasha ran to Zoe, hugging her. 'Are you okay, babe? Let's get this chain off.' She forced the crowbar between the links of the chain, but it wouldn't give.

'The padlock. Force it against the padlock on the wall.' Zoe croaked, as she pointed to the metal plate on the wall.

With a resounding bang, the padlock fell from the chain and the chain fell loosely to the floor. 'Come on, Zo, let's go. Can you walk?'

Zoe's eyes were wide with fear as she stared past Sasha.

Even as Sasha knew it was him, she was grabbed from behind.

'Oh no, you don't, Sasha. You're coming with me.

He punched her hard in the head and, dizzy and disorientated, she felt him pull her down the stairs. Her back slammed against the stairs as he dragged her, sending pain shooting through her body. She tried to resist him but a further blow to her head knocked her into unconsciousness, just as she heard the distant sound of sirens.

TAKEN

Sandra directed the officers as they poured from their vehicles, 'He's already here, in the house. He went after Sasha. Her friend's on the top floor.'

An officer held her back, as she tried to go with them. 'You're hurt. Stay here and wait for the ambulance.'

After what seemed to Sandra an interminable length of time, Zoe was brought out of the house wrapped in a blanket. Sobbing and resisting the officers, she kept repeating the same phrase. 'He's taken her.'

The paramedics took charge, gently lifting Zoe into the waiting ambulance. Sandra pushed the paramedic away as he tried to attend to her shoulder wound. 'Zoe? I'm Sandra, I work with Miles. Sasha told me everything. Where is she?'

But Zoe shook her head, before slumping onto the stretcher. 'She's gone. He took her. He was always going to take her...'

A voice came over the radio of the officer nearest them. *We've got a body in the basement.*

Zoe struggled to sit up as Sandra stared at him in horror. 'Is it Sasha?' they both cried.

After an anxious wait, the same officer returned to them. 'It's not Sasha, not unless she's been dead for a few weeks.'

Relief that it wasn't Sasha was met with guilt and revulsion at the thought that Miles had killed a woman and left her in the basement. 'All this time, while he kept me here, he had a dead body in the house? But where's Sasha? Have you found her yet? You have to find her.' Zoe howled, giving in to hysteria, as Sandra tried to calm her by placing her good arm around her thin shoulders.

But the paramedics separated the two women, it was time to take them to the hospital.

~

Sasha came round as Miles threw her on the ground and, catching sight of some gravestones, realised that she was in the cemetery behind the house. She tried to crawl away from him but blacked out again as his boot made contact with her head.

Miles unlocked the door of the van, congratulating himself on his forethought. He never brought his car to the house, always used the van, a plain white transit van that no one paid any attention to, certainly not anyone who visited the cemetery. Sliding the door open he picked up Sasha and threw her inside before climbing in after her. He grinned at her small moaning sounds. 'Little Sasha, everything's going to be okay, I've got you now.' He closed the handcuffs around her wrists, securing her to the side of the van, before crawling through to the driver's seat.

Trying to calm his agitation at the turn of events, he started the engine and took a deep breath before pulling out of the parking area and leaving the cemetery grounds. His head hurt, as well as his balls. He had to hand it to Sasha, she was a feisty little bitch, and she'd almost beaten him at his game – but she hadn't in the end. Admittedly he'd been impressed that she'd found the house already – having had to delay his planned abduction of her, he'd been planning on spicing things up by dropping a few more clues to lead her in the right direction – and how the hell *had* she found it? She just had to go there with big plans to rescue her stupid little friend, right when he was in Birmingham, hadn't she? But Miles was too sharp for her. Always a step ahead. He frowned. Until now, that is. He had to come up with a plan, and fast. He drove carefully, not wanting to attract attention, as he considered his options.

'Why, Miles?' Sasha's voice was calm, although weak. 'Why have you done all this? What's it all for? When did Zoe or I ever hurt you? And that poor child, Molly, how could you? And the woman in the basement? What did she do? And Eric? He was your friend. And all the other women you tortured, or killed, why did you do it? You owe me an explanation at least.'

'Why? What did you ever do? You rejected me, Sasha.' Miles's voice was shrill as he let his emotions erupt. 'You made a big mistake. You were supposed to choose me not Eric. But you never even noticed me. I was stuck with your stupid whore friend, while you and Eric played happy couples. I wanted you but I had to sit back and watch that slob paw you and slobber all over you while that little tart tried to stick her tongue down my throat.'

'All this, it's about you and Zoe, and me and Eric?' Sasha's voice was incredulous. *Keep him talking*.

'There never was a me and Zoe,' Miles roared. 'I put up with her to be close to you. But you thought you were so high and mighty. And then you dumped Eric. I was there, you know – when you moved on to the next guy. I watched you. You never saw me because I was so insignificant to you.'

'What? You were there? Where?' Chills took hold of Sasha and she shivered. Was he in Parva Crossing while she was there, while Chantelle was missing? Was he watching her? How could she have missed this? And then recollections came to her, a man bumping her chair roughly in a coffee shop, the back of a man's head at the inquest, her feeling that there was something vaguely familiar about him...

'You think it was a coincidence that I bumped into you at the service station? You're dumber than I gave you credit for,' Miles sneered. 'I've always been there, Sasha, waiting for the right moment.'

'The right moment for what, Miles?' She strained against the handcuffs but they were tight around her wrists.

'The right moment to reel you in, you stupid cow. And you played right into my hands. Couldn't resist, could you? Think you're so good at solving mysteries. Well, not this time. Now shut up, I need to think.' Switching on the radio, he turned up the volume.

~

Eric was frantic. Why wouldn't anyone answer his calls? Sasha's phone just rang off every time. What did that mean? Was she okay? And the police officer, Wendover, no reply from her either. Frustrated, he fell back onto his pillows, picking up the remote control and flicking through the various channels. Sitting upright, he clicked back to the news as they reported on the scene unfolding in South Ealing. He stared at the screen in horror – this was it, this must be the house, it had to be. He turned up the volume, ignoring the complaints from the bed next to him.

'Tell me something, for God's sake!' Eric yelled at the television. 'Useless bloody reporters. Give me some news, dammit!' He scowled at the reporter on the screen, trying to figure out what was happening. Had they got him? Was Sasha alright? And Zoe? What was going on there?

A nurse appeared beside his bed, not looking at all pleased with him. 'Eric, you're disturbing the other patients, we'll have to turn that off for now, okay? You're supposed to be resting, not shouting at the television.' She picked up the remote and with a firm click switched off the television.

'No, please, you don't understand. Look, I'm sorry, okay? I'll keep it low. But my girlfriend's there, in that house, the one on TV. I need to know what's happening. I need to know that she's safe.'

After a little further convincing, the nurse nodded, handing him back the remote. 'But keep it low, any more problems and I'll take it away.'

Eric stared at the television, his one finger repeatedly pressing the redial button on his phone. *Pick up, Sasha, pick up*. A thought occurred to him, could she have blocked his number? Picking up the handset beside his bed he tapped in her number and began calling again from the landline.

~

Sandra was lucky, her shoulder wound was superficial, she must have strong bones, the doctor had said. A police officer appeared to take a statement and she told him everything that she could, explaining that Detective Inspector Wendover already had all the background information. Advised that she could go home, Sandra went in search of Zoe.

Zoe was also being interviewed by the police as a nurse stood grimly by, overseeing the questioning. Sandra was allowed a moment with Zoe and the two women gingerly hugged, assuring each other that they were alright. Concern for Sasha was etched over both their faces as they expressed their fear for her safety to the officer. But with no further information available concerning Sasha's whereabouts, Sandra was sent home and Zoe was asked to think back over everything that Miles had ever said to her for any clues that might give them an idea where he might be taking Sasha.

Zoe promised them that she'd rack her brains for anything useful but then a thought occurred to her. 'You need to speak to his friend, Eric. If anyone knows anything it'll be him, he's known him for years. He's probably at work but he should have his mobile on him.' Frustrated, she realised that she didn't know Eric's number and without her phone, which that sick bastard had taken from her, she had no way of contacting him.

But the officer cut into her thoughts. 'Would that be a Mr Eric Latimer?'

Surprised, Zoe nodded. 'Yes, how did you know? Have you already spoken to him then?'

Realising that Zoe couldn't know what had happened to Eric, the officer's expression softened as he spoke gently. 'I'm afraid that Mr Latimer was found badly beaten in his flat last night. He's currently in hospital – this hospital actually – and I understand he's going to be okay.'

Zoe's expression was one of disbelief. 'Eric's been beaten? *It was Miles. It had to be.* And he's here? I need to see him. Right now!'

'I'm not sure that's a good idea, Miss.'

'I don't care! Nurse!' She called out, pressing her call button. 'I've been held against my will for weeks so I seriously don't need anyone telling me what I can and can't do right now.'

The nurse hurried in, looking enquiringly at Zoe and the officer. 'I need to see Mr Latimer. I know he's here. He's my friend. Please can you help me?' Zoe gestured to the drip in her arm. 'Can I walk with this?'

The officer nodded at the nurse and, once the nurse had settled Zoe into a wheelchair, the officer wheeled her through the corridors to Eric's ward.

~

Sasha's body bumped and rolled as the van moved, hurting her wrists. She still had the tin opener stashed in her boot, for what good it would do, but it certainly wasn't much use to her there. Suddenly she became aware of a vibration against her buttock. Her phone! Amazed that Miles hadn't thought to check for it, she tried to think how she could access it. She attempted to wriggle her bottom lower, hoping that she could slide her phone out. Someone was trying to call her. If she could manage to press a key, any key, it would answer the call.

Finally, she managed to manoeuvre her phone out of her back pocket and with some careful wriggling, not helped by the swaying motion of the van, positioned the phone between her feet. If she could just manage to hit a button with her heel...

~

Miles's brain worked frantically as he drove out of London. He was beginning to formulate a plan. He didn't like it when he wasn't in control of a situation, when things didn't go as planned, but he had an idea now. It wasn't perfect, but the more he thought of it the more he realised that it could work. It was the last place anyone would think of looking, a remote Scottish island, and the time of year was perfect too as there would hopefully be few tourists around.

~

Eric looked up in amazement as Zoe was wheeled into his room. 'Zoe! Oh thank God, you're okay! Where's Sash?' He looked behind her as if expecting to see Sasha walking in. But as Zoe began to weep and shake her head, he groaned. 'No! Tell me. Where's Sasha? What's happened to her? Is she–? She's not–?' He couldn't formulate the words and looked at Zoe helplessly.

'Oh, Eric, I'm so sorry. She's gone. Oh no–' She hurriedly explained, at his expression of despair. 'She's not– Eric, he took her. Miles took her. She saved me, and he took her.'

Eric thumped the bed covers in anger and frustration as Zoe recounted everything that had happened, firstly relating the events of the day to him before going back over her own ordeal.

Not even realising that his finger was still doing it, he'd been hitting redial constantly on the hospital's phone, and suddenly, in a lull in their conversation, they became aware of a sound coming from the handset. 'Shhh!' Eric held up his hand. 'Sash? Sash, can you hear me? Sasha are you there, baby? Talk to me!' He put the phone on speaker as the officer moved in beside him.

They waited, holding their breath, trying to make sense of what they were hearing. Music, a little distant, possible a radio. Eric shouted into the phone, 'Sash, it's Eric!'

She could hear something – a voice on the end of the phone. Straining as far forward as the handcuffs would let her, she tried to shout into the phone. 'My name is Sasha Blue. I've been kidnapped from South Ealing. I'm in a white transit van. Call the police.'

'They all looked at each other in frustration. 'Anyone?' Eric smashed his fist into the bed covers. 'It's her, she's alive, but did anyone hear what she said?'

'Sasha!' Zoe yelled into the phone. 'It's Zo, where are you?'

The van jolted and Sasha's phone slid across the floor. 'Is anyone there? My name is Sasha Blue, I'm in a white van, please help!' She glanced at the back of Miles's head, thankful that the sound of the radio prevented him from hearing her, but aware that it was also probably preventing whoever was on the other end of the phone from hearing her too.

'You can stop with the shouting, Sasha, no one's going to hear you.' Miles turned around and grinned at her as his eyes clocked her position – straining forward, her eyes locked on something at the back of the van. 'You little bitch, what have you done?' Pulling over and switching off the engine, he clambered through to the back, smashed his fist into Sasha's head and picked up her phone. In the sudden quiet of the van, he could hear Zoe's voice. Grinning into the phone, he spoke. 'Hello, Zoe.'

But even as Zoe shrank from the sound of his voice and Eric opened his mouth to shout at him, they realised he'd rung off.

'Well, it's something, we know she's alive, and her phone is with her. I'll get a trace put on the phone right away, see if we can track it,' the officer said as he wrote down Sasha's number.

REMEMBER

Miles shook his head sadly. 'Oh, Sasha, you don't give up, do you? And look what you made me do to you.' He gazed at her inert form crumpled at his knees as he smashed the heel of his boot into her phone. Removing the sim card, he broke it in half and threw the pieces out of the window as he climbed back into the driver's seat.

He began to drive again, working out how long it would take him to get to the ferry, and cautiously put his foot down.

~

Steph Wendover was frustrated. The sim card was inactive, no doubt broken and disposed of by Miles as soon as Sasha had made her call. The last known location told them nothing – North West London – what could they do with that? They needed information on Miles, something that could indicate where he might be headed with Sasha. She needed to talk to Eric Latimer and Zoe Pullman. Grabbing her coat and bag, she left the station.

~

'I swear I'll kill him.' Eric was fuming, his helplessness driving him crazy. 'Zoe, think, did you pick up anything that Sasha said? She said her name, I'm sure, which means she probably didn't even know it was me calling. But what else? Kid something maybe? Kidnapped? That's all I've got.'

'Same.' Zoe shook her head. 'Maybe she said the word police, but I couldn't hear. Oh, Eric, I feel so terrible, Sasha came to help me and now he's taken her. He could be going anywhere. How are the police ever going to find her?'

'We need to think back to everything we know about Miles, anything he said that might give us a clue about where he might go. Although he's been living a lie for years, so anything he told us was probably a lie too. But it can't be easy, lying all the time, maybe he slipped up, and if he did that's what we need to remember.'

Zoe nodded and the two sat quietly for a while, thinking back over their relationships with Miles.

They looked up as a police officer walked up to them. 'I'm Detective Inspector Stephanie Wendover, but please just call me Steph. Eric, we've met before, when you were found in your flat, but you won't remember of course, and we spoke on the phone earlier. And you must be Zoe, I presume?'

With introductions made and information shared, Steph came to the point. 'We need more information. At the moment it seems that you're the only two people who might be able to tell us something. You know Miles – or Blake, to use his real name – but for simplicity let's just call him Miles. Eric, the two of you were friends, I need you to think back over every conversation you ever had with him, see if there's anything that sticks out as odd, or memorable – anything that he might have said that can help us. And the same for you, Zoe, I understand you were in a relationship with him for a while?' At Zoe's regretful nod she continued. 'Try to think back over your conversations, from where you went together, to what you did, and see if there's anything you can tell me that feels strange. And I mean anything, guys, however small, okay?'

'What about his flat?' Eric leaned forward. 'Are you going to check it out?'

Steph nodded. 'We have officers there now, as well as at his place of work, and obviously, they're still working the scene at the house in South Ealing – if there's anything to find that will help us, they'll find it, but I suspect he's been careful, he'll have certainly had enough practice of that what with living under a new identity for all these years. I'm afraid that the two of you are currently our best chance of helping Sasha. And I don't need to tell you that time is of the essence.'

When she'd gone, Eric and Zoe looked at each other helplessly. Zoe shrugged, 'It's like you said, Eric, we're the only ones who might be able to help by remembering something Miles let slip. Guess we'll have to get to work, although remembering my relationship with him is the last thing I want to do.' She sighed. 'But for Sasha, I'll do anything.'

~

Checking the time, he nodded. He was making good progress but he'd need a rest at some point. He congratulated himself on having his 'go bag' always ready with everything he needed but cursed himself for never having gone and looked at the place he was heading for. It must be habitable, after all his nan had lived there until she'd died and left it to him. It was the last place anyone would think of looking for him – he'd never told a soul about it – no one apart from Charles – and would suffice until he could come up with a better plan.

He drove for a little while longer before pulling into a service station. Parking in a dark corner of the parking area, he checked on Sasha. She was groaning, but not fully conscious. He'd get some food for them both and then make a plan to keep her quiet.

The smell of onions hit her nostrils and she stirred, feeling dazed. 'Eat.' Miles thrust the burger and chips at her as she realised he'd undone her handcuff. Not wanting to do as he told her, but knowing that she needed to keep her strength up, plus she was hungry, she took a bite from the burger and stuffed some chips in her mouth.

'Miles, give it up. There's nowhere you can take me that they won't find me. They'll be tracing my call, your best chance is to let me go.' Her eyes fell on her smashed phone on the floor of the van before looking at Miles. Her heart sank as his grin told her that he'd made sure no one would be tracing her. She couldn't even be sure that whoever had called her had even heard anything she'd shouted at them. Despondency overcame her. She was on her own. She picked up the bottle of water and drank thirstily before finishing her food.

'I'm going to fill up with fuel, Sasha, and I'll need you to be quiet, can you do that? Probably not, knowing you as I do, so we'll just take an extra precaution.' He peeled off some duct tape and stuck a strip over her mouth, before handcuffing her again.

After a short rest, he used his phone to check on ferry times and then hit the road again. They'd take the first ferry from Ardrossan in the morning.

~

Zoe said goodnight to Eric and went back to her bed, hoping that she might be able to remember something by lying there quietly.

Eric lay in his bed, his mind going back over everything he'd ever known about Miles, every time they'd gone out, trying to recall their conversations. The more he tried to remember the more he realised that it had been him, Eric, who'd always done most of the talking. Miles had always been the quiet one, never giving much away. How had they even become mates? Well, that was easy, it had been in a pub. Yes, Miles had been sitting on his own having a pint and Eric had started up a conversation with him. He couldn't stand being on his own with no one to talk to and was always making new acquaintances. For some reason, he'd taken a liking to Miles, probably because he let Eric steal the spotlight all the time. Whatever. He shook his head, it didn't matter, somehow they'd ended up good mates and the rest was history.

~

Miles drove into the ferry terminal and opened his window as he arrived at the kiosk. 'I don't have a ticket, will I be able to get on the ferry leaving at seven?' Nodding, he pulled over and parked where directed, before walking to the office to pay. He paid with cash and returned to the van, moving it into the short line of vehicles waiting to cross. Not many people travelled across to Arran at this time in the morning apparently.

Sasha strained to hear what was going on around her. She could hear voices, the sound of vehicles, possibly trucks, and, was that a seagull? A loud boom carried across the air. It was a horn! They were getting on a ferry. But where were they? And more to the point, where were they going? She strained against her restraints hopelessly, knowing that she was trapped. The van began to move and Sasha's body was thrown about as the van moved onto the ramp and up into the ferry. She could hear men shouting directions, the sound of doors slamming and could feel the throb of the ferry's huge engine as it waited to take them across the water. Memories of childhood holidays flooded her mind as she remembered the excitement that she and her sister, Tess, had always felt on these occasions. She felt no such excitement this time, only despair that every move Miles made took her further away from any hope of help and rescue.

A BEAUTIFUL PLACE

Eric woke up in a bad mood. He'd spent a restless night filled with disturbed images of Sasha and Miles. Miles beating him half to death, Miles with Sasha, Miles embracing Sasha, kissing her. He groaned. Miles had been seeing Sasha, they'd been in a relationship. That meant he'd been sharing her bed. The thought made him feel sick. And what was he doing to her now? It was all his fault. If he hadn't behaved like such a prick maybe he and Sasha would still be together and Miles would never have entered her life. But it was no use thinking like that – Miles had obviously had a plan – he'd wanted Sasha – and Zoe had been a pawn in his larger game. Poor Zoe, he wondered how she was this morning. He pressed the button for the nurse. He'd had enough of being stuck in bed.

Zoe woke after a similarly fitful night. She had nothing. No idea of where Miles might be taking Sasha. He'd never really told her anything about himself or his past – his fabricated past – she reminded herself. The more she thought about it the more she realised that Miles had let her be the loud one in their relationship. It had suited her, of course, she was outgoing, she loved to talk, and he'd let her. Why hadn't she pushed him to talk more? Why hadn't she asked more questions? Because she'd always been too busy telling him about herself. Well, she'd learnt her lesson, if she ever had another relationship in her life, and that was a huge 'if', she'd never make that mistake again.

Eric appeared in her room, angrily thumping his crutches as he made his way towards her. 'How are you doing, Zo? I told the nurse I wasn't spending another minute stuck in bed. If they didn't give me my freedom, I said I'd be the worst patient they'd ever had. So here I am. Hopalong bloody Cassidy, that's me.' He dropped the crutches and fell into the chair beside Zoe.

~

Well, they'd arrived, wherever it was. Sasha was again swayed and jolted as the van moved off the ferry and onto dry land. She tried to listen for a clue. A French accent maybe? Or a Belgian one? Where else might Miles have gone? She sniffed the air, but the windows were closed in the front of the van and all she could smell was stale air and her own sweat. Her nose wrinkled in disgust, even though she knew how she smelt was the least of her worries.

~

Miles headed out of the terminal, following the directions on his phone. Under other circumstances, he might have enjoyed taking in the scenery around him but for now, all he was interested in was in reaching his destination. He'd need to get some provisions in, he acknowledged, but first, he needed to find the villa and check it out.

What a weird place, hardly any vehicles, the sea, always the sea, on his right and, worryingly, no shops since he'd left the main town. Cursing, he realised that he should have stopped for provisions before leaving the town. He drove through a small village, noting a fish and chip kind of establishment, closed though until later in the day. But no food stores. Nothing. A little further on the road slowly drifted inland, hills and low mountain ranges appearing on both sides. Well, he'd picked the right place for isolation. He checked his phone again, frowning as the screen appeared stuck, the map no longer responsive.

A whisky distillery appeared on his left, well that would be useful he thought, suddenly longing for alcohol oblivion. He must be close now, he realised, remembering the simple route that his phone had shown earlier, and turned right into a smaller road before crossing over a stream. The road narrowed to a single lane and he wondered where the hell he was headed. A final turn left and a few isolated villas appeared on his right. Glancing across the calm water on his left he was surprised to see what looked like an old castle perched on a promontory. His nan had lived here. Unbelievable. He'd never met her, only heard mention of her when he was a small boy. But she'd left him her home when she'd died, for some reason known only to her, and regardless of his new identity, the details of her bequest to her grandson had found their way to him through the legal channels protecting him. Well thanks, Nan, it's going to come in handy.

He crawled slowly along the small lane, looking at the villas on his right as he tried to read their names. He was almost at the end of the lane, now little more than a track. Had he missed it? The track widened slightly into a parking or turning area and he pulled the van in, switching off the engine. It wouldn't do to trawl a van up and down, some local or other might become suspicious. Better to walk casually along, as a tourist would.

~

Sasha woke up at the sudden lack of motion and sound. Where the hell were they? And had she seriously been asleep? During her own abduction? Well, that was clever, a fine detective she made, not even managing to track her own movements. She winced as Miles slammed the van door closed, the sound of his footsteps, crunching gently on gravel, slowly becoming fainter.

~

Frustration was building in him now. Where was the wretched villa? He retraced his steps towards the van, noting a slight movement behind a curtain at the window of a small stone cottage bearing the sign 'Seal Cottage'. A sign of life at least, he was beginning to think the whole place was deserted – better if it was though, if he was honest. A barking sound reached his ears and he looked down towards the rocks poking above the water. Seals. Well, that explained the name.

The track continued a little farther on from the turning area, a larger villa appearing to be the last building just beyond where he'd parked. He headed along the track feeling angry. How could the place just not exist?

~

Ann-Marie Campbell watched the man from her window as he walked along, her hand reaching to stroke the soft fur of her companion. Angus purred, rising on his hind legs to gently nuzzle the woman's neck. She picked him up and carried him to the kitchen, putting the kettle on as he mewed hopefully. 'You're a naughty wee thing, Angus.' She chuckled as she removed the kippers from the gas, turning them onto the plate already laid with bread and butter. 'Your mammy's going to have her meal now, and there'll be some for you too if you're a good boy.' Taking her tray, she settled herself down in front of the television with Angus perched contentedly on the arm of her chair. She'd watch the next episode of Taggart from her boxset, she thought, feeling as content as Angus.

~

He almost missed it, so overgrown was the garden, the driveway itself a mass of tall weeds, leading to a dilapidated garage. He'd been about to turn back after checking the name of the large villa, but something had made him walk on just a little farther. The small garden gate, its paint peeling, hanging by one hinge, led the way to an overgrown path which in turn led to a similarly neglected front door. Pushing the foliage away from the sign beside the door he could just make out the faded words, 'Castle View'. He'd found it. Relief flooded him as he took the key out of his pocket.

~

Eric and Zoe hugged each other goodbye as the orderly waited to wheel Zoe down to the waiting taxi. 'You're sure you'll be okay, Zo?' Eric asked anxiously, as she smiled at him.

'I'll be fine, there's nothing really wrong with me, I just need to get my head straight and deal with what happened to me. I've been given my orders from the rather cute doctor – rest, healthy food, and light exercise. I think I can manage that. But what about you? When are they going to let you go home?'

'They haven't said but I don't see why I can't go, no need for me to be stuck in here. I'll be seeing the doctor in the morning and I'm planning on being in my own home tomorrow. For one thing, I'm dying for a drink or two.' He grinned, hugging Zoe again. 'Go. Get out of here, I'll call you tomorrow, okay? And keep thinking about that bastard, between us we'll remember something I'm sure of it, Miles can't have been that careful, he'll have let drop something we just need to recall it.'

Eric lay back on his bed thinking about opening a can of cold lager, as the tea trolley came round. Resignedly he accepted a cup of tea, sipping it broodingly as he mulled over his conversations with Miles. He had to remember something, Sasha's life depended on it.

~

Miles walked around the cottage pulling open faded curtains and letting the dull daylight in. It had begun to drizzle and the cottage felt damp and cold. Testing the light switch he wasn't surprised to find that there was no power. To one side there was a small living room and on the other, separated by a small passageway, a dining room. The passageway led to a galley kitchen on the one side and a bathroom on the other. A back door led to a small garden, the ground rising sharply at the end of it. Climbing the stairs, he checked out the bedrooms – one on each side – one of which had clearly been his nan's room, the other a spare room with a single bed and a jumble of stuff piled here and there. Opening the large wardrobe, he found a small pile of bed linen and some towels, all damp to the touch.

Returning downstairs he tested the kitchen tap, relieved to find that it still had water. The living room had a fireplace so he could buy some wood he thought, shivering. That would mean smoke though, which in turn meant drawing attention to the fact that the cottage was occupied. Now for the garage. Unsurprisingly the doors to the garage were locked and he didn't have a key. There must be a key in the cottage somewhere but it was time to bring the van up the small track and into the driveway out of sight from prying eyes.

~

Her wrists had begun to bleed from her futile attempts at freeing herself. She thought of the tin opener in her boot but had no way of reaching it. *Come on, Sasha, he'll be back any minute.* But it was too late, the door slammed and Miles started the engine, the van moving slowly along a bumpy surface before drawing to a halt a moment later.

Sasha blinked in surprise as Miles pulled her from the van, her eyes accustomed to the dark interior. Drizzle fell on her face and a chill hit her body. He pulled her roughly towards the door of the cottage as she struggled, trying in vain to look around at her surroundings. Managing to turn her head as he pushed her inside, she glimpsed an expanse of water and something rising through the mist – a building of some kind, an old building. A castle? A ruined castle? The air smelt of rain, and something else, something familiar, what was it? A smell of wet earth – wet, peaty earth – and bracken. Stumbling as she stepped inside, Miles yanked her upright and pushed her into the bathroom.

'You've got two minutes, don't try anything, I'm right outside the door.' While she used the bathroom, Miles hurried back to the van, grabbing the few bits he needed, and was waiting for her when she opened the door.

'Miles, what the hell are you doing? Where are we? How can you think you'll get away with this?'

'Shut up!' His fist smashed into her face, flinging her head back, and he manhandled her up the narrow stairs and into the spare room. He looked grimly around the room, knowing already that he had nothing else to secure her to apart from the old iron bedstead.

With Sasha handcuffed to the bed and a fresh piece of tape fixed over her mouth, Miles used the bathroom himself, before falling into one of the old armchairs in the living room. He'd made a huge mistake. What had he been thinking? They were trapped on an island which meant that if anyone noticed anything suspicious there was nowhere to run to. The sound of a ferry horn reached his ears and he stood to look out of the window. Another ferry, right here, just across the small expanse of water. How had he not known about this? He cursed himself for his lack of preparation. Well, he knew about it now and would find out more later. First of all, he had to buy some provisions.

~

Ann-Marie picked up her plate from the floor where Angus was still busily licking it, laughing softly. 'It's all gone, my boy, nothing left, you've licked the plate clean. Let's go and make ourselves a cup of tea.' While the tea brewed, she placed another log on the fire, shivering slightly. 'Winter's come early this year, Angus and that's a fact.' She walked to the front window, gazing out. 'Well, that man and his van have gone. Perhaps he was a workman having his break. And there's no nicer spot for it and that's a fact.' With her tea beside her chair, a blanket over her knees, and Angus purring on her lap, Ann-Marie felt tiredness wash over her. She sipped her tea, pondering her day ahead. Mary had asked her to visit for the afternoon, that would be nice, just a short walk around the loch. She'd need her raincoat she thought as her head nodded sleepily and she fell into a doze.

~

Sasha listened to the sounds of Miles exiting the cottage, starting the van and pulling away. Now was her chance. But her chance for what? Angrily she pulled at the handcuffs holding her prisoner on the bed. She pulled with all her might, the iron bedstead banging and clanking as it pounded against the wall behind it. The pain from her bleeding wrists made her wince but she carried on, trying to call out from behind the duct tape he'd replaced across her mouth.

~

Miles retraced his route, cursing at his lack of planning. Why, oh why, hadn't he just stopped for provisions when he'd driven off the ferry? He wasn't thinking clearly, that bitch had ruined his careful plans and look what she'd done. It was her fault and he'd make her pay later. The thought gave him a frisson of pleasure. He allowed himself to picture what he'd do to her. This was just the beginning of the fun he was going to have with her, the fun before he finished her. Maybe he'd indulge for a few days, not too long, and then he'd go, somewhere, anywhere. He'd done it before, he could do it again.

Pushing his trolley around the supermarket he threw in the basics, tea, milk, bread, butter, cheese, ham, eggs, bacon, and a couple of frozen pizzas. He grinned, Sasha's favourite, he'd tell her it was her last supper. Remembering that the cottage had no power he threw in some candles and a couple of torches before heading for the cashier. He paid with cash, noting that he didn't have a large amount remaining. Another reason not to prolong the pleasure.

~

'Now you be a good wee boy, Angus, I won't be very long, I'm off to see our Mary for a while. When I get back, we'll see about supper, maybe some nice chicken, you'd like that wouldn't you?'

Angus mewed appreciatively, rubbing up against his owner's legs as she pulled on her raincoat.

Ann-Marie walked along the lane, enjoying the smell from the fresh rain and smiling at the seals as they rested on the rocks by the shore. Not a day went by when she didn't feel thankful for living in such a beautiful place. She glanced at the cottages as she walked along, aware that many of them were unoccupied at this time of year. It was a different matter in the summer months, occupants changed weekly as holidaymakers arrived, bringing with them the inevitable resultant noise and disruption. Still, it was nice to have activity, it could feel rather isolated during the winter months. Her mind wandered to the man she'd seen earlier as she pondered why he'd been walking up and down. Oh well, she was just getting a bit nosy in her old age. He had as much right as anyone else to stop there for a bit and take a walk, she didn't own the road, now did she? It was just... he had been staring rather intently at all of the cottages...

She arrived at her friend's home to a warm welcome, a roaring fire, and a fresh pot of tea. Now that was just what the doctor ordered. The two women, friends since their school days, hugged each other and sat down for a good chat.

~

On the way back he stopped in the village where he'd clocked the fish and chip shop, walking inside and picking up two portions. It smelt wonderful and his stomach growled in hunger. His final stop was the whisky distillery shop where he declined the offer of a tasting, taking two bottles of single malt and paying with his dwindling supply of cash.

Driving back to the cottage he was pleased to see that no curtains twitched from any of the cottages. Whoever had looked out at him earlier certainly wasn't keeping watch for him. He carried his shopping in and called out to Sasha. 'Honey, I'm home!'

~

Sasha froze, stopping her frenzied struggling. He was back and she was as stuck as she'd been when he'd left. Weariness overcame her. She'd never escape while she was handcuffed. It would have to be when he uncuffed her for the bathroom. Sounds reached her ears of cupboard doors banging, crockery clinking, and then his footsteps climbing the stairs. She sniffed the air, her stomach rumbling. Was that the smell of fish and chips?

She ate hungrily, using her one freed hand to break off pieces of the battered fish, the food warming her frozen body a little. Miles hadn't spoken a word to her, not that she was complaining. At the back of her mind was fear – fear of what he planned to do to her. She knew he'd killed Molly as well the poor elderly woman across from her flat whose name she'd never known despite smiling and waving every day. And then there was the dead woman she'd found when she'd entered the house where Zoe had been kept. All those deaths and he clearly felt no remorse. She now knew what he was capable of, she'd read the old newspaper articles and she'd seen the photographic evidence with Zoe.

Thoughts of Zoe stopped her in her tracks. Zoe must be okay, they'd have taken her to hospital. Oh, she hoped she was alright, the poor thing. The irony of her situation hit her, making her want to laugh. Miles had held Zoe captive, taunted Sasha so that she tried to save Zoe by hunting him down, all the while trusting him, and she'd succeeded in saving Zoe and getting herself caught. And now here she was. Damn, these fish and chips were good. She licked her fingers after picking up the last of the chips. At least he'd given her something to eat.

And now here she was, she thought again. And where was this exactly? Her mind was beginning to compute everything that had happened since he'd taken her. They'd driven for hours before taking the ferry, which meant – well, it meant they didn't take the ferry from Dover. So where else could they have departed from? Ferry crossings weren't her strong point but she had an idea you could take a ferry from Portsmouth or Newhaven, which told her exactly nothing. And then there were ferries to the Scottish islands. That familiar buzz fizzled through her body. Scotland. Could he have driven to Scotland? And if so, which island were they on? Something familiar hovered in the back of her mind but she couldn't quite grasp it...

She thought back to when he'd pulled her from the van and she'd recognized the smell in the air – it had been bracken – wet bracken to be exact. A smell she was extremely familiar with from her childhood. And seawater, without a doubt. About to examine her thoughts and memory further, she was prevented from doing so by the arrival of Miles.

COTTAGES AND CASTLES

It felt better to have tidied up a bit, Zoe thought, picking up the pile of papers from the kitchen counter to give it a wipe. The key fell out onto the floor and she picked it up, a shudder coursing through her body as she looked at the red ribbon she'd tied through it, remembering how she'd given it Miles, thinking that the red bow was a nice touch. 'Now you're mine,' he'd said, smiling, and she'd thought that was sweet. The sinister meaning behind his words was clear to her now and made her want to throw up.

A couple of hours later she wiped her eyes in tiredness, looking at the pages of notes in front of her. She was determined to think of something that would help find Sasha. Making herself another cup of tea, she jumped when the doorbell rang. Panicking for a moment, she realised it would be her shopping delivery and she opened the door after checking from the front window to be sure.

The delivery man's smiling face brought an answering smile from Zoe as she took her bags in, thanking him. His accent was quite strong and she wondered where he was from. Italy, she decided, his tanned and handsome face giving credence to her guess. And what she wouldn't give to be sitting on the terrace of an Italian villa right now, sipping ice-cold wine with Sasha...

Sitting back down with her tea she stared at her notes, desperately trying to think of more clues to where Miles might have taken her friend.

~

Eric tossed his empty yoghurt pot onto the trolley table across his bed. He was getting out of here tomorrow no matter what. He wanted a few cold lagers and some real food, a kebab and chips would go down well. He switched off the television irritably, feeling frustrated. He'd come up with nothing about Miles, zip, nada, and the thought of Sasha being held captive by him was driving him crazy. *Come on, Eric, think.*

~

'Undress.' Miles stood looking at her impassively after removing her handcuffs, his arms folded.

'What?' Dread filled Sasha.

'Strip. Take your clothes off. Now, you little bitch.'

She had to try. 'Miles, we can talk about this. We've shared stuff, been intimate together, we cared for each other. This isn't what you want.' His fist came from nowhere, slamming into her gut and knocking the air out of her. Doubling over, she pleaded with him. 'Miles, come on, there has to be a way we can–'

'Don't tell me what I want. I'm in charge. I've had enough of little miss clever Sasha know-it-all. Now take your clothes off.'

Feeling nauseous, Sasha pulled off her shirt, followed by her tee shirt, and then unzipped her jeans. Remembering the tin opener in her boot, she bent down to ease her boots off. It was no good as a weapon against him, but if she could slip it under the bed cover maybe she could use it somehow to try to open her handcuffs later, but she'd need to distract him... 'Miles, look around you, we're in some stupid cottage that looks like it belongs in the fifties–' She didn't get to finish. His roar and fist against her jaw sent her crashing onto the bed.

'Shut up! Shut up! Hurry up you little slut, and keep your mouth shut. No more talking.'

She smiled to herself through the pain. The tin opener was under the pillow. Her tongue flicked over her lip, bringing the metallic taste of blood into her mouth. With no other option, she slipped off her jeans and stood shivering in her bra and knickers.

'Take them off,' Miles snarled.

Dreading what was coming she removed her underwear and stood in front of him naked. Hard to believe she'd lain in bed with this man, desired him, and cried out in pleasure at his touch. Now the thought of him touching her made her skin crawl. Dare she attempt to distract him any further? 'Miles, who was the woman in the basement? Why did you kill her?'

'That dumb bitch?' He laughed cruelly. 'She was a practice run that was all, but a pretty boring one, no spunk, the stupid little whore just kept crying all the time. She was no fun at all, but at least I got to refresh my skills a little before I played with that little slapper, Zoe. Lay face down on the bed,' he commanded. 'Stretch your arms and legs out.'

She felt him pull her arms and secure them to the bedpost, and then do the same with her ankles. If they'd still been a couple, if he hadn't turned out to be a complete psycho, this was something they might have done for a little kinky pleasure. Now she just wanted to throw up. 'And Molly? The young girl? And my elderly neighbour? How could you?'

'Oh please,' he sneered. 'That stupid little girl almost spoilt everything with her pathetic detective games. She deserved it. Couldn't have some interfering kid ruin my plans. And your nosy neighbour? Yes, well, I felt bad about that, for about two seconds.' He laughed manically. 'She'd seen me on your balcony, that's why. You were supposed to disappear and no one was supposed to suspect me. But that stupid old woman kept looking over and waving, didn't she? She's only herself to blame.'

She felt his weight on her legs and a white-hot pain shot across her thigh. What did he just do? She could hear him moaning, his hands rubbing her thigh and moving onto her buttock. She turned her head sideways, trying to look, but he pushed her head into the pillow. His weight moved upwards so that he was straddling her, his hand still pushing her head into the pillow.

His moans increased in volume and she could hear his heavy breathing. Feeling revulsion at what he was going to do, she lay there helplessly.

'You dirty little whore,' he murmured, grabbing a fistful of her hair and grinding her head hard into the pillow. 'Disgusting, filthy little slut.' His movements increased but still he didn't enter her.

He's masturbating, she thought in relief. She shuddered in disgust as he cried out, warm fluid oozing onto her exposed back. All was quiet apart from his breathing. Her head was released suddenly and she turned to the side for air. Sounds of him dressing reached her ears and still she lay still, not wanting to draw attention to herself. Her thigh was stinging. Had he cut her? Finally, her wrists and ankles were released from their restraints and she sat up, wrapping her arms around her knees.

'I need to use the bathroom.' She couldn't bear to look at him. When he grunted in agreement she stood, grabbing her knickers and shirt. She was desperate to have a wash and wondered if he would allow her to use the shower. She may as well try, not much to lose at this point.

Relieved, she stood in the freezing bathroom feeling shaky. The shower was a rubber attachment over the ancient bath and after a while of running the tap, she was forced to acknowledge the fact that there was no hot water. Well, what the hell, it would have to do. Taking a deep breath for courage, she forced herself to stand under the icy jet, hurriedly soaping her face and body using the cracked bar of soap on the corner of the bath and noting the red hue of the water as it ran into the plughole. Gingerly she felt her thigh, wincing as she found the cut. Great.

A brisk rubbing down with a musty-smelling towel and she was dry and feeling warmer. The bathroom cabinet above the basin revealed some ancient wound ointment which she rubbed onto the cut before quickly pulling on her scant clothing. Upon opening the door, she was met by Miles's sneering face.

'You can get dressed again for now.' He pushed her towards the stairwell but she managed a quick glimpse into the room on either side as she passed. Upstairs, once dressed, her wrists were cuffed together and one ankle was cuffed to the foot rail of the bed. He left her without a word.

~

Fury raged through him as he sat slumped in the armchair. He should have taken her. But his hardness had been momentary and he'd known he wouldn't be able to see it through. The thought of her mockery, if she'd known, fuelled his anger and he opened the bottle of whisky roughly before pouring himself a large measure. The amber liquid burned his throat as he swallowed and then the warmth hit him. Leaning back, he lit a cigarette and pondered his situation.

~

Sasha sat on the bed looking out at the clear, calm sky, her eyes fixed on the ruined castle standing proud just across the small loch. She knew where she was. She bloody well knew where she was and it was absurd and crazy and the most amazing coincidence ever and it was just so unbelievable that she found herself laughing.

A momentary rage bubbled up inside her at the thought that he'd dared to bring her to this place that had always represented happiness and that was filled with precious memories – this place where she'd always felt safe – *oh, the irony of that* – but she quashed it firmly. Now was not the time for emotion but the time for expediency – she had to focus on herself, her situation, and her escape.

~

Jumping up, Miles went into the kitchen. The key to the garage must be somewhere and he needed to hide the van. He yanked drawers open, rifling through junk, but found nothing. Where the hell would an old woman keep the key? And the key to the back door, that must be somewhere. He pulled the sprigged curtain aside from the glass in the back door and smiled. Good old Nan. Unhooking the small bunch of keys, he first tried the door lock, unlocking it with the second key.

Triumphantly he pulled open the garage doors, his face turning to dismay when faced with the interior. The entire garage was stacked to the brim with old furniture, boxes, and shelves loaded with yet more boxes – there was no way he was hiding the van in there. He'd just have to hope that no one walked along and noticed it. Unlikely, he told himself, surely not many people bothered to walk along here, it was a dead-end, wasn't it?

Returning to his armchair he poured himself a full glass of whisky and picked up his phone. He'd investigate this other ferry and find out where it went to. If the need arose it could prove a useful escape route. But his phone refused to cooperate. Frowning, he peered at the screen, realising that it had no signal. Where was this place? World's bloody end? Fuming, he threw it across the room and took another swig of whisky.

~

Ann-Marie Campbell walked slowly home, enjoying the calm of the early evening, not bothered by the swarms of midges surrounding her. It would be dark soon no doubt. As she neared her cottage, she made a decision, she'd just walk along to the end of the lane and make sure that all was in order. Poor Flora's cottage had sat empty since her passing and the Fergusons were away in Spain or some such place. Anyone would think they didn't enjoy the weather here the way they were always off to sunnier climes. And there'd been something about that man that had bothered her, she just couldn't put her finger on it.

But a movement at her window distracted her. Och, Angus, you poor wee thing. You'll be missing your mammy to be sure. Angus stretched up at the window, his paw raised, and her heart melted. He was such a sweet cat, a true companion. Not able to bear his disappointment if she continued past her cottage, she turned in at her gate and unlocked her front door to a warm furry welcome. She'd take a walk along tomorrow and see that everything was as it should be.

~

Usually a night owl, Zoe found herself yawning quite early in the evening, no doubt the after effects of her ordeal. She'd promised herself that she wouldn't go to bed until she'd thought of something that could help the police find Sasha, but the thought of her bed was extremely appealing. Maybe she could lie in bed and just rest, she could still keep thinking and jotting things down. She took a large mug of hot tea with her and pulled on some soft pyjamas, feeling the need for comfort clothes. Ensconced in her bed and sipping her tea, she stared at her notes, her eyes feeling heavy.

~

Eric's doctor arrived at his bedside on his evening rounds and Eric, not having expected to see the doctor until the following morning, took the opportunity to put his case for going home in the morning, which the doctor finally agreed to rather unhappily, but conceded that there was no urgent medical reason for him to remain in hospital if he was insistent on leaving. Strict instructions were given on various points and Eric was left to spend his last night in a hospital bed. He took the pills from the night nurse and threw them down his throat, he might as well knock himself out he figured. He'd failed to come up with anything about Miles and was feeling quite useless. The pills began to take effect and he lay back, enjoying the floaty feeling washing over him. As his eyes closed, his mind replayed a night he'd spent in a pub with Miles. Images of a laughing Sasha and Zoe swam across his brain. Celebrating. They'd been celebrating something he recalled drowsily. Miles had won something? No. Miles had... he was almost asleep. Miles had inherited something... He tried to fight the tiredness. Miles had inherited a property somewhere. He tried to wake up, tried to claw his way out of sleep, this was important, it was the key. But it was too late, the pills had done their job and he drifted off, snoring gently.

~

Zoe jolted awake, surprised to find her lights on. It took her a moment to orientate herself and she looked around feeling a little discombobulated. Her eyes fell on a travel brochure lying on the floor, one she'd kept with an idea of booking a mini-break somewhere, which in turn made her think of the Italian delivery driver for some reason, as if he was important. She reached over and picked up the brochure, thumbing through its pages and finding the section on Italy. As she looked at the pretty villas a crystal-clear memory shot into her head.

It was the night she and Sasha had met Miles and Eric – the men had been celebrating the fact that Miles had inherited a property from his nan. And not just any property – a villa. She could remember it all. Miles had tried to stop Eric from talking about it. Miles owned a villa somewhere – that's where they'd find Sasha, she was sure of it! But where was the villa? She strained to recall what had been said. Had Eric let slip where the villa was? No, Miles had changed the subject, had been pretty antsy about the whole thing if she recalled correctly – he'd clearly wanted to keep it a secret. She'd clean forgotten about it until this moment and Miles had never referred to it.

Villas meant Italy, or France, or Spain, or, well, probably anywhere in Europe. She picked up her phone excitedly and called Eric, maybe he would remember. But Eric's phone was off and she garbled a message for him to call her as soon as he got her message. She played with the card Detective Inspector Wendover had given her, wondering if she should call. And tell her what though? That Miles owned a villa somewhere in Europe? She simply couldn't justify a call at two in the morning with such vague information. No, she'd wait for Eric to call and hopefully he'd know a bit more.

RUN, BABY, RUN

Miles looked at the whisky bottle through hazy eyes, reaching for it to refill his glass, surprised to find it was almost empty. He should go upstairs and show that bitch that he was in control. Stumbling slightly, he stood and clambered up the staircase.

Sasha froze as she heard him climbing the stairs. She slipped the tin opener back under the pillow, grateful for the darkness preventing him from seeing the scratches on the bed frame where she'd been working at the old fittings. She threw herself back onto the bedcovers just as he stumbled into her room, closing her eyes and feigning sleep.

He stood there looking at her in the darkness, contemplating. She needed to be punished, they all did, but especially her, the little stuck-up bitch. He reached out his hand and stroked her body, his hand resting on her breast. Desire rose in him and he was pleased to feel his body responding. Clambering on top of her he unfastened his jeans, freeing himself and feeling powerful.

Sasha lay dead still, revulsion coursing through her veins. Maybe if he thought she was asleep he'd just do what he did earlier and leave her alone. Her skin crawled as he unzipped her jeans and pulled them down, together with her knickers. She shuddered as he pulled her top up and forced her bra up above her breasts, her vulnerability terrifying her. A cry escaped her lips as he twisted her nipple painfully.

'Awake are we, my little bitch?' Miles slurred as he frantically touched himself. He couldn't lose it now. He forced her legs apart and lowered himself onto her, fumbling as he tried to push himself inside her.

She could smell his whisky breath. Sod this, she wouldn't let it happen, not if she could help it, and to hell with the consequences. 'Miles, you're not capable, you're not man enough. You can't get it up let alone keep it up.' She laughed, taunting him. 'You're not a man, I can't wait to exchange notes with Zoe about what a pathetic, impotent little–' Pain shot through her skull as his fist made contact with her face.

'Shut up!' He shouted in rage, even as he felt his hardness ebb away. Furious and emasculated, he pummelled her with his fists, her laughter filling his ears. 'You're lucky I don't kill you right now.' He landed a final punch into the side of Sasha's face before climbing off her and stumbling from the room. This wasn't how it was supposed to be. He'd been fantasising about this moment for so long, why was she ruining it for him? He crossed the small landing to the other bedroom and threw himself onto the bed, the room spinning in front of his eyes.

Tears filled Sasha's eyes and pain suffused her body. She curled up, drawing her knees into her chest, sobbing quietly. It had been worth it though, he hadn't been able to take her forcefully – he had a trigger and she'd found it – mockery of his manhood. But how long before he lashed out too violently and killed her? She forced herself to sit back up, pulled her clothes together as best she could and began to work on the bed frame again whilst keeping one ear out for any sounds of Miles returning.

~

Miles passed a fitful night in his nan's old bed, tossing and turning, waking from his alcohol-fuelled dreams feeling nauseous and with a sense of loss of control of the situation. Shame filled him as he remembered his failure of the night before, and not just that but her mockery of him. He couldn't let her get away with that, he had to stay in control. He needed her to feel shame and pain for everything she'd done to him since they met. The thought of it made him feel marginally better. And he couldn't stay long in this place, it was too small, he'd stick out like a sore thumb, and it was absolutely freezing.

Stepping to the window he stared out at the rain, as it fell in sheets from the grey cloudy sky, and at the palm trees forced almost horizontal by the wind. Palm trees? In this place? He shook his head. Right now he needed some warmth and some food. Then he'd go and find out about the ferry – he needed a forward plan. Tonight would be the night he decided. He'd cause her real pain, he'd take his time and enjoy it. He stopped mid-thought, that was why he'd failed – he hadn't indulged, he'd rushed. Tonight he'd take his time and savour every cut, every punch, every time she cried out in pain. And when her body was slick with her blood and she was begging for mercy, his arousal would be ultimate, then he'd take her triumphantly. *And then he'd kill her.*

~

Her ears strained to hear what he was doing. He was moving around which meant he might check on her at any minute. Carefully Sasha balanced the iron rod at the end of the bed, pushing the blanket in either side to hold it upright. She just needed a little more time, it was so loose now. Desperately frustrated she lay down and waited, trying to stop her body from shivering.

~

He paused at her doorway, glancing in but not wanting to face her right now, before heading down the stairs. He'd take a chance with the fire, no one in their right mind would be out in this weather so there'd be no one to notice the smoke. Once he'd lit the fire, he tested the gas stove. Nothing, of course, he should have guessed. But a thought occurred to him. He stood at the back door and checked outside the kitchen wall. Yes, there it was, a gas cylinder.

Slipping on the moss-covered path he twisted the valve on the cylinder and hurried back inside. He tested the gas again, a gentle hiss rewarding his efforts, and he struck a match, jubilantly bringing a flame to life.

He was beginning to enjoy himself, the promise of the evening's delights filling him with hungry anticipation, and he found himself humming as he melted butter in a pan and dropped in some bacon rashers. It felt like a holiday, camping but without the tent, he thought, as he cracked eggs in the pan and buttered some bread. With the kettle sitting on another of the gas burners, he sat down to his breakfast.

There was no point in feeding the bitch, she wouldn't need food soon anyway. He wiped his mouth on a tea towel and gulped his tea, leaning back in the kitchen chair contentedly before putting his mug down with a frown. He needed to dress her. How could he have forgotten? It was all part of it, the dress, the underwear, the shoes, all were needed to make everything perfect. Well that was easy, he'd drive back through to the main town and buy what he needed, there must be a clothing store or two there, surely, then he'd check out the ferry situation on his way back.

~

The smell of bacon and eggs made Sasha realise how hungry she was. She couldn't take the risk of loosening the rod any further in case he appeared with food for her, so she forced herself to stay lying down, pulling the blanket tightly around her as she listened to the rain pelting against the window.

~

Ann-Marie awoke to the gentle nuzzling of Angus and his purring face staring directly into hers. 'Good morning, my boy, aye, you'll be wanting your breakfast.' She sat up, cuddling the cat, and listened to the sound of the rain against her window. 'Well, we'd best get on with it.' She left the warmth of her bed and pulled on her dressing gown as she slipped her feet into her slippers, laughing as Angus tried to hurry her downstairs.

Once Angus was cleaning himself on the window sill, content after his meal, Ann-Marie sat herself down with her tea and slice of bread, thickly buttered, her breakfast ritual for more years than she cared to remember. She'd finish her tea and get herself dressed, then maybe she'd just stroll along and check on the cottages. The rain wasn't that bad by Arran standards and it would be nice to take in a little fresh air.

~

Dressed and ready to go, Eric realised that he hadn't switched his phone on and quickly did so. He called for a cab and was wheeled to the entrance to wait for his ride. Racking his brain, he tried to remember what it was he'd thought of last night. It had been something important about Miles. His phone pinged and he listened to Zoe's garbled voicemail, her words bringing to mind his own muddled recollections. He hurriedly called her back. 'Zo, it's Eric, I just got your message. You're right, I remembered something about it as well. He did inherit a property. It was from his nan, a villa somewhere. Look, I'm leaving the hospital now, shall I come straight to you? Have you got anything to eat? Eggs will be perfect, and put the kettle on, will you? I'll see you soon.'

~

With her raincoat on, Ann-Marie left her cottage and began to walk along the lane. The rain was falling harder now, ominous sounds of thunder rumbling around her. Looking ahead to where the end cottage was hidden by trees, she paused. Was that smoke drifting from the chimney? Yes, it was, so someone was there, but was it the man she'd seen? She had no reason to think so, just one of her feelings. Maybe she should pop along and introduce herself to whoever it was, no harm in that, after all, Flora had been her friend. But a loud crack and flash of lightning brought a sudden torrential downpour and she turned back. She'd have to wait for the weather to calm. She rushed back into her cottage and closed the door, rain dripping from her coat onto an unhappy Angus.

~

Sasha jolted from her stupor as the door slammed. Come on, Sash, stay with it, you can't give in to this. Sitting up, she listened intently, trying to guess what he might be doing. Was he going out? Or was he just fetching something from the van? It was hard to hear above the sound of the heavy rain, so she got herself into a standing position on the bed from where she was able to see down into the lane in front of the cottage. He was going out, she thought with relief as she watched the white van reverse into the lane and head back along the loch. Her gaze fell on the rain-blurred outline of Lochranza Castle, memories of her and Tessa playing in and around it as children bringing her a fond moment of nostalgia. But she shook her head, no time for that now. One good thing was that Miles had absolutely no idea that she knew, and loved, this island, that she was familiar with Arran from the many years of family holidays spent here.

With no idea how much time she might have, Sasha set to work, feverishly forcing the tin opener into the loosened section of the rod repeatedly. Mustering all her strength she bent the rod first one way and then the other, feeling it give a little more each time. *She could do this.*

~

Entering her living room, the sound of a vehicle brought Ann-Marie to her front window and she was just in time to see the rear end of a white van pass on its way back around the loch. So it was him, well that was that part of the mystery solved, for now. She decided to make some more tea and sit down to watch the news.

~

Eric and Zoe hugged awkwardly around his crutches before moving into the kitchen. With a plate of eggs and toast in front of him and a steaming mug of tea for each of them, they both began talking at once. Zoe took the lead, as Eric chewed on a mouthful of his breakfast, presenting her list of possible countries where Miles might have inherited a villa in the hopes that one of them might ring a bell with Eric.

'So, I looked it all up early this morning and countries that call houses villas seem to be mainly Mediterranean. We're talking about Spain, France, Italy, Portugal, Greece, Turkey, then there's Malta, and Croatia...' She looked at Eric hopefully.

'Pthwrrsh.' Eric tried to swallow the large mouthful as he spoke.

'What?'

'Sorry, jumpers, that's what I was trying to say.'

'Eric, I'm not following you, what have jumpers got to do with anything?' Zoe felt exasperated, if Eric wouldn't take this seriously then she was wasting her time.

'Jumpers, Zo. The famous jumpers. They're made on some island somewhere. That's where he inherited his villa. I remember now, he mentioned the name of the place and I immediately thought of the jumpers. I never asked him about it, that's when we met you and Sasha — we kind of had other things on our mind, like chatting you two up.' He grinned, before looking anguished. 'I swear, Zo, we have to find her, I can't bear it.'

'D'you mean Aran jumpers?' Zoe looked at him incredulously. 'That's like, hold on, where— oh, the Aran Islands isn't it? Where the hell are they? Somewhere colder, not the Mediterranean at all!' She began to search on her phone, bringing up the information. 'Okay, so the jumpers take their name from the Aran Islands off the west coast of Ireland. Hold on... there are three in the

Galway Bay. Could this be it, Eric? Think. Did his nan live in Ireland?'

'Eric held his hands out, 'Damned if I know, Zo, but yeah, could be? Maybe they call houses villas there too?'

Zoe tapped in the phone number for Detective Inspector Steph Wendover and waited impatiently for her to answer. 'Hi, Detective Inspector Wendover? Steph? It's Zoe, here, Zoe Pullman, Sasha's friend. Yes, we've remembered something. Eric thinks that Miles inherited a property, well a villa, from his nan, and we think it's on one of the Aran Islands. Yes, Ireland, so we thought–' nodding she listened to the other woman speak, before thanking her and saying goodbye. 'Eric, put the TV on, she's going live on the news in a few minutes, about Sasha.'

They sat and watched the news, images of Sasha and Miles appearing on the screen, as Steph Wendover announced what they knew already, that their friend had been abducted by someone believed to be dangerous. Even as they watched, she added in extra information, that there was a possibility she'd been taken to an island off the west coast of Ireland, one of the Aran Islands.

'Wow, that was fast.' Zoe was full of admiration. 'She thanked us, by the way, said they've been looking into everything about Miles but this was news to her. They're going to look into inheritance stuff now, however they do that, but she said they'll immediately alert the Irish Garda. She wants you to keep thinking though, see if you can remember anything else that might narrow it down.

~

Miles rolled his eyes as he left yet another so-called clothing shop, his good mood fast dissipating. Did these people wear nothing other than thick fleeces and walking boots? He'd give it up, pity though, he'd liked the idea of dressing up his little bitch whore doll for the grand finale, would've made for some nice photos to keep on his phone as a keepsake. He may as well head back and investigate the ferry. Then he'd spend a little time taunting her, give her an idea of what to expect later. The thought excited him and he hurried back to the van.

~

It had taken her another two hours or more but she'd done it – the rod was free of the frame at last! She slipped the cuff from the bottom of the rod and stood up. There was nothing she could do about her hands being cuffed together, and he could be back at any minute. She needed to get out of the cottage now and find someone in one of the other cottages to help her. She stumbled down the stairs, dizziness forcing her to reach out to the banister for support. Weak from lack of food and water, Sasha went into the kitchen, quickly looking for something, anything, that she could stuff into her mouth for energy.

She grabbed the cheese slices from the fridge, slapping them between two slices of bread and took a large bite, before filling a mug with water from the tap. Having gulped some water, she rushed to the front door. Frustrated she pulled at the handle. Locked – she'd have to go out the back. Glancing out of the small window beside the front door she had a sudden clear view across the loch. The rain had stopped suddenly and the sun shone brightly. In dismay, she saw the white van driving along from the small ferry terminal. He was on his way back, she had to get out now. Back in the kitchen, she searched frantically for the keys to the back door, hampered by her cuffed wrists.

~

Miles hummed as he drove along. It was all working out. He'd take the ferry tomorrow, he'd never been to Kintyre, maybe he'd spend a day or two taking in the scenery before deciding where to go next. And now the sun was shining, just for him, that was more like it. An image of Sasha came into his mind and he threw his head back, guffawing loudly as he imagined her corpse positioned on a chair in his nan's cottage. It could be years before anyone discovered her. It would be his magnum opus.

~

Ann-Marie came to, the television still on, to find herself looking at a photo of the man she'd seen walking along the road. Horror brought goosebumps to her skin as she listened to what he'd done, followed by dismay as the policewoman announced that he was believed to be somewhere in Ireland, possibly on one of the Aran Islands. No, not the Aran Islands, he was right here, on Arran! Oh dear, and the poor girl, she must be in Flora's cottage, held captive, and who knew what he'd done to her, or what he'd do to her. She had to help her. Flustered she stood up, disturbing a sleeping Angus who stalked indignantly over to the windowsill and jumped up.

Looking up his number in her phone book, Ann-Marie dialled her nephew Callum's mobile phone. Never had she been more relieved that her nephew was a policeman. While she waited for him to answer she stroked Angus as he purred his forgiveness for the undignified ejection from her lap, glancing out of the window in time to see a white van heading from the direction of the small ferry terminal across the loch.

~

Callum mopped up the last of the baked beans with his toast, appreciatively, before taking a huge gulp of tea. His phone rang and he smiled, it was his Aunty Ann-Marie, or Lochy as she'd been fondly called since they were kids. 'And what can I do for you on this fine morning, Lochy?'

'Oh, Callum, you have to come quickly, you'll have seen the news? About the poor wee girl? The man that's taken her? He's right here, Callum, he's here in Lochranza. They're saying he's taken her to the Aran Islands, but they've got it all wrong. Oh dear.'

'Slow down, slow down, start at the beginning. Now, where did you hear this? On the news you say? Alright, I'm on my way, now don't you go getting in a state, I'm coming over. It'll take me a while, I'm over in Brodick, just had my breakfast. I'll see you in about half an hour. Stay inside and lock your doors, Lochy, I'm serious.' Callum ended the call, frowning, it wasn't like his aunt to be dramatic. 'Pop the news on there would ye, Shona?

~

Locking the front door behind him, Miles frowned at the blast of cold air rushing into the small hallway. In a few strides, he was in the kitchen, staring at the open door in dismay. No, no, no. He turned and raced upstairs, knowing his captive would no longer be where he'd left her but wanting to see it with his own eyes. He flew back down the stairs and out of the kitchen door, staring frantically to his left and right. To the left was nothing, wilderness, the end of the island surely, she'd never have gone that way. She'd have gone over the small wall on the right to the cottages, trying to ask for help. Leaping over the wall he told himself to remain calm. The cottages looked pretty much unoccupied but she wouldn't know that. She'd probably pass through each garden to stay out of his sight from the road and try to knock on back doors. Scanning the garden he was in, that of the big villa next to Point Cottage, he climbed over the wall and into the adjoining garden, rage flooding through him. He couldn't lose her, not now.

~

As Callum drove, he called his fellow officers and filled them in on the situation before calling his father. 'Dad? Callum. I'll be needing some men, the more the merrier, call my brothers, will you? I've got just me and three officers today. Fergus has gone to the mainland with the wife and Niall's sick today can you believe it. I'm headed for Lochy's from Brodick, she says she's seen the man on

274

the news, the one who took the lass from London. Reckons he's holing up at old Flora's cottage. I've never known Lochy to be wrong about anything. Thanks, Dad, and you all be careful, I'll see you there.'

Next, Callum called mountain rescue, filling Bruce Currie in as quickly as he could. Finally, he called the number Detective Inspector Wendover had given out during her announcement. As he waited for someone to answer he looked worriedly out at the menacing clouds gathered once more in the sky, even as large raindrops fell on his windscreen.

~

Trembling, Sasha edged out from behind the door of the small pantry. Her ruse had worked but how long would it be until he figured it out? Which way to go? Front or back? Panicked thoughts crashed about inside her head as adrenaline fuelled her movements. She rushed to the front door, tugging at it in vain – he must have locked it when he came back in. But she'd have been exposed if she ran onto the road – no, better to go through the back, but her plans to reach a cottage for help had been thwarted, she'd caught a glimpse of him leaping over the wall to the next property while she'd been hiding in the pantry. She had no choice but to head towards the point. Carefully exiting the kitchen and crouching low, Sasha scrambled over the low stone wall as the rain began to fall once more. Stumbling in panic, she tripped numerous times as she made her way through the wet bracken, her clothes snagging on the thorny gorse bushes. Finding her way to the narrow footpath she began to run, memories of hikes along this very path with her sister filling her mind. Drenched now, her hair slick to her head, and her breathing ragged, Sasha forced herself into a manageable rhythm as she headed towards Newton Point.

~

With a start, Ann-Marie realised that her back door was unlocked. Tutting to herself she went through to the kitchen and turned the key, glancing out of the window and seeing a movement in the garden to her left. It was the man and he appeared to be searching the garden. A banging sound reached her ears and she realised he was knocking on the back door of the neighbouring cottage. Hurriedly scooping up Angus she climbed the stairs and closed him in her bedroom before quietly stepping to the small window at the end of the landing.

A loud banging made her jump and she realised it was her own back door. Taking a step back she waited, her heart racing. Once it had stopped, she peered out of the window in time to see him clambering over her wall to make his way onward. Had the girl escaped? She must have, oh the poor thing, and where was she? Well, drenched to the core that was a fact. She willed Callum to arrive as the man disappeared from her view.

~

Steph Wendover thanked Sergeant MacKinnon and instructed officers to call the Garda with an update and apologies. Now how to help the band of men on the Isle of Arran to find Miles, and more importantly, to find and rescue Sasha Blue. This was assuming that the woman on the island was correct in her identification. She pulled up a map on her computer and zoomed in on Lochranza as she called Eric.

'It's Steph.' Eric answered his phone, pacing the floor as Zoe looked on anxiously.

'Eric, we've received some more information and I want you to think carefully. Could it be that the place Miles inherited his villa was actually on somewhere called the Isle of Arran? It's in Scotland. Could you have associated the name with the jumpers by mistake d'you think? Only someone has called saying they think they've spotted Miles on the island.'

Eric slammed his palm against his forehead in exasperation. 'Yes! Yes! The Isle of Arran. They sound the same, yes, I'm sure of it now. Scotland you say? Yes, it makes sense, how could I have got it so wrong? He told me his nan's name, it was Flora, that's Scottish, isn't it? I'm guessing they call houses villas there too then. I think I even joked about him wearing a kilt. But we'd been drinking, he stopped talking about it suddenly, and we got totally pissed, I forgot all about it and I think he forgot that he ever told me, he certainly never referred to it ever again. Dammit, why didn't I remember? What about Sasha? Have they caught him? Have they found Sasha, is she okay? Why did I not remember any of this before, I feel terrible, it'll be my fault if anything's happened to her.'

'Listen, don't blame yourself, it's not confirmed yet. There are four police officers on the island and they're headed to a place called Lochranza where a resident says she saw him.'

Eric shouted jubilantly. 'That's it, Lochranza, it makes sense! He said it was on the water. And, wait, this is going to sound weird, but– is there a castle there by any chance? I don't even know why that's come into my head.'

'How did you–?' Looking at the map on her computer Steph nodded. 'An old ruin, Lochranza Castle, on the loch. Miles was spotted around the other side of the loch at the end of the road there, possibly hiding in a villa called Castle View – ah, that's how you knew about the castle – he must have told you the name of the property. Newton Road is the name if you want to look it up. Okay, thanks, Eric, you've been very helpful, I'll keep you posted.' About to ring off, she was interrupted by him.

'Did you say there are four police officers on the island, like, that's it? Not four men for the whole island surely?'

'Well, yes, it seems there's not a whole lot of crime there, it being a small island. But mountain rescue are heading to the area as well and I believe some other local men are assembling as we speak. There's not much we can do from here, unfortunately.'

Filling Zoe in on the news, the two of them brought up a map of Arran on her laptop, poring over it and zooming in on Lochranza to stare in amazement at where Miles had taken Sasha.

A FEW GOOD MEN (AND WOMEN)

Mrs Pringle, in the village of Parva Crossing, was enjoying a rare afternoon off, having left Sheila in charge at the chemists. She'd caught up with her ironing, had a dust through, and now had the kettle on for a cup of tea which she planned to accompany with a toasted teacake slathered in melted butter. Humming happily, she switched the television on and plumped the cushions on the couch in readiness for her break.

A name spoken on the television made her lift her head sharply, her senses immediately in overdrive. She knew that name. Oh dear. Oh no. That poor girl. Agitated, she paced the room, not sure what to do with the information. The sister would know all about it, surely. But what if she didn't? She'd never forgive herself if she didn't do her community duty. Picking up the phone Mrs Pringle dialled Beedham's department store in Rentham.

~

Sasha's teeth chattered uncontrollably as she tried to control her shaking body. She passed Newton's Point and continued on the path, gasping as the ground became bog-like underfoot. Reaching Fairy Dell she paused, trying to make out the small cottages through the thick fog that had crept in. Maybe she should try and get into one of the old fishermen's cottages and shelter, she thought longingly. But if he was following her, and surely he was by now, it would be the first place he looked. No, she should plough on.

The ground became steeper and Sasha struggled to scramble over the large boulders, hampered by her handcuffed wrists and lack of visibility. Slowly, slipping and sliding, she made her way towards the cock of Arran, the sound of the waves crashing to shore telling her that it must be high tide. Gradually the terrain levelled and she felt the flatter unique sandstone formations of this part of the coastline underfoot.

Weary now, Sasha felt filled with dread. She'd made a terrible mistake. How could she hope to survive out here on her own in these terrible weather conditions? She needed to find shelter, and fast, so turned inland and pushed her way through the bracken. Tessa's voice suddenly filled her ears, a younger Tessa. They were here on holiday and the two girls were hiking along the coastline. 'Let's go and find Ossian's Cave!' And now Tessa's voice was stronger in her head, an older Tessa. 'Go to the cave, Sash. You'll be safe, he won't find you there.'

A rustling in the bracken ahead of her made her look up and peer ahead into the fog, and suddenly she found herself looking into the eyes of a red deer as it stepped into her path. The beautiful creature stopped for a moment and stared at her with its gentle eyes, shook its body and snorted softly before turning and disappearing.

She scrambled in the direction of the deer, her feet gradually finding their way from memory and, finally, she found the boulder-like steps that would bring her to the hidden cave. Moaning with exhaustion, and barely able to make it another step, Sasha reached the entrance to the cave and pushed through the wet bracken obscuring its opening. Collapsing, she forced herself to crawl forward on her knees before falling over and curling up in a tight ball. She heard Tessa's voice again— 'You'll be safe,' and passed into unconsciousness.

~

Seething, Miles watched the vehicles converge in front of the cottages from his higher vantage point and watched the men emerging to gather together in a huddle, clearly discussing their next move. They knew he was here. But how? That meant they knew about Sasha as well. He watched as a woman emerged from one of the cottages and spoke to a police officer. She pointed to his nan's cottage and then to the gardens of the cottages, her hand movements telling him she'd observed him as he made his way through the gardens. There was no way he was going to be able to retrieve his van he realised, as a group of men headed to the cottage. He either had to head inland or try to make it to the ferry on foot in time for the last crossing. And what about that bitch, Sasha? Was he just going to let her get away? She must have gone in the other direction but whatever the hell lay that way he couldn't imagine. Should he try to catch up with her? He weighed up his options, all the while watching the activities of the men down below.

Gradually he lost sight of the men, and realised that fog was enveloping him and his surroundings little by little. Great. But wait a minute. If the fog came right in, he could make it to the ferry without being seen...

~

'I don't think she's in the cottage, Callum, he was looking for her, I'm sure. I reckon she'll have headed along to Newton Point, although where she hoped to get to, I don't know, poor lass. You must find her, and hurry, she'll be drookit by now to be sure, Callum.' Ann-Marie wrung her hands in worry as she talked to her nephew.

'Aye, you're right there, Lochy, the poor girl will be soaked to the skin. Don't you worry now, you get back inside in the warm and let us do our job.' Callum returned to his band of men and organised groups to search for Sasha as well as Miles. They set off in their various directions and Ann-Marie returned to Angus, holding him tightly as she stared anxiously from her window into the thickening fog and rain.

~

Von put the phone down and called Tessa over from where she'd just finished serving a customer. 'Tess, darling, have you spoken to your sister lately?'

'Not for a few days, why, has something happened?' Ever since her daughter Chantelle had disappeared, and thankfully been returned to her, Tessa had lived in a state of constant anxiety.

Placing her arm around Tessa's shoulders Von steered her away from the counter. 'Something's been on the news about her and I think you'd better know about it.'

Racing to the staff room, Tessa put the news on while at the same time bringing up the information on her phone. She read in horror of Sasha's abduction and the possible sighting of her and her abductor on the Isle of Arran. She called Zoe.

Zoe had just made them more tea when her phone rang and she snatched it up, seeing Tessa's name on the screen. 'Tessa, hi, it's Zoe, oh I should have called you, it's just that so much has happened.'

'Zoe, tell me, is it true? About Sash? Why didn't you call?' The two women spoke at the same time.

For the next couple of minutes, Zoe gave Tessa a canned account of what had been happening – from her abduction at the hands of Miles to her rescue by Sasha, and Sasha's subsequent abduction. She finished by confirming that it was now believed that Miles was holding Sasha in a cottage on an island in Scotland.

'Yes, yes, I saw the news,' Tessa was impatient in her anxiety. 'I know the Isle of Arran – *we* know Arran, we used to holiday there and often stayed in Lochranza as children so Sasha knows the area well. Zoe, I have to speak to someone in charge. I am so sorry about what happened to you, it must have been a terrible ordeal, I can't imagine what you went through, but right now I need to speak to someone who can tell me exactly what's going on.'

~

Steph Wendover answered her phone and listened to Tessa explain who she was. Having given Tessa a brief update, no more detailed than Zoe's, she promised to find out the latest and call her back.

~

Charles Priestley yawned, stretching his arms above his head as he glanced out of the window at the rain. Checking his watch, he estimated that he had just enough time to finish up the last file on his desk and he pushed his chair back to go and make himself a coffee.

While he waited for the kettle to boil, he wandered through to the staff lounge adjoining the kitchenette and switched on the television, changing the channel to the news, his jaw clenching as he listened to the reporter relay the fact that the manhunt on the Aran Islands had been halted due to new information. Unaware that the kettle had switched off, he stood transfixed as the newsreader informed him that the man wanted for the abduction of Sasha Blue had been allegedly sighted on the Isle of Arran, in Scotland, and that all efforts were being directed there as it was believed that he was holding the woman hostage in a property on the island. It took him a moment to realise that someone was talking to him.

'Earth to Charles! You're a million miles away, want a coffee?' Shelley stood in the doorway, her eyebrows raised in mock exasperation.

'What? Oh, yes, thanks, Shelley, I was just about to make myself one and thought I'd watch the news while I waited for the kettle to boil.'

'Ye-es... I can see that, Charles.' Shelley shook her head in amusement as she walked up to stand beside him. 'What's got you so mesmerized? Oh, it's that manhunt, terrible, isn't it? Apparently, he'd taken a couple of women and done all sorts of dreadful things to them, and they're saying he killed one of them. And now he's taken another one, poor thing, but they're onto him now. Don't reckon it'll be long 'til they catch the bastard now. Anyway, I'll make that coffee.'

Forcing himself to maintain control, Charles smiled tightly and switched off the television before joining Shelley in the kitchenette where he added milk and sugar to his coffee, thanked her and returned to his office.

He couldn't concentrate on work now. He clicked onto the internet and hunted for the story online, wondering if there was anything that he should do. Bringing up a map of the island he homed in on the place mentioned in the news, wondering what had forced Miles to travel there to his nan's villa of all places. He must have had no choice – must have had to make a snap decision. What were his chances of evading capture? And what of the woman? Poor Miles, his heart ached for his friend.

Answering his phone as he stared at the screen, he registered his wife's voice and smiled into the phone. 'Megan, everything alright? Kids alright?'

A few minutes later he switched off his computer, slipped into his overcoat and left his office, putting his head over the partition to speak to his secretary. 'I'm off a little early, Shelley, Megan's coming down with a cold and wants me to pick up something for dinner on my way home.'

~

Being an astute woman, Ann-Marie analysed everything she'd observed of the man's activities, and her senses honed in on the fact that she'd seen a van, his van surely, driving from the direction of the ferry terminal. Had he been planning on taking the ferry over to Kintyre? Would he still try to escape that way on foot? She looked at the thick fog now blanketing the lane in front of her home. No one would see him if he made his way along there now and that was a fact. She picked up her phone to call Callum and tell him what she was thinking.

~

Tessa listened to everything that Detective Inspector Wendover had to tell her, from the location of the cottage where they believed Sasha had been held; to the belief, now confirmed, that she'd managed to escape; that groups of men including mountain rescue were currently searching for her; and that Miles had been spotted searching for her but that his whereabouts were unknown at this time. When she'd told Tessa everything she could, it was Tessa's turn.

'We used to holiday on Arran, and we often stayed in Lochranza, we even rented a cottage along Newton Road once, right on the shore there. Unknown to that sick freak Miles, he took her to the one isolated place that she knows inside out. If, as you say, Sasha managed to escape, and Miles was spotted searching for her in the gardens of the cottages and banging on their doors, he obviously assumed that she'd tried to get help from someone in one of the cottages. Well yes, that's probably what she would have done normally, but if she knew he'd go that way then she will have gone the other way. She'll have headed along the path to Newton Point, a hike we often took as girls. There are the old cottages at Fairy Dell, but if she thought he would eventually head back along that way then they're too obvious, he'd easily find her if she was in one of them. No, I think she'll have gone to Ossian's Cave. He couldn't know a thing about it and would never find her there. She'll be safe for now. She's probably waiting there until the coast is clear. Then she'll make her way round to Sannox knowing that he would never guess that she could get there via the coastline. Please Steph, ask your men to check Ossian's Cave, I know my sister, that's where she'll be, I'm sure of it.'

Steph Wendover thanked Tessa and immediately called Callum MacKinnon, telling him everything that Tessa had told her. Callum then radioed Bruce Currie and his team, advising them that there was a high chance that they'd find Sasha at Ossian's Cave. It was heartening to hear that they weren't too far from it and should be there in about half an hour.

~

'Lochy, I can't talk now, we've got a lead on the woman, you just stay put alright? I'm busy instructing the guys and I'll be along with an update all in good time, alright? You've been a great help, Lochy, you truly have, I'll see you in a while.' Callum was gone before Ann-Marie could utter one word.

Tutting and exasperated, *when would the boy learn?* Ann-Marie went to plan B. 'Mary, aye, it's me, listen, where's your Gordy at? Oh, they are, they won, did they? That's good, well now, let me fill you in quickly. You'll have to move fast, Mary, there's no time to waste and no other help coming.' She proceeded to fill her friend in.

~

Mary Kennedy put the phone down, slipped her feet into her outdoor shoes and put on her raincoat. Leaving her cottage, she walked the short distance along to the hotel bar and entered, looking around for her son and his rugby teammates.

'Gordy, you and the boys are needed and I'm sorry for interrupting your celebrations, but there's something we need you to do. Can we get the news on the television or can you find it on your phone there?' Mary explained everything to her son and he called the men together, showing them the photo of Miles on his phone.

Well, thought Mary, they might have had a few beers, but they were still a force to be reckoned with. She watched the group of burly men leave the pub, knowing that if the man was headed for the ferry, as Ann-Marie believed he was, then her Gordon and the lads would get hold of him alright. Perhaps she should have a wee dram while she was in the bar, yes, she could do with it after all that excitement. 'Kyle, pour me a measure will you? And then will you get our Ann-Marie on the line across the loch there? There's something I need to tell her.'

~

Ann-Marie nodded and thanked Mary. It was up to Gordon and his boys now. Perhaps she'd pour herself a wee measure of whisky after all the excitement and wait for Mary to let her know when they'd got him – and what did Angus think about that she wanted to know? But Angus was asleep, unaware of all the excitement unfolding around him.

PROVIDENTIAL, DEAR

Eric paced the floor of Zoe's flat – if hobbling on crutches could be called pacing. 'What should we do? Do we phone Steph again? Or Tessa? What about Tessa, maybe she knows a bit more now that she's spoken to the officer? I mean, we can't just wait around. Someone must know something dammit! I need a drink. Have you got any lager, Zo?'

Calmly Zoe fetched a can from her fridge, pouring herself a large glass of wine at the same time. This would be her first drink for what felt like forever and she wished with all her heart that she was pouring one for Sasha too.

'Oh hell, have you got any smokes, Zo? I've got nothing on me.' Eric channel-hopped, desperately hoping to find an update on the news, looking up hopefully as Zoe's phone rang.

It was Steph Wendover with an update for them. Zoe thanked her and recounted everything to Eric, telling him about Tessa's certainty that Sasha would have headed to a cave along the island's coastline if she'd been unable to make her way back past the cottages. There was no sign of Miles, they were still searching, and the mountain rescue team were on their way to the cave in the hopes that Tessa's theory was proved correct. Yes, she agreed, to Eric's frustrated fuming, it did sound like something out of a famous five adventure story, but didn't someone once say that truth was stranger than fiction? And if anyone could carry it off, Sasha could.

~

Miles quietly slipped along the road, grateful for the fog which shielded him from prying eyes. It had stopped raining and as the outline of the castle appeared to his right, he realised that the fog was thinning and might be gone soon. He increased his speed, passing a pub to his left and thinking what he wouldn't give for a drink right now. It couldn't be much farther he thought, as a crowd of boozed-up guys exited the pub behind him and headed in the same direction as him.

The noise and laughter from the men increased, with two or three of them running around him, one holding a rugby ball. The other two tackled the ball carrier a little further up the road, shouting and generally making a huge scene. This was all he needed he thought, about to discreetly veer to the side of the road in preparation for passing them as unobtrusively as possible.

Someone called out from behind him and it took him a moment to realise that the person was addressing him.

'Excuse me, mate, d'you happen to have a light by any chance?' The speaker was directly alongside him now, a cigarette in his mouth as he passed cigarettes to the men still behind him.

Sighing inwardly, Miles made a show of patting his pockets and was about to hold out his hands apologetically when he realised the group of men were now uncomfortably close and surrounding him. As warning bells rang, he saw their nods and without a chance of escape felt their hands grab hold of him firmly.

'You'll be coming with us, it seems you've been a bit of a bad boy, what with taking girls and hurting them and suchlike. Miles, isn't it?'

The men's iron grip on his arms gave him no recourse but to accompany them back to the pub, and once there, amidst much hooting and applause, he was roughly pushed into the beer cellar where ropes were provided and he found himself secured to a chair. *It was over, he knew that now.*

~

Mary excitedly updated Ann-Marie on the phone and the two women congratulated each other on their planning, they made a good team they agreed. Perhaps Mary would visit tomorrow and they'd celebrate with a drop of the good stuff. She'd stop off at the distillery and pick up a bottle of single malt on her way.

~

With promises to Mary that she'd let her know once Callum and the men were on their way round to the pub to take charge of the prisoner, Ann-Marie turned to Angus, who had woken at the sound of his mistress's laughter, and gave him all the details as he blinked and purred happily.

~

Callum waited anxiously for news from Bruce Currie, having organised the ambulance to come through in readiness. He'd also been on to the air ambulance and it too was on its way so that it would be ready to transport the patient from Brodick to the hospital in Glasgow. He radioed the other guys to check for updates on the manhunt for Miles and was dispirited to hear that no one had located him so far. Frustrated, he paced the ground, relieved that it had stopped raining at last and that the fog had now cleared.

~

Bright lights and the sound of a man's shouts reached her exhausted senses and Sasha groaned, shifting slightly on the cold rocky ground. He couldn't have found her, he couldn't. But wait, unless her ears were playing tricks on her this was more than one man, and they had Scottish accents. So, not Miles. Someone called out loudly as a hand gently touched her face. A soothing voice spoke to her.

'Sasha, you're alright. We've got you. You're safe now. My name's Bruce Currie, I'm with mountain rescue. The men and I are going to look after you now alright? I just need to check you over a little.' Frowning, when he saw the handcuffs around Sasha's wrists, Bruce called for someone to get them off, as well as the cuff on her ankle.

Her outer wet clothing was then carefully removed and they manoeuvred her into a sleeping bag before placing a foil blanket around her. She felt herself being gently lifted onto a stretcher and tried to ask if they'd caught Miles, but she was crying and the slurred words wouldn't come out properly. A bottle of water was held to her mouth and she drank a little, before taking a bite of the energy bar someone handed to her. A hand stroked her forehead as the team moved her from the cave and began their return to Lochranza, the swaying of the stretcher gradually rocking Sasha into exhausted sleep.

~

'That's fantastic news, Bruce, to be sure. Great work by you and the men. The ambulance will be waiting when you get here.' Callum grinned, what an excellent result. Now they just needed to find the man, and where in the hell was he?

Thinking that perhaps everyone could do with some hot tea, he decided to head back along to Lochy's and ask her to get some water on to boil. As he walked, he contacted Detective Inspector Wendover, pleased to be able to give her the good news about Sasha. She thanked him profusely and wished him continued luck in the manhunt.

~

'Sorry.' Eric lunged for Zoe's phone, grabbing it and raising his eyebrows in apology. 'Yes? Steph? Eric here with Zoe. Any news on Sasha? There is? They've found her? Oh, thank God. That's the best news it really is! Is she okay? Has she spoken? Has he hurt her?' He listened to Steph's update, grinning with relief, as Zoe impatiently waited for the full details.

'They've found her, Zo, she's safe, what a relief, and she's alright, a touch of hypothermia, exhaustion and stuff, but she's safe!' His shoulders shook as he allowed himself relief from the tension that had gripped them both for hours. Holding out a hand he clasped Zoe's.

Zoe collapsed in tears, blowing her nose and telling him to get on with it, to tell her everything.

'I'm so glad, oh poor Sasha. Where are they taking her now? And what about him? What about that sick bloody bastard? Please tell me they've got him? Eric?'

But Eric shook his head. 'They haven't found him yet, they're still looking.' Eric studied Zoe's tear-stained face in sympathy. Poor girl, she'd been through a horrendous ordeal and hadn't said one word about it. 'Zo.' He spoke gently. 'You're going to need to talk about what happened to you, you know that right?'

She nodded grimly. 'I'm not ready to do that at the moment. I don't even know what he was doing half the time. I mean, he'd do things, horrible things, and he'd take me to places—' She stopped, shaking her head. 'No, I don't want to know, not right now, not until it's all over and everything's back to normal.' A ring on her doorbell interrupted her and Eric followed her to the door.

~

A TV reporter had been busy following leads since the announcement of Sasha's abduction and having found out everything she could at the hospital where Zoe and Eric had been treated, she'd made her way to Zoe's, planning on heading to Eric's next. Finding them both standing in the doorway of Zoe's flat filled her with delight. Two for the price of one.

Her cameraman began filming as she spoke to them. 'Zoe Pullman? Eric Latimer?' At their confused nods, she continued. 'I'm live right now, here with Sasha Blue's best friend Zoe Pullman, and Sasha's boyfriend Eric Latimer. What can you tell me about Sasha? You must be so relieved that she's been found safe. And Zoe, you were held captive by the same man, that must have been awful for you, tell us about it. Eric, it must have been terrible knowing your girlfriend had been taken by a man you'd believed to be your friend, who we also understand almost killed you? How did that make you feel?'

The questions continued non-stop as Eric answered them as best he could, quite enjoying the attention now that he knew Sasha was safe. Zoe had stepped quietly back out of sight after a question or two, not wanting her horrendous experience to be turned into a freak show with her as the star.

~

Steph Wendover called Tessa, thrilled to have good news to tell her about her sister, and thanked her for her help in guiding them in the right direction.

~

At home now, Tessa slumped onto the couch in relief that her sister was safe. She'd been told about the Graffic account and how it had been used to lure Sasha into hunting for the woman in the photos – who had turned out to be Zoe. Zoe herself had told her much of it, the policewoman filling in the rest. For a fleeting second, she wondered why her daughter, Chantelle, hadn't seen anything about it, before remembering that Chantelle's phone had been taken and broken during her own abduction. They'd bought her a new phone but had kept it from her so far, on Doctor Singh's orders, it being felt that she needed some time away from the news whilst recovering from her terrible ordeal and the loss of her best friend.

Picking up her phone, Tessa wondered how she could access this Graffic account but was saved from the complication when Chantelle came downstairs and asked her what was going on.

Once Tessa had told Chantelle what had been happening, she decided it was time for her to have her new phone, and a delighted Chantelle immediately began setting it up.

A little later they sat together, staring in horror at the photos in which Sasha had been tagged. They looked in disbelief at the pictures of Zoe and were still in shock when Dave, Tessa's husband, arrived home from work. Switching the television on to see if there was any more news they were greeted with Zoe's and Eric's faces as they were interviewed outside Zoe's flat.

~

Leaving the train an hour later at Walthamstow Central, Charles Priestley headed home, stopping to pick up a takeaway on the way. Unlocking his front door, he was met by his wife's exhausted face and the sound of children squealing. He embraced his wife before releasing her and raising his eyebrows.

'You poor thing, Meg, you look terrible, have you taken medicine? And what the hell are the kids screaming about? Go and sit down, I'll dish the food up in a moment, let me just get changed and shut those little rascals up.'

After their meal had been consumed and her husband had cleared everything away, Megan blew her nose for the umpteenth time and leaned back on the couch, sighing. 'Thanks for doing everything, Charles, I feel like a wet rag tonight.'

Charles bent down and kissed his wife. 'That's alright, darling, now, I'm going to make the tea, settle the kids in bed and then we can watch the news.'

'Oh, not the news.' Megan groaned. 'It's so depressing, it's all about some awful man who's been abducting women and torturing them, even killing them, really, Charles, it's too miserable for words, can't we watch something else?'

From the kitchen, Charles forced a smile as he returned with the tea tray. 'Of course, just for a few minutes though, you need an early night.'

'You're so good to me.' Megan smiled lovingly at her husband as he handed her a cup of tea, before watching him head upstairs to make sure the children had brushed their teeth before going to bed.

Finally, he thought, half an hour later, having convinced Megan to get into bed. Relaxing his strained shoulders, he switched to the news and poured himself a large whisky.

He stared intently at the screen, absorbing everything. How had the bitch escaped? Where was Miles? He continued to watch, pouring himself whisky after whisky as his family slept upstairs.

~

Ann-Marie opened her door to Callum's knocking and he charged in full of the good news about Sasha. 'She seems alright as far as Bruce can tell, apart from some mild hypothermia and general exhaustion. They'll be along with her shortly and the ambulance will take her through to Brodick for the air ambulance. Then it's off to the mainland with her, Glasgow I don't doubt, where they'll take good care of her and do a full examination of the poor lass.'

Ann-Marie opened her mouth to speak but Callum ploughed on. 'I'm sorry about earlier, Lochy, but you caught me at a bad time, now you must tell me what's on your mind. And–' he continued, as Ann-Marie opened her mouth again, 'I thought we might get the kettle on, it's a cold night, the men will appreciate a hot cup of tea I reckon.'

'I've got two pots of tea here ready, Callum, milk, sugar, and mugs all set out. You just let them know to come and help themselves. There's some shortbread here as well, they could do with some sustenance. I'm sure. Now, if you're quite finished, there's something I've been wanting to tell you.'

Callum finally slowed down enough to notice his aunt's grinning face. 'What's that then, Lochy? You look like the cat that got the cream and that's a fact.'

'We've got him. We've got your man, Callum. He's over at the pub right now as we speak, tied up in the cellar.'

Callum looked incredulously at his aunt. 'Say that again, Lochy?'

So she did, this time giving him all the details, including the part that Mary had played, as well as her son, Gordon, and his fellow teammates.

Shaking his head from side to side, Callum whistled in admiration. 'You're a one, Lochy, you really are.' He pulled her into a bear hug, holding her tight until she pushed him away, laughing.

'Go on with you. Now, what'll it be? Tea? Or d'you want to get round there and take that man into custody?'

Callum poured himself a mug of tea and called P.C. Wendover with the good news, knowing that there were friends and family of Sasha's waiting anxiously for updates. 'Now, I've not seen it with my own eyes mind, but I'm reliably informed that our man is in custody. If you'll believe this, he was apprehended by a local rugby team and is currently tied up in the cellar of the pub across the loch. The whole operation was orchestrated by two women, one of whom happens to be my aunt. What's that you say? Yes indeed, we've got an amazing bunch of people on this island and that's a fact.' With his call finished, he turned to his aunt.

'Right, I'm off round to the pub now, Lochy. You, Mary, and the lads are local heroes that's what you are.' He radioed his officers, advising them of the latest and instructing them to meet him at the hotel bar.

~

Ann-Marie switched her television back on to see if news of Sasha's rescue had reached the networks yet and was just in time to catch the interview with Zoe and Eric. She watched, smiling, as the man on crutches talked about his girlfriend, Sasha, of how much she meant to him and how he couldn't imagine life without her. He's got it bad, that one, she thought, head over heels to be sure. And what a lovely girl standing beside him, her best friend by all accounts. She smiled to herself, nodding, yes, the lass would be in good hands when she got home to London.

~

She was a feisty one, thought Bruce, as Sasha asked him yet more questions. 'Sasha, you need to rest, you've been through a horrific ordeal. He sighed, giving in. How did we know you were here on Arran? Well, that was all something to do with old Mrs Campbell along at Seal Cottage there. Seems she noticed something amiss about the fellow who took you, I think. I don't know, maybe she took a disliking to his appearance, and then there was the van, the white one, it kind of stood out a bit. And then you were on the news, photos of you both, reckon she tied it all up from there the clever old stick.'

'Thanks.' Sasha's slurring was less pronounced as she struggled to sit up, while Bruce tried to keep her lying down. 'But how did you know to look in the cave?'

'Well, that would be your sister over in England. She said that's where you'd be. Turns out she was right – we'd have checked the cave, of course, but she sent us straight there. Here's the ambulance, I'll need you to get in and not cause us any trouble.' He was grinning, amused by Sasha's indomitable spirit, and pleased that her speech was returning to normal.

Stunned, Sasha remembered hearing Tessa's voice telling her to go to the cave, that she'd be safe there. 'Bruce, can I see her? Mrs Campbell? I'd like to thank her.'

She smiled hopefully at him. 'I promise after that I'll get into the ambulance like a good girl. Please?'

Nodding, Bruce spoke to the paramedics. 'Keep an eye on her, she's not keen on following instructions this one. She wants a word with Ann-Marie along the way, I'll walk ahead. He turned back to Sasha, grinning, 'In the ambulance now, you needn't think we're carrying you along to Ann-Marie when there's a perfectly good ambulance here to take you. They'll stop for you to have a word.'

Ann-Marie smiled down at Sasha, her eyes filled with sympathy. 'I'm just pleased you're alright, love. You're a tough one and that's a fact.'

Sasha squeezed Ann-Marie's hand. 'Thank you, Ann-Marie, without you– without you, I wouldn't–'

'Now, stop those tears.' Ann-Marie patted Sasha's hand. 'It was providential, dear, that's what it was, to be sure. You're alright now. They've got him, the man who took you. Got him trussed up like a turkey round at the pub. We don't take kindly to people like him coming onto our island, abducting girls and the like.'

Trying to climb off the stretcher, Sasha couldn't hide her relief. 'They've got him? I can't believe it! You mean it's all over?' Feeling overjoyed, she brushed the swarms of midges away from her face – even they felt wonderful – but hands gently pushed her back down onto the stretcher.

'It's all over.' Ann-Marie nodded. 'Now you let them get you off to the hospital. And I want you to bring that handsome boyfriend of yours back here for a holiday soon, you hear me? And make sure you come and visit me.'

Sasha sat up. 'My boyfriend? Who–?'

'Why, the nice young man on the news, standing there on his crutches, Eric isn't it? And your best friend Zoe? Worried sick they've been. Between them, you'll be in the best hands and that's a fact. Go on with you now.' Ann-

Marie leaned over and kissed Sasha's cheek before turning and heading back inside her cottage.

Sasha fell back onto the stretcher dumbfounded. What had Eric been saying? And on TV as well? The ambulance doors were slammed closed and she felt the vehicle begin to move. For a moment anxiety took over as memories of being held in Miles's van came into her head, but she shook them away. It was over. Her thoughts returned to Eric and suddenly she could think of nothing nicer than being held in his strong arms. And Zoe, her dearest friend, she so badly wanted to see her. The sedative administered by the paramedic began to take effect and she drifted off with Eric's and Zoe's faces in her mind.

~

This time it was Zoe who lunged for the phone and from her delighted shrieks, Eric guessed immediately that Miles was in custody. When she'd thanked Detective Inspector Wendover, she told Eric how Miles had been captured by a bunch of islanders and the two of them laughed gleefully at the image of him tied up in a pub.

'We could do with a photo of him like that going viral on Graffic, talk about payback–' Eric spoke without thinking, stopping at Zoe's questioning look as he realised that she was probably still unaware of the photos Miles had taken of her. 'I just mean that he deserves to be publicly shamed for what he's done,' he ad-libbed quickly.

Zoe's expression darkened. 'Too right, but nothing will ever be enough payback for what he did to me and Sash and so many others.' She started. 'Oh, Tessa will be waiting for news, I'll call her quickly.'

~

Tessa turned to Chantelle and Dave, smiling. 'They've caught him. It's over. Now we wait for news on Sasha once she gets to the hospital.' About to put the kettle on, she thought of Mrs Pringle who'd first alerted her to Sasha's plight. The woman was a notorious busybody but she had a kind heart and she'd be anxiously waiting for news. She'd give her a quick call.

Dolly Pringle pounced on her phone, hoping it was good news and was relieved to hear Tessa's happy voice telling her that Sasha was safe and her abductor had been caught. 'Oh, I'm so pleased, what a relief. Now dear, tell me everything, start from the beginning, that's right.' Picking up her pen and notepad she made notes as Tessa talked, murmuring accordingly as the story unfolded.

Tomorrow was going to be a wonderful day. She could hardly wait to tell Sheila when they opened up in the morning. And word would spread and people would find excuses to visit – oh yes, it was going to be very pleasant indeed. She'd better make sure they had a good supply of teabags and custard creams in.

Tessa came off the phone grinning. 'No prizes for guessing what the topic of conversation is going to be at Pringle's Chemist tomorrow. Now, I should put the kettle on, we could do with a cup of tea after all this excitement.' She put her hand to her mouth. 'Good grief, I'm beginning to sound like the woman. Stop me, quickly!'

Dave laughed. 'Forget the tea, I'll open a bottle of wine, we should celebrate.'

~

The noise in the bar was huge as Callum and his men walked in. Amidst the cheering, he tried to make himself heard by holding his arm up in the air. 'It's been an amazing effort by everyone today and I want to thank you all. Mary, you've been a star, you and Lochy are a force to be reckoned with and that's a fact. And Gordon, you and the guys should be proud of yourselves, you apprehended a dangerous criminal. Great work to be sure.' More cheers went up as beer glasses were held aloft. 'Our lass, Sasha Blue, has been found, Bruce Currie and the guys have brought her back from Ossian's Cave and she'll be going off with the ambulance now around to Brodick, then off with the air ambulance to the mainland. Now, let me see this bastard you've got tied up in your cellar, Neill.'

The barman nodded, grinning, and led Callum through to the cellar and a fuming Miles.

'We'll be reading you your rights now and taking you into police custody. You came to the wrong island, we've no time for your type here. We've found the woman you abducted and I'm pleased to tell you she'll be just fine. With everything you've done, you'll be going away for a long time and if I had my way you'd never get out. Roy?' He nodded at his officer and Roy MacGill stepped forward to do the honours.

It was time for a drink, Callum decided, he was officially off duty now. 'I'll take a double, Neill, and the same for our Mary here.'

She'd end up drunk at this rate, Mary thought, nonetheless accepting the glass of whisky with a smile and a nod of thanks.

~

'You'll drink me out of tea, lads, if you carry on like this, and that's a fact.' Ann-Marie was laughing with the men as Callum walked back into her cottage, a bottle of whisky in each hand. Cheers went up and she grinned, exchanging the mugs for glasses.

A while later and the somewhat out of tune lyrics from the Irish ballad, 'whiskey in the jar', could be heard clearly across the other side of the loch as glasses were refilled and everyone, including Ann-Marie, did their very best to ensure a hangover for the following morning.

The only occupant of the cottage not partaking was Angus, having taken himself upstairs to curl up on his mistress's bed and await her arrival when she regained her senses.

~

'Charles! What on earth are you doing?'

Megan's shocked voice reached him as if from a distance and it took him a moment to focus. He turned his head to find his wife standing in the doorway of the lounge in her dressing gown. Following her gaze, he looked down at his hands as they held the remains of one of his daughter's dolls.

'Megan, I– what are you doing out of bed?' He dropped the doll to the floor and tried to focus through his whisky haze.

'What am I doing? I came down to find some aspirin. What are you doing? What have you done to Lucy's doll?' Picking up the pieces, Megan looked at him, a strange expression on her face. 'Charles, are you drunk? This is her favourite doll, oh, you've pulled its arm right off – and torn its dress – and what's happened to its foot? Is it–? You didn't–? Did you bite it, Charles?' Megan was aghast.

But Charles couldn't tear his eyes from the television, even though he knew he should.

Distracted, his wife looked at the screen. 'Oh good, they've caught him. I hope he suffers after what he's done. And they've found the woman he took, oh, I'm so relieved, the poor thing, I can't imagine what she must have gone through. Charles, are you going to say anything? Oh, forget it, I'm going back to bed, but you'd better buy Lucy a new doll to make up for this. Really, I don't know what's got into you.'

Charles Priestly held it together until his wife climbed the stairs and he heard their bedroom door close, before giving in to his emotions. Picking up a cushion he pressed it against his mouth as he wept, great shuddering sobs racking his body and threatening to escape as howls of despair.

His best friend – and mentor – had been caught. It was all over and he couldn't bear it.

THE MORNING AFTER

There were quite a few sore heads the following morning, Eric's and Zoe's among them. Eric sat up, groaning, from where he'd passed out on Zoe's couch. He'd have to head to his flat this morning having yet to return since he'd left the hospital. But first, he thought hopefully, maybe Zoe could be convinced to cook up some eggs and bacon.

~

Dave Watson in Parva Crossing, although feeling the effects of the previous night's drinking (one bottle of wine having turned into two or more), was up early and had a pot of tea ready for his girls. He'd made some phone calls and excitedly called them from their beds. 'Come on, girls, we're going on a road trip!'

~

Angus eyed Ann-Marie disapprovingly from his perch on her bedroom windowsill.

'Alright, alright, my boy, your mam's getting up now. Yes, I know it's a little late and you want your breakfast. Just let me take it slowly this morning, I've a sore head and that's a fact.'

Purring, he forgave her tardiness, jumping down and entwining himself around her legs as she stood up, before leading her determinedly down to the kitchen and jumping up onto the kitchen counter.

~

Mary Kennedy also woke up with a headache – it had turned into quite a party down at the bar last night after all the excitement. Nursing a strong cup of tea, she phoned her friend. 'Lochy, and how are you this morning after all the fuss? Me too, we're a pair are we not?' The two women giggled like schoolgirls as they chatted, feeling the years slip away as they ran through the events of the night before. 'Breakfast you say? Well, that would be grand, I'm sure. I'll bring some eggs with me, freshly laid.'

~

Sasha had been awake for hours, impatient to get the day started and to get back home. There wasn't really anything wrong with her, she felt fine. Smiling, she greeted the nurse and was told that breakfast would arrive shortly. Shocked, she realised that she had no idea which hospital she was in. Where was she?

'You're in Glasgow, sweetie,' the nurse informed her as she bustled out and a tray was brought in.

Glasgow? How the hell was she going to get home from here? She looked at her breakfast miserably. Yoghurt, bland-looking cereal, and a banana.

~

Tessa, Dave, and Chantelle tucked into their full English breakfasts at the service station feeling like they were on holiday. They had a few hours of driving ahead of them still, but they'd be with Sasha by the afternoon.

~

'Thanks, Zo, that was delicious.' Eric mopped up the last of his egg with some bread and took a swig of tea as they watched the news about the events on Arran detailing Sasha's rescue and Miles's capture. 'It's done the trick, my head feels better already. How about you? I'll need to get back to my flat this morning, although I've no idea what kind of mess it's in. I remember things getting smashed during the struggle with Miles, that's all.'

'I'll come with you. I feel fine after that breakfast, best remedy for a hangover if you ask me. I can help you tidy up, you'll never manage on those crutches on your own, Eric. But first, we need to find out where Sash is, and what we're going to do about getting her home.'

That issue was rapidly resolved by Tessa's phone call to Zoe a few minutes later, informing her that they were on their way to Glasgow to be with Sasha and would bring her back to London.

~

The delicious smell of bacon reached Mary's nostrils as she entered Ann-Marie's and her stomach rumbled. The two women hugged and while Ann-Marie expertly turned the tattie scones on the hot griddle, Mary cracked eggs into the frying pan.

'You can throw a couple more of those in the pan, Mary.' A male voice boomed out as the front door slammed. 'Morning, Lochy.' Callum leaned down and gave his aunt a peck on the cheek. 'Sounds like you two misbehaved yourselves a bit last night by all accounts.' He grinned. 'If you give me breakfast, I'll not arrest you.'

'You cheeky lad.' Ann-Marie tsked happily, laying out another setting at the kitchen table.

Once the three were seated and tucking into their breakfast, Callum teased the women. 'So, Mary, what's this I hear about you leading a singsong in the bar last night then?'

Mary giggled. 'Well, we did have a bit of a shindig after you left, you know. And don't forget it was you who got me started on the double whiskies.'

Ann-Marie opened her mouth to laughingly tick her friend off but was stopped by her nephew.

'And you can watch it, Lochy, the lads tell me the party carried on a bit after I left you last night. Good thing you don't have any neighbours to complain about the racket you were all making.' He leaned back, smiling. 'But it's all good, and well deserved I'd say. Our prisoner is being transferred to the mainland today to face his fate. And Sasha is in Glasgow and none the worse for her ordeal. I'd say we all did our island proud.'

~

Finally, the doctor appeared and Sasha's first question was when could she leave.

'Well, they warned me about you, said you hadn't stopped asking questions since you got here, seems they were right.' He smiled. 'Everything's looking good on your charts, Sasha, you've bounced back incredibly quickly for someone who was admitted with mild hypothermia. The wound on your thigh is healing nicely and will only leave a tiny scar. I'll be happy for you to leave but we'll need to arrange to get you back to London. There's also the issue of clothing – you don't actually have any at the moment, apart from the few items that arrived with you, I'm afraid. But all this can be sorted out, I'm sure. Just take it easy today while we organise things.'

Dammit, thought Sasha, after the doctor had left, I don't have a phone. Hell, I can't even remember anyone's phone number. I'm stranded in Glasgow with no clothes and no phone. There was a funny side to this, she acknowledged, she just wasn't feeling it yet.

~

Miles spat his breakfast out. Cold porridge, they'd done this deliberately. He was freezing cold and the thin blanket he'd been given offered no comfort. Pushing the porridge bowl away he huddled on his bed, knowing that complaining would get him nowhere, he'd get no sympathy from anyone.

He didn't care, not really, the only thing that he cared about was the fact that she'd got away, that she'd ruined his plans and taken away from him his planned moment of pure pleasure as he found that absolute bliss whilst watching the life fade from her eyes. Where was she now? Being fussed over and cosseted somewhere no doubt, the centre of attention and lapping it up like the little show-off that she was. He smashed his fist into the thin mattress. It wasn't over. They couldn't lock him up forever. And when he got out, he'd hunt her down and finish what he'd started. This time he wouldn't make any mistakes. He was still grinning when the officers took him from his holding cell and signed him over for transfer to the mainland.

~

Zoe left Eric with promises to pop back with some shopping for him a bit later. She'd cleaned up his flat as best she could, changed his bed, and removed the dried, blood-caked cloths from the utility room where the paramedics had dropped them. Although she'd mopped the floor it was still stained, but that was too bad, Eric could live with it, she was sure.

A feeling of tiredness washed over her. Three friends, three flats left deserted suddenly as each of them had fallen prey to Miles's psychotic behaviour. Well, her own flat could wait, she'd dealt with the basics there. For now, her main concern was to get over to Sasha's flat and to make sure it was ready for her return.

Standing at the door to Sasha's flat a little later, she tried her spare key in the lock again to no avail. Sasha must have changed the lock. She wondered why.

~

She was so bored. She'd watched enough daytime television to last her a lifetime, eaten her lunch of chicken salad like a good girl, and even had a nap. Time for another walk around the hospital corridors in her lovely nightgown. She wanted out of here. She wanted pizza and she wanted wine, lots of it. And hell, she wanted a smoke. And she'd get none of these while she was stuck in here, she thought miserably. It was as she was returning to her room, pausing to gaze out of the windows into the parking area below, that she heard voices. And not just any old voices, these were familiar, they sounded like–

'Sash!' Tess's voice yelled out in happiness as she ran to her sister, hugging her, and being rapidly joined by both Dave and Chantelle.

Much chat ensued, tears, laughter, and more hugs until they calmed down and got down to practicalities.

'I've brought you some of my clothes, at least we're about the same size.' Tessa took the bag from Dave and placed it on the bed. 'There are toiletries in there, everything you need. So hurry up and get changed and let's get out of here!'

'What?' Sasha looked at her sister in surprise. 'Get out? What now? And go where? Does the doctor know? Oh wow, you guys, I can't believe this, you've saved my life!'

'Well technically that was a bunch of people on the Isle of Arran according to the news, but anyway, just get dressed, and yes, the doctor does know, let's go.' Tessa was laughing, relieved to be with her sister and thrilled to have surprised her. She turned to Dave and hugged him. 'Thanks, darling, this was the best idea you could ever have had.'

They bundled into the car and Dave drove them along to the hotel they would spend the night at. 'Meet you girls in the bar once you've been to your room?'

Sasha and Chantelle nodded and dropped their stuff off while Chantelle took photos of everything, posting onto her Graffic account excitedly.

'Chants, you know to be careful on that, right?' Sasha watched her niece worriedly, wondering how much she should tell her about what had happened in the recent weeks.

'Don't worry, Sash, I've seen the photos, I know the sort of stuff that can happen and I know to be careful.'

Pulling her in for a hug, Sasha thought about Chantelle's recent experience and how close she'd come to not seeing her again. Now was not the time to tell her about Molly. 'Let's get down to the bar, your aunt needs a giant glass of wine!'

'So, who's going to tell Sasha why we chose this hotel?' Dave was grinning, his arm around his wife as he emptied his beer glass. 'And it's all thanks to my daughter's expert research by the way.'

'Um, because it's got a bar?' Sasha winked at Chantelle. 'No, I've no idea, but I love it anyway. Come on, Chants, spill.'

Looking pleased with herself Chantelle spilled. 'They do a build your own pizza in the restaurant.'

'No! That's my girl, that's why I love you.' Squeezing her niece's shoulders, Sasha finished her glass of wine. 'Oops, I think I need a refill.'

'Well, I think I deserve some praise too, I bought you these.' Tessa dropped the packet of cigarettes on the table, grinning. 'Not that you should smoke, sis, but I reckon you deserve it right now.'

'I think I've died and gone to heaven, you guys. Thanks, Tess, you're a star, you don't mind if I–?' She waved the packet, giving Dave a wink, who looked at Tess with a shrug.

'Well, I think Sash could probably do with the company...' Dave ducked as Tess pretended to whack him.

'Go on you two, go and have your smoke, I'll get some more drinks in. Chants will give me a hand.'

Sitting in the restaurant later, Sasha leaned back happily. 'I honestly can't thank you guys enough. This was so what I needed, a fabulous pizza, plenty of wine, and being with you all. You're the best family a girl could ask for.'

'Talking of family,' Tess began. 'What's all this about Eric being your boyfriend? We saw him and Zoe on the news. I thought that was all over. Anything you need to tell us?'

Sasha felt herself blushing. 'Well, honestly? I don't know what made him say that. It's all been rather complicated lately, it was his friend that I was with, and well, we all know how that turned out. I've always said I had bad luck with men, but to be in a relationship with a guy who abducts you and wants to kill you is a bit steep, even for me. I think that even trumps being with a guy who turns out to have a pregnant wife. And let's not forget that it was Eric who actually forgot he was out on a date with me once and went home alone, leaving me in the pub.' She rolled her eyes as she continued.

'But Eric tried to help me, he realised that something was wrong I think, but Miles manipulated everything so I never gave Eric the time of day. And it was Eric that I turned to for help when I was trying to rescue Zoe. I knew that Miles was on his way to the house where he'd been keeping her, and I'd got into the basement and found a–' She stopped herself just in time, noticing Chantelle's face losing colour. There was no way she could talk about finding a dead woman in the basement after Chantelle had lost her best friend under similar circumstances. 'No, it doesn't matter, the main thing is that Eric really came through for me. Maybe he's more reliable than I gave him credit for.'

'Well, he was so sweet on the TV, maybe you should give him another chance, he's obviously besotted with you. And I'm not saying you need a man, but you could do with some fun and having someone to take care of you after everything.' Tessa yawned and looked at her watch. 'I think I'm ready for bed. And Chants, you ought to be getting to bed too.'

'I'm not a baby, Mum.' Chantelle laughed. 'And anyway, me and Sasha are going to stay up all night talking.'

'Whoah, I'm getting a bit old for that, Chants, but maybe just for a while. Come on then, let's go and see who's getting which bed.'

A GIRL'S BEST FRIENDS

They arrived at Sasha's flat in the late afternoon of the following day and Sasha shuddered, trying to shake off the memories of Miles. A note had been pushed through the letterbox from Zoe, telling her she'd tried to get into Sasha's flat to prepare it for her but her key hadn't worked. That was something she was going to have to explain to Zoe, if she didn't know by now about the photos Miles had taken and posted of her.

While Tessa and Chantelle bustled around changing Sasha's bed and preparing the bed settee in her office, Dave went out for groceries and Sasha took the opportunity to call Zoe from her home phone. She'd have to get a new mobile tomorrow, the second one in only a few short weeks she thought unhappily, wondering what state her bank account was in.

The two friends chatted excitedly, assuring each other that they were fine, and Sasha asked Zoe if she wanted to come round. Zoe's tentative mention of Eric was met with casual enthusiasm from Sasha who said why not call him and invite him too. So Zoe did, and they arrived in a taxi together a while later.

With so much hugging, kissing, and talking going on, it was chaotic, and Eric took the opportunity to pull Sasha aside. 'Sash, I've so much to thank you for I don't know where to begin. If you hadn't come round to my flat to check on me, well, I might not be standing here now, albeit on two crutches.' He hugged her tightly and she allowed herself to sink into his chest, breathing in his familiar scent.

'Eric, honestly, it's the other way round. You came straight to the party, you got the police onto the house where he'd held Zoe, you helped them to find me, between you, Zoe, and Tess, and the most wonderful woman and a bunch of other people on Arran, I owe so much to so many of you that I don't think I can ever repay it.'

'I can think of a way,' he murmured into her hair. 'Come out with me for dinner this week. Give me another chance, Sash, I've changed, I promise. No more bad behaviour from me. Hell, I don't even get drunk anymore.'

'That's a lie!' Zoe appeared, wrapping her arms around them both, laughing. 'He got drunk the night before last, Sash, but we have to let him off, I overdid it too. We were so relieved to know that you were safe.'

'Food's here!' Chantelle yelled as she and Dave carried the takeaway bags into the kitchen.

Much later, filled to the brim with curry from Sasha's local tandoori restaurant, the group sat around her table finishing off their fourth bottle of wine. It had turned into a wonderful night of family and friendship, love and laughter, and Sasha felt she had to pinch herself for being so lucky.

'So, what happens next, guys? Sadly, we have to head home tomorrow, but what do you have lined up?' Tessa spoke as she tidied the plates into a pile.

'Oh hell, I have to see if I have any clients, I need to earn some money.' Sasha groaned.

'Well, I'm pretty stuck for a while.' Eric ruefully indicated his crutches.

'I'll tell you what's going to happen.' Zoe looked around the table with an enormous grin. 'Sash, Eric, we're going to take a holiday in a few months, when we've all recovered. I've already looked into it. We're going to a Greek island for a week!'

'What?' Sasha looked at Zoe incredulously.

'Yep.' Zoe was pleased with herself. 'But not the awful old taverna on Corfu that Sasha and I stayed in when we were younger, the one where we never got any breakfast and had to buy our own loo rolls. And the one that played a crucial role in probably saving my life.' She stopped at this point, as quizzical faces stared at her, while she and Sasha explained how Zoe had managed to cryptically convey a message to Sasha while she was held captive by Miles.

'That's amazeballs.' Chantelle was in awe. 'And Sash, you knew that Zoe was lying about the taverna but Miles didn't? And that's when you knew she wasn't off on holiday? But what if you hadn't remembered it right?'

'I was never going to forget how terrible it was, Chants. We laughed so much about it at the time, and have often enjoyed a good laugh about it since. It was run by this mad old woman who just cackled all the time when we asked for breakfast or loo rolls, or for our room to be cleaned. It was our worst experience ever, but also the one that's given us the most laughs ever since. But Miles had no idea, so he thought I believed Zoe. Of course, I didn't know that Miles was the one who'd taken her, not then, not for a long time, but I was certain then that she was the girl in the photos–' She stopped talking as Zoe looked at her strangely.

'The girl in the photos? Is that what he did? I haven't–' Suddenly she stood up and walked over to Sasha's couch, sitting down and feeling the cushions on either side of her. 'He brought me here,' she whispered. 'He brought me here and took photos, that's why you changed your lock.' She looked at Sasha with wild eyes. 'How many pictures did he take of me?' She covered her face with her hands, her voice muffled as she groaned. 'Not now.' She stood up, resolutely. 'I just want to block it all from my memory at the moment. Nothing's going to spoil this night. Let's open another bottle of wine.'

Cheers met Zoe's suggestion, and Dave grabbed another bottle as everyone quickly glanced at each other. There would be no more talk of Miles this evening. A lot of talking would be required and a lot of healing would be needed, but all in good time. Tonight was special and nothing else would be allowed to spoil it.

Eric slipped his hand under the table and found Sasha's, winking at her as she looked at him with a smile.

Warmth filled her and she clasped his hand tightly. Maybe they would try again...

MALUS PASSUUM

December – one month later

They'd all received the same message from Detective Inspector Wendover asking them to meet her for an update, and the three of them travelled to her office together.

'Sasha, Zoe, Eric, thanks for coming and it's nice to see you all looking so well. I thought you'd like to know the latest regarding Blake Selim, or Miles Bleak as you knew him.' At their expectant nods, she continued.

'I'll keep it fairly brief and just run through the points one by one. First of all, Blake was taken into foster care at a young age and repeatedly had difficulties settling in. He bounced between adoption homes and families and was with his third foster family and living in Liverpool when he abducted his first victim, nineteen-year-old Sharon Contell. She was kept locked up by him for two weeks, in a derelict building, and abused repeatedly. He moved on, repeating the pattern until he'd held captive, abused, tortured, and repeatedly raped, eight women in total. One of these died as a result of his torture. In all cases, he took photographs of the women during their captivity.

His particular fetish was to dress his victims up, specifically in suggestive clothing such as short dresses or skirts, high heels, etc. In fact, Sasha, it seems that his inability to be able to purchase such clothing on Arran may have helped save your life, strange as that sounds. He complained about that a lot during his interviews saying that if he hadn't wasted time trying to shop for the clothing that he'd needed for his special time with you, to make everything perfect, to quote his words, then he would have got back to the cottage much quicker and you'd not have had the chance to escape him.'

Chills ran through Sasha at Steph Wendover's words and Zoe gasped, before speaking haltingly. 'He dressed me up, it made my skin crawl, especially as I'd dressed up for him in the past when we were a couple. But he never, he never–'

Nodding, Steph helped Zoe out. 'He never raped you, Zoe, thankfully, nor you, Sasha. The psychiatrist thinks it's tied up with the fact that he'd previously had relationships with you both and that somehow this resulted in impotence when he took you each captive. It's something to be grateful for at last.

Anyway, to continue – he was caught and served twelve years as a minor, before being released under supervision for a further eight years. At this stage, he moved to London as Miles Bleak and began to lead, to all intents and purposes, a normal life.

He abducted Sally Birchmont, aged thirty-four, whilst in a relationship with Zoe, and kept her at the property in Nun's Lane. We estimate that he held her for about four weeks, subjecting her to torture before he killed her. Sasha found her body in the basement of the property when she was searching for Zoe. We found photos of Sally on another phone which was in his possession when he was apprehended. We believe that she was killed before Zoe was brought to the property.'

The shock on their faces, and the collective gasps, caused Steph to pause and give them time to assimilate the information. Once satisfied that they were ready, she continued.

'Zoe, I'm afraid that you became his tenth victim when he abducted you and held you captive. The young girl, Molly Townsend, then became his eleventh victim when she was killed, as you know, in a traffic accident in Leicester Square. We do believe that she was pushed into the path of an oncoming vehicle by Miles. Eric, you were his only male victim, to our knowledge, and number twelve. He believed he'd killed you and expressed a huge amount of anger when confronted with the knowledge that you were alive and well. His thirteenth victim was Maureen Jarvis, Sasha's elderly neighbour. She lived across the street from Sasha's flat and had seen Miles with Sasha on more than one occasion. We suspect that he was planning his imminent abduction of Sasha and making sure that no one would be witness to it. We don't think he intended either Eric or Zoe to be alive and witnesses to his involvement, so he could come across as the bereft boyfriend eventually when he'd accomplished his goal. And that goal was you, Sasha, his fourteenth and last victim.'

Stunned at the sheer number, the three of them sat in silence, shaking their heads. Finally, Sasha spoke.

'That night, before he went to Birmingham, he kept checking outside on the balcony and asking me all about the other people in my building. That's what he was doing, working out when to take me with no one seeing. He went out in the middle of the night and murdered poor Maureen Jarvis, that sweet old lady, and then got back into bed with me – that's why he was so cold. I hope the sick bastard's going away for life for what he's done.'

'Oh, he will, don't you worry.' Steph Wendover smiled grimly. 'We've got more than enough evidence to put him away for good, plus he's confessed to everything. He's so angry about his plans being thwarted that he complains constantly, raging about the unfairness of it all. The more he rants and raves, the more he gives us.'

'Why did he do it? Does anyone know?' Zoe spoke quietly.

'Well, he's been psych evaluated and has given us some information pertaining to that, plus we've been able to get hold of records from his childhood due to the extenuating circumstances. Usually, these would have been sealed, of course. His mother raised him on her own and apparently didn't know who his father was. She worked nights at a bar and would leave Miles alone at home, but we suspect she also worked as a casual prostitute too, possibly bringing her clients to her home. From some of the things Miles has said, it seems he may have secretly watched her with her clients – which would account for his need to dress his victims in clothing possibly similar to that which his mother wore for those occasions. If we build in the likeliness that some of her clients would have engaged in bondage with her, or were violent in some way, well, then it may explain his own warped and violent behaviour. Explain, not excuse, of course.

His mother had another child – a girl – when he was four years old and he was jealous, the usual story. She was sleeping and woke to hear her baby crying. She found her baby tied up with her stockings and Miles poking it with a knife. Superficial wounds but enough to draw blood. He was spreading the blood over its body with his hands. I suppose, if we want to be technically correct, his baby sister was actually his first victim, poor little thing.'

Sasha shuddered, thinking about the little girl, and her own knife wound on her thigh and how he'd rubbed the blood over her.

Steph continued. 'His mother didn't want him anywhere near her child and social services became involved, resulting in him entering the care system, where we received the same story from each foster family when we interviewed them. All the dolls in the house would disappear. They would eventually find them dressed up in odd items of doll's clothing but torn and damaged, the dolls dismembered, daubed with red lipstick to replicate blood, and sometimes tied with various kinds of twine. It caused a lot of upset as you can imagine and there were hints that some of the young girls may have had unpleasant experiences at his hand, although nothing was ever reported so there's no real proof about that. No family was happy having such a disturbed child with them, hence his repeated returns to the orphanage. Oh, and he had a camera that someone had given him. One of those instant cameras? They found photographs of the damaged dolls hidden at each home. Of course, none of it necessarily explains his psychopathic behaviour, many people subjected to childhood abuse, whatever its form, grow up to lead perfectly normal lives, but some people like him could just be born that way I guess.'

Steph Wendover looked sympathetically at the three. 'It's a lot to take in and all terribly shocking, I know, notwithstanding, of course, your own personal experiences at his hands. I'm hoping that none of you will be required as physical witnesses due to the large amount of incriminating evidence and witness statements, together with his full confession. So that's it, I hope it helps in some way in putting this all to rest for you all. And if there's anything else that you need at any time, please give me a call, okay?'

Remembering something, Sasha wondered if Steph knew by any chance. 'His account on Graffic – his name – what did it mean, do you know?'

Steph rifled through her papers. 'Hold on, it's here somewhere, I'm sure. I think the psychiatrist made a note. Yes, here it is. Malus Passuum – roughly translated to mean Bad Miles. From the Latin apparently. I guess he was trying to be clever.' she shrugged.

'It was right there,' Sasha breathed. 'He told me from the start. I never even tried to find out what it meant. That must have been part of the thrill of the game for him, wondering if and when I'd work it out. But I never did. Well, he got something right, he is bad.'

'He's not just bad, he's downright bloody sick, twisted and evil, and what's the Latin for that I'd like to know,'

Eric exclaimed angrily, before summing up everyone's feelings by announcing that he planned to get extremely drunk. He followed this up rapidly with an apologetic look at Sasha, who grinned and said that under the circumstances she'd let him off as she and Zoe would be joining him. Detective Inspector Wendover laughingly declined her invitation to join them, thanking them nonetheless, as she regrettably had work to do, it being a busy time of year for crime. After much hugging and thanks and everyone's wishes for a good Christmas having been expressed, the trio left and headed for the nearest pub.

~

Frank and Irene Weatherall gratefully accepted the cups of tea from their son, Scott, and looked around at their almost empty living room.

'Fifty years, old girl, not bad going, eh? If these walls could talk, I bet they'd have some stories to tell.' Frank squeezed his wife's hand as their minds filled with memories of the many children who had come and gone through the doors of their foster home over the years.

'Mum?' Scott appeared, carrying a stack of old photo albums. 'What shall I do with all these?'

'Now where on earth did you find all those? They must have been up in the attic. Leave them here for me, will you, love? I'll just have a look through them. I don't suppose we can–?'

But Scott shook his head. 'You can't keep everything, Mum, you know that – you just won't have the space.' His expression softened at his mother's sad face. 'I tell you what, have a look through and put aside any photos you really want to keep and I'll get Beth to make you up one album to take with you, how's that?'

'That's the ticket, son.' Frank smiled gratefully at Scott. 'Come on, girl, let's take a look at all our children, bet this'll bring back some memories, we must have photos of every single one of them in these books, going right back to our first foster. Now, let's see how many of these you can remember. Who was this little chap? Let's see now, that would have been...'

Scott tiptoed quietly away, pleased to hear his mum identifying the children by name. Leaving his parents to their trip down memory lane he went in search of his wife to see how she was getting on with packing up the bedrooms.

'How's it going?' Beth appeared with a pile of linen which she dropped into a packing case. 'Any problems with your mum?' She looked at him sympathetically.

'She's having quite a good day today, I left them going through the old photo albums, sounds like she can remember the names of most of the children. Funny that – she can remember details from all those years ago but can't remember what she had for breakfast and keeps forgetting where they're moving to. I've had to tell her three times today. Oh, I told her you'd make up one album for her of the photos she wants to keep. Sorry.' Scott raised his eyebrows apologetically.

'That's okay, it must be hard for them, and everything will be so strange at the retirement home, they'll need some familiarity around them, something to give them an anchor to their past when they need it.'

Scott swooped his wife into a hug, pressing his mouth into her hair. 'You're a wise woman, Beth Weatherall, and kind with it.'

~

Later that night, Irene tossed and turned in bed, the bed covers twisting around her legs as thoughts rushed in and out of her head. What was that? Had she just heard one of the children cry out? Climbing out of bed she pulled her gown on and padded along the landing, checking in each of the bedrooms. Where were all the children? Confused, she headed down the stairs, looking in the kitchen before moving to the lounge, her eyes lighting on the photo albums and she sat down, opening the top one and turning the pages.

There was little Blake, he'd been a troubled one, that one, poor little thing. She shook her head sadly, it hadn't been often that they'd had to relinquish their care of a child, but little Blake had caused so much disruption. And there he was with his friend – joined at the hip those two had been. Now, what was his name? He'd followed Blake everywhere, hero-worshipped him really, copying everything that he did. Her hand stilled, about to turn the page. Charles. That was it, Charles Priestley – a sweet little boy with the most angelic smile – but she'd had concerns about him. Copying everything that he did – the phrase repeated itself in her head. She'd known that he'd been involved with Blake in the whole issue over the dolls – the dismembering and stabbing and suchlike – but she'd kept it to herself. He'd been such a sweet boy and she'd felt that with Blake gone he would be alright – it had been Blake who had the darkness inside, not dear Charles. Of course, there'd been a couple of minor incidents which she was sure he'd been responsible for, after Blake left them, but no harm had been done, not really. No, Charles had thrived under her and Frank's care and had surely grown to become a wonderful young man.

Thinking of him as an adult brought Irene back to the present and in a clear-headed moment, she remembered the policewoman coming to talk to her about Blake. Should she have mentioned Charles? Yes, she thought, chastened, she should have.

Moving to the dining table and Beth's 'administration centre for their move', as she called it, Irene picked up a pen and began to write on a sheet of paper from a notepad. When she was finished, she enclosed the photo of Blake and Charles and sealed everything in one of the envelopes sitting beside the notepad. She hesitated – who should she address it to? What had the police officer's name been? It had been a pretty name, a bit like a flower. Stephanie – the name came to her suddenly – Stephanie something – something like Wednesday. Was that it? Or was it Wentworth? That sounded right, she nodded to herself. But where did she work? Somewhere in London surely?

Addressing the envelope to Police Officer Stephanie Wentworth, London office, Irene placed the envelope into her handbag beside the couch. She'd post it when she took the children to school.

'Irene?' Beth placed her hand on her mother-in-law's shoulder in concern. 'I saw the light on. What are you doing down here? Are you alright?'

Glancing down in puzzlement at her bare feet, Irene looked up at Beth, confusion crossing her face. 'The children – I have to wake the children for school, I–'

'That's alright, come on now, I'll do that for you today, let's get you back to bed shall we?' Beth guided her mother-in-law towards the stairs as Scott appeared, his hair tousled from sleep. His eyes met Beth's in sadness as he took his mum's hand and led her up the stairs.

GRAFFIC LIVES AND GRAPHIC LIES

February

The few funeral guests sipped their tea and politely ate a sandwich as they expressed their condolences to Scott and Beth Weatherall, before quietly departing.

'Two months,' said Scott, sadly. 'I can't believe it, first Dad, then Mum two weeks later.'

His wife squeezed his arm. 'They really loved each other, my darling, and they're together now. At least we had one last Christmas with them. They had a good life and did so much good.' She sighed, 'We'd better clear their last few personal bits from their room.'

Picking up Irene Weatherall's handbag, Beth had a brief look inside, removing the worn purse, a tube of peppermints and a comb and shook it over the waste bin to remove the bits of fluff and old paperclips residing in the bottom. She then placed it into the box for charity, together with some boxes of unopened handkerchiefs, a virtually full bottle of Irene's scent, some of her pretty neck scarves and Frank's brand-new slippers they'd bought him and which he'd never worn. With a last look around the room, Beth and Scott left.

~

March

Sheila Johnson examined the bag, turning it this way and that. It wasn't often that you found a good quality second-hand leather handbag these days. This one was nice and strong, well-made, with lots of useful pockets inside – and black was so versatile, it would go with just about anything. Approaching the lady at the counter she placed it down while she counted out the four pounds in coins, handing them over and leaving the charity shop with her purchase.

Once home, Sheila spread some newspaper on the kitchen table, sat the bag on the paper, and gave it a good wipe-over with disinfecting wipes, making sure to clean inside its many pockets. Well, there was a surprise – another pocket, flat against the bag's lining – she'd almost missed it. Slipping her hand in to wipe it out her fingers touched against paper and she withdrew an envelope.

Popping her reading glasses on she read the spidery writing addressing it to Police Officer Stephanie Wentworth, London office. Well, this wouldn't do, it wouldn't do at all. Taking a postage stamp from her purse, she affixed it to the envelope. She'd post it tomorrow when she returned her library books she decided, after all, it might be important and she was nothing if not a dutiful citizen.

~

April
Irene Weatherall's letter arrived at the central London sorting office where, unable to be sorted by the automated machines, it was passed on for hand-sorting, together with the many thousands of incorrectly addressed mail which ended up there. A postal worker, picking up the letter a few days later as it reached the top of the pile, decided that it should go to the Metropolitan Police London HQ and it arrived there the following day.

The mailroom at Police HQ wasn't quite sure who to pass the letter to and it languished in the room for a few days until an earnest new employee decided to take it to the Criminal Investigations Department, for want of a better idea.

No one had heard of a police officer by the name of Stephanie Wentworth and there was no such name in the employee system, but one of the officers happened to have worked with a Stephanie Wendover before her promotion to Detective Inspector and her subsequent transfer to Hammersmith.

Slipping the envelope, together with a covering note, into an inter-office mail pocket, the officer dropped the pocket into the tray for collection, pleased to have passed off the problem.

~

May – Paxos, Ionian Islands, Greece

The two couples walked back along the beach, suntanned and carefree, carrying their baskets and beach towels.

'I can't believe it's our last night, it's gone too quickly.' Sasha swatted Eric's hand away from the tie on her bikini brief, laughing.

'Me too, I never want to leave.' Zoe looked back at her, smiling, James's arm firmly around her shoulders, as she took their photo. 'Anyone who sees all our photos on Graffic is going to be so jealous.'

He's been so good for her, thought Sasha fondly, just what she needed after Miles. Hugely attractive, and extremely well-off, James had purchased a couple of artworks from Frame, the gallery where Zoe worked. He'd asked her out for a drink but Zoe had been understandably wary of men after her horrific ordeal and had declined. Nonetheless, he'd persisted, and finally, her boss, Flavia, had phoned Sasha in desperation, begging her to talk to Zoe, saying that he was driving her mad coming into her gallery every day. She'd also claimed that he was the perfect man for Zoe and just what she needed.

Flavia had been right. Sasha had conducted undercover surveillance of James and investigated everything about him, right down to where he worked and where he lived (something which he'd jokingly never let her forget, once he knew about it). Finally, satisfied that he was the real deal, she'd convinced Zoe to meet him, with her and Eric there as back-up. That was two months ago and they were now inseparable.

'Let's walk down into the town tonight and have a blow-out meal. What d'you say, guys?' Eric had become addicted to a local speciality, bourdeto, and took every opportunity to indulge.

'I'm game.' James loved his food, and his drink, and seemed to have a huge capacity for Ouzo, but his favourite part of every meal was ordering a bottle of Theotoki Aspro, the white wine produced on the Ionian Islands and made famous by James Bond in one of his movies. It was the considered opinion of the other three that his attempt at sounding like 007 was a dismal failure, but it always made them laugh.

They reached their villa and, hot after the walk up from the beach, jumped into the pool for a cooling dip before heading inside to shower and get ready for their evening.

Eric nuzzled Sasha's bare shoulder as she tied her sundress halter behind her neck. 'You smell gorgeous, babe. Don't tie this yet, we've got some time...'

Half an hour later they joined Zoe and James on the terrace where James had poured them ice-cold glasses of Ouzo. 'You two took your time.' he grinned, winking at Sasha who blushed. He raised his glass. 'Yamas!'

'Yamas!' they all repeated, clinking their glasses and laughing.

Wandering along the harbour promenade a while later, they finally decided on the Taverna Spiros and took seats at an outside table close to the bobbing yachts. Eric immediately ordered them a round of Ouzo and James ordered two bottles of Theotoki Aspro, giving them the usual laugh. With starter platters of spanokopita and tiropita ordered, they sat back and relaxed, enjoying the ambience around them.

Much later, after moussaka, bourdeto, souvlaki, and stifado, accompanied by fries and huge Greek salads, and followed up with baklava and halva, they groaned at their full stomachs.

'I'm on a diet starting tomorrow,' sighed Zoe, as Sasha agreed. The two men had gone inside to pay the bill and they watched them huddled in conversation. James threw his arms around Eric, laughing, a huge grin on his face, and the girls looked at each other, raising their eyebrows.

'Those two.' Sasha giggled. 'It's like they were separated at birth, I can't believe what good mates they've become.'

'Oh no,' Zoe groaned. 'They've bought more wine. I'm not sure I can absorb any more.'

'Come on, let's go back to the villa and celebrate our last night.' James handed one of the bottles to Eric and they pulled the girls up out of their chairs.

'Celebrate? I thought that's what we just did. I'm not sure I can even walk straight at the moment.' Sasha giggled as Eric pulled her close, kissing her long and hard.

Once back at the villa, Sasha and Zoe were told to relax on the terrace while the men found glasses and ice. Dreamily, Sasha found herself thinking about Eric. Less than a year ago she'd had enough of him, enough of his neglect, of his extreme drinking, of his flirting with other women, and yes, he probably had cheated on her... So much had happened since then, there'd been Cal... she allowed herself a moment to picture him, his dark eyes twinkling into hers, his sexy smile, long hair... his kiss... and then she forced herself to picture him with his pregnant wife standing beside him. She sighed and Zoe dragged her eyes from the ocean glittering in the moonlight below their terrace.

'What is it, Sash?'

'Oh, nothing... just... thoughts.... you know? You and James seem so happy, you're perfect together, Zo.'

Zoe smiled. 'I can't believe how lucky I am. And you and Eric, you're so good together this time around. He's a good bloke, Sash. He was so worried about you when– you know... It's like you were his whole world and without you, he was lost. You make the perfect couple.'

Nodding, Sasha agreed. 'He is a good bloke. He's good-looking, fun, a little crazy, and he's definitely been trying not to get so hammered like he used to, he's, well he's making an effort all round. We do work well together...' Her voice faded away as her private thoughts took over.

Eric *was* a good bloke. She was lucky. And they did make a good couple. Maybe she should just let down any remaining barriers and give in to how good she felt when she was with him. And she should forget the past and everyone in it. The clinking of glasses brought her out of her reverie.

'Cheers, guys. Here's to the fab week we've spent together, to friendships, to my beautiful Zoe, and to you guys, Sasha and Eric.' James held up his glass as they followed suit, collectively shouting 'Yamas!' as their glasses clashed and wine slopped over the brims.

Zoe picked up her phone and began casually taking photos, grinning manically, as Eric appeared to have dropped something, fumbling on the floor on his knees in front of Sasha.

'Eric, what are you–?' Sasha was laughing as Eric held open the small box, a glint of something sparkling prettily. His serious expression stopped her laughter. 'Eric?'

'Sash, you're the most wonderful woman in the world and when I thought I might lose you I realised how much you meant to me. I love being with you, I love talking to you, I love making you laugh and I love driving you crazy. Hell, I even love your addiction to pizza. But more than anything, I just love you. Will you marry me, Sasha?' He held out the ring, taking Sasha's left hand in his, his eyes filled with love.

All was silent as they awaited her reply. Sasha looked from Eric to Zoe, who nodded encouragingly, beaming.

She looked back at Eric, feeling loved and happy. This could work. Hadn't she just been thinking about how lucky she was, how good they were together, how good he made her feel?

'Yes.' She spoke instinctively. 'Yes, I'll marry you, Eric Latimer!'

Eric slipped the ring onto her finger and pulled her close, kissing her, as Zoe and James whooped and clapped. From somewhere, James magically produced a bottle of bubbly, opening it with a loud pop, as Zoe brought out champagne glasses.

'Photos!' yelled Zoe, snapping away as they kissed and laughed happily.

~

D.I. Wendover yawned. It was late but they'd cleared most of the offices in readiness for the long-overdue refurbishment. All that remained were boxes of files, mainly closed cases, to be put into storage and the new young officer, Graham Barnes, had instructions to take them there, a chore he was currently busy with.

With a last glance at the familiar grubby walls with their remnants of sticky tape from posters and at her old desk with its lop-sided drawer, Steph Wendover picked up her bag and jacket, left the offices and headed down the stairs. Calling out goodbye to the officer on the reception desk, she smiled her thanks to the inter-office courier as he held the door open for her and stepped out onto the pavement, wondering what to pick up for a late supper and looking forward to her two week's leave.

~

Graham Barnes raced to pick up the phone as he returned once more to the old offices to collect the last box of files. Huffing in irritation he told the receptionist that he'd be right down and took the stairs rather than wait for the lift.

Blast. He looked at the name on the mail pocket in irritation, D.I. Wendover had just left. Back upstairs he turned the pocket over in his hands, not sure what to do. Tearing it open he read the short note accompanying the hand-written envelope addressed to Stephanie Wentworth. Anxiously he deliberated his options. It might not be for her at all, but then again it might, but she was now on leave for two weeks and everything was in storage. He decided to open the envelope.

Glancing at the photo of two young boys, he squinted his eyes as he tried to decipher Irene Weatherall's spidery handwriting. Something about two boys – concern about a boy called Charles Priestley - Stephanie's recent visit – but the letter was undated and the postmark on the envelope was smudged – then a name jumped out at him – Blake Selim. He smiled – the gods must be smiling on him today, he thought, as he turned to look at the remaining box of case files containing, unbelievably, the Blake Selim casework – closed now, of course.

Well, that was simple, he decided – he'd slip the letter and photograph into the box for safekeeping where it could easily be found should it ever be needed.

Pleased at his resolution to the problem, Graham picked up the last box, switched off the lights with his shoulder, and took the box down to storage.

~

Jules finished wiping down the bar counter of The Spotted Dog in Parva Crossing and picked up her phone to scroll through the pictures on her Graffic feed. A photo of Sasha on holiday on Paxos appeared. She sighed, looking at a smiling Sasha and Zoe, thinking that a holiday would be nice. The sound of the door opening made her look up and, about to say the bar was closed, her face broke into a large grin of surprise instead. 'Cal!'

'Hi, Jules!' A grinning Cal swept Jules up into a bear hug. 'You don't happen to have a room available, do you?'

'Of course I do, you can have your old rooms, they're empty, they've been waiting for you. How long are you back for? And what happened? Is it just you, or–?" she looked quizzically at Cal before glancing behind him.

'It's just me. It's a long story. Any chance of a pint?'

But Jules had beaten him to it and passed him the filled glass, before pouring herself a glass of wine.

A short while later Cal was finishing off his brief update to Jules. 'So that's it in a nutshell, I'm free of her, and them.' His face darkened for a moment before he shook his head to dispel the memories. 'I can't believe she tried to pretend the baby was mine. Hell, I hadn't seen her for almost a year. And I lost Sasha because of it, I never got the chance to explain.'

While Cal carried his bags up to his old rooms, Jules made a quick decision. She wasn't one to interfere usually but she'd seen how good Cal and Sasha had been together – and they probably still would be, if that woman hadn't turned up and ruined everything. She knew Sasha was on holiday with a girlfriend, having just seen their photo, but she could still send her a message and let her know...

~

Tessa looked up from her phone as Dave, her husband, walked in from his late shift. 'Hi, babe, how was work, okay?'

Dave yawned. 'Yeah, no problems. What are you up to?'

'Oh, I'm just sending Sash a message, giving her the exciting news from Parva Crossing. She gets home from her holiday tomorrow.'

'Well, here's some news for you. Remember the old woman, Dorothy Newton, old George's wife? The one who caused all the trouble with her letters, who went mad and ended up in Meadowvale? You're not going to believe this but she's been murdered.' At Tessa's stunned expression he continued. 'Yep, total shocker. I bumped into P.C. Crossley, or Detective Sergeant Crossley now, I should say. They're completely non-plussed at the moment, don't know where to start. As he said, how d'you go about interviewing a bunch of old crocks, half of who don't know what day it is, let alone find out who might have killed her? Fancy a glass of wine?'

At Tessa's distracted nod, Dave went to the kitchen to pour the wine, while Tessa absorbed the news. She should tell Sash, she'd spent some time with Dorothy, she'd want to know. Maybe she'd come up for a visit and help look into it... She carried on typing her message, including the news about Dorothy, and sent it to Sasha.

~

With another pint of lager in front of him, Cal finally asked the question he'd been dying to ask since he'd arrived at the pub. 'Have you heard from Sash at all? How is she?'

'She's actually doing great, and I can do better than just tell you, I saw a photo of her with a girlfriend, they've obviously been on holiday together. Oh, and she looks great by the way. Hold on, I'll find it. Here it is, oh–'

As they looked at the photo of Sasha and Zoe, the feed refreshed and a new photo appeared.

Cal stared at the photo of a smiling Sasha and Eric, a ring glinting on her left hand, with the caption 'We're engaged!'

'Well that's that then,' he said sadly. 'But you're right about something, she does look great.'

'Oh, Cal, I'm sorry, I had no idea.' Jules felt terrible. 'But you know, photos don't always tell the true story...'

'It looks pretty true to me.' He downed his pint miserably, wondering if he should move on and forget about Sasha.

~

Sasha leaned back in the hot tub on the roof and gazed at the stars. She was completely drunk. I'm going to suffer in the morning she thought, as she reached for her cigarettes.

Picking up her phone she scrolled through the graphics and photos, marvelling at how perfect everyone's lives looked on social media. Our Graffic lives... our graphic lies... now why did she just think that?

Eric reappeared with more drinks and she admired his suntanned naked body as he slipped back into the bubbling water. Searching for cigarettes, he picked up an empty packet, crumpling it and throwing it into a nearby pot plant. Her old irritation at his carelessness hovered in the back of her mind even as her phone pinged twice in rapid succession. She reached for it.

'Leave it,' he whispered, nuzzling her neck as his hand reached under the water for her leg.

'It might be important, I'll just check.' She read Tessa's message, gasping in shock at the news.

'What is it, babe?'

'Someone's been murdered, someone I knew, an elderly lady from Parva Crossing. Tess thought I might want to go and help look into it.'

'Not that stupid little place again.' Eric leaned back in satisfaction. 'Boring, boring, I reckon it's time I took you to bed. You need to start doing as I say,' he teased. 'You'll be my wife soon. And the first rule is no going to Parva bloody Crossing to investigate the deaths of mad old ladies.'

Slight irritation at his comment about Parva Crossing as well as his lack of concern for someone's murder fluttered across Sasha's mind. Oh, a message from Jules, she thought warmly, clicking on it.

Hi Sasha, thought you should know. Cal's back. It's a long story, but he's single and the baby wasn't his. He misses you. So do I. Call me. Jules xx

Reeling in shock at the message, she looked at the ring glinting on her left hand.

'Come on, babe, I'm getting lonely over here, can you leave the murdered old ladies just for tonight? Sod it, I'm getting another drink.' Eric stumbled from the hot tub, slipping on the wet tiles and laughing as his wine glass shattered.

Have I just made a terrible mistake? thought Sasha.

EPILOGUE

Miles Bleak smiled as he watched Charles Priestley enter the visitors' room at Wakefield Prison, his friend's eyes scanning the inmates as he looked for Miles. The two men greeted each other fondly as Charles sat down at the small table.

'I've missed you, Miles, I can't bear it. Will you ever get out?' Charles's voice broke into a sob of despair.

'One day.' Miles smiled calmly. 'For now, it's up to you. Did you bring them?' His eyes stared hungrily at the envelope which Charles pulled from his pocket.

Taking his time, as if with a glass of fine wine, Miles savoured the first photo of Sasha. It was taken from a distance but he could still make out her smile as she turned to someone beside her at the entrance to a restaurant. The next photo brought a scowl to his face as he recognised Zoe laughing with Sasha as they entered a pub. His scowl turned to anger when he picked up the next photograph and gazed at a grinning Sasha, realising that it was Eric's arm around her shoulders. Forcing himself to remain calm he held the last photo. This was perfect – Sasha stood on her small balcony as she smoked a cigarette, leaning on the railing and gazing wistfully into the distance.

'You've done well, Charles.' He smiled approvingly at his protégé as he slipped the photos into his pocket.

Beaming with pride, Charles leaned forward eagerly. 'D'you want me to take her for you? Just say the word – I can do it on my own, I know I can – you said so with the last girl we took, the one we left in the basement of the house.'

'No, not just yet.' Miles's eyes glazed over thoughtfully. 'Where is she now?'

Smirking, Charles couldn't resist a little boast. 'I followed her to the hair salon and pretended I was trying to find out prices for my wife. I was standing right next to her when she told the stylist that she was off to Parva Crossing. It was like taking candy from a baby.'

Miles suppressed the fleeting feeling of irritation that Charles's words evoked, reminding him, as they did, of his own incarceration. 'Keep taking the photos for me while I think about what to do with Sasha Blue. I've got all the time in the world.'

Back in his cell, Miles fixed the photo of Sasha standing on her balcony onto his wall. Sitting down on his narrow bed he stared at it until it became too dark to see.

AFTERWORD AND A FEW INSIDER SECRETS!

When I began writing Graphic Lies, I had no idea that Sasha Blue would take us all on such an adventure – and certainly not that she would find herself on the Isle of Arran. Such is the fun of writing a book – especially a mystery.

As you will know, if you've read Village Lies, I like to slip in the odd fond anecdote, memory, and a little fun, into my stories, and I've shared the origins of a few of those that featured in Graphic Lies with you below.

Sasha recognises her own bedroom, in one of the photographs, from the battered copy of The Thorn Birds by Colleen McCullough, which is sitting on the bedside table. My own much-loved and damaged copy is tattered and faded, with stained pages falling loose from the worn spine, from the many times I read it as a young girl. Memories are held forever within the pages of our old books and although I could have replaced it with a new copy, I've preferred to keep my original book, complete with splashes of sun tan oil and evocative memories, just as Sasha did.

When I was sixteen, we moved from Dartford to Hartley Village and a Waitrose opened in Longfield, just down the hill. We loved their mini-baguettes like mad people. Add into the mix holidays in France where a piece of baguette slathered with unsalted butter and topped with Emmental cheese and fresh tomato made the perfect repast, and you have the lunch which Sasha eats out on her balcony.

When Sasha tackles her side case of a missing wife, she emerges from Chancery Lane tube station and gazes at Staple Inn Hall, before heading along Leather Lane. The market trader's call of 'Going cheap. Cheep cheep,' is a direct memory from my time as a junior accounts clerk, at the grand age of seventeen, for The Institute of Actuaries, which was housed within the beautiful Staple Inn Hall, when a wander through Leather Lane market was a regular lunchtime experience. I can still hear that market trader's voice after all these years.

One of the unsolicited messages that Miles finds on Sasha's phone is for 'hip broadening cream'. This is a real thing. I still have the clipping from a newspaper in Zambia (I know, weird, right?) where an advert was placed for Hips Booster – 'to redefine the shape of a woman by broadening the hips and thighs'. I find differences between cultures fascinating and confess that I was amused by this, as women in many parts of the Western World struggle to achieve quite the opposite.

Zoe's deliberately incorrect description of the Greek holiday that she and Sasha enjoyed, which convinced Sasha that Zoe was the girl in the photos, was taken from an experience I shared with my great childhood friend. As soon as were old enough to holiday without our parents we enjoyed a number of Greek island holidays. One such trip was a real bargain – a room above a taverna on Corfu, complete with only the most basic of furniture, and breakfasts which never materialised – and yes, we did have to buy our own loo rolls!

Sasha's abduction, by Miles, to the Isle of Arran, allowed me to indulge myself a little more in my love for a very beautiful part of the world, although the fact that even the swarms of midges felt wonderful to Sasha, when she was rescued, may have been a stretch too far...

Bobotie is a popular South African dish consisting of spicy mince with a baked egg topping. Sasha makes it in one of her mad cooking sessions and it's delicious served with rice. You'll find my husband's mum's own recipe on my blog under the recipes tab, if you'd like to try making it yourself.

I'll finish with Ann-Marie's comment in response to Sasha's tearful thanks for her part in her rescue, that of 'providential, dear,' complete with a pat on the hand. This is a sweet nod to my grandma on my dad's side, as it was her response to everything that worked out in the way it was supposed to. It's become a catchphrase for those of us who loved this very kind and gentle lady, and a small way of remembering her.

I could go on, but it's time to tell you about Sasha's next mystery – Old Lies.

DON'T MISS THE NEXT SASHA BLUE MYSTERY!

Old Lies

It's been said that everyone has something to hide, and the residents of Meadowvale retirement home, on the outskirts of the village of Parva Crossing, are no exception.

The murder of Dorothy Newton, whose poison pen letters caused so much harm during Sasha's first visit to the village when her niece went missing, brings Sasha back once more, to hunt down the killer.

Newly engaged to on and off boyfriend, Eric, Sasha is conflicted about her feelings, especially when she resumes residence at The Spotted Dog pub, only to find that Cal, the man she'd developed feelings for during her last visit, has also returned.

With the local police seemingly non-plussed, Sasha is determined to find out who Dorothy's murderer is, and so begins an investigation into the lives of the elderly residents, where old lives and old lies are slowly uncovered.

But it's not just the varied residents, among whom are a writer, a retired accountant, and a pair of spinster sisters both vying for the attentions of an eligible, if somewhat elderly, bachelor, who Sasha must investigate, there are also the relatives who visit regularly, as well as the staff.

Secrets, greed, love affairs both old and new, and another murder, all test Sasha's detective skills, even as she suspects that there is someone in the village who wishes her harm. Or possibly more than one person...

Old Lies is the third book in the Sasha Blue Mystery Series. Although each book may be read as a standalone there are ongoing connections between the stories which make them more enjoyable when read as a series.

ABOUT THE AUTHOR

Linzi Carlisle grew up in Dartford, Kent, in the UK, before moving to South Africa where she met her husband. They lived in Zambia for many years before settling in South Africa in the beautiful town of George, part of the Garden Route, nestled between the Outeniqua Mountains and the Indian Ocean – the perfect spot for writing her books. They share their home with their two beautiful cats.

A MESSAGE FROM LINZI…

Thank you so much for choosing to read Graphic Lies, the second book in the Sasha Blue Mystery Series – I hope you enjoyed it.
To stay in touch and keep up to date with new releases see the list below.
I'd love to see your photos of your book on social media and if you can take a moment to review Graphic Lies anywhere that would be fabulous.
Sharing book recommendations is one of the ways I've been able to enjoy and share many great books over the years.
Nothing beats word of mouth – sharing your thoughts is a great way for readers to find out about my books.
Thank you.

Website: www.linzicarlisle.blogspot.com
Instagram: @linzicarlisleauthor
Facebook: www.facebook.com/linzicarlisleauthor

www.ingramcontent.com/pod-product-compliance
Lightning Source LLC
Chambersburg PA
CBHW050903130726
47900CB00015B/1896